MALICE

Books by Lisa Jackson

See How She Dies
Final Scream
Wishes
Whispers
Twice Kissed
Unspoken
If She Only Knew
Hot Blooded
Cold Blooded
The Night Before
The Morning After
Deep Freeze
Fatal Burn
Shiver
Most Likely to Die
Absolute Fear
Almost Dead
Lost Souls
Left to Die
Wicked Game
Malice

Published by Kensington Books

LISA JACKSON

MALICE

KENSINGTON BOOKS
www.kensingtonbooks.com

KENSINGTON BOOKS are published by

Kensington Publishing Corp.
850 Third Avenue
New York, NY 10022

All Kensington titles, imprints, and distributed lines are available at special quantity discounts for bulk purchases for sales promotion, premiums, fund-raising, educational, or institutional use.

Special book excerpts or customized printings can also be created to fit specific needs. For details, write or phone the office of the Kensington Special Sales Manager: Attn. Special Sales Department. Kensington Publishing Corp., 850 Third Avenue, New York, NY, 10022. Phone: 1-800-221-2647.

Kensington and the K logo Reg. U.S. Pat. & TM Off.

ISBN-13: 978-0-7582-3649-4
ISBN-10: 0-7582-3649-2

First Trade Paperback Printing: April 2009

10 9 8 7 6 5 4 3 2

Printed in the United States of America

Acknowledgments

There are many people I would like to thank for their expertise and help in the writing and publication of this book. Special thanks to Rosalind Noonan, fellow author and friend, for her tireless help, and to everyone at Kensington Publishing for their patience, especially my editor, John Scognamiglio. Also, in no particular order, thanks to Nancy Bush, Ken Bush, Matthew Crose, Niki Crose, Michael Crose, Larry Sparks, Ken Melum, Kelly Foster, Darren Foster, and my agent, Robin Rue.

If I've missed anyone—hey, no surprise there, but please accept my apologies.

Author's Note

I know I've bent the rules and played around with the police department procedure just to keep my story moving; this book in no way reflects the actual police departments of Los Angeles, California, or New Orleans, Louisiana, or their procedures.

PROLOGUE

Culver City, a Suburb of Los Angeles
Twelve Years Earlier

"So you're not coming home tonight, is that what you're getting at?" Jennifer Bentz sat on the edge of the bed, phone pressed to her ear, as she tried to ignore that all-too-familiar guilty noose of monogamy that was strangling her even as it frayed.

"Probably not."

Ever the great communicator, her ex wasn't about to commit.

Not that she really blamed him. Theirs was a tenuous, if sometimes passionate, relationship. And she was forever "the bad one," as she thought of herself, "the adulteress." Even now, the scent of recent sex teased her nostrils in the too-warm bedroom, reminding her of her sins. Two half-full martini glasses stood next to a sweating shaker on the bedside table, evidence that she hadn't been alone. "When, then?" she asked. "When will you show up?"

"Tomorrow. Maybe." Rick was on his cell in a squad car. She heard the sounds of traffic in the background, knew he was being evasive and tight-lipped because his partner was driving and could overhear at least one side of the stilted conversation.

Great.

She tried again. Lowered her voice. "Would it help if I said I miss you?"

No response. Of course. God, she hated this. Being the pathetic, whining woman, begging for him to see her. It just wasn't her style.

Not her style at all. Men were the ones who usually begged, and she got off on it.

Somewhere in the back of her consciousness she heard a soft click.

"RJ?"

"I heard you."

Her cheeks burned and she glanced at the bedsheets twisted and turned, falling into a pool of pastel, wrinkled cotton at the foot of the bed.

Oh, God. He knows. The metallic taste of betrayal was on her lips, but she had to play the game, feign innocence. Surely he wouldn't suspect that she'd been with another man, not so close on the heels of the last time. Jeez, she'd even surprised herself.

There was a chance he was bluffing.

And yet . . .

She shuddered as she imagined his rage. She played her trump card. "Kristi will wonder why you're not home. She's already asking questions."

"And what do you tell her? The truth?" *That her mother can't keep her legs closed?* He didn't say it, but the condemnation was there, hanging between them. Hell, she hated this. If it weren't for her daughter, their daughter . . .

"I'm not sure how long the stakeout will be."

A convenient lie. Her blood began a slow, steady boil. "You and I both know that the department doesn't work its detectives around the clock."

"You and I both know a lot of things."

In her mind's eye she saw him as he had been in the bedroom doorway, his face twisted in silent accusation as she lay in their bed. Sweaty, naked, she was in the arms of another man, the same man with whom she'd had an affair earlier. Kristi's biological father. Rick had reached for his gun, the pistol strapped in his shoulder holster, and for a second Jennifer had known real fear. Icy, cold terror.

"Get out," he'd ordered, staring with deadly calm at the two of them. "Jesus H. Christ, get the hell out of my house and don't come back. Both of you."

He'd turned then, walked down the stairs, and left without so much as slamming the door. But his rage had been real. Palpable. Jennifer had escaped with her life, but she hadn't gone. She couldn't.

Rick hadn't returned. They hadn't even fought about it again. He'd just left.

Refused to answer her calls.

Until today.

By then it had been too late.

She'd already met her lover again. As much out of retribution as desire. Fuck it. No one was going to run her life, not even Rick-effin'-Bentz, superhero cop. So she'd met the man who was forever in her blood.

Slut!

Whore!

The words were her own. She closed her eyes and hung her head, feeling lost. Confused. Never had she planned to cheat on Rick. Never. But she'd been weak, temptation strong. She shook her head and felt black to the bottom of her soul. Who was she so intent on punishing? Him? Or herself? Hadn't one of her shrinks told her she didn't think she deserved him? That she was self-destructive?

What a load of crap. "I just don't know what you want," she whispered weakly.

"Neither do I. Not anymore."

She saw an inch of liquid remaining in one martini glass and drank it down. The noose tightened a notch, even as it unraveled. God, why couldn't it be easy with him? Why couldn't she remain faithful? "I'm trying, Rick," she whispered, gritting her teeth. It wasn't a lie. The problem was that she was trying and failing.

She thought she heard a muffled footstep from downstairs and she went on alert, then decided the noise might have been the echo in the phone. Or from outside. Wasn't there a window open?

"You're trying?" Rick snorted. "At what?"

So there it was. He did know. Probably was having someone tail her, having the house under surveillance. Or worse yet, he had been parked up the street in a car she didn't recognize and had been watching the house himself. She glanced up at the ceiling to the light fixture, smoke alarm, and slow-moving paddle fan as it pushed the hot air around. Were there tiny cameras hidden inside? Had he filmed her recent tryst? Witnessed her as she'd writhed and moaned on the bed she shared with him? Observed her as she'd taken command and run her tongue down her lover's abdomen, and lower? Seen her laughing? Teasing? Seducing?

Jesus, how twisted was he?

She closed her eyes. Mortified. "You sick son of a bitch."

"That's me."

"I hate you." Her temper was rising.

"I know. I just wasn't sure you could admit it. Leave, Jennifer. It's over."

"Maybe if you didn't get off bustin' perps and playing the superhero ace detective, maybe if you paid a little attention to your wife and kid, this wouldn't happen."

"You're *not* my wife."

Click.

He hung up.

"Bastard!" She threw the phone onto the bed as her head began to pound. *You did this, Jennifer. You yourself. You knew you'd get caught, but you pushed away everything you wanted and loved, including Kristi and a chance with your ex-husband, because you're a freak. You just can't help yourself.* She felt a tear slither down her cheek and slapped it away. This was no time for tears or self-pity.

Hadn't she told herself that reconciliation with Rick was impossible? And yet she'd returned to this house, this home they'd shared together, knowing full well it was a mistake of monumental proportions. Just as it had been when she'd first said "I do," years before.

"Fool!" She swore under her breath on her way to the bathroom, where she saw her reflection in the mirror over the sink.

"Not pretty," she said, splashing water over her face. But that really wasn't the truth. She wasn't too far into her thirties and her dark hair was still thick and wavy as it fell below her shoulders. Her skin was still smooth, her lips full, her eyes a shade of blue-green men seemed to find fascinating. All the wrong men, she reminded herself. Men who were forbidden and taboo. And she loved their attention. Craved it.

She opened the medicine cabinet, found her bottle of Valium, and popped a couple, just to take the edge off and push the threatening migraine away. Kristi was going to a friend's house after swim practice; Rick wasn't coming home until God knew when, so Jennifer had the house and the rest of the evening to herself. She wasn't leaving. Yet.

Swoosh.

An unlikely noise traveled up the staircase from the floor below.

The sound of air moving? A door opening? A window ajar?

What the hell was going on? She paused, listening, her senses on alert, the hairs on the back of her arms lifting.

What if Rick were nearby?

What if he'd been lying on the phone and was really on his way home again, just like the other day? The son of a bitch might just have been playing her for a fool.

The "stakeout" could well be fake, or if he really was going to spend all night watching someone, it was probably her, his own wife.

Ex-wife. Jennifer Bentz stared at her reflection in the mirror and frowned at the tiny little lines visible between her eyebrows. When had those wrinkles first appeared? Last year? Earlier? Or just in the last week?

It was hard to say.

But there they were, reminding her all too vividly that she wasn't getting any younger.

With so many men who had wanted her, how had she ended up marrying, divorcing, and then living with a cop in his all-too-middle-class little house? Their attempt to get back together was just a trial. It hadn't been going on long and now . . . well, she was pretty damned sure it was over for good.

Because she just couldn't be faithful to any one man. Even one she loved.

Dear God, what was she going to do? She'd thought about taking her own life. More than once. And she'd already written her daughter a letter to be delivered upon her death:

> *Dear Kristi,*
> *I'm so sorry, honey. Believe me when I tell you that I love you more than life itself. But I've been involved with the man who is your biological father again, and I'm afraid it's going to break Rick's heart.*

And blah, blah, blah . . .

What a bunch of melodramatic crap.

Again she thought she heard something . . . the sound of a footstep on the floor downstairs.

She started to call out, then held her tongue. Padding quietly to the top of the stairs, she held on to the railing and listened. Over the smooth rotation of the fan in her bedroom she heard another noise, something faint and clicking.

Her skin crawled.

She barely dared breathe. Her heart pounded in her ears.

Just your imagination—the guilt that's eating at you.

Or the neighbor's cat. That's it, the scraggly thing that's always rooting around in the garbage cans or searching for mice in the garage.

On stealthy footsteps she hurried to the bedroom window and peered through the glass, seeing nothing out of the ordinary on this gray day in Southern California, where the air was foggy, dusty, and thick. Even the sun, a reddish disc hanging low in the sky over miles and miles of rooftops, appeared distorted by the smog.

Not the breath of a breeze from the ocean today, nothing stirring to make any kind of noise. No cat slinking beneath the dry bushes, no bicyclist on the street. Not even a car passing.

It's nothing.

Just a case of nerves.

Calm down.

She poured the remains of the shaker into her glass and took a sip on her way to the bathroom. But in the doorway she caught sight of her reflection and felt another stab of guilt.

"Bottoms up," she whispered and then, seeing her own reflection and the glass lifted to her lips, she cringed. This wasn't what she wanted for her life. For her daughter. "Stupid, stupid bitch!" The woman in the mirror seemed to laugh at her. Taunt her. Without thinking, Jennifer hurled her drink at her smirking reflection. The glass slammed into the mirror, shattering.

Crraaack!

Slowly, the mirror split, a spider web of flaws crawling over the slivered glass. Shards slipped into the sink.

"Jesus!"

What the hell have you done?

She tried to pick up one of the larger pieces and sliced the tip of her finger, blood dripping from her hand, drizzling into the sink. Quickly she found a single, loose Band-Aid on the shelf in the cabinet. She had trouble as her fingers weren't working as they should, but she managed to pull off the backing and wrap her index finger. Yet she couldn't quite stanch the flow. Blood swelled beneath the tiny scrap of plastic and gauze. "Damn it all to hell," she muttered and caught a glimpse of her face in one of the remaining jagged bits of mirror.

"Seven years of bad luck," she whispered, just as Nana Nichols had foretold when she'd broken her grandmother's favorite looking glass at the age of three. "You'll be cursed until you're ten, Jenny, and who knows how much longer after that!" Nana, usually kind, had looked like a monster, all yellow teeth and bloodless lips twisted in disgust.

But how right the old woman had been. Bad luck seemed to follow her around, even to this day.

Spying her face, now distorted and cleaved in the shards of glass that remained, Jennifer saw herself as an old woman—a lonely old woman.

God, what a day, she thought thickly.

Heading for the broom and dustpan, she started downstairs, nearly stumbling on the landing. She caught herself, made her way to the first floor, and stepped into the laundry room.

Where the door stood ajar.

What?

She hadn't left it open; she was sure of it. And when her lover had left, he'd gone through the garage. So . . . ? Had Kristi, on her way to school, not pulled it shut? The damned thing was hard to latch, but . . .

She felt a frisson of fear skitter down her spine. Hadn't she heard someone down here earlier? Or was that just the gin talking? She was a little confused, her head thick, but . . .

Steadying herself on the counter, she paused, straining to hear, trying to remember. Good God, she was more than a little out of it. She walked into the kitchen, poured herself a glass of water, and noticed the hint of cigarette smoke in the air. No doubt from her ex-husband. How many times did she have to tell him to take his foul habit and smoke outside? Way outside. Not just out on the back porch, where the damned tobacco odor wafted through the screen door.

But Rick hasn't been here in two days . . .

She froze, her gaze traveling upward to the ceiling. Nothing . . . and then . . . a floorboard creaked overhead. The crunch of glass.

Oh, God, no.

This time it wasn't a guess.

This time she was certain.

Someone was in the house.

Someone who didn't want her to know he was there.

Someone who wanted to do her harm.

The smell of cigarette smoke teased at her nostrils again.

Oh, Jesus. This wasn't Rick.

She slid on silent footsteps toward the counter where the knives were kept and slowly slid a long-bladed weapon from its slot. As she did, she thought of all the cases Rick had solved, of all the criminals who had channeled their wrath toward him and his family when they'd been arrested or sentenced. Many of them had vowed to get back at Detective Bentz in the most painful ways possible.

He'd never told her of the threats, but she'd learned from other cops on the force who had gladly repeated various criminals' promises to seek revenge.

And now someone was in the house.

The back of her throat turned desert dry.

Holding her breath, she eased into the garage and nearly tripped on the single step when she realized that the garage door was wide open to the driveway, a blatant invitation. One the intruder had accepted.

She didn't think twice and slid behind the wheel, where the keys were already in the ignition.

She twisted on the keys.

The engine sparked.

She threw the gear into reverse and gunned it, tearing out of the driveway, nearly hitting the neighbor's miserable cat and just missing the mailbox.

She glanced up to the master bedroom window as she crammed the van into drive.

Her heart froze.

A dark figure stood behind the panes, a shadow with a cruel, twisted smile.

"Shit!"

The light shifted on the blinds and the image was gone—maybe just a figment of her imagination.

Or was it?

She didn't wait to find out, just hit the gas pedal, racing down the street as old Mr. Van Pelt decided to back his ancient tank of a Buick into the street. Jennifer hit the brakes, her tires screeched, and then once past the startled neighbor she floored it.

"There was no one in the window. You know that," she tried to convince herself. "No one was there."

Driving with one hand, she searched the passenger seat for her purse and cell, which, she now remembered, sat in the bedroom where she'd seen the dark figure.

"Just your imagination," she said over and over as she drove out of the subdivision and onto the main highway, melding into the thick traffic. Her heart pounded and her head throbbed. Blood from her hand smeared the steering wheel. She checked her rearview often, searching for a vehicle following her, looking through the sea of cars for one that seemed intent on chasing her down. Metal glinted in the sunlight and she cursed herself for not having her sunglasses with her.

Nothing looked out of the ordinary. Tons of cars heading east: silver, white, black sedans and sports cars, trucks, and SUVs . . . at least she thought that was the direction she was going. She wasn't sure. She hadn't paid a lot of attention and she was starting to relax, starting to think she'd eluded whoever had been after her. If anyone really had.

Just another Southern California day. She spied a dark blue SUV coming up fast and her heart jumped, but it sped by, along with a white BMW on its tail.

She flipped on the radio, tried to steady her nerves, but she was sweating, her finger still bleeding. The miles passed, nothing happened, and she began to breathe easier . . . really relax. She drifted a bit, nearly sideswiping a guy who hit the horn and flipped her off.

"Yeah, right, whatever," she said, but realized she shouldn't be driving, not in all this traffic in her altered state. At the next exit, she turned off . . . dear Lord, where was she? . . . in the country? She didn't recognize the area, the sparseness of the homes, the stretches of brush and farmland. She was inland somewhere and the Valium had kicked in big-time. Blinking against the sunlight, she looked in her side-view mirror and saw another big blue SUV bearing down on her.

The same one as before?

No!

Couldn't be.

She yawned and the Explorer behind her stayed back, following her at a distance on the two-lane road that led into the hills.

It was time to turn around.

She was so damned tired.

The road before her seemed to shift and she blinked. Her eyelids were so heavy. She'd have to slow down and rest, try to clear her head, maybe drink some coffee . . .

There was a chance no one had been in the house. Jeez—God, the way she was imagining things, the way her nerves were strung tight these days, the way guilt was eating at her, she was probably letting her mind play tricks on her. Her thoughts swirled and gnawed at her.

She saw the curve in the road and she braked. As she did, she noticed the dark Explorer riding her ass.

"So pass, you idiot," she said, distracted, her eyes on the rearview mirror. The rig's windows were tinted and dark, but she caught a glimpse of the driver.

Oh, God.

Her heart nearly stopped.

The driver stared straight at her. She bit back a scream. It was the same intruder she'd seen in the upstairs window of her house.

Scared out of her wits, she tromped on the accelerator.

Who the hell was it?

Why was whoever it was following her?

She saw the corner and cut it, hoping to lose the SUV, but her judgment was off and one of the van's tires caught on the shoulder, hitting gravel. She yanked on the wheel, trying to wrestle the car onto the road, but the van began to spin.

Wildly.

Crazily.

Totally out of control.

The van shuddered. Skidded.

And then began to roll.

In slow-motion certainty, Jennifer knew she was going to die.

More than that, she knew she was being murdered.

Probably set up by her damned ex-husband, Rick Bentz.

CHAPTER 1

"Talk to me in six weeks." Melinda Jaskiel's voice was firm. Clear. Propped on his good leg on the back veranda, his cell phone nearly stuck to his ear in the sweltering bayou heat, Rick Bentz realized his boss wasn't going to budge. Sweat dripping off his nose, he balanced on one crutch, the thick rubber tip wedged between two flagstones. His back ached and walking was a strain, but he wouldn't admit it to a soul—especially not to Jaskiel. As head of the homicide division in the New Orleans Police Department, she had the authority to put him back on active duty. Or not. It was her call.

Once again, Melinda Jaskiel held the fate of his career in her hands.

Once again, he was begging. "I need to work." Jesus, he hated the desperation in his voice.

"You need to be at a hundred percent, maybe a hundred and ten to be back on duty."

His jaw tightened as the intense Louisiana sun beat down on the back of his neck and a fine mist rose from the swampland that backed up to the cottage nestled into the woods. Jaskiel had given him a job when no one else would touch him after the mess he'd left in L.A. And now she was shutting him down.

He heard her mutter something under her breath and thought for a split second she was reconsidering. "Look, Rick, I don't see you pushing papers at a desk from eight to five."

"I've been in P.T. for a couple of months now, strong as ever."

"Strong enough to chase down a suspect? Wrestle him to the

ground? Break down a door? Hit the deck, roll, draw your weapon, and cover your partner?"

"That's all TV BS."

"Is it?" Jaskiel's voice was skeptical. "Seems to me you were doing just that kind of 'TV BS' when you ended up in the hospital." She knew him too well. "You know the drill. Bring in a doctor's release and we'll discuss your reinstatement. *Discuss*. No promises. You know, retirement's not a bad idea."

He snorted. "Gee, Melinda, I'm getting the idea you're trying to get rid of me."

"You're still in physical therapy and you're wound too tight. End of subject. I'll talk to you later." She hung up.

"Son of a bitch!" He flung his crutch across the flagstones of the veranda, where it skidded, clattering noisily and startling a mocking-bird from a nearby magnolia tree into flight. "Son of a goddamned bitch." His fingers clenched over his cell and he considered hurling it into the swamp, but didn't. Hell, he didn't want to explain *that*. So far, the department only questioned his physical ability. He didn't want to give the powers that be an insight into his mental state.

No shrinks. No soul searching. No pouring out his heart. No thank you.

He stood with difficulty, his balance not what it had been before the accident, despite what he'd told Jaskiel. And sometimes his leg hurt like hell. He knew he wasn't really ready for active duty, but he was going out of his freakin' mind staying at home. Hell, even his relationship with his wife Olivia was beginning to wear thin. Her biological clock was ticking like crazy and she was pressuring him to have a kid. His own daughter, Kristi, was in her twenties. He wasn't sure he wanted to start over.

No, what he needed was to get out of the house and back to work. It had been nearly three months since the accident and he couldn't take sitting around another second.

"So do something about it," he ordered himself.

Gritting his teeth, he took a step unaided.

First one foot, then the other.

None of the namby-pamby putting one foot forward with the walker and dragging the second one up to it. No way. He was going to walk across this damned patio one foot in front of the other if it killed him. He'd show them all. In a month he'd be running across these stupid stones. A crow sat on one of the roof's gables and cried noisily, its raspy caw echoing through the scrub oak and pine.

Bentz barely noticed.

A third step.

Then four.

He was sweating now. Concentrating hard. The heat was oppressive, sun beating down, the dank smell of the swamp heavy in his nostrils. The crow kept up his incessant, mocking caw. Irritating bastard.

Another step and Bentz looked up, away from uneven stones and to the bench, his destination. He was crossing his patio on his own two feet.

Just as he would have if he hadn't been injured.

Just as he would have if he hadn't nearly lost his life.

Just as he would have if he hadn't been forced to consider early retirement.

He moved forward again, more easily, more confidently.

And then he felt it.

That cold certainty that he was being watched.

His gut tightened as he looked over his shoulder. Dry, brittle leaves rustled on the windless day.

The crow had disappeared, its scolding cries silent.

A flicker of light between the branches. Something in the thicket, just on the other side of the veranda, moved. A shadow passed quickly, darting through the undergrowth.

Oh, sweet Jesus.

Instinctively, Bentz reached for his sidearm.

His hand came up empty as he rounded to face the woods.

He wasn't wearing his shoulder holster.

Not in his own house.

He squinted.

What the hell was it?

Sunlight played through the lacy canopy of needles and leaves. His heart thumped crazily. The spit dried in his mouth.

It was just his imagination.

Again.

Right?

But the goose bumps crawling over his flesh and the tightening of every muscle in his body told him otherwise.

Idiot! You're in your own damned backyard.

He turned slightly, trying to make out if the intruder were an opossum, or a deer, or even an alligator crawling up from the swamp, but he knew deep in his soul that this was no wild creature wandering too close to his house.

Uh-uh.

The shivering leaves stilled on this hot, breathless day.

Bentz squinted into the forest. He had no doubt that he would see her.

Again.

He wasn't disappointed.

Through the shimmering heat her image appeared. Dressed in that same sexy black dress, flashing him the barest of smiles, she stood between the bleached bark of two cypress trees.

Jennifer.

His first wife.

The woman he'd sworn to love through all his days.

The bitch who had betrayed him . . . And she was as sensual and gorgeous as she had been all those years ago. The fragrance of gardenias wafted through the air.

He swallowed.

Hard.

A ghost?

Or real flesh and blood?

The woman, a dead ringer for his first wife, stood deep in the woods, staring at him with wide, knowing eyes and that sexy little smile . . . God, that smile had turned him inside out.

His heart went still as death.

An eerie chill slid through his veins.

"Jennifer?" he said aloud, though he knew his first wife was long dead.

She arched a single eyebrow and his stomach dropped to his knees.

"Jen?" Bentz took a step forward, caught his toe on an uneven rock, and went down. Hard. His knees hit first. *Bam!* His chin bounced against the mortar and stone, rattling his jaw, scraping his skin.

Pain exploded through his brain. The raven cackled, as if laughing at him. His cell phone skittered across the flagstones.

"Shit!" he muttered under his breath as he lay still for a second, taking in a couple of breaths, telling himself he was a goddamned idiot, a freak who was seeing things that didn't exist. He moved one leg, then the other, mentally assessing the damage to his already racked-up body.

Not that long ago he'd been paralyzed, the result of a freak accident in a lightning storm. His spinal cord had been bruised, not severed. Slowly he'd recovered to this point and he hoped to hell that he hadn't reinjured his damned back or legs.

Painfully he rolled over and pushed himself onto his knees while staring over the edge of the veranda toward the spot where he'd seen her.

Jennifer, of course, had vanished.

Poof.

Like a ghost in an old cartoon.

Using a bench for leverage, he pulled himself to his feet and stood, solid and steady. Gingerly, ignoring the pain, he walked closer to the edge of the veranda. Squinting into the shadows, he looked for something, anything to indicate she'd been out there. Tempting him. Teasing him. Making him think he was going crazy.

But nothing moved in the forest.

No woman hid in the deep umbra.

No drop in the temperature indicated a ghost had trod upon his soul.

And, beyond all that, Jennifer was dead. Buried in a plot in California. He knew that as well as his own name. Hadn't he identified her himself over twelve years ago? She'd been mangled horribly in the accident, nearly unrecognizable, but the woman behind the wheel in the single-car accident had been his beautiful and scheming first wife.

His stomach twisted a bit as a cloud passed over the sun. High in the sky jets streaked, leaving white plumes to slice the wide expanse of blue.

Why now had she returned—at least in his mind? Had it been the coma? He'd lain unconscious in the hospital for two weeks and he remembered nothing of those fourteen lost days.

When he'd finally awoken, staring through blurry eyes, he'd seen her image. A cold waft of air had whispered across his skin and he'd smelled the heady aroma of her perfume, a familiar scent laced with gardenias. Then he'd caught a glimpse of her in the doorway, backlit by the dimmed hall lights, blowing him a kiss and looking as real as if she were truly still alive.

Which of course she wasn't.

And yet . . .

Now, as he stared into the shaded bayou where shadows length-ened and the steamy scent of slow-moving water filtered through the leaves of cypress and cottonwood, he second-guessed the truth. He doubted what he'd been certain was fact; he questioned his sanity.

Could it be the pain pills he'd been taking since his accident as his daughter—*their* daughter—had insisted?

Or was he just plain going nuts?

"Crap." He glared at the woods.

No Jennifer.

Of course.

She was all a part of his imagination.

Something that had been triggered by nearly half a month of tee-tering on that razor-sharp edge between life and death.

"Get a grip," he told himself.

Man, he could use a smoke right now. He'd given up the habit years before, but in times of stress nothing gave him a clear sense of what needed to be done like a hit of nicotine curling through his lungs.

Grimacing, he heard a series of sharp barks. The dog door opened with a click, followed by the scratch of tiny paws flying across the stones and a high-pitched yip. Hairy S, his wife Olivia's terrier mutt, streaked across the veranda, sending a squirrel squawking loudly up the bole of a scraggly pine. Hairy, who had been named in honor of Harry S. Truman, Olivia's grandmother's favorite president, was going nuts. He leaped and barked at the trunk of the tree, his mottled hair bristling as the squirrel taunted and scolded from the safety of an upper limb.

"Hairy! Shh!" Bentz wasn't in the mood. His head was beginning to pound and his pride had already suffered a beating with the fall.

"What the hell are you doing?" Montoya's voice boomed at him and he nearly tripped again.

"I'm walking without a damned cane or crutch. What's it look like?"

"Like a face plant."

Bentz turned to find his partner slipping through the side gate and striding across the flagstones with the irritating ease of a jungle cat. To add insult to injury, Olivia's scrappy little dog diverted from the squirrel to run circles around Montoya's feet, leaving Bentz to dust off his pride. He tried not to wince, but his knees stung where his skin had been scraped off. No doubt bruises were already forming. He sensed the ooze of warm, sticky blood run down his shins.

"I was watching from over the top of the gate. Looked to me like you were attempting a swan dive into the concrete."

"Very funny."

"I thought so."

Bentz wasn't in the mood to be ridiculed by his smart-assed partner. Make that his smart-assed *younger* partner. With hair that gleamed black in the afternoon light, reflective sunglasses covering eyes that were as sharp as they had ever been, Montoya was younger and more athletic than Bentz. And not afraid to remind his older partner of it.

When he walked, Montoya damned near swaggered and the diamond stud in his earlobe glittered. At least today he wasn't wearing his signature black leather jacket, just a white T-shirt and jeans. Looking cool as all get-out.

It bugged the hell out of Bentz.

"Olivia at work?"

Bentz nodded. "Should be home in a couple of hours." His wife still worked a couple of days a week at the Third Eye, a New Age gift shop near Jackson Square that had survived Hurricane Katrina. She'd completed her master's in psychology a while back and was considering starting her own practice, but she hadn't quite made the transition to full time. Bentz suspected she missed the hustle and bustle of the French Quarter.

Montoya found Bentz's cell phone near a huge ceramic pot filled with cascading pink and white petunias. "Looking for this?" He dusted off the phone, then handed it to him.

Glowering, Bentz muttered, "Thanks," then jammed the damned phone into his pocket.

"Bad news?" Montoya asked, suddenly sober.

"Jaskiel doesn't think I'm fit for duty."

"You're not."

Bentz bit back a hot retort as a dragonfly zipped past. Considering his current state, he couldn't argue. "Is there a reason you came all the way out here, or did you just want to give me a bad time?"

"Little of both," Montoya said. This time his teeth flashed white against his black goatee. "They're reassigning me. Making Zaroster my"—He made air quotes with his fingers—"'temporary' partner."

Lynn Zaroster was a junior detective who had been with the department a little over two years though she was barely twenty-six. Cute, smart, and athletic, Zaroster was filled with enthusiasm. She was as idealistic as Bentz was jaded.

"Change of pace for you."

"Yeah." Montoya's smile faded. "Sometimes I feel like a goddamned babysitter."

"You're afraid this might be permanent." Because Bentz was being pushed out of the department.

"Not if I have my say, but I thought I'd tell you myself. Rather than you hearing it from someone else."

Bentz nodded, wiped the sweat from his face with the sleeve of his shirt. From inside the house, through the open window, he heard the sound of Olivia's parrot, which, like the dog and this little cottage, she had inherited from her grandmother. "Jaskiel's been hinting that I should retire." His lips twisted at the thought of it. "Enjoy what's left of my life."

Montoya snorted. "You're not even fifty. That's a whole lotta 'left.' Thirty—maybe forty—years of fishing, watching football, and sitting on your ass."

"Doesn't seem to matter."

Reaching down for Bentz's crutch, Montoya said, "Maybe you could retire, draw a pension, and then get your P.I.'s license."

"Yeah . . . maybe. And you can keep babysitting." Ignoring the preoffered crutch, Bentz started inside, the little dog hurrying ahead of him. "Come on, I'll buy you a beer."

"Have you gone off the wagon?" Montoya was right beside him, hauling the damned crutch.

"Not yet." Bentz held the door open. "But then, the day's not over."

CHAPTER 2

Bentz was slipping away from her.

Olivia could feel it.

And it pissed her off. Yes, she was sad, too, she thought as she tore down the road in her old Ford Ranger, a relic with nearly two hundred thousand miles that she would have to trade in soon.

She loved her husband and when she'd vowed to stick with him through good times and bad, she'd meant it. She'd thought he had, too, but ever since the accident . . .

She braked for a curve on the long country road winding through this part of bayou country on the way to her home, a small bungalow built near the swamp, one she'd shared with Grannie Gin before the old lady had passed on. She'd lived in it alone for a few years, but eventually, when she and Bentz had married, he'd moved from his apartment to the bungalow tucked deep into the woods.

His daughter had lived with them for a while, though that hadn't worked out all that great. Kristi was a grown woman and had needed her own space. But they'd been happy here for the past few years.

Until the damned accident.

A freak occurrence.

Lightning had cleaved an oak tree and a thick branch had come down on Rick, pinning him and nearly severing his spine. Even now she shuddered thinking of those dark days when she hadn't been certain whether he would live or die.

He'd clung to life. Barely. And in that time she and her stepdaughter had finally bonded, clenching each other's hands in the hospital when the doctors had given Bentz a dire prognosis.

She'd thought she'd lose him, expected him to die. And in those heart-rending days, she'd regretted not having a child with him, not having a part of him to carry on. Maybe it was selfish. But she didn't care.

She caught a glimpse of her reflection in the rearview mirror. Worried amber-colored eyes stared back at her. She didn't like what was happening.

"So do something about it," she said. She'd never been one to hold back. Her temper had been described as "mercurial" on more than one occasion. By Bentz. The first time she'd met the man, she'd gone toe-to-toe with him, reporting a murder she'd witnessed though her visions. That had set him back a bit. He hadn't believed her, at first. But she'd convinced him.

Somehow now, she had to convince him of this as well.

She put the truck through its paces and tried not to dwell on the fact that the warmth in their home had seemed to fade after he'd woken from the coma. He'd become a different man. Not entirely, of course, but somehow changed. At first, she'd passed off his lack of affection as worry. He'd had to concentrate on getting well. But things hadn't gone as she'd expected. As the weeks had passed and he'd gained strength, she'd noticed a sense of disillusionment in him. She'd told herself his mood was sure to change the minute he was back to work, doing what he loved, solving homicides.

But as the weeks passed she became concerned. Though they had talked about having a baby together, he'd become less and less interested. Bentz had always been a passionate man; not as hot-tempered as his partner, Montoya, but steadfast, determined, and courageous.

In bed, he'd been an eager lover who had derived some of his own pleasure from hers.

But all of that had changed.

She didn't doubt that he loved her; not for a second. But instead of mellowing with age, their relationship had grown . . . stale, for lack of a better word. And she didn't like it.

She flipped down her visor. Sunlight dappled the warm ribbon of pavement meandering through this lowland and a jackrabbit hopped into the underbrush at the side of the road.

She barely noticed.

What her relationship with Bentz needed was a kick-start. Or maybe her husband just needed a well-timed kick in his cute behind.

She turned in to the drive, her tires splashing through a puddle from an early morning shower. She parked in the garage and walked inside where a Bryan Adams song from the eighties was blasting. Her husband, sweating in a T-shirt and shorts, was working out on a small weight machine tucked into the den. He glanced over as she walked to the doorway and leaned against the doorjamb. "Hey, Rocky," she said, and he actually laughed.

A rarity these days.

"That's me." He finished a set of leg lifts, his face straining, the muscles bulging in his thighs. For the past three weeks, ever since his boss had suggested he might want to retire, Bentz had redoubled his efforts, throwing himself into regaining his strength with a vengeance. For the most part he'd ditched his crutch and was using a cane, though sometimes he walked unaided, just as he had when he was supposed to be using a crutch. He'd ignored his doctor's warnings and pushed himself harder than he was supposed to. Big steps, but not big enough to satisfy him.

Olivia couldn't help but worry about him, aware that exercise had become one of the few de-stressors in his life. His sleep was restless, his only connection to the department, Montoya, was busy with the job and his own family commitment. Even his daughter Kristi was wrapped up in her own life as she planned her wedding. "What do you say I take you out to dinner?" she asked.

"It's Monday."

"That's why we're celebrating."

He snorted but smiled as he climbed off the machine and swabbed his face with the towel. "Life must be pretty boring if Monday is cause for a celebration."

"I thought you might need to get out."

He arched an inquisitive, thick brow. Yeah, he was in his forties, and yeah, he'd had more than one life-threatening scare in the years that she'd know him, but he was still a hunk. Big-time. Still turned her inside out when he made love to her, which, unfortunately had been spotty since the accident. She thought about trying to seduce him right here and now, but knew he'd suspect she had an ulterior motive of getting pregnant. Which wouldn't be too far from the truth.

"How about Chez Michelle?" he suggested.

"Oooh, upscale. I was thinking more like a hole-in-the-wall kind of place where they serve curly fries and spicy Cajun shrimp in buckets."

His dark eyes flickered with the memory of their first "date." With a chuckle, he said, "That's what I like about you, Livvie, you're a true romantic. You're on." He snapped his towel at her as he passed and made his way to the bathroom.

Two hours later they were seated at a table in a brick courtyard where doves cooed and pecked at crumbs while the sun began to set. Shadows crept through the pots of herbs that bloomed and scented the air.

The restaurant itself was narrow and dark, its walls strung with fishing nets, the tables butting up to huge tubs of shaved ice packed with bottles of beer. Luckily, this place had been spared the wrath of the hurricane.

Olivia sipped from a glass of iced tea and ate heartily from the spicy Cajun shrimp and crisp French fries. Conversation buzzed around them and rattling flatware echoed through the courtyard. It was her favorite place, one they patronized often. Bentz had walked into the courtyard without the use of his cane and his movements were surer now, steadier. But there was still something bothering him, something that he was keeping from her.

And she was sick of waiting for him to open up. It wasn't happening.

"So," she said, pushing her plate aside and wiping her fingers on the lemon wedge and napkin provided. "What's going on with you?"

"What do you mean?"

"Don't do this, Rick." She met his gaze. "You and I both know that things are strained. I suppose it's partly due to the accident. Heaven knows you've been through a lot, but there's more to it."

"Using your ESP on me?" he asked, taking a slug from his zero-alcohol beer.

"I wish I could." She tried to keep the irritation out of her voice, but she knew him well enough to sense when he was being evasive on purpose. "You've been shutting me out."

One of his bushy eyebrows quirked. "You think?"

"I know."

"See . . . it's those extra powers of perception you've got."

"You and I both know that whatever 'powers' I had quit working years ago." She didn't want to think about that time, when she'd first met Bentz and she could see the horror of a series of grisly murders through the killer's eyes. At first he'd openly scoffed at her visions, but eventually he'd learned differently. And he never let her forget it. "Don't try to change the subject. It's not gonna work." She shoved her plate to one side and set her elbows on the table. "It's more than you suffering from your injuries after the accident. Something's eating at you. Something big."

"You're right. I can't stand not working."

"Really?" She didn't buy it. His attachment to work didn't explain the distance she felt between them. Besides, he was too quick with his answer. "Anything else?"

He shook his head. Stonewalling her.

"You'd tell me if there was?"

"Of course." He offered her that lazy grin she found so charming, reached across the table, and squeezed her hand. "Be patient with me, okay?"

"Haven't I been?"

His gaze slid away.

"Is it that I want a baby?" She'd always been a straight shooter, saw no reason not to acknowledge the problem they'd avoided discussing. For the first few weeks after his accident Bentz had been impotent. Hell, he'd barely been able to walk, much less make love. But that problem had corrected itself.

"I think I told you about that. I'm pushing fifty, out of a job at the moment, still using a damned cane some of the time, and I've got a grown kid who's about to get married. I don't . . . it's not that I don't want a child with you, it's just that I'm not sure the timing's right or that I want to start over."

"But I do. And I'm in my late thirties. My biological clock isn't ticking, Bentz. It's tolling like thunder in my ears. I don't think I have time to wait, to mull things over. If I want a child, and I do, then we have to try."

His jaw slid to the side and he took a swallow from his bottle, then looked away, as if the roofline of the restaurant were suddenly fascinating. She felt the gulf between them widen and when she saw the waiter seating a young couple and their three-year-old toddler, her heart twisted painfully.

"What the hell's happening to us?"

A muscle worked in his jaw and her heart clutched. He was struggling with something, weighing if he could trust her with the truth. Her stomach dropped. "What is it?" she asked, her voice a whisper, a new fear chasing after her, burrowing deep into her heart. She believed he loved her, she did. But . . .

And then he closed her out again. "I've just got a lot to deal with."

Translation: *Stop bothering me and for God's sake, don't pressure me into a decision about having a baby.*

"I'm a psychologist. I can feel you blocking me out."

"And I'm a cop. A detective. Or I was. I've just got to figure out a few things." He looked at her again, the expression in his eyes unreadable. But this time when he touched her, he held fast. "Trust me."

"I do. But I think you're depressed and no one can blame you. Maybe we need a change of scenery, a new start."

"And a baby? Look, I don't think that will solve the problem." He met her gaze evenly. "You can't run from problems, Livvie. You know that. Sooner or later they catch up to you. Mistakes have a way of chasing you down. Even ones from a long time ago."

"That's what you think's happened?" she asked, her mind spinning to tiny references he'd made lately. "Your past in L.A. finally finding you?" She pulled her hand away from his.

"I don't know what's happening. But I'm working on it. Right now, it's the best I can do." He signaled a passing waiter for the bill and the conversation was effectively ended. They settled up and Bentz walked stiffly, though unaided, through the dark restaurant toward the street where his Jeep was parked. He'd insisted on driving and had done a fair enough job on the way to dinner. Though now, on the way home, Olivia whispered a few Hail Marys as he pushed the speed limit on the freeway and she accused him of driving like Montoya.

He flashed her a grin and stepped on it.

They drove home in relative silence, the radio playing softly, the engine humming, each of them lost in thought. At the house he walked her up the front steps, held the door for her, and outwardly seemed attentive. Even loving.

They went through their usual routine. She took care of the pets and went upstairs to read in bed; he watched the news before coming up to their room. They didn't say much; uncertainty and the tension between them still simmered in the air.

From the corner of her eye Olivia watched Bentz strip down to his boxers, noticing that he winced a little as he slid into bed. She dog-eared the page she'd been reading, folded the book closed, and placed it on her nightstand. "I don't want to fight," she said, reaching to turn out the light. She lay still a moment as her eyes adjusted to the darkness. "I don't want to go to sleep angry."

"Are you?"

A breeze lifted the curtains at the window as it blew in from the bayou. "Yeah, a little. And frustrated and . . . worried, I guess. It seems like . . . like you're right here but I can't find you."

The mattress creaked as he turned to her. "Keep looking," he whispered into her hair, his breath warm as it brushed over her skin. One big hand smoothed over the curve of her waist. "Don't give up on me."

"Don't give up on us," she said, feeling the sting of tears in her eyes.

"Never." His arms surrounded her as he pulled her close. His lips found hers in the dark and he kissed her hard, with a pulsing intensity that ignited her blood.

She shouldn't do this, fall into this sexual trap when she was riddled with angst over their future. But his touch, as always, was seductive, the feel of his body comforting. His tongue pressed hard, then slid through her teeth, touching and dancing with hers.

Don't do this, Livvie. Don't fall for this sex in lieu of conversation.

He began tugging her nightgown ever upward, his fingers grazing her skin. Still kissing her, he skimmed one warm hand over her thighs, her hips, and higher still to her waist.

"I don't know if this is a good idea," she whispered.

"It isn't. It's a great idea." He yanked the damned nightgown over her head, tossed it to the floor, then quickly settled over her, his body stretching the length of her. "Don't think for a second I would give up on us," he said against her skin as she tore off his boxers, her fingertips skimming his tight buttocks and sinewy legs.

She wanted to believe him. With all her heart.

"Feel good," he said, and she closed her eyes and gave herself up, body and soul, to his touch.

Later, she was still awake. The ceiling fan whirred above the bed, forcing the air to move.

God, she loved this man. Her heart ached with the burden of loving him. But she wouldn't let that love destroy her.

She ran her fingers through his coarse hair and listened to him gently snore. His eyes were moving rapidly behind his lids, his body hardening, muscles tense rather than relaxed. "No," he said aloud. "No . . . oh . . . God. Stop!"

"Shh," she whispered. "It's all right."

"Stop! Please! Don't!" He was frantic, his breathing wild. "Jennifer!" He yelled her name without waking, then settled into a troubled slumber.

But Olivia didn't sleep a wink.

The sound of his voice yelling Jennifer's name echoed through her mind. She slid from beneath the covers and walked downstairs. She wrapped a fuzzy blanket around her, stretched out on the couch, and let the dog curl into her lap as she stared out the window at the rising moon.

Olivia didn't know what was going on with her husband, but realized that somehow, some way, Rick's first wife was causing a rift between them.

It was ridiculous. She'd met Bentz long after Jennifer had died and though she suspected he carried some guilt for his young wife's death, for living when she lost her life, he seemed to have handled it well.

Until he'd spent two weeks in a coma.

Something had happened in those lost days when he'd been unconscious. Rick Bentz had changed. Which wasn't unusual, considering the circumstances. He'd nearly died.

No one could escape such a trauma without some emotional scarring. Withdrawal and introspection were normal. The man had faced death, for God's sake, so Olivia had granted him ample time to heal, not just physically, but emotionally as well.

But what the hell did Jennifer Nichols Bentz have to do with it?

She must've dozed because she was surprised to notice dawn seeping over the horizon. Deep shades of magenta and lilac streaked the eastern sky and she couldn't stand lying on the couch another second. Her head ached and she decided to start the coffee. Decaf, she reminded herself as she walked into the bathroom and pulled out the small wastebasket beneath the sink.

Lying on the top of a pile of wadded tissues was the remains of her most recent pregnancy test, the package unmistakable, the test stick with its pink line still giving a positive reading, indicating that yes, indeed, Olivia Bentz was pregnant.

CHAPTER 3

"*Help me.*" *Jennifer's voice was as clear as it had been the last time he'd seen her alive.* "*Rick . . . help me.*" *She was lying in the car, her face bloodied, her body broken, unmoving. And yet he'd heard her voice.*

"*You'll be okay,*" *he said, trying to move closer to her, but his legs were leaden, weighted as if in quicksand. The harder he tried to reach her, the more distant she was, her face disintegrating before him.*

Suddenly, her eyes opened.

"*It's your fault,*" *she said as the flesh peeled away, revealing only a skull with damning eyes.* "*Your fault.*"

"*No!*"

Bentz's eyes flew open and he found himself in bed. Alone. His heart was thundering, pounding in his brain, but over it all he heard the rumbling of a truck at the edge of the drive, then the clatter of garbage cans being lifted.

What the hell time was it?

Sunlight burned through the windows and he glanced at the clock. After nine. He'd finally slept. Fitfully, but for a long while. He rubbed a hand over the stubble on his jaw and tried to dispel the nightmare of Jennifer.

Olivia had already left for the day.

Because she still has a life.

He curled a fist, angry at the world, then slowly straightened his fingers.

Oh hell, Bentz, get over your sorry self. This poor-pitiful-me act is wearing thin.

He gave himself a swift mental kick, used the john, then hobbled downstairs where coffee was still warming in a glass pot. She hadn't left a note, but he knew she was meeting with a friend, a woman who worked with her in the shop. She and Manda had a standing date for café au lait, beignets, and gossip at the Café Du Monde on Decatur. They read the paper and people-watched as they sipped their steaming brews from outdoor tables.

Bentz poured himself a cup of coffee, let the dog outside and, while Hairy S sniffed around the edges of the veranda, he stared into the woods where only a few days earlier he'd been certain he'd seen Jennifer.

Or someone who looked so much like her it stole the breath from his lungs.

Of course she hadn't been out there; he'd checked the spot where she'd stood between the two bleached cypress trees. There had been no footprints on the ground, no bit of trace evidence left to indicate anyone had recently been in the spot where he would've sworn on his daughter's life he'd seen his first damned wife. *Ex*-wife. They hadn't been married at the time of her death.

If she'd really been killed in that freak accident.

Bentz had always thought the "accident" had been Jennifer's way of escape. A suicide, though it was a damned messy way to take care of things.

He figured she'd felt so guilty not so much about cheating on him—more than once—but because she'd been caught in bed with another man. Bentz's own half brother. Even now, years later, he still felt the rage that had ripped through him as much from the sting of her infidelity as the fact that he'd been stupid enough to trust her again.

So she'd taken herself out, left him to raise their daughter alone. She'd even written a suicide note, explaining her actions, her guilt.

At the time Bentz had been certain that the woman behind the wheel of the battered van had been Jennifer, and he'd buried her as such. There had been no DNA tests, no blood taken. Just his word that his wife was the driver.

Now, as he stared at that area at the edge of the swampland where he'd witnessed his latest "Jennifer sighting," he felt a little tickle upon the back of his neck, as if someone were silently observing him. He turned quickly, teetering slightly, his eyes trained on the windows of his home.

Nothing.

No one was watching him from inside the house.

Or standing behind a magnolia tree outside peering at him.

He let out his breath slowly.

Ignored the sense of panic that gripped him.

For the love of God, Bentz, pull yourself together!

Was he going completely around the bend?

He knew he'd seen Jennifer, not just a few weeks earlier in this very spot and at the hospital, but other times as well. Once when he was sitting in the front seat of Olivia's truck, waiting while she was taking in the dry cleaning, he'd been certain he had caught a glimpse of her. There was Jennifer, handbag clutched to her chest, hair scraped back in a ponytail, hurriedly crossing the street and disappearing into an alley. He'd gotten out of the truck, hobbled to the entrance of the alley, but had only spied a white cat slinking through a rotted fence while trash cans stood overflowing behind an old garage.

Another time he'd been sure he'd seen her strolling through a park, walking slowly around a fountain as sunlight caught in her hair, firing up the dark strands to a rich auburn. She had turned and looked over her shoulder and a slow, steady smile had stretched across her lips.

Her eyes had twinkled with a catch-me-if-you-can dare. He'd stopped his Jeep, double-parked and, using his cane, followed after her past the fountain only to find that she'd once again vanished.

Then there had been the incident in the woods near his house.

She'd seemed so real.

He was cracking up. That was it. Or hallucinating from the drugs he'd been prescribed. Trouble was, he'd kicked those damned pain-killers a month ago.

Long before he'd seen Jennifer standing just off the edge of his veranda.

Or her ghost.

No way.

He didn't believe in ghosts or anything the least bit supernatural or paranormal. He'd even had trouble swallowing his wife's visions at the time a serial killer known as The Chosen One had terrorized New Orleans.

Yet he was certain that he'd seen her.

Really? Then she hadn't aged much in the last twelve years, right? What's up with that? Come on, Bentz, face it, you're losing it.

"Hell's bells," he muttered under his breath, then took a long swallow before tossing the dregs of his cup into a flowerbed filled with flowers in shades of periwinkle and deep purple.

He was tired of thinking about Jennifer, sick of wondering why his subconscious was so determined to dredge her up again. He'd tried to ignore her. Told himself that he must've just caught glimpses of a woman who resembled her, that because he'd thought he'd seen her during the day, his dreams at night had been haunted by her.

But that didn't explain catching sight of her in the woods the other day. Nor running into an alley or strolling through a park, but here, alone with him in his own backyard. The times he'd caught glimpses of her in public places might have been brushes with someone who looked similar, but the two times he'd seen her alone at the hospital and in the yard had been different—not a play of sunlight and shadow, not easily dismissed.

Was the woman who had been standing in his backyard a figment of his imagination? A product of wishful thinking? Misfiring synapses from an injured brain?

Who knew?

"Get over it."

Whistling to the dog, he walked inside, showered, shaved, and, spying the exercise equipment in the den, promised himself he'd work out in the afternoon. Today he intended to drive into the city, to plead his case with Jaskiel again, get out of the ever-shrinking rooms of this cozy little cottage.

He brought his cane.

Melinda Jaskiel had asked for six more weeks and half that time had slowly passed. He didn't think he could wait any longer. He was on his way to try to convince his boss that he was ready to work, at least part-time, but just as he was climbing into his Jeep, ignoring the pain in his leg, his cell phone beeped.

Caller ID said it was Montoya's personal cell.

"Hey," he said into the phone.

"Back atcha. You got a minute?"

Bentz waited a beat. No doubt his once-upon-a-time partner was being a wiseass. "Just one," he said dryly.

"Can you meet me in . . . say . . . an hour?" No joking now. Montoya was dead serious.

"At the station."

"No. How about the Cat's Meow?"

"I can be there in half an hour."

"Good." Montoya clicked off and Bentz was left with a gnawing in his gut. Something was up. Was there a rumor circulating that Bentz was going to be forced into retirement? "Shit," he said and switched on the ignition.

The thought of turning in his badge soured his stomach. He wasn't ready for retirement, damn it, and he didn't see himself as a P.I. He threw his SUV into reverse, did a quick turn, and drove down the lane to the county road, where he stepped on it and headed to New Orleans and whatever bad news Montoya had to offer.

The Cat's Meow was a bar off Bourbon Street that, after the hurricane, had been restored to its original lack of splendor. The brick walls, even newly scrubbed, looked as if they might crumble. Wood floors, though refinished, had the patina that comes with overuse and age. Surrealistic pictures of jazz singers hanging over the bar had been retouched to appear as if they'd collected decades' worth of smoke. The end one, of Ella Fitzgerald, was still hung crookedly, as if the owner of the bar prided himself in all things in the world being imperfect.

The air conditioner wheezed loudly, ceiling fans slowly rotated, and smoke drifted upward from tables where groups of patrons huddled over their drinks.

Montoya was waiting for him in a booth with a cup of coffee sitting neglected in front of him. He gave Bentz the once-over as he tried not to wince while sliding in opposite the younger cop.

"What's up?" Bentz asked without preamble, then ordered a sweet tea.

"Got some mail for you."

"You did?" Bentz asked.

"Well, the department did."

Montoya waited for the server to deposit Bentz's drink before reaching into his jacket pocket and withdrawing a manila envelope: Eight-by-ten with Bentz's name written on it in block letters, the address listed as the Homicide Department of the New Orleans Police Department. Across each side was a stamp that pronounced the contents: PERSONAL.

The packet hadn't been opened.

"This came today?"

"Mmm." Montoya took a sip of his coffee.

"Scanned?" Meaning for explosives or foreign substances such as anthrax.

"Yeah."

Bentz's eyes narrowed. "By you?"

"That's right. I spotted it in the mailroom, figured it was no one's business but yours, so . . ." He raised a shoulder.

"You lifted it."

Montoya wiggled a hand beside his head. Maybe yes. Maybe no. "It's postmarked to you. Thought it would be best if you got it before Brinkman or some other jerk-off caught a glimpse." He slid a glance at the envelope. "Probably nothin'."

"If you thought that, you wouldn't have bothered."

Again a shrug of one leather-clad shoulder. "You gonna open it?"

"Now?"

"Yeah." Another swallow of coffee.

"So that's it, you're curious."

"Hey, I'm just covering your back."

"Fine." Bentz studied the postmark. It was smudged and the lighting in the bar was too dark to see much. But he had a penlight on his key chain, and as he shined its small beam over the postmark his gut tightened.

The name of the town was unreadable, but he recognized the zip code as the one in which he and Jennifer had lived before her death.

Using a house key, he slit the envelope open and gently tugged the contents within. A single piece of paper and three photographs.

He sucked in his breath.

His heart stilled.

The pictures, complete with dates, were of his first wife, Jennifer. Dear God, what was this?

He heard his pulse pounding in his brain. First the "sightings" and now this?

"Is that—?"

"Yeah." The photographs were clear and crisp. In color. Jennifer walking across a busy street. Jennifer sliding into a light-colored car, make and model undetermined. Jennifer sitting at a tall café table in a coffee shop. The last picture was taken from the street, her image captured through the window of the shop. In front of the window was a sidewalk with pedestrians passing by and portions of two newspaper boxes in the foreground. He recognized one as *USA Today*, and the other the *L.A. Times*.

Narrowing his eyes, Bentz looked for a reflection of the photographer in the large window, but saw none.

This was nuts.

"Old pictures?" Montoya asked.

"Not if the dates from the camera are right."

"Those can be changed."

"I know."

"And with Photoshopping and image altering and airbrushing, pictures can be made to look like anything someone wants them to. Other people's heads on someone else's body."

Bentz looked up from the disturbing photos. "But why?"

"Someone just fuckin' with ya."

"Maybe." He turned his attention to the document and his jaw grew hard as granite. The single page was a copy of Jennifer's death certificate. Scrawled across the neatly typed document was a bright red question mark.

"What the hell is this?" Montoya asked.

Bentz stared at the mutilated certificate. "A sick way of telling me that my first wife might not be dead."

Montoya waited a beat, watching the expression on his partner's face. "You're kidding. Right?"

"Does this look like a joke to you?" Bentz asked, pointing at the death certificate and scattered pictures."

"You think this is Jennifer? Nah!" Then eyeing his ex-partner, "You're messing with me, right?"

Bentz filled Montoya in. Until this point only his kid, who had been in his hospital room at the time he'd awoken from his coma, had any idea that Bentz had seen his first wife. Kristi had dismissed his vision of Jennifer as the result of his coma and too much medication. After that first sighting, he'd kept his mouth shut and his daughter, caught up in preparing for her wedding, hadn't brought up the subject again.

"Wait a second," Montoya said when Bentz paused to take a drink. "You're saying you believe she might actually be alive?"

"I don't know what to believe."

"Otherwise you're chasing a ghost."

Bentz scowled. Felt the heat of Montoya's stare. "I'm not chasing a ghost."

"Then?"

"And I'm not going out of my mind."

"Which leaves . . . what? You believe that someone's dressing up to look like your ex and then gaslighting you? Is that what you're thinking, that you're caught up in some kind of weird scenario straight out of a Hitchcock movie?"

"As I said, I don't know what to believe."

"You tell this to Olivia?"

"No." He looked away. "Not yet."

"Afraid she might have you committed?" One of Montoya's dark eyebrows raised as he finished his coffee.

"Nah, just that she wouldn't understand."

"Hell, I don't understand."

"Exactly."

Pushing his empty cup aside and resting his elbow on the table, Montoya asked, "So what do you want me to do?"

"Keep it quiet. For now. But I might need some favors."

"Such as?"

"A few things. Since I'm on leave, I can't get information as easily as before. I might need you to do some digging."

"In finding this woman?"

"Maybe," Bentz said. "For starters, I'll need someone to have this letter fingerprinted and checked for DNA—lift the stamp and the envelope flap. Can you get me a copy of everything?"

"Sure." Montoya looked at the document.

"And have the lab check, see if the photographs have been altered. They should be able to tell, right?"

"Probably." He eyed the pictures. "At least I'll give the lab guys a run at it. There's one tech—Ralph Lee—specializes in all kinds of photography."

"Good. After I take copies, have him look at the originals. Blow them up, sharpen the focus if possible, find details that might help me pinpoint the locations and time they were taken. See if there are street names, license plate numbers, clocks on the buildings, or the position of the sun, anything that confirms the time and date of the original pictures."

Montoya frowned. "What're you gonna do with the copies?"

"Not sure. I'm still working on it."

Bentz returned the eight-by-tens and the death certificate to the manila envelope. He wasn't even certain himself what he needed, not yet, but he was sick of jumping at shadows, of feeling that his brain was fraying, bit by bit. He just couldn't sit back and let whoever was behind this run with it. "So, for now, don't say anything. If Jaskiel or anyone else at the department thinks I've been seeing things, it'll take a whole lotta convincing for me to get back to work."

Montoya scratched at his chin and pushed his chair back, the diamond stud in his earlobe catching the light.

Bentz saw a flicker of doubt in his partner's dark eyes. "You don't believe me."

"Me? A doubter? No way. Not my style." He offered a quick, hard-edged Montoya grin. "But as you said earlier, it's strange. I'm like you. I don't know what to believe."

CHAPTER 4

The postmark from Southern California really bothered Bentz. Burned in his brain as he drove away from Bourbon Street. He'd found a Quickie Print and taken several copies of the photographs and death certificate, even using the enhance and enlarge options to get more definition. Then he'd handed the originals to Montoya.

He was convinced that someone from his past, or Jennifer's past, was tracking him down. But who? Why? And why screw with his mind?

He slowed for a red light, brooding as the Jeep idled. Overhead, dark clouds scudded slowly across the sky and the smell of the Mississippi River reached his nostrils through the open window.

He remembered Jennifer's image as she'd stood in the woods skirting his backyard. So close to his house—Olivia's home. And now the photographs. He glanced to the passenger seat. The picture of Jennifer crossing the street met his eye. Either the woman in the photo was his ex-wife or a dead ringer.

Ghosts don't show in photographs.

Crazy manifestations aren't real images and therefore cannot be caught on film.

So she was real?

His gut tightened.

So who had been in the backyard of his home, the house that Olivia had brought into the marriage? All in all, this latest encounter was too close for comfort. Too close to Olivia.

He didn't like the thought of his wife being dragged into this, whatever the hell it was. She lived here, too, and just the inkling of her safety being the least bit compromised didn't set well. Olivia had always felt safe at this house. Though Hairy S was useless as a guard dog, they did have a security system Bentz had insisted she install years ago. They rarely used it, but that would have to change.

The light turned green and he waited for an elderly woman on a scooter who was still in the crosswalk. Once she'd eased out of the way, he took the corner fast, then stood on the brakes. A jaywalking teenage boy in a baggy T-shirt and shorts loped across the pavement while plugged into his iPod. The kid never noticed that Bentz had nearly mowed him over.

Bentz cruised past the station and noted that Brinkman had parked in the spot Bentz usually claimed. No big surprise there; Brinkman, though a good cop, was always a pain in the ass. And who could blame the prick? It's not as if Bentz could use it anyway. "Have at," he said, then drove to a coffee shop with Internet access. He linked up as he sipped iced coffee. Crunching ice cubes, he searched for any information he could find on his first wife, even Googled himself in the process. For the most part, he was considered a hero, having solved more than one serial murder case since being hired by the New Orleans PD.

But there was some bad press, too. From L.A., stories surrounding a cop with a tarnished badge, who had left the department with a high-profile case still unsolved.

Then there was the shooting when he'd mistaken a twelve-year-old boy with a toy gun for a killer intending to take down his partner. Bentz had warned the kid, then fired.

The boy, Mario Valdez, had been pronounced DOA at the hospital.

Bentz had poured himself into a bottle and, his badge blackened, had left the department. Thankfully Melinda Jaskiel here in New Orleans had seen fit to give him a second chance.

So he'd relocated.

The rest, as they said, was history.

And now someone was intentionally drawing him back to L.A. He didn't doubt for a second that whoever was behind the photos and mutilated death certificate was intentionally luring him to Southern California.

But *why?* And *why now?*

He finished his coffee, then phoned Montoya's cell and left a message on his voice mail asking Montoya to return the call. He scanned the small bistro where people clustered around tall café tables or sat in overstuffed chairs near the window. Two women in their forties were sharing a doughnut. Three teenagers, a boy and two girls, were slouched in the big chairs and sipping mocha-looking drinks piled high with whipped cream drizzled with chocolate. Without a break in their conversation they were all sending text messages at the speed of light.

Fortunately, his first wife—or her ghost—was nowhere to be seen.

Not that he'd be surprised when she showed up again.

However the answer to the enigma of Jennifer rested in California. He pulled out the photos again. Definitely L.A. There was a palm tree visible in the corner of the shot of her running across the street, and a California license plate on a parked car. In the photo of her in the coffee shop, there was a bit of a street sign visible and he saw the letters *ado Aven.* Some avenue, probably. It could be many places, he thought, but his mind raced, old memories surfacing. Mercado, or Loredo or . . . His stomach dropped as he thought of Colorado Avenue in Santa Monica.

If that was it, someone was really screwing with him.

He and Jennifer had spent a lot of Saturday afternoons at the Third Street Promenade just off Santa Monica Boulevard. About a block and one major shopping mall away from Colorado Avenue. If he remembered right, the mall was accessible from Colorado. He felt that little buzz, like a caffeine rush, at the thought that he was connecting the dots.

Too easily.

He wasn't that smart.

But it was true that Santa Monica, with its outdoor shopping area, long beach, and trendy restaurants, had been one of Jennifer's favorite cities, and significant to them as a couple.

"Crap." He rubbed a hand around the back of his neck and knew that, like it or not, he had to return to Southern California.

Someone was luring him.

Someone wanted him back.

"Son of a bitch," he muttered under his breath. He'd left a lot of turmoil in Southern California. A lot. Most of it unresolved. Few people in the LAPD were sorry to see him leave.

And now he was seeing ghosts and getting anonymous mail from the area near his former residence, a place he'd sworn never to set foot in again.

Something definitely smelled rotten in the Golden State.

And he needed to find out what it was, even if that meant he was playing right into some sicko's hands. That bugged the shit out of him, but there was no way around it.

He clicked off the computer and realized Olivia was due to clock out at the shop in fifteen minutes. Which was perfect. Like it or not, it was time to tell her what the hell was going on.

Outside, the day had taken a turn for the worse, the clouds overhead thickening darkly. The air was dense and sultry, threatening a storm. He climbed into his car, rolled up the windows, and drove toward the French Quarter, where he managed to find a parking spot two blocks from Jackson Square.

Using his damned cane, he made his way to the shop, little more than a tourist trap, at least in his opinion. Olivia liked meeting people and working with Tawilda, a thin, elegant black woman who had been at the store forever, and Manda, a later addition to the staff at the Third Eye. So Livvie had decided to stay on while finishing school and setting up her practice.

The place gave Bentz the creeps.

The little storefront was filled with shelves displaying an assortment of New Age crystals, religious artifacts, books on voodoo, Mardi Gras beads, and tiny alligator heads complete with glittering eyes. Then there were the dolls—all kinds of dolls that reminded him of dead children with their painted faces, false smiles, and eyes that were shuttered by squared-off fake lashes. The dolls were a recent addition to the store and, according to Olivia, a hit, the rare, high-priced ones boosting the shop's profits.

Bentz didn't get it.

He'd once made the mistake of asking, "Who the hell buys this voodoo garbage?"

Olivia, standing at the kitchen window while adding seeds to her parrot's feeder, hadn't been offended. She'd just looked over her shoulder, offered him an enigmatic smile, and said, "You wouldn't want to know. Careful, Bentz, someone you crossed or sent up the river might want to place a hex on you."

"I don't believe in that crap."

"Not yet. Just wait until you break out in a rash, or . . . your eyes turn red, or . . . oh, I don't know . . . you lose your ability to make love, even to the point that your favorite appendage just drops off," she'd teased, raising a naughty eyebrow. That was all it had taken.

"You're asking for it," he'd warned, advancing on her.

"Oh, yeah, and who's gonna give it to me?"

He'd grabbed her then, swept her off her feet, while the seeds scattered over the counter and floor. Chia had squawked and the dog had barked crazily as Bentz carried his wife up the stairs. Squealing, Olivia had laughed, her sandals falling to clatter noisily on the steps.

Once he'd reached the bedroom, he'd kicked the door closed and fallen with her onto the bed. Then he'd gone about showing her that his male parts were still very much fully attached and working just fine.

God, he loved her, he thought now as the first drops of the rain fell from the leaden sky and he made his way along the busy sidewalk skirting Jackson Square. Yet now their relationship was strained and lacked the vitality, the easy, flirtatious fun that had once infused it.

There was still passion; just not the spontaneity or quirky playfulness that they'd enjoyed.

And whose fault is that, Detective Superhero?

His leg began to ache as he walked past the open doors of restaurants, hardly noticing the strains of jazz music and the peppery scents of Cajun cooking that wafted into the street.

He had considered confiding in her about the whole weird Jennifer thing, but he'd never been much of a talker, wasn't a person who expressed all his hopes and fears. Now all that had changed. Push was definitely coming to shove.

He wended through a collection of artists displaying their work on the outside of the wrought iron fence surrounding the square. As a saxophone player blew out a familiar song, his case open for donations, a tarot reader was hard at work laying down cards in front of a twenty-something eagerly listening to the fortune-teller's every word.

Another day in the Quarter.

As the rain fell, Bentz crossed the street behind a horse-drawn carriage, then stepped into the open doorway of the Third Eye. Olivia was just ringing up a sale, several T-shirts, a little box of sand complete with stones and a rake for relaxation, and a baby alligator head. Along with two antique looking, frozen-faced dolls.

Eyeing the ghoulish merchandise, Bentz thought it was high time his wife started expanding her psychology practice. Time to get out of this shop of weird artifacts and start talking to people with problems.

"Hey." Olivia spied Bentz as he tried to move out of the way of the customer, a bag-toting woman who bustled past a display of oyster-shell art on her way to the door.

"Hey back at you."

Olivia grinned, that same smile that could stop his heart. "What're you doing here? Slumming?"

"Looking for a hot dinner date."

"Moi?" she asked coyly, pointing an index finger at her chest.

Frowning thoughtfully, he pretended to look her over, head to toe. "Yeah, I guess you'll do."

"Nice, Bentz," she said with an easy laugh. "I guess you'll do, too."

"Damned straight."

"The male of the species, always so humble," she said to Manda as she clocked out. That done, she crossed the shop and gave her husband a quick kiss on the cheek. "What's this all about?"

"You asked me what was going on and I thought it's time you knew."

Her smile faded. "Should I be worried?"

He hesitated, wanting to reassure her. But in the end he decided to play it straight. "Not really. At least not yet and not about our relationship, but there is something pretty weird going on." He spied her umbrella by the door and snagged it, then, taking the bend of her arm, escorted her out of the shop. Rain peppered the sidewalk and coursed through the gutters. Artists, tarot readers, musicians, and performers quickly covered their wares with plastic tarps or folded up their tables for the day before scurrying for cover.

Bentz opened the umbrella and held it high over Olivia's head as they dashed along the sidewalk. Rain slid down his back as he tried like hell to avoid both puddles and pedestrians. A bicyclist raced by, cutting in and out of traffic. A horn blasted and somewhere a horse whinnied nervously.

In a second the shower turned into a downpour.

Half-running to the restaurant, Bentz felt the familiar pain in his hip, a constant reminder that he wasn't a hundred percent.

The shoulders of his jacket and hems of his pant legs managed to get soaked despite his efforts.

Olivia was laughing, her eyes sparkling with wicked delight at being caught in the storm. "You're soaked," she said as they reached the doorway of the restaurant.

"That's because I was being gallant and keeping you dry."

"Which I appreciate. Thanks." She winked at him. "I'll return the favor sometime."

"Yeah, right." Beneath the cover of a striped awning, Bentz shook the rain from the umbrella, then held the door for her. Inside, tiny lights were strung from the open rafters, appearing like stars over-head, and the walls were paneled with warm reddish wood compli-menting areas of exposed brick.

A hostess led them to a far corner where they were seated at a window table. Outside the rain continued to pour down, gunmetal-gray clouds huddling over the city, water running wildly in the gutters. Inside, beneath lazy paddle fans a waiter brought water and menus, then lit the single candle before promising to return.

"So, about what's happening," Olivia prodded, once they were alone again. "Why do I have the feeling I'm not going to like it?"

"Because you're a very smart woman."

"Mmm."

"And you're some kind of kook psychic."

"Whom you love," she reminded him.

"Right."

"Make that adore."

"Now you're pushing it."

"You're avoiding the subject."

"Waiting for the right moment," he said, eyeing the menu and not bringing up Jennifer until after they ordered. Once the waiter had re-treated again, Bentz laid it all out. He started with the moment he'd woken up in the hospital and felt the drop in temperature before wit-nessing his dead wife in the doorway. He told Olivia about the other sightings as well. Finally, he admitted to spying Jennifer again just off the veranda a few days earlier, then just recently receiving the marred death certificate and photographs.

With each of his confessed sightings, Olivia became more and more serious. "I don't understand," she whispered, her gaze seeking his. "How? Why?"

He handed her the copies he'd kept and watched her face turn ashen. "I wish I knew the answer to that."

"Jennifer's dead." She glanced up at him for confirmation.

"Yes."

"There was a suicide note, you made the ID on the body."

"I know."

"Then . . . ?"

"An imposter, probably."

"Or . . . your imagination."

"Don't think so." He tapped the pictures with a finger. "These are real."

"Or someone faked them."

"That's possible."

"Rick, she's *not* alive!" She cleared her throat and leaned back in her chair. "Did you . . . have you told Kristi?"

"She was there when I woke up and she thought it was hallucinations from the drugs or aftereffects from the coma. Said it was all a 'bad trip.' I didn't want to upset her, so I haven't mentioned it again. Neither has she."

But then his daughter was caught up in writing her book and planning her wedding. Kristi didn't want to think that her father had lost his marbles. Because, even though now he was certain he was being tormented by an outside force, he also suspected deep inside that some of his visions of Jennifer had been conjured in his mind.

Maybe outside influences had tripped a latch in his brain and, though he was loath to admit it, he didn't know what was real and what was a figment of his imagination.

"She hasn't seen these?" Olivia motioned to the photos.

"No."

Slowly letting out her breath, Olivia stared at the marred death certificate, then the pictures once more. Her eyebrows pulled together to form little lines in her forehead and her full lips twisted in revulsion. "This is really sick."

"Can't argue that."

"Do you have any idea who sent these?" She held the photos and certificate up, then shook her head and handed everything back to Bentz.

"No. But Montoya's having the lab check out the originals. Finger-prints, DNA, photo-altering—anything else the department can find out including what kind of red pen was used to write the question mark." He tucked the envelope into the inside pocket of his jacket just as the waiter delivered the first course.

"You think she's alive?" Olivia asked.

"No." He stirred his seafood stew and shook his head. "But I don't think she's a ghost, either."

"Obviously. So . . . an imposter. Someone messing with you." She nodded to herself, picking up her fork. "Who?"

"That's the million-dollar question."

Irritated, she stabbed bits of lettuce and shrimp onto her fork. "So you think there's someone *here* in Louisiana pretending to be Jen-nifer, and she makes herself visible to only you. And you think she showed up at the hospital months ago, at the precise moment you woke up. Nonetheless, the pictures and death certificate were mailed from L.A." Her eyes narrowed as she bit into her salad. "Is that about it?"

"Yeah. About."

"So why go to all that trouble? Why not mail the package from here in New Orleans?"

"Jennifer died in Southern California."

"If it was her in the van."

"It was."

"You say she hasn't aged, right? But how close were you to her?"

Good point. "Not close enough."

"Hmm. And the photos, they make her look young, but again, they could've been doctored. Or her face superimposed over an-other woman's body."

"The answer is in L.A."

"Although you saw her in Louisiana?"

"These shots were taken around L.A."

"Maybe."

The whole Photoshop thing again. "Her body is buried in Califor-nia," he said and watched her reaction.

"Jesus, are you thinking of exhuming her?" Revulsion showed on her face. "Because you *think* you saw her? Because you received some pictures and a marked-up death certificate with a postmark from the town where you lived. Isn't that a little extreme? I mean, would anyone even order it?"

"I don't know, but I think so."

"So you're thinking of going to California," she guessed, shaking her head.

"Yeah. While I'm off duty."

"So soon."

He nodded. "Montoya will watch my back here, look after you."

"You think I need looking after?"

"No. But . . ."

"But just in case I feel abandoned, he's around. Right?" she mocked. "In the off chance that I feel you're on a wild goose chase, or following a ghost or . . . I don't know, dealing with all those old feelings you haven't quite laid to rest, I can count on your partner, not you. Is that what you're saying?"

He felt the muscles in his back tighten.

"I don't need to be babysat or coddled, okay? I've lived in that house most of my life. A lot of it alone. I don't need 'looking after.' Sometimes I wonder if you've lost your mind!"

That makes two of us.

"Maybe you should just let the cops handle this."

"I'm a cop."

"No, not this time." She shook her head, golden strands of her hair catching in the candlelight. "This time I think you're the victim."

"Listen, Livvie—"

"To what? Some excuse to go chasing after a woman who's dead? Some trumped-up rationale? This is a situation for the police," she said, pointing to the death certificate and photographs of Jennifer. "And as for 'seeing' Jennifer, maybe you should take that up with your doctor or, heaven forbid, a shrink. These photos . . . they have to be fakes!"

"Olivia—"

"I hear what you're telling me, Bentz. Word for word. But it's what you're *not* telling me that is drumming through my head, pounding in my brain, and ripping a damned hole in my heart."

"Wait a second."

"No, I'm not waiting. Not a second, not half a second. You're going to hear me out. The way I see it, what's going on here is that you're hell-bent for leather to chase after your past. Face it. If we've had a problem in our marriage it's been Jennifer. Kristi's mother. A woman you divorced because she was cheating on you, then took back, even though she couldn't be faithful. You've been fighting emotions that have been eating at you for over a decade: Guilt. Guilt that you're alive and she's not."

"Is that your professional opinion?"

"Nothing professional about it. Common sense." She looked about to say something more, then pushed the rest of her salad aside. "Look, if you need to go, then go. Figure it out. Because, you know, I've tried to be supportive and understanding and upbeat, but this has been eating at you. So go. Find out what it is. That's important, yeah, but what's really important to me is that you deal with the past and put it away."

He felt a tic near his temple. "If you don't want me to go—"

"Oh, no, you don't. Don't you dare go there. This is your deal, not mine. You feel this is something you need to do, then do it."

"I thought you wanted me to open up, to tell you what was bothering me."

"Yeah," she admitted, nodding, then waiting as their entrées were served. "I did want to know, but I thought it might happen a little earlier, you know, before you'd already mentally packed your bags to take off for La La Land."

"I told you, if you don't want me to go, just say the word."

She hesitated, then leaned forward. "No, Rick. I want you to go. As happy as we've been, and we have been happy, there's always been that little bit of doubt on my part. And guilt on yours. Look, if Jennifer were still alive we might not be together. So now we get to find out just how strong our marriage is."

"I think it's damned strong."

"Do you?"

"Yes."

"But you can't commit to a child."

"I have a child." He was about to say more but saw by the darkening of her eyes that he'd wounded her. Instead he reached across the table to take her hand. "This just isn't the time."

She pulled her fingers from his. "But it is for me, Bentz," she said, her jaw jutting a bit. "It's really now or never."

He considered giving in. After all, she'd make a wonderful mother, he knew that. And so what if he was so old he'd qualify for Social Security when the kid graduated from high school? People did it all the time. He slid his jaw to the side. "I'll think about it."

She grabbed her purse and pushed away from the table. "Then think fast."

CHAPTER 5

She should have told him.

She shouldn't have chickened out.

Olivia stepped out of the shower and toweled off. Steam covered the window in the bathroom and she cracked it a bit, all the while second-guessing herself. Bentz had left earlier in the morning and even now was winging his way to Los Angeles.

She never should have let him go without mentioning the baby. But the thought of being *that* woman, a clinging female who would use any excuse, even her unborn child, to try to keep a man from doing what he wanted stuck in Olivia's craw. She didn't believe in reining in someone she loved. It just didn't make sense. She wasn't into using guilt to hang on to him, and he'd certainly made it clear how he felt about becoming a father again.

It wasn't as if she'd intentionally gone behind his back and gotten pregnant. There'd been no trick involved; she simply wasn't taking any measures to prevent pregnancy. He knew she wasn't on the pill. Though Rick usually took care of birth control himself, there had been a few times he hadn't bothered with a condom, several instances where passion had overruled sanity. And, Olivia thought, brushing her teeth and seeing her reflection in the foggy mirror, she was thrilled to have this new life inside her, having been worried that, given their ages, it might be difficult to conceive.

Nonetheless, she hadn't used the baby as a means to stop him from going on his damned quest to L.A.

She spat, leaned her face under the faucet, rinsed her mouth, and straightened. The woman standing in the misty reflection stared back at her and silently accused her of being a coward. Guilty. But she'd kept mum for good reason. She had wanted to avoid a fight, and couldn't bear to witness the disappointment—even resentment— in his eyes. She didn't believe he'd suggest abortion, but she couldn't begin to deal with the idea of terminating her pregnancy.

"And I thought you were a straight shooter," she said aloud to her own watery image. "Aren't you the one who never backs down? What the hell happened to you?"

She let her hands fall to her flat belly.

A baby . . . a life that right now was growing inside her.

And her husband didn't even know she was pregnant. Didn't want to know.

"Jerk," she muttered under her breath. "Good riddance." She pulled a comb through her hair, wrapped a towel around her body, then opened the door and nearly tripped over the dog. Hairy S had camped out in the hall in front of the bathroom. "Not smart," she said to the dog and petted his furry head. "But don't worry about it; there's a lot of stupidity going around in this house these days. A lot. You're not the Lone Ranger."

Hairy thumped his tail against the floor, then followed her to the bedroom, where she dressed and tried not to think about the fact that her husband was nearly a continent away, chasing demons who had haunted him for twelve long years.

The flight was uneventful.

Once, after dozing, Bentz thought he smelled gardenias. He took a long look around the cabin of the 727, eyeing all the passengers, half expecting Jennifer to be calmly seated near the window, reading a book. She would, of course, upon feeling his gaze upon her, look up and smile with that sexy little grin that had always gotten to him. Without saying a word she would tell him that she knew he'd follow her.

It didn't happen.

No one on the plane remotely resembled his first wife . . . *ex*-wife he reminded himself. *Ex.* They had been divorced, though living to- gether, at the time of her death. But those arrangements had been about to end. Because she hadn't been able to give up her lover.

The plane touched down at LAX with a soft bump as the back

wheels hit the tarmac, then even less of a jar as the wheel under the nose of the plane found the pavement. As the 727 taxied to the gate, most of the passengers were already turning on cell phones, unbuckling their seat belts, and shifting the luggage at their feet. After spending the entire trip with her nose in a book, the woman in the seat next to Bentz swung a purse the size of Guatemala onto her lap and scrounged for her cell frantically. Touchdown propelled her into frenzied mode and she hastily dug through her huge purse. Bentz barely avoided being knocked over by the bag as he pulled his computer from beneath the seat in front of him and she located her phone and clicked it on, immediately making a call.

He couldn't help but overhear her conversation, a one-sided affair in which she was trashing her ex's latest girlfriend.

Fortunately, the plane emptied fairly quickly.

On the way to baggage claim Bentz called Olivia and left a message that he'd landed safely. He found his one bag, then rented a small SUV with a G.P.S. already installed. He'd done it all without using his cane and, though his hip ached, he ignored the pain and threw the damned walking stick that he'd brought along into the backseat.

As he exited the rental lot in the Ford Escape, he slipped a pair of sunglasses onto the bridge of his nose. The scenery was familiar, the tightness in his chest new. Years ago he'd left L.A. with a bad taste in his mouth; now all those old feelings came back at him in a rush. Guilt over Jennifer's suicide, remorse over the death of a twelve-year-old kid with a toy pistol, gnawing frustration that he would have been able to solve the Caldwell twins' double homicide if he'd been at the top of his game, and the fog of too many numbing shots of whiskey.

He'd been a mess. Jack Daniel's had become his best friend and that friendship had damaged every other relationship. It had also compromised his job performance and his ability to see clearly.

Though officially he'd quit the LAPD, the pressure to resign had been palpable, the tension in the department thicker than the smog that blanketed the city. Even his remaining friends, the few coworkers who "had his back," had been relieved to see him leave. His departure had been better for all concerned. Especially him.

Except that he'd left some unfinished business behind.

It had been years since he'd been in Southern California, and though the area had changed, the royal palm trees and space-age arches of the Encounters restaurant at LAX were reminders of a time he'd tried hard to forget.

As he maneuvered onto the freeway he couldn't see the surrounding hills through the layer of smog that hovered over the area. He fiddled with the air conditioning to combat the rising temperature as buildings rose ghostlike through the shimmering heat waves. By instinct he headed toward his old neighborhood, which wasn't too far from Culver City.

The area had changed a little. The shrubs and trees were larger, the neighborhood as a whole seeming to have gone a little downhill, evidenced by the cracked sidewalks and wrought-iron bars on some windows.

His old house looked pretty much the same. Sometime in the past twelve years, it had been painted a dove gray, but now was in dire need of another coat. The garage door was blistered and didn't quite close, the yard overgrown and dry. Weeds turned brown in the sun-bleached bark chips near the tired front porch. A FOR RENT sign was wedged into the grass, but it too was fading beneath the intense California sun.

Leaving his cane in the rental, Bentz walked around the house and peered through the dirty windows to spy dusty floors and dingy walls, some the same color they had been a dozen years earlier. Stepping backward and shading his eyes, he gazed up to the window and was bombarded by memories of images within his former bedroom, the scene he'd walked into more than a decade ago. Twisted sheets of the unmade bed and slivers of broken glass spattered beneath the gaping hole where a mirror once hung. In his mind he retraced the path to the spare bedroom on the second floor, the guest room Jennifer had used as her office. He remembered that it had taken a while to find the note that she'd left, not in an obvious location on a table or a counter, but tucked away in her desk drawer, written to Kristi and signed in Jennifer's flowing hand.

He'd always wondered about that.

The suicide note to their daughter that had been tucked away in the pages of the latest self-help book Jennifer had been reading. *The Power of Me,* or something just as self-centered.

All the advice in the world hadn't helped his screwed-up ex-wife.

But she hadn't left the note out in the open.

As if she'd had second thoughts.

Or was waiting. Hadn't yet made a final decision.

At the time he'd discovered the note he'd pushed aside the nagging questions and had rationalized that in her pursuit of death, as in so many facets of her life, Jennifer had done a lousy job. But now he had renewed doubts. What if Jennifer's death hadn't been suicide? What if she hadn't been driving the car? What if the woman he'd identified as his wife and buried six feet under had been someone else?

Just who was decomposing in that grave?

His gut twisted at the thought and he didn't let his mind wander too far down that dark, rocky path.

He returned to the Escape and drove nearly five miles to a cemetery, the spot where he'd thought Jennifer had been laid to rest. Parking in the shade of a live oak tree, he fished out his wallet and found a battered card for Detective Jonas Hayes of the LAPD. He'd carried the damned card around for twelve years and remembered the day Hayes had pressed the card into his palm. "Hey, if you ever need anything," he'd said after the burial as clouds had rolled in and rain had started to fall. So long ago . . . and now Bentz wondered if Jennifer were truly entombed in the casket lying under the granite headstone.

He walked through the drying grass and found the plot, read the simple inscription, and felt a strange pang in his heart. Had he made a mistake? Did the corpse beneath his feet belong to someone else? He glared down at the grass, as if he could see through the sod and six feet of dry earth to the casket where a woman's body had been decomposing for twelve long years.

A whisper of a breeze slid across the back of his neck and the scent of gardenias was suddenly heavy in the air. Did he hear someone whisper his name? He turned, expecting to see Jennifer beckoning with that come-hither naughty smile that had been her trademark. But she wasn't leaning against one of the taller headstones, her auburn hair shimmering in the afternoon sunlight. Nor was she standing anywhere within the wrought-iron fencing surrounding the silent graveyard.

He was alone at his ex-wife's final resting place. The cemetery was empty, not a soul besides himself visible. Some of the plots displayed fresh flowers. A few had been adorned with plastic bouquets and others were festooned with tiny American flags that had faded in the harsh sunlight. However, no other person, nor ghost for that matter, stood inside the ominous black wrought-iron fence.

Of course not.

She's dead, Bentz. Dead. You know it. You identified her body with your own eyes, for Christ's sake! And you don't believe in ghosts. Try remembering that one, will ya?

He lingered a few more minutes, trying to piece together what was happening to him. He didn't think he was cracking up, and he knew he didn't believe in ghosts. Dead women did not just reappear.

So why come here, to the cemetery?

Without an answer he returned to the car, which was now sweltering from the sun. Leaving the driver's door open, he sat behind the wheel and turned on the engine to get the A/C pumping. As the car cooled, he eyed Hayes's business card. On one side was the official information for Detective Jonas Hayes of the LAPD; on the other was a phone number scratched hurriedly a long time ago.

Bentz punched the private number into his cell and was rewarded with a message from a lifeless voice that told him it was no longer in service. "Great." Bentz flipped the card over and tried again, this time phoning the police department directly and asking for Detective Jonas Hayes.

Without too much fuss he was put through to Hayes's voice mail. He left a message saying he was in town and wanted to meet. Afterward he called and left another message for Olivia. As he hung up he had the uncanny feeling that he was being watched, that hidden eyes were observing his every move. He scanned the cemetery as he drove off, checked his mirrors and saw no one tailing him, no one tracking his movements.

"You're an idiot," he told himself, then went in search of a cheap, clean motel.

Jonas Hayes swore under his breath. He was tired. Dead tired. He'd spent too many hours the previous day trying to hammer out details for the custody of Maren, his daughter, then hadn't slept a wink before pulling a full shift. And now he had Rick Bentz calling him.

"Hell," he muttered. There were a lot of reasons he didn't want to return the call. He waited until his shift was over and he was in his car miles away from the department before he dialed the cell number Bentz had left.

On the third ring, Bentz answered. "Rick Bentz."

"The death-defying Rick Bentz, who lives through a lightning strike?" he joked, though truth to tell there wasn't anything remotely humorous about Bentz calling.

"Not exactly accurate, but close enough. Bad news travels fast."

"Gossip has no bounds. These days with the Internet, cell phones with cameras, traffic lights with cameras, security cameras everywhere, you have no privacy. You can't take a leak in New Orleans without someone putting it up on YouTube for all of us out here to view."

"Is that right?" Bentz said. "Then how the hell don't we get the suspects on film?"

"We do. A lot of times. At least the stupid ones. That is, when we get lucky."

"So you got dinner plans? I'm in town and I'll buy."

Hayes saw it coming. Big as life. And he didn't like it one bit. "Sounds like you need a favor."

"Maybe."

"No maybes about it. That's why you rose from the dead, Bentz. Admit it."

"We'll talk about rising from the dead over steaks. How about Roy's if it's still around?"

Roy's had once been a hip, happening place, an homage to the days of the great westerns. "It's around and seedier than ever. But the food's still good and happy hour drinks are five bucks."

"That's a bargain?"

"In Hollywood? Yeah. But tonight won't work. I'm already booked. Is the offer still good tomorrow?"

"Sure. I'll meet you there . . . say, around seven?"

"That'll work. Tomorrow at seven. See ya there."

Hayes hung up, opened the console between the two front seats of his old 4Runner and found a bottle of Rolaids he kept in the glove box. His heartburn was acting up and the call from Bentz didn't help.

Hayes poured out a few and popped them into his mouth, downing them with the remainder of this morning's coffee, the dregs of which had settled into the bottom of his travel cup. The taste was bitter, but tolerable. He slid his shades onto his nose, glanced in his rearview, checking traffic, then eased onto the street.

If Rick Bentz was in L.A., something was coming down.

Something that wasn't good.

I really have to congratulate myself.

Job well done!

Rick Hot-Fucking-Shot Bentz is back in L.A.!

No big surprise there.

Like a hungry lion leaping onto a weak gazelle, Rick Bentz took the bait. Just in time.

I check the calendar and nod to myself. Feel a little thrill race down my spine. It didn't take long and he's still recuperating, not quite agile or fleet-footed, still using a cane, which is just damned perfect. I can't help but experience a wave of pride. In myself. Not just for this, his return, but for my patience. I had to wait until the timing was right, but now I think I can pour myself a drink, a strong one.

Let's see . . . how about a martini? That would be fitting. I walk to the bar and find the vodka and curse myself for being out of olives. Oh, damn . . . well, who cares? I find the vermouth and pour just a whisper, then shake the concoction with ice and pour . . . mmm. Since there are no olives I settle for a twist of lemon . . . perfect.

I walk to the full-length mirror, where I see myself and lift my glass toward the woman in the glass. She's beautiful. Tall. Willowy. The ravages of age not yet apparent. Her dark hair falls to her shoulders in easy waves. Her smile is infectious, her eyes those of a woman who knows what she wants and always gets it.

"To new beginnings," I say touching the rim of my glass to the mirror and hearing the soft little click of glass on glass. "You and I, we've waited a long time for this."

"That we have. But no longer," she replies, arched eyebrows lifting conspiratorially.

I tingle inside knowing that everything we—I—have worked for is about to come to fruition.

The window is open and I feel evening settling in the rising moon, a ghostly crescent glowing in the twilight sky.

"Cheers," my reflection says back to me, her eyes twinkling in naughty anticipation as she holds her glass aloft. "May we be successful."

"Oh, we will," I assure her, smiling as she grins back at me. "We will." Then we drink as one, feeling the cool cocktail slide so easily down our throats. Together we think of Rick Bentz.

Handsome in a rugged way. Athletic and muscular rather than thin. With a square jaw and eyes that could cut through any kind of lie, he's smart and pensive, his emotions usually under tight rein.

And yet he has an Achilles heel.

One that will bring him down.

"Bravo," I say to the mirror. Because I know that soon, that sick son of a bitch will get his.

CHAPTER 6

Bentz had a lot of ground to cover and he didn't want to waste time.

First things first: He had to find a place to stay. He decided to stick close to where he'd lived with Jennifer and in the area of the zip code on the envelope that had been sent to him.

Though hotel prices in Southern California were through the roof, he found a motel in the older part of Culver City that advertised, "inexpensive, clean rooms." The So-Cal Inn was a long, low-lying stucco building that, he guessed, was built in the decade after World War II, and offered, along with weekly rates, a swimming pool, air-conditioned rooms, cable TV, and wi-fi. The place also claimed to be "pet and kid friendly."

Everything he needed and more.

Bentz parked in front and walked into the small reception area, where a glass pot of coffee sat congealing on a hot plate. A kid who looked no more than fourteen was working, fiddling with the remote to a television mounted on the wall over a display of brochures for activities in the area. "Mom," the teen yelled toward a half-open door behind the long desk, then pointed the remote at the television and pressed down over and over again, in rapid-fire succession, with the agility of the generation that grew up with text messaging and video games. However, the TV channel or volume didn't change and the boy's frustration was evidenced in his red cheeks and set jaw.

As Bentz reached the counter a woman slipped through the open door. Her red hair was piled high on her head, her mascara so thick her eyelids appeared weighted down. She looked to be in her mid-thirties. Perfumed by cigarette smoke, she was trim and lithe in shorts and a print top that wrapped around her chest to tie under one arm. Pinned over one of her breasts was a nametag that read: REBECCA ALLISON—MANAGER. "Can I help you?" she asked, her shiny lips curving into a friendly smile.

"Lookin' for a room. For one. Nothing fancy."

"We have a few that have wonderful views of the pool," she said, quickly flipping into salesperson mode. "They've each got a sliding door to a private sitting area that opens up to the pool."

"Are they the cheapest?"

Her smile didn't falter. "Well, no. If you'd like something less expensive, I've got several that overlook the parking lot," and she quoted him the daily and weekly rates.

"One of those will do fine," he said. "For the week."

"Great." She ran his credit card while the kid muttered something under his breath about friggin' cheap-ass remotes, and the deal was sealed.

Rebecca sent the boy a sharp look, then turned back to Bentz. "Here's a map of the area. We serve a continental breakfast here from six until ten in the morning, and coffee's available all day."

He resisted another glance at the sludge pot.

"If you need anything, just call the main desk."

"This damned thing—" the kid said.

"Tony!" Rebecca said sharply. "Enough."

The boy went immediately into pout mode, turning his back on his mother and shaking the remote as if he could somehow make the bad connections spark.

Bentz walked out and squinted into the white haze. For the next week, at least, he was a resident of Southern California.

Hayes strode across the lush lawn in front of his ex-wife's apartment as the sun settled over the hills to the west. He clicked the remote lock for his SUV and nearly ran into a woman walking two beagles who tugged their leashes taut. "Hey, watch it," she said, sending him a withering glare. He barely noticed as he yanked open the driver's door.

The interior of his car was blistering, the steering wheel almost too hot to touch. But the temperature inside his 4Runner was nothing compared to the heat churning in his gut. Jesus, he was mad. Who the hell did Delilah think she was, pulling out of the marriage because she couldn't hack being married to a cop any longer? She'd known he was a career man with the LAPD when she'd married him twelve years ago.

But then she'd been pregnant.

And they'd both wanted the kid.

That part, he thought, considering his daughter, they'd gotten right. The rest had been up and down, a roller-coaster ride exacerbated by his career and Delilah's mood swings.

So now they were divorced. Shit. Making him a two-time loser. He'd already been married once before to Alonda, his college sweetheart. That had ended when he'd found her in bed with her best friend and she'd admitted to him that she was gay. Had been all along. It wasn't that she didn't love him, but . . .

Great.

He'd stormed out and filed papers the next day. At least there were no kids from that first doomed union.

Two years later he'd met Delilah and fallen head over heels. But he'd been careful. He hadn't wanted to make the same mistake twice. He hazarded another glance at the apartment building, a four-story pink-tinged stucco building with arched windows and tile roof, a nod to old California. She was on the top floor, two bedrooms and a thousand square feet of vaulted ceilings and new carpeting. There, she asserted, she could "start over" and "find what she really wanted in life," whatever the hell that meant.

With a flick of the ignition his Toyota fired up. He pulled out of his parking spot, a rare commodity here in Santa Monica, twenty-six blocks from the beach. High rent, in Hayes's estimation, but Delilah had money. She owned half of a modeling school, where runway moms sent their daughters to learn the tricks of the trade. Delilah, once a print-ad model herself and a natural salesperson, had helped make the school a raging success.

What did she need with a workaholic cop for a husband? Their divorce, had been finalized six months earlier. Now if they could just straighten out the custody schedule.

To be truthful, Jonas had already started dating. This time he'd taken up with Corrine O'Donnell, a fellow cop, a woman who understood the rigors and demands of the job. She'd been a detective, but since her injury she'd been assigned to a desk job in missing persons. She claimed she didn't mind. He wondered.

He slid his SUV into traffic, attempted to rein in his fury over Delilah's latest custody demand, and angled the 4Runner toward the Santa Monica Freeway. He wanted to do a little more checking on Bentz before he met with him tomorrow.

Rick Bentz hadn't just shown up out of the blue.

The few quick calls Hayes had made earlier had confirmed what Hayes suspected: Bentz was on leave from the New Orleans Police Department and there was talk that he wouldn't be returning. He'd been injured, spent a couple of weeks in a coma and a few months in physical therapy. If he ever got back to work, he'd probably be stuck behind a desk and the Rick Bentz Hayes had known, back in the day, would have shriveled up and died if he hadn't been in the field.

Hayes surmised that hadn't changed.

But he'd do some checking. The way he remembered it Bentz had fallen apart after his ex-wife's death and the shooting of the Valdez kid. Bentz had been cleared of any charges; the boy had been taking aim at Bentz's partner, Russ Trinidad, but the weapon had turned out to be a very authentic-appearing toy. Though exonerated of any crime, guilt had eaten away at the detective and it looked as if his ex-wife's suicide had pushed him over the edge. He'd lost interest in anything except his kid and had left the department with a couple of black eyes—the Valdez kid's death and a double-murder investigation that had gone too cold too fast.

Bentz had given up his badge in L.A., and though no one could really pin the blame for either event on him, people took their shots. Even some of those closest to him had thought he'd lost his edge when he'd taken his ex-wife back. After the fact, people had blamed the Valdez kid's death on Bentz's lack of good judgment, his lack of focus, but, bottom line, it was just a tragedy.

Hayes didn't know what to think as he cut toward the Ten. He saw his entrance and passed an old Volkswagen bus belching blue smoke before gunning it onto the freeway.

His cell phone rang and he snagged it. "Hayes."

"Hey, how'd it go?" Corrine asked. She was one of the few people who knew he was still hammering out a change in the custody arrangements.

"It went," he said and smiled a bit. Corrine, another cop who knew the ropes, had become his rock.

"You okay?"

Never, when dealing with Delilah. He hated to think it, but his shrink seemed to think he was still hung up on her. "I will be."

"So, you're coming over later? I've got *First Blood* on DVD. Thought it might help get out some of your aggressions."

He actually laughed. "I'll bring the raw meat."

"I think you need to come up with something . . . uh, what's the quote . . . about what Rambo ate?"

"I think it's something that would make a billy goat puke."

"Yeah, that's right." She chuckled. "We can barbecue whatever it is . . . roadkill maybe."

"I'll work on it." He felt a little better as he glanced at the dashboard clock. "Look, I have a couple of things I've gotta do. I'll be there in little over an hour."

"Why do I have the feeling that this is because Rick Bentz is in town?"

He probably shouldn't have told her that Bentz had called, especially because she and Bentz had "a history." But the truth would have gotten out sooner or later, and Bentz had dated several women in the department before he met and married Jennifer. Hayes decided it was best if Corrine heard it from him first. If he'd learned anything from his two failed marriages, he now knew it was better to stick to the truth. It was also a whole lot better to be the bearer of bad news than let the woman in his life be blindsided from some other source.

"You figured out the Bentz connection," he teased. "Proof that you're a crack detective."

"Yeah, right. Missing Persons wouldn't be the same without me."

She played along. "Don't think that kind of sweet talk will make up for the fact that you'll be late."

"Wouldn't dream of it."

"I'll fire up the DVD player. At least I can count on Rambo showing up."

"Ouch! I'll be there. Soon."

"Just as long as you know I'm not the kind of woman who sits around and waits forever."

"What's wrong with ya?" he joked and she chuckled.

"Jerk!"

"Yeah, but you love me."

"And that's the problem. I'll see you soon."

He hung up feeling better. Corrine O'Donnell wasn't the love of his life and he doubted that she ever would be. Besides, he'd sworn off marriage for good. Twice was enough and being a bachelor wasn't all that bad. She seemed to feel the same; at least for the time being she wasn't making noises about moving in together or getting married. But then, she, too, had taken her turn in the divorce department.

Jockeying through traffic, Hayes turned his thoughts to Bentz again and decided the guy deserved some kind of break. Hayes would meet with him and see what Bentz wanted. Even if he already knew he wasn't going to like it.

To say Bentz's new accommodations were less than five-star would be a vast understatement. Room 16, overlooking the sun-cracked asphalt with its faded parking stripes, would be hard pressed to earn two stars, but Bentz didn't care. The two double beds had matching, if washed-out, paisley spreads and faux oak headboards screwed into the wall. There was a sad desk and bureau from which a TV straight out of the eighties eyeballed him. The attached bath was tiny, with barely enough room for him to turn around. The towels were thin, but it all looked clean enough. Probably not up to Olivia's standards, but good enough for Bentz.

He was unzipping his bag when the phone rang and the number of Olivia's cell flashed on the display.

"Hey," he answered. "I was beginning to get worried."

"Were you?" She sounded lighthearted, and for that he was re-lieved. In the past few days she'd tried to be supportive, even joke with him. Most of her attempts had fallen flat and he knew she was concerned, even troubled, about the trip. Twice he'd offered to can-cel and both times she had insisted he follow through. "You just do what you have to do, and when it's over come back home, okay?" Olivia was not the kind of woman who would sit around and wait for a man. This time, though, she was attempting to do just that, though it went against all her natural instincts. He appreciated her sacrifice and had promised her he'd wrap things up and return as soon as he could.

"You'd better be working 'round the clock," she said sternly.

"I've only been here a few hours."

"And it's seemed like an eternity," she whispered. For a moment he almost bought into her act, but she blew it by chuckling. "I'm sorry, I couldn't help that."

He swallowed a smile. At least she was joking, kidding around with him. "Okay, fair enough. You got me."

"So what do you know?"

"Nothing yet." They talked a few minutes and she told him she'd had dinner with Lydia Kane, a friend she'd met while in grad school. He gave her the name and number of his motel and promised to call her the next day.

"Be careful," she said. "To be honest, I don't know what to wish for. That you find Jennifer is dead and that someone is just playing a sick game with you . . . or that she's really alive."

"Either way will be messy."

"I know. I mean it, Rick. Don't take too many chances. We need you."

"We?"

She hesitated just a second. "Yeah, all of us. Kristi and me, well, and Hairy S and Chia, too."

"I'll be home soon," he promised, but they both knew he was just placating her. He had no idea when he'd return to New Orleans.

"Just let me know how many wild geese you catch."

"Funny girl."

"Sometimes," she said.

"Most of the time. I'll call you."

He hung up and considered taking the next plane east. Why not? She was right. He was still chasing a ghost and he was either being set up or losing his mind.

He bet on the first.

And knew he was going to ride it out.

He had to.

CHAPTER 7

For Bentz, dinner consisted of the prepackaged cheese and crackers and diet Coke he found in the vending machine in the breezeway leading to the pool area.

He bit off the cellophane as he walked back to his room, then went to work. He'd already made lists of the people Jennifer had been closest to. He would start trying to track them down while munching on the oily crackers and processed cheddar.

He figured some of Jennifer's nearest and dearest might still be in the area, so he could set up meetings. That was, if anyone was willing to talk with him. No doubt he'd be considered persona non grata with most of them. As for the acquaintances who had moved, he'd have to hunt for them and make an attempt to contact them by phone.

And what will you say to them? That you think you've seen Jennifer even though you buried her twelve years ago?

He didn't have an answer for that one, he thought. He set up his laptop with its Internet card on the scarred Formica desk, cracked the blinds so that he could view the parking lot, and settled into the straight-backed chair.

Dredging a cracker through one of the tiny plastic troughs of cheese, he noticed a blue Pontiac from the late sixties pull into one of the parking slots. The guy behind the wheel, wearing a plaid driver's cap and a goatee, grabbed a couple of bags from the front seat and climbed out. Immediately a tiny spotted dog that looked like it had a little bit of Jack Russell terrier in it hopped onto the pavement and danced at its owner's feet. With surprising agility, the man locked the car with his key, then, whistling and calling to "Spike," hauled his two plastic bags and a small briefcase into the room adjoining Bentz's.

Once the door closed Bentz turned his attention back to the laptop and the issue at hand—Jennifer's acquaintances. He'd have to play it by ear with them. He didn't plan to tell any of Jennifer's friends that he'd thought he'd seen her, not unless they volunteered some sort of information about fake "hauntings" first.

But getting them to open up would be a trick.

Anyone who knew anything about Jennifer's death would have maintained silence for twelve years, keeping the truth not just from him but from his daughter and the police. Bentz, ex-cop and ex-husband, would be hard-pressed to pry anything from those who had known her.

He'd already put together a short list of friends pared down from all her known acquaintances. These women had been the closest to Jennifer. They would most understand her, most likely to have been her confidantes.

Shana Wynn, whose last married name he knew of was McIntyre, had been one of Jennifer's best friends and, as Bentz recalled, a real bitch. Beautiful. Smart. Out for number one. She and Jennifer had been college roommates and they'd had a lot in common. If anyone knew that Jennifer had faked her own death, it would be Shana.

Tally White also made the "must interview" list. Tally's daughter Melody had been a friend of Kristi's in elementary school. Jennifer and Tally had gotten close. Real close. Both women had been divorced.

Fortuna Esperanzo had become a friend of Jennifer's when they'd both worked briefly at an art gallery in Venice.

Then there was Lorraine Newell, Jennifer's stepsister, who hadn't liked Bentz from the get-go. A dark-haired prima donna with a princess complex, Lorraine hadn't been particularly close to Jennifer, either, and hadn't bothered to keep in contact with Kristi since Jennifer's death.

There were others as well, but these four women were at the top of his list. He just had to find them. Which was easier said than done. So far his online searches had only turned up one plum: Shana McIntyre's current address. He clicked open a file with information on her and jotted the street number and name on the envelope he used to carry his photos. Hopefully, Shana was in town and would be willing to see him when he paid her a visit.

Bentz slid the photos out of the envelope and fanned them out on the desk. Tapping the photo of Jennifer looking out of the coffee shop, he did an online search of coffee shops on Colorado Avenue. Bingo! Plenty to choose from. A cup of coffee would be his first order of business in the morning.

He worked late into the night, finally gave up, and flopped onto the thin mattress with a sinkhole in the center. Propping himself up with pillows, he turned on the television, watched some sports updates, and, with the latest scores flashing across the screen, drifted off.

The remote was still in his hand when the bedside phone rang, jerking him awake. He picked up, knowing it couldn't be good if someone was calling so late, phoning at the motel and not on his cell. "This is Bentz," he said, cobwebs still in his mind, some kind of cage fighting on the TV screen. For a second he heard nothing. "Hello?"

He hit the television's mute button.

Soft crying was barely audible.

"Hello?" he said again. "Who is this? Are you okay?"

More muffled sobbing as he pushed himself up in bed. "Who are you trying to reach?"

"I'm sorry," she whispered, her voice raspy and raw. For a second he thought she was apologizing for calling the wrong person, but then she said, "Please forgive me, RJ. I didn't mean to hurt you."

What? His heart nearly stopped. "Who is this?" he demanded, his pulse pounding in his ears.

Click!

The phone went dead in his hand. "Hello?" he said, and hit the button on the receiver's cradle in rapid succession. "Hello?"

Nothing.

"Hello? Hello? Damn!"

She'd hung up. With suddenly sweating hands, he replaced the receiver and felt as if a cold knife had sliced through his heart. The voice had been familiar. Or had it?

Jennifer.

She'd been the only one in his entire life to call him RJ. Holy crap. He swallowed hard. Told himself not to panic.

It has to be someone impersonating her.

What the hell was going on? He rolled out of bed, threw on a T-shirt and the pair of khakis he'd draped over the back of the desk chair. Zipping up, he walked barefoot to the office under the lone security lamp mounted high over the neon sign for the motel. Only a few cars rolled by and the night air was cool, felt good against his skin.

Inside the reception area the lights were on—dimmed, but on. Less than a cup of coffee sat like oil in the bottom of the glass pot in the coffeemaker. No one was behind the desk. Following instructions inscribed into a metal plate on the counter, he rang the small bell. After waiting half a minute, he rang it again, just as Rebecca slipped through a locked door marked EMPLOYEES ONLY.

Devoid of makeup, her lipstick faded, her hair falling past her shoulders, she looked much younger than she had earlier. And crankier. "Can I help you?" she asked, then glanced pointedly at the clock. "Is something wrong?" She was already reaching for another key to his room, assuming that he'd locked himself out.

"I just need to know if you have a record of incoming phone calls to the rooms."

"What?" She stifled a yawn, trying not to sound cross but failing. Obviously the staff at the So-Cal was stretched thin.

"Someone called me and didn't identify herself. I need to know where the call came from."

"Now?" Looking at him as if he were certifiably crazy, she opened a drawer and pulled out a pack of cigarettes and a lighter. "It's the middle of the night."

"I know. It's important." Reaching into his pants pocket, he withdrew his wallet and showed her his badge.

"What?" She was suddenly wide awake. "You're a cop?" Worry slid through her eyes as she slapped the cigarettes onto the counter.

"New Orleans Police Department."

"Oh, Jesus, look, I don't need any trouble here."

"There won't be any." He second-guessed flashing the badge, but at least it was getting her attention.

"Look," she said, licking her lips nervously as if she did have something to hide. "This . . . this isn't a big operation. We're not, like, the Hilton, you know."

"But you have a central switchboard that calls come through, right?"

"Yeah, yeah . . . we do." She was thinking hard.

"I assume there's some sort of caller ID on it." She was nodding. "So, I need to see origin of the calls that have come to my room."

She pressed two fingers against one temple. "Can't this wait until morning?"

"If it could, I wouldn't be here."

"Okay." With a tired sigh, she nodded. "Just give me a sec, okay?" She disappeared behind the door again. Bentz paced through the lobby past brochures of fishing trips, movie studio visits, and museums. He could only hope the badge had made an impression. Nervously jangling the change in his pocket, he walked to the large plate-glass window and peered out. He saw only a few cars parked between faded stripes in the parking lot.

"Okay, here ya go." Rebecca returned to the lobby with a business card. Handing him the card, she said, "Only one call."

"Only had one. Thanks." He scanned the number jotted in her neat handwriting. A local number.

"Anytime," she said without the slightest bit of enthusiasm. "Anything else?"

"This'll do."

"Good." She scraped her pack of Marlboro Lights and her lighter from the counter, then followed Bentz outside.

He heard her lighter click as he reached his room.

Inside, using his cell phone, he dialed the single number listed on the printout. It rang ten times. He hung up; hit redial. Twelve more rings, no answering machine, no voice mail. He hung up and tried one last time, counting off the rings. On the eighth, a male voice said, "Yeah?"

"Who is this?" Bentz demanded.

"Paul. Who is *this?*" Indignant.

"I'm returning a call."

"What the fuck are you talking about?"

"Someone called me from this phone."

"Big surprise," the guy said, his speech slightly slurred. "Duh. It's a pay phone."

A pay phone? *Probably only a handful of those dinosaurs left in the country and you get a crank call from one.* "Where?"

"What?" the stranger, Paul, demanded.

"The phone you're on right now. Where is it?"

"I dunno . . . uh . . . in L.A. What do you think? Here on Wilshire. Yeah . . . there's a bank on the corner. California Something, I think."

"What's the cross street?"

"Who the hell knows? It's around Sixth or Seventh, I think . . . hey, look, I gotta use the phone, okay?"

Bentz wasn't going to let the guy go. Not yet. "Just a sec. Did you see a woman using this phone, say, twenty minutes ago?"

"What is this?" The guy on the other end was getting pissed.

"I thought you might have been waiting for the phone and seen someone. A woman."

"Shit, dude, I said no! Oh, for Christ's sake!" He hung up, severing the connection.

Bentz clicked off his cell phone, gathered his keys, and slipped into his shoes. He didn't know what good driving around L.A. in the dead of night would do, but he sure as hell wouldn't be able to get back to sleep any time soon. Rebecca was just crushing her cigarette into the large ash can by the front door. The night air was still tinged with the faint smell of smoke as she watched him climb into the Ford.

Familiar with the area, he drove to Wilshire and cruised down the wide near-empty boulevard. A cop car screamed by, lights flashing. He kept his eyes on the street-level storefronts of buildings rising toward the night sky. In the blocks around Sixth and Seventh his gaze swept over the sidewalks and plazas of the massive buildings of steel and glass, searching for a damned pay phone. He wasn't sure what he expected to find, but he knew he wouldn't spot the woman who had called him. Unless she was an idiot. His gut told him that she'd be long gone by now. Still he felt the need to view the pay phone for himself.

He missed it on the first pass, but then, spotting California Palisades Bank, he wheeled around in their empty lot . . . and there it was. His tires squealed slightly as he tore from the parking lot and steered straight to the modern booth. Three sheets of dirty, graffiti-covered Plexiglas on a pole, in front of an edifice with a Korean market on the first floor.

Few people were on the street, but he parked and walked around the pay phone as a city bus sat idling at a bus stop.

Who was she?

Why had she called him? What was the purpose? To get him to track her down here? He scanned the area, dubious. No point in getting him here among these office buildings sitting like sleeping giants in the night, security lights casting eerie beams beyond tinted glass. On the avenue only a smattering of cars passed. Traffic lights glowed green and red down the broad boulevard while tall streetlamps rained down a fluorescent lonely atmosphere.

He saw nothing unusual.

Only that someone was seriously messing with his brain.

Who the hell was doing this to him?

And, more importantly, why?

CHAPTER 8

"I just don't know why you didn't tell me," Kristi fumed on the other end of the wireless call.

"Do you know what time it is?"

"Yeah. Eight in the morning."

"There. It's barely six here," Bentz grumbled, eyeing the digital clock as he rolled to the side of the uneven mattress. He'd barely slept since falling into bed after his late-night drive down Wilshire Boulevard. "Two hours difference, remember?" His back ached and he hadn't gone to bed until nearly 2 A.M. and now his kid was calling at dawn.

"Okay. Sorry." She didn't sound it. "But come on, Dad, what's this all about? I asked Olivia about it, but she was kinda secretive. You know how she gets, all 'this is between you and your father,' which is just such BS." Kristi must've been standing outside, maybe outside the apartment she rented in Baton Rouge while attending All Saints College. Bentz could hear the sounds of traffic and the soft call of a mockingbird in the background.

"I just need to work things out."

"So this is like . . . what? A separation?"

"What? No." He rubbed a hand over the stubble on his jaw and walked to the window to crack open the blinds. Immediately bright sunlight streamed through the dusty glass. "I just have some things to do."

"What things?" Kristi demanded.

"Just catching up on some old cases. I'm meeting with one of the guys I worked with tonight."

"Why? I thought you hated L.A. The way I remember it you couldn't get out of the place fast enough."

"I was going stir crazy."

"So suddenly, after all these years, you hop on a plane and head west? Save me, Dad," she said with a theatrical sigh. "Just tell me this doesn't have anything to do with Mom, okay?"

"It doesn't."

"And you're a bad liar. A real bad liar."

He remained silent, wondering what had tipped her off. Of course . . . he'd told Kristi he'd seen Jennifer in his hospital room after he'd woken from his coma. Though they'd never discussed it since, Kristi was bright enough to put two and two together. She was also on the verge of being paranoid now that she possessed her own little bit of ESP. Ever since an accident that nearly took her life, Kristi claimed she knew when a person was about to die, that the victim would "bleed from color to black-and-white." That had to be scary for her, and Bentz didn't want to add to her worries.

"Aren't you supposed to be planning a wedding or something?" he asked.

"Don't deflect, Dad. It doesn't work with me."

"So why did you call? Obviously not just to tell me to have a nice trip."

"Very funny."

"Thought so," he said as he moved to the bathroom where a single-cup coffeepot was wedged onto a slice of countertop. Tearing open the packet of coffee, he listened as Kristi kept firing questions at him: Why was he in L.A.? When was he coming back? Were there problems with Olivia? How worried should she be? He plopped the packet of "fine roast" into a basket, added a cup of water to the pot, and pressed the on button.

"I'm fine. Olivia's fine. Nothing to worry about," Bentz insisted as the coffeepot gurgled and hissed. He needed to take a leak, but decided not to freak his daughter out any further and waited until she hung up.

It took another five minutes, but she finally told him "to keep in touch," before taking another call. He relieved himself, hopped in the shower, and dressed. With his cup of coffee in hand, he decided to hunt up breakfast. He figured a coffee shop on Colorado Avenue might be a good place to start.

After breakfast he would continue trying to locate the women on his list. First up: Shana McIntyre . . . well, after some digging last night he discovered that her name had changed a couple of times. She'd been Wynn before she married her first husband and became Mrs. George Philpot. After that divorce she'd become Mrs. Hamilton Flavel, and now, she'd taken the name of her current husband, Leland McIntyre. Bentz recognized her type—a serial wife.

Last night he'd found a number for her and had tried it, only to get her lofty voice on the answering machine. "You've reached Leland and Shana. Leave a message. We'll get back to you . . . sometime."

Nice, he'd thought and didn't bother leaving his name or number. His cell would show up as "restricted call" and he wanted to catch her off guard. Didn't want to give her time to make up answers or avoid him.

By the time he walked outside, the sun was already rising in the sky, glare bouncing off the pavement. His car was warm, its interior collecting heat more quickly than a solar panel in the middle of the Sahara. He rolled out of the parking lot and headed toward Santa Monica and Colorado Avenue, which he'd tentatively identified in one photo of Jennifer.

He'd already done some Internet research. An online map had shown three coffee shops in a twelve-block stretch.

Within twenty minutes he spotted it—a cafe on a corner that matched the photo. The Local Buzz, it was called. Two newspaper boxes stood by the front door, and tall café tables were positioned near the windows.

This was too easy, he thought. Whoever had taken the picture had lured him here without too much finesse.

He parked on a side street and made his way inside, where the smell of ground roast was overpowering. Jazz competed with the hiss of the steamer and the gentle din of conversation. The booths were full and several patrons had their laptops open, taking advantage of the free wi-fi connection. Bentz ordered a black coffee and waited while a surge of customers ordered lattes and mochas, everything from macchiatos and soy caramel lattes to plain coffee. Once the crowd dissipated, he approached the baristas again, this time showing them his pictures of Jennifer.

Neither coffee server claimed to have ever seen her. They were certain. The tall girl in frumpy suede boots and shorts barely glanced at the photos as she wiped off the hot milk nozzle and shook her head. But her partner, a shorter, rounder woman of around fifty, studied the shots thoughtfully. Above her rimless glasses her eyebrows drew together. "She could have come in when we were busy or when someone else was working, but she's not a regular. At least not a morning regular. I would know her." She went on to explain that there were six or seven servers on staff, so someone else might have helped the woman in the picture.

He glanced at the table where "Jennifer" had sat in the photo, went to the window and stared out at the street. To the left, a dozen or so blocks from here, the streets ended at the Pacific Ocean. He and Jennifer had spent some lazy afternoons there, walking the Santa Monica Pier and the path that cut alongside the beach. Long ago he'd considered Santa Monica their special place, a spot where, near the jutting pier, he and Jennifer had first made love in the sand.

He sipped his coffee and tried to imagine what Jennifer—no, make that the woman posing as Jennifer—had been doing here, and why he'd been led to this spot. What was the damned point? He stared out the window for a few minutes more, then left with his too-hot coffee and a feeling that he was being worked.

Shana, breaking the surface after swimming underwater the length of her pool, drew in a deep breath, then shook the wet hair from her eyes. Forty laps. She was congratulating herself on keeping in shape when she heard the doorbell peal.

She wasn't the only one. At the first bong of the dulcet tones Dirk, her husband's damned German shepherd/rottweiler mix, began barking his fool head off. He'd been lying at the edge of the pool, but was instantly on his feet, the hairs at the back of his neck bristling upward.

Great.

Just what she needed—a surprise visit by some stranger. She

hoisted herself onto the tile strip near the waterfall, then climbed to her feet. She was naked, not even the small pieces of her string bikini covering her body. The housekeeper had the day off, the gardener had already left, so she'd taken her alone time to sunbathe for a perfect tan, one completely devoid of lines or shading. She'd just swum her laps after lying on her back on her favorite chaise. Had she not been interrupted, she would have lain facedown, toasting her backside.

"Later," she promised herself as she scooped up her white poolside robe, jammed her arms down the sleeves, and cinched the belt around her slim waist.

The doorbell rang once more, setting off Dirk all over again. "Hush!" she commanded to the dog, then louder, "Coming!"

Quickly wringing the excess water from her hair, she slid into her low-heeled mules near the French doors before clicking through the sunroom, hallway, and foyer. Dirk was two steps behind. The loyal dog loved her for some unknown reason when she really didn't much care for him, or any dog for that matter. All that hair, the dirt, and the poop in the yard bothered her. When the big mutt drank from his oversized water dish, the laundry room floor was splashed with a trail of drool-laced water that ran to the entry hall. If it were up to her, there would be *no* pets, but Leland wouldn't hear of getting rid of his 150-pound, often snarling "baby."

"Stay," she ordered and the dog stopped dead in his tracks. Peering through the beveled glass sidelight, she locked gazes with her visitor.

"I'll be damned."

The last person Shana had expected to find on her doorstep was Rick Bentz. But there he was in the flesh, arms folded over his chest, legs slightly apart as he stood between the gigantic pots overflowing with trailing red and white petunias. A pair of aviator-type sunglasses were perched on the bridge of a nose that had been broken at least once, probably a couple of times. He'd trimmed down, too, lost maybe fifteen or twenty pounds since she'd last seen him a dozen or so years ago at Jennifer's funeral.

He'd been a mess then.

Pouring himself into a bottle.

Filled with self-pity and self-loathing, or so she suspected from the psych classes she'd taken at the community college after George, her first husband, had left her for a little flit of a thing named, of all things, Bambi. For the love of God, how much more clichéd could a guy get?

Well, at least she'd learned from that experience.

Now, she unlocked and opened one of the heavy double doors. "Rick Bentz." She felt her lips twist down at the corners, though a small part of her, that ridiculous, jealous, super-competitive feminine part of her, was secretly interested. She'd told herself that she'd never liked the man. He had a way of staring at her and, without words, urging, almost forcing, her to speak. She became much too glib and nervous around him. It was the whole cop thing. Cops *always* made her uneasy. But she had to admit he was sexy. In that raw, rugged way that Hollywood was always trying to exploit.

"Shana." He nodded. Forced a smile. "It's been a while."

"More than a while. What're you doing here?"

"In town for a couple of days. Thought I'd look you up."

"And what? Catch up?" she asked, feeling one of her eyebrows lift of its own accord. She knew bullshit when she heard it. "Come on, what is this? Some kind of official business?" She stood in the doorway, blocking Bentz and also keeping Dirk, who couldn't keep from growling a bit, at bay.

"Nothing official." His smile was damned near disarming. "I'd just like to talk to you about Jennifer."

That floored her. "Really. Now? After she's been gone for what? Ten or twelve years? A little late, isn't it?" She folded her arms under her breasts, felt them lift upward. Good. They were incredible and she knew it. "You know, it seems to me you didn't pay her a whole lot of attention when she was alive, so why would you want to talk about her now?" She eyed him critically. The guy favored one leg as he stood. What the hell was his deal?

"That's what I'd like to talk to you about."

Hmm.

More out of morbid curiosity than an urge to help, Shana moved out of the doorway, grabbing Dirk's collar and dragging him toward the patio. She figured she might as well work on her tan while she was at it. The dog gave off another low warning growl as she led Bentz down the hallway and through the French doors to the patio. Dirk definitely didn't make it easy, the big beast. Behind her Bentz limped a little, she noticed, though he tried like hell to hide it.

Once outside, she let go of the dog. "Leave us alone, Dirk. Go!" she said and snapped her fingers, motioning toward the side of the patio where a thicket of palms provided some shade. The dog hesitated for just a second, then padded obediently to a spot in the grass. After a quick circle he laid down, chin on his paws, eyes focused on Bentz.

"Pretty big dog," Bentz observed, staring at Dirk's massive head.

"My husband's. Has him for protection." A little stretch of the truth there, but hey, why not? "Really, all he does is bark at the neighbor's yappy little Chihuahuas. I guess I should offer you something to drink. Something . . . nonalcoholic?" she asked, smiling through her barb at his affinity for the bottle.

"I'm fine."

She doubted it. Otherwise he wouldn't be here. "So what's up?" She settled into one of the faux-wicker chairs surrounding a large glass table and motioned him to have a seat. "What is it you want to know about Jennifer?"

Bentz sat in the shade of an oversized umbrella. "Her suicide," he said.

Shana frowned, felt her lips pull into a knot of frustration.

"You were one of her closest friends. I thought you could tell me her state of mind before her death—did she really want to end it all?"

"Wow. That's it? You want my take on what she was thinking?"

"Yeah."

Okay, he asked. Shana rolled the years back in her head, remembered Jennifer—fun and naughty and terminally sexy. "It never made sense to me. She was too full of life, too into herself to want to end it."

"We found a note."

"Oh, pooh!" She swiped at the air as if a bothersome fly were buzzing around her head. "I don't know what that was all about. Sure, she told me she fought depression at times, but . . . I didn't think it was that serious. Maybe I was wrong, but I would have bet at the time she wrote the note it was just a way to get attention, you know? She was big on that. I mean who kills themselves by driving into a tree?"

He was listening, not bothering to take notes.

"She could've had an accident, I'll grant you that. She was known to drink a little and then there were pills, but . . ." She looked him straight in the eye. "If you're asking me if I think Jennifer was capable of suicide, I'd say no. Just like I said pretty loudly at the time she died."

Bentz nodded. As if he remembered.

"I lived with Jennifer at Berkeley and then afterward when . . . you know she was dating Alan Gray? No, not just dating. I think they were engaged for a while, right?"

She saw the narrowing of his eyes, the quiet assent behind his shaded glasses.

"But she didn't move in with Alan, probably because she met you. Personally, I thought she was crazy. I mean, Alan was this super-rich real estate developer. God, he must've been worth tens of millions. Yet, she fell for you. A cop. Threw the millionaire over. Go figure." Shana sighed theatrically. "But then who could figure our girl out? Jennifer was nothing if not a dichotomy." Shana remembered Jennifer the flirt. Jennifer the extrovert. Jennifer the wild. But never could she recall Jennifer the morose. "However, I never considered Jennifer someone who would hurt herself. Not intentionally. I mean I just don't think she was capable of it. She would do a lot of things for attention. A lot. But never really self-destructive." Shana caught herself and sighed. "Well, unless you mean the affair." She met his gaze, but she doubted it so much as flickered behind his shades. "James was definitely her Achilles' heel." She looked away to the pool where sunlight danced on the water, clear and aquamarine. "Look, it's been a long time and really, I don't know what was in her head at the time. I just doubt that it was suicide."

Bentz asked her a few more questions about her friendship, then, when she looked at her watch, came up with the bombshell.

"Do you think Jennifer could have faked her death?"

"What?" She was shocked. "Are you kidding?" But he wasn't. His face was stone-cold sober. "No way. I mean, how would she go about it?" Her thoughts swirled. Goose bumps rose on the back of her arms. Was this some kind of trick question? But Bentz's expression told her differently. "Okay, I don't know what you're getting at, but no, I don't think she could have . . . what? Staged the accident? Put someone up to it? Killed another woman? No . . . that's nuts, Rick." She felt her insides churning. This was just too weird. "Weren't you the one who identified her body?"

He nodded, his lips tightening just a bit.

"Well, then, did you make a mistake?"

"I don't know," he said and she let out a long breath. "She didn't talk to you about it? Didn't show up afterward?"

"No! For the love of God!" Was the man bonkers? Holy crap! "What kind of dope are you smoking, Bentz? Jennifer's dead. We both know it."

"If you say so."

Shana leaned back in her chair and eyed the man who had been Jennifer's husband. He hadn't been known to hallucinate. At least, not before all his problems. At one point he'd been the shining star of the LAPD, but that star had been tarnished, along with his badge.

Today, though, he looked like the old Bentz. Handsome and hard-edged. Oh, he was a little more shopworn around the edges, the years starting to show. But this Bentz was clear-eyed and determined. Passionate. Some of the qualities Jennifer had been drawn to in the first place.

"What makes you think Jennifer is alive?" she asked. This conversation was weird, weird, weird.

He withdrew something from an envelope—photos that he fanned over the glass-topped table. Shana's heart nearly stopped. The woman in each shot was Jennifer, or her goddamned identical twin. "Where'd you get these? I mean . . . you're saying these are recent?" she asked, her mind boggled. Jennifer was dead.

"Someone sent them to me. I thought you might have an idea who."

"Not a clue . . . but . . . this can't be . . . I mean, she's dead. You were the one who—" She picked up the shot of Jennifer crossing the street. A chill slid down her spine.

"I'm just looking into her death," he said as she eyed the pictures, looking for flaws, some hint that this was a twisted hoax.

"Where did these come from?" she asked.

"Postmarked Culver City."

"Where you lived." She swallowed hard. Heard the dry wind rustling the palm fronds. Felt cold as death inside. "This has to be an illusion."

"I know, but I have some time, so I thought I'd check into it a little deeper."

"Why?"

He didn't answer, just asked, "Is there anything you can tell me about the last week or so of her life that was unusual or different?"

"Aside from the fact that she died?" Shana asked bitterly, then eyed the pictures again. The truth of the matter was that she missed Jennifer. She wasn't crazy about talking to Jennifer's ex-husband, a real son of a bitch who'd been distant from his wife, always putting his work before his damned family.

She felt an allegiance to Jennifer, even now when she was no longer with the living. Discussing her with Rick seemed a betrayal somehow. Shana glanced away from Rick Bentz's intimidating glare to the garden where heavy-blossomed bougainvillea clung to an arbor, the leaves rustling in a soft breeze.

But what was the point to keeping mum now? Her allegiance was long over. Jennifer was gone.

"All I know is that Jennifer talked about leaving a lot. She mentioned giving herself a break and you your freedom." To his credit, the man winced, if only slightly. "She thought you were more cut out to be a parent than she was, even though you worked too much, got too involved with your cases, and drank a whole lot more than you should." Shana lifted her hair up, letting the breeze skim across her nape. "She was smart enough to realize you were a good father. For what that's worth."

Crossing one leg over the other, she wondered, could those pictures be real? No way. The woman in the pictures was too young. Or she had an exceptional plastic surgeon. Shana dragged her gaze away, got back to skewering Bentz. "You already said you know she had a lover." From the tightening of Bentz's jaw, Shana knew she had hit a nerve. "She was planning to cut it off with him, too. Her life was getting too complicated and since James was your half brother . . ."

"And the father of my daughter."

Jesus, he was way ahead of her. Shana shrugged and wished she'd made a pitcher of margaritas. She was suddenly thirsty as well as nervous. "Well, she knew that her affair, with him being a priest and all, only spelled trouble for both of them."

"Did he know she was going to end it?" Bentz asked gravely.

"Suspected it, I think. She hadn't actually done the dirty deed, but he'd sensed it was coming. He was beside himself."

Bentz's jaw slid to the side and she knew she was getting to him. Good. The bastard deserved it for ignoring his wife, probably sending her to an early grave, and then showing up here on Shana's doorstep out of the blue. He was sexy, though, in that earthy way she found fascinating, if a little dangerous. Rugged and tough . . . despite the fact that he was a cop. Shana leaned forward, making sure her robe gaped open a bit, displaying a hint of her perfect décolletage, her latest investment since her damned boobs had started going south sometime after thirty-five.

"So what did he do?"

"Father James?" she asked coyly, suddenly glad to get back at this bastard.

"Yeah. Him."

"He was upset, of course. They had a couple of fights. He was . . . out of control."

There was a slight tic in Bentz's jaw. "You think he had something to do with her accident?"

"I . . . I wouldn't say that," she hedged, but then what had she known about a priest who had continually broken his vow to God and church? Hadn't she asked herself that very same question? She decided to change the subject. "You know, that brother of yours, he was damned sexy and passionate. A problem, I think, since he happened to be a priest." She fluttered her fingers. "That vow of celibacy tends to get in the way. It can be a real bummer."

Bentz was silently seething and she loved it. She decided to push it a bit. "You know, they sometimes met up on the Santa Monica Pier, or somewhere around there. I believe that's where they first really hooked up. On the beach maybe, not far from the amusement park." She saw Bentz flinch and knew she'd hit a mark. Good. She went on. "Let's see, and then . . . Jeez, what was it that she was always talking about?" she asked and noticed the tightening of the corners of Bentz's mouth. "Oh, I know! This was a biggie for her for some reason. They used to meet at some inn at San Juan Capistrano, I think."

He tensed even more, his eyes, behind his shades, squinting. "You know the name?"

"No, but I remember Jennifer saying it was part of an old mission. Not the main one that's there. It's a smaller church that was sold and remodeled into an inn." She tried to recall the details. "Wait a sec. Didn't she tell me they always stayed in room number seven? It was, like, their lucky number, or something."

"Number seven?" he repeated tightly.

"Yeah, I think so, though why I remember that, I don't know." But suddenly a conversation she'd had with Jennifer after one of her trysts came back to her now. Jennifer's eyes had been bright with mischief, her lips curved into an aren't-I-naughty smile as she sipped a martini and spilled a few juicy details of her secret life. And the name of the motel in Capistrano? It floated to her, then away. So damned elusive. "I think the name of the inn was Mission San . . . San Michelle." That didn't sound right. What the hell was it? "No . . . no. Wait!" She snapped her fingers as it came to her. "Mission San Miguel, that was it! It was special to them. They'd been there the first time, you know, when she got pregnant and then again, when they restarted the affair." She saw the revulsion that Bentz was trying so hard to mask and she felt a thrill of satisfaction.

The jerk deserved a dose of cold, hard reality. He was the reason Jennifer had been so messed up; his distance had forced her into the arms of another man. She leaned a bit closer and said in a throaty stage whisper, "It's kind of ironic, don't you think, being as Father James was a man of God and all. I guess he could sleep with Jennifer, break all kinds of vows, and then head on over to the confessional to cleanse his soul." She wrinkled her nose. "I'm not Catholic, but that is how it works, isn't it?"

"I don't know." He seemed to be making a mental note. "Any other place?"

"Oh, I think there was some little no-tell motel over on Figueroa, somewhere near USC, but I'm not really sure." Maybe she was telling him too much. Maybe she should keep her mouth shut. Nothing she said would bring Jennifer back.

His jaw was set. Rock hard. Eyes as steady as his voice. The cop. Cold. Distant. Had seen it all. "Anything else you remember?"

"Only that she was sorry," she said in a moment of bare, honest-to-the-bone truth. "For hurting you."

He looked at Shana as if she were yanking his chain again.

Who could blame the guy?

"I'm serious, Rick. She loathed herself for what she referred to as 'her curse,' her need to throw away all that was good in her life. Yeah, she was self-centered and vain, but deep down there was a very good person. In her own weird way, Jennifer loved you. A lot."

CHAPTER 9

That day Bentz saw Jennifer for the first time in L.A.

After leaving Shana's Beverly Hills estate he'd driven southwest, deciding to find Figueroa Street and satisfy his own morbid curiosity.

He was still mentally digesting everything he'd learned from Shana, trying to cull the facts from the fiction, or at least from Shana's very slanted view of things, as he wended his way through the early afternoon traffic. One thing was clear from his meeting with Shana McIntyre; the pictures of Jennifer had unsettled her. No way had Shana faked her reaction. That had to mean something.

And in her catty way she'd reminded him to check out Alan Gray, the man Jennifer had professed to love.

For a while.

A developer who had made his money in the seventies and eighties, long before the recently stalled economy, Alan Gray had been in and out of Jennifer's life. Bentz reminded himself to look the mogul up and see what good old Alan was doing these days. He would be in his late fifties or early sixties by now, possibly retired.

Bentz would check.

Squinting against the bright sun, he flipped down his visor and spotted several motels that could well have been one of the spots where Jennifer and James had met for their trysts. Unfortunately, there would be no records to prove that any of the stucco-faced buildings had been the private spot where they had met.

And so what if they had?

It had been over twelve years.

In that span of time places had changed hands, old buildings torn down and new ones sprouting up. He was just about to turn toward Culver City when he caught a glimpse of a slim, dark-haired woman in a yellow sundress and dark glasses standing at a bus stop.

So what? he thought initially. But as he drove past, he saw her profile and his heart stopped. The nose and chin . . . the way she held her purse as she stood near a bench, her eyes trained down the street where the approaching bus lumbered and belched blue smoke. She lifted one hand to her forehead, shading her eyes even further.

Just as Jennifer had always done.

Shana's words rushed back to him: "In her own weird way, Jennifer loved you." He'd been stunned then and was still.

This is crazy, his mind warned. *It's not her. You* know *it's not Jennifer. Power of suggestion, that's all it is!*

With one eye on his rearview mirror and the other trained ahead, he searched for a parking space as the bus slowed to a stop.

"Oh, hell." Gunning his car into a parking lot for a strip mall he nosed his rental into the first available space, an area that warned that the lot was for customers only. The doors to the bus were open. Two teenaged boys plugged into iPods laughed and pushed each other as they hauled their skateboards onto the bus.

Bentz threw himself out of the car and hitched his way across the street.

She was gone.

The woman in the yellow dress was nowhere to be seen.

The doors of the bus closed and the driver turned on the flashers to signal that she was heading into traffic.

"No!" Bentz pushed into the street, his bad leg aching as he hobbled after the city vehicle. He reached the stop just as the bus rumbled noisily away.

Was she aboard?

As it pulled away from the curb, Bentz stared through the dusty windows. He scanned the face of every passenger he could see, but recognized no one. There wasn't anyone remotely resembling his ex-wife.

Bentz took note of the bus number and the time, then studied the surrounding landscape. No dark-haired woman in a lemony sundress was strolling along the sidewalk or walking quickly around a corner or climbing into any of the vehicles lining the streets.

He felt a prickle of déjà vu run through his soul.

As if he'd been here before.

As if he'd been chasing Jennifer along these very streets.

He stared after the bus as it disappeared from view, considered chasing it down, trying to outrun it and board at the next stop.

Get a grip, he silently told himself. *It wasn't her. It's just the power of suggestion, all because of Shana, the bitch. Jennifer, living or dead, is* not *on that bus. Come on, man, get real! When in known history did Jennifer ever take public transportation?*

"I just don't like it, that's all," Kristi admitted. She was driving with one hand, her cell phone in the other as she talked with Reuben Montoya, her father's partner.

"He needed to get away."

"Why?" she demanded, working her way through the narrow streets of Baton Rouge as she drove toward All Saints College.

"He just said he needed some time away. He was going stir crazy not being able to work."

"Why go back to L.A.?"

"Ask him."

"I did and he stonewalled me." Kristi was beginning to panic. Something was wrong, really wrong. Ever since the accident her dad hadn't been himself. She'd thought—no, *hoped*—that after he worked through physical therapy he would return to normal, but that wasn't the case.

"Your father can handle himself," Montoya said. "Don't worry about him."

"Trust me, I don't want to." She hung up and drove into the parking lot of her apartment building, which faced the campus. A once-grand old house, the building had been cut into single units, each one becoming a basic collegiate apartment. She lived here alone with her cat, punctuated by the occasions when Jay taught forensic science at the college. Those nights he stayed with her. The rest of the time he lived in New Orleans and worked for the crime lab.

Once they were married this December and she was finished with school, they would live in New Orleans. Fingers crossed that the first draft of her true-crime book would be finished by then.

But first, her father. God, what was Bentz doing? She mulled it over as she pulled out a sack of groceries from the back of her Honda hatchback and hiked up to her third-floor studio. She toyed with the idea of calling Olivia, her stepmother, but their relationship hadn't always been smooth. It would be better to talk with her in person, but who could find the time?

As she was placing the last of her cheapo low-cal meals-for-one in the freezer, she saw Houdini outside the window. The black cat slunk inside and she picked him up, stroking his head as her phone chirped. "Hello?" she said as her quirky feline hopped down to the floor.

"Hey, Kristi, it's Olivia."

Perfect.

"Hi."

"How're things at school?"

What was this? Olivia never called. "All good," Kristi said tentatively.

"And the wedding?"

"Everything's on target." Kristi kicked out a chair at her café table and sat down. "How about with you?"

"Good."

Time to cut out the crap. "So why's Dad in L.A.?"

"Well, that's the thing. I can't really say," Olivia admitted, "but it seemed like something he had to do." Her voice faded for a moment, as if she were looking away from the phone. Kristi's heart began to drum as she anticipated what was to come: that her father and Olivia were getting a divorce. "He didn't tell you about it?"

"He didn't tell me anything. Just some BS about old cases in L.A. and that he'd be back soon. It all seemed bogus and I was wondering what was going on. Thought maybe there was something wrong between you."

A beat. No answer. Kristi's heart hit the floor.

"Your dad . . . he's struggled since the accident. Can't stand sitting around here, so I think he needed to do something to give himself a new perspective or . . . think things through."

"What things?" Kristi asked cautiously. There was an undercurrent to this conversation she didn't understand.

"I'm not sure. I don't even think he knows, but when he does, I'm sure he'll tell us."

I wouldn't bet on it.

"Anyway, I was calling to see if you wanted to get dinner some-time, or coffee? Maybe the next time you're in New Orleans."

"Sure." It wasn't as if Olivia hadn't tried to bridge the whole step-mother gap with her before. They'd done some things together, but usually Dad was along. This was a little out of the ordinary. "I'm com-ing down in about a week," Kristi offered.

"Then let's make a date. If your dad's back, maybe we'll let him join us." She paused a second, then added, "But maybe not."

"You got it." Kristi hung up. *If your dad's back,* Olivia had said. So she was in the dark, too. Kristi didn't like it. Whatever her father was going through, it wasn't good.

After a long day of classes Laney Springer threw her books onto the tiny café table one of her roommates had donated to the cause of their shared apartment. God, it had been a day from hell, starting with Professor Williams's dullsville lecture on the Korean War. Why she'd ever thought Modern History: American Politics in the Twenti-eth Century would be an interesting way to fill her schedule was be-yond her. Thankfully, the semester was wrapping up. Professor Williams would soon be history—literally.

She walked to the refrigerator and peeked inside. The contents were pathetic: dried-out pizza in its box, the pieces of pepperoni al-ready picked off. A bag of celery was turning brown beside some half-drunk bottles of Diet Pepsi.

Gross.

She shut the door and decided she shouldn't eat anyway. Not if she wanted to fit comfortably into her tight, tiny, shimmery silver dress tonight. And she did. If nothing else, she wanted to look hot, hot, hot.

Forget the old pizza.

This was her big night. Well, technically not just hers, but her twin sister Lucy's, too.

At midnight both of them would turn twenty-one. Finally *legal!*

Of course there were still over six hours of waiting until the clock struck midnight. The witching hour. Kind of a reverse Cinderella syn-drome. She had fake ID, but tonight, she was going to burn her fraudulent Oregon license.

The good news was that she wouldn't have to wait an extra four-teen minutes after her twin sister took her first legal sip. Lucy always lorded it over Laney that she had been born at 12:47 while Laney hadn't come along until 1:01. But tonight it didn't matter. It was the date, not the time.

There was going to be a big party; all her friends would be there, even Cody Wyatt, the really cool guy in her English Lit class. Good. Because she knew she'd have to put up with Lucy's creep of a boyfriend, Kurt Jones. What a loser! A thirty-year-old high school dropout who had never married the mother of his kid and, accord-ing to Lucy, didn't want anything to do with his three-year-old son. Now Kurt was hanging out with Lucy and she was making all kinds of excuses for him. No doubt he was her dealer. Lucy was really getting into weed and who knew what else.

It worried Laney.

A little marijuana was one thing; the other stuff could be a huge problem. But tonight, if Kurt showed up, Laney figured she'd ignore the prick. Who cared what he did?

Weed, meth, coke, pills, he does it all.

She hoped Lucy would dump his ass.

For good.

Keyed up, she decided to work out, stretch muscles that had been cramped into uncomfortable desks all day. She'd get enough cardio tonight on the dance floor, but she wanted to tone her body. So first she'd lift some weights, then she'd pop in her yoga DVD and stretch out. Afterward, she'd take a long shower and wash her hair and spend as much time as she wanted with her makeup. It was, after all, almost her birthday. Correction. Make that *their* birthday. Hers *and* Lucy's.

She found her iPod in her book bag and slipped the player into the sound system her roommate Trisha owned. The music was loud, but all the renters in the triplex were college kids; no one com-plained about music, parties, or even pets that were strictly forbid-den.

On her way to the bedroom she shared with Trisha, Laney grabbed the communal free weights from the bookcase. Kicking a clear spot on the rug in the small space between the foot of her unmade bed and Trisha's dresser, Laney started working on her arms to a song by

Fergie. No flapping wings for this girl. Not ever. If she had to do a thousand triceps curls when she was eighty, so be it. Eighty. Wow. Like sixty years into the future. Fifty-nine as of tonight!

The reps came easy at first and she closed her eyes. The song and mood changed. She got lost in the beat and melodies of Justin Timberlake, then Maroon 5 . . .

One more set; she was really feeling it now.

Come on, come on, she encouraged herself as the music pounded through her brain. *You can do it; don't give up.*

She was breathing hard, sweating big-time.

Once her biceps and triceps were screaming, she stretched out on the floor and started with leg lifts.

She thought she heard someone come in and yelled, "I'm in here!" over the throb of bass and a long keyboard riff, then kept working out until her body was covered in sweat and her legs ached.

Only after doing all the reps she'd planned did she spring to her feet. *Good girl! Way to go!* She grabbed her towel and headed to the living area where the music was still blasting. Time to stretch these muscles. Besides, she wanted to give Trish or Kim a chance to wish her a happy birthday.

But she didn't see either of her roommates flopped on the second-hand couch Kim had found. And they weren't nuking popcorn or boiling ramen in the kitchen.

Odd.

Hadn't she heard one of her roommates return?

Dabbing at the sweat on her face, she strode over to check Kim's room. Empty.

Snap!

A strange sound. Muted.

Had her iPod skipped?

She backed out of Kim's room, pulled the door shut behind her, and headed back to the living area. On her way to the stereo she noticed a hint of cigarette smoke in the air. No big deal. They all had taken up cigs.

Snap!

Behind her?

In the hallway?

Fear sprayed through her blood.

"Kim?" she said starting to turn.

In a split second she saw that the door she'd just shut, the one to Kim's room was open and someone was looming in the darkened hallway. Someone who hadn't been there an instant before.

"Hey! Who the hell are—" The words died in her throat when she noticed the belt in his hands. "Oh, Jesus!"

She screamed, but her attacker was on her in an instant. He slipped the thin belt over her head and looped it around her neck in a snap, cutting off her air, stifling her cry.

Oh, God! This jerkwad was going to hurt her! Rape her! Kill her! Fear curdled her insides.

She kicked, landed one blow with her heel and her assailant let out a hiss of pain.

Good!

She tried again but was jerked roughly to one side, her airway cut off, the pain in her lungs hot and tight.

This can't be happening, she thought wildly. She was coughing and gasping, digging at the strap, struggling and flailing, throwing her weight around. Anything to loosen the ever-tightening collar!

No! No! No!

Kicking crazily, trying to land another blow on his shin, she slipped. He used the chance to wrench her up by the belt, holding her in the air. Dangling like a doll.

Hit the creep. Get the belt off your neck! Save yourself! Though her lungs were on fire, she flung her fist backward, trying to hit the monster in the nose or eyes or anything! The fingers of her other hand were scratching at the strap on her throat.

She couldn't breathe, couldn't think.

Help me. Please, someone, anyone *help me!*

She wasn't a wimp, but her strength was fading, the pain excruciating.

Passing out would be better.

No!

Don't give up!

Fight!

Oh, God, the pain . . . I can't breathe! Help! Please help me!

She gave up hitting and used both hands to try and free herself from the constricting strap.

Her fingers clawed at her neck.

Dug deep.

But it was too late.

Her lungs were bursting.

Pain screaming through her body.

Her heart thudding.

Blackness converging over her.

In that horrid instant, Laney knew. She knew she would never see her twenty-first birthday.

CHAPTER 10

Hayes had been right.

Roy's had definitely gone downhill, Bentz thought, driving past the restaurant.

Still a little shaken from his recent "Jennifer sighting," he found a ridiculously small parking spot a couple of blocks from the restaurant. He wedged the Ford Escape into it and fed the meter. Ignoring the pain in his leg, he managed to avoid a couple of speeding skateboarders who whipped by, the wheels of their boards grinding against the concrete as he hitched his way to the front doors.

Named for its original owner and not Roy Rogers as many people thought, the place still had a western facade complete with Dutch doors that looked as if they belonged on a barn. There had once been a plastic rearing horse mounted over the front awning, until some smart-ass had climbed up on the roof in the middle of the night and painted the white stallion's private parts fire-engine red.

That had been the end of the white stud.

Now the awning displayed a sign that simply said: Roy's.

Good enough, Bentz figured as he pushed open the doors and stepped back in time.

Inside, the dark restaurant seemed dingy. Twelve years ago all the cowboy memorabilia gathered from the sets of old westerns and television shows had been retro-cool. Now the worn saddles, fence posts, cowboy hats, and chaps that adorned the place looked dusty and worn.

The crowd had changed, or at least aged, just like the old plank floors.

A long bar, complete with brass foot rail, swept along one side of the establishment. Tables and booths took care of the rest.

He found a booth, settled in, and ordered a nonalcoholic beer from a waitress who was splitting the seams of her cowgirl costume.

Before she could return, Bentz spied Jonas Hayes pushing through the front doors. Hayes, too, had aged. African American and six-four, he was still imposing, if slightly thicker around the middle than he had been when he was a rookie cop or a running back for UNLV. His close-cropped black hair showed a few bits of silver, and when he took his shades off, crow's feet were visible at the corners of his eyes.

But he still dressed as if he were a model. Expensive suit, polished shoes, silk tie knotted to perfection.

Bentz waved him over and stood, stretching out his hand. "Helluva long time."

Hayes nodded and clasped Bentz's fingers in a strong, sure grip. "What's it been? Eleven? Twelve years?"

"'Bout that."

They sat down on opposite sides of the booth. "And then you show up outta the blue. Lookin' for a favor."

"You got it."

Waitress Pseudo-cowgirl returned, her mood not appearing to have improved as she took Hayes's order for a scotch on the rocks.

"Friendly," Hayes observed once she'd huffed away.

"Don't think she likes the getup she has to wear."

"Can't blame her. You still on the wagon?" Hayes nodded toward Bentz's bottle.

"Yep. Gave it up after Jennifer died."

"Probably a good thing."

Bentz raised an eyebrow. "Yeah. Well, most of the time. Trinidad still with the department?"

"A lifer and then some." Hayes was nodding as the waitress, forcing a false smile, returned with Hayes's drink and plastic-encased menus. She rattled off a couple of specials and was about to turn away when Bentz asked, "You still have the T-Bone and steak fries?"

Without an ounce of enthusiasm, she said, "It's, like, been on the menu forever."

"Thought so. I'll take it. Medium rare. Blue cheese dressing on the salad."

She didn't bother writing it down, just looked at Hayes, who scanned the menu and folded it closed, ordering the barbecued pork chop special.

Once she'd disappeared again, he turned dark eyes on Bentz. "Okay, so what gives? What's this 'favor' you want from me?"

"I want you to look at Jennifer's death again."

"Jennifer? As in your wife?"

"Ex-wife, but yeah." Bentz settled back against the cushions and took a swallow from his bottle.

"That was twelve years ago, man. She died in a single-car accident. Probable suicide." Again Hayes searched Bentz's face with those black eyes. Cop's eyes.

"That's what we all thought at the time, but it's a helluva way to kill yourself. Messy. Sometimes doesn't get the job done right and you end up a vegetable, or taking someone else out with you, or spending the rest of your life in a wheelchair. Not a usual form of suicide. Why not just run the car in the garage or take pills? Slit your wrists in the tub? Hang yourself in the closet?"

"She was your wife. You tell me."

Bentz was shaking his head. "Besides, she wouldn't have wanted to mess herself up that way. Too vain."

"She was killing herself, man. On pills and booze. Not thinkin' right. She didn't give a good goddamn about how she looked and she might have taken the car out cuz she didn't want you or your kid to come home to it, y'know? Not a good thing for her daughter to find her dead."

"She didn't have to do it at home. There are other places. Motels." He thought about the shabby condition of the So-Cal Inn, a perfect place for a suicide. Cheap. Private. Poolside view if you wanted it.

Hayes rotated his drink between his palms. "Okay, let's cut the crap here. What's going on?"

Bentz took another swallow of his beer, then reached into his jacket pocket and withdrew a copy of the marred death certificate. Quickly he explained that it had been sent to the station, mailed from Culver City.

"So what?" Hayes said. "Someone messin' with ya."

Bentz nodded. "But it's more than that." He placed the photographs of Jennifer on the table. "I think someone is gaslighting me."

"Oh, hell! These are Jennifer, right? And recent, I assume?"

"That's what whoever sent them to me wants me to think."

Hayes looked at him. "Dead ringer?"

"Perfect."

"But . . . dead ringer from twelve years ago? No extra pounds, no more wrinkles."

"You got it."

"Son of a bitch." Hayes stared at the pictures, then gave the death certificate a longer look, his eyes narrowing. At least he was listening now.

"Someone's pretending to be Jennifer."

"But why?" Hayes asked.

"Don't know, but she's not in this alone. Someone's taking pictures."

"So now it's a conspiracy? To make you nuts."

Bentz nodded.

"This is so far-fetched," Hayes said, though his eyes strayed to the photographs again. "Man, oh, man. You and JFK? Okay, I'll bite. Start from the beginning."

Bentz filled him in. From waking up in the hospital, to see and smell and feel Jennifer in the room, to the sighting in his backyard. He left out the woman at the bus stop, worried that it was too vague, that she could have been anyone.

As he was wrapping it up, Hayes said, "And you think this person has been in New Orleans and L.A. She somehow knew the moment you would wake up from your coma . . . and then she hurried back to L.A. for a photo shoot around town?"

"No. If the dates on the photos are legit, she was back and forth between L.A. and New Orleans."

"Then there should be plane tickets."

"I've got someone looking into it; so far nothing."

"Could've used an alias."

"Jennifer Bentz is the alias," he said, trying to convince himself. "I've got to find out who she really is and what she wants."

"And you need my help." Hayes was wary.

"Yeah."

"How?"

Bentz brought up the call from the pay phone. "So what I'd like to see is photos from traffic cameras in the area, or security tapes from local businesses, or better yet, satellite images of the street."

"You don't want much, do you? As far as I can see, no crime has been committed."

"Unless the woman in Jennifer's grave isn't her."

"That's a big leap."

Bentz couldn't argue the point, though he tried. The waitress returned and slid large platters onto the table. She warned them that the plates were "really hot," asked them about refills and if they needed anything else.

"I'm good," Bentz said and Hayes nodded, agreeing.

"Okay, just let me know if you change your mind." With a quick turn, she moved toward a table where four women were being seated.

Once she was out of earshot, Hayes said, "So you want me to use the resources of the department to help you find whoever's screwing with you."

"You could work with Montoya, in New Orleans. As I said, he's already started."

"Right. We'll form a joint task force to solve . . . oops, there's been no crime." Hayes stared at his pork chop, cornbread, and applesauce. "So basically you came to California because of a postmark and some photographs."

"Seemed like the logical place to start."

"As I said, someone's just fuckin' with you."

"No doubt. But why?"

"You tell me."

"That's what I'm trying to find out." Same old Hayes; the guy needed a firm push. "So the long and short of it is I need to know if Jennifer is in that casket."

"What?" Hayes nearly dropped his fork.

"She was buried before we could do the DNA matching we do today," Bentz said around a mouthful of steak. "All the testing was still in its infancy."

"And you want her tested because you think what?" Jonas asked, his fork tines jabbed in Bentz's direction. "That Jennifer might not be in there? That she might really be alive?"

"This is just a place to start."

"Hell."

"So you'll get me the file on her suicide?"

"Remind me again why I would do this for you?"

"Because I saved your sorry black ass more than once in the past." And it was true. When Hayes had been going through his divorce with his nutcase of a first wife, Alonda, Bentz had covered for him. The fact that his wife had left Hayes for another woman had really messed the guy up. Bentz figured adultery was adultery, no matter who you slept with, but Hayes, always a ladies' man, had been devastated. He'd spent a couple of months partying until dawn, proving his manhood by picking up a lot of different women, and literally fucking up.

Fortunately he'd pulled himself together, but it had been touch and go for a while.

"Okay," Hayes said reluctantly. "I'll see what I can do."

"And I might need a little help with the exhumation order."

"Exhumation? Lord, this just keeps getting better and better," Hayes complained, but he didn't offer further argument as he finished his drink, ordered another, then cut into what had to be a cold piece of pork.

Snap!

Lucy Springer turned, eyeing the edge of the park as she hurried along the sidewalk to her apartment. She saw nothing alarming in the shadows, just an old man walking his dog about a block down the street. The dog, a skinny greyhound, it seemed, was relieving itself on a tree. But the night was thick and dark, the hint of fog rolling in, making everything in the bluish glow of streetlamps appear out of focus and ghostly.

Goose bumps pimpled her scalp. Her pulse elevated.

The street was just too . . . quiet.

"Jeez." Inwardly she told herself she was being a big wuss, or pussy as her boyfriend Kurt would say. She needed to get over her case of nerves. Cell phone in hand, she paused at the corner, waiting for the light to change.

With the press of a button, she located her sister's cell phone number and started texting.

Snap!

Her head whipped up and she looked over her shoulder. What was that sound? Not someone stepping on a twig. More like a sharp, hard click. Something she should recognize.

But she saw no one. Just the old man and dog ambling off in the opposite direction.

There wasn't much traffic so she stepped into the street against the light and kept texting Laney.

Where R U?

Almost 21.

Legal.

Meet at Silvio's! 11 p.m. Drinks on me @ midnight.

Party on!

It was strange that Laney wasn't texting or calling back. They'd been planning this celebration forever! Well, make that twenty-one years. Finally she and her twin were going to be adults! So why the hell was her sister avoiding her?

It was odd.

Not like Laney.

Lucy unlocked the gate to her building and walked through as her phone chirped. She glanced down to check it, vaguely aware of the gate clanging shut behind her.

A text from Laney!

Finally.

It was a picture-text and she clicked it open to see a fuzzy shot of her sister. Laney's eyes were wide and round with fear and some kind of red gag was pulled tight over her mouth. She looked scared to death!

What?

"Oh, God," Lucy whispered, her heart pounding crazily, horror creeping up her spine.

What was this?

And then she got it.

This sick picture was Laney's idea of a joke. "Bitch," Lucy muttered under her breath. Though she had to hand it to her younger twin; the look on Laney's face was one of pure terror. Well, of course. Wasn't Laney going to USC and majoring in theater? Didn't she have an acting scholarship, for God's sake? Hadn't she done a few acting jobs in commercials? Laney knew how to convey emotions perfectly and she had friends in the school who were experts in makeup and film.

Still, it scared the crap out of Lucy. "Not very funny," Lucy said aloud and then stiffened as she heard the tiniest of noises . . . Breathing?

No way. The gate had latched behind her . . . right?

She reached her door and as she mounted the steps, began texting like crazy.

U really had me going for a sec.

C U later!

She reached in her purse for her keys and saw the neighbor's cat perched on the rail of Chuck's small porch. It stared at Lucy, its round eyes reflecting the porch light. "Hey, kitty."

The silver tabby froze for a second, then dropped to the concrete and started to slink under the bottom rail. But it paused at the edge of the shadowy bushes, turned its sleek head toward Lucy and let out a long, low growl.

Crazy cat! "Hey, Platinum, it's me, Lucy."

Arching her back, Platinum hissed, showing needle-sharp teeth and round, wild eyes before scurrying madly under the fence.

"Oh, for God's sake, Platinum, what's wrong with you?" Lucy asked before she smelled it, a whiff of something foreign in the air. Cigarette smoke? Or . . .

Snap!

This time the noise was so close to her ear that she actually jumped.

She nearly screamed

From the corner of her eye, she saw something move in the darkness. A figure, shadowy and shimmering, leapt at her.

What!!!

In its big hands was a thin leather strap.

Oh, God, no!

She tried to yell for help, knew she should run, but it was too late. He grabbed her arm, yanked her hard against him. "Oooph," she gasped, forcing a weak scream from her airless lungs just as the strip of leather slithered around her neck and grew taut.

What was this?

Pain sliced through her.

She couldn't breathe, couldn't scream. Couldn't cough. *Oh, dear God, the pain!*

She clawed at the noose, trying to get her fingers under the smooth leather. The deadly strap didn't budge.

She felt her attacker breathing fast and hard, getting off on her pain, yanking the leather hard.

Who? Who would want to kill me?

Why?

Her lungs burned and strained for oxygen. She kicked wildly, crazily, hoping her heel would connect with her attacker's shin or anything nearby. She gasped hoarsely, trying to drag in any whisper of air.

Help me! Please, someone, help me!

Tearing at the damned ligature, she scratched her throat. A fingernail ripped. Blood welled. Her head was in a vise. And her lungs, oh, God, her lungs . . . her lungs were about to burst! With a cruel jerk her assailant pulled tighter and the leather bit into the soft flesh beneath her chin.

Her eyes bulged.

Raw, searing pain ricocheted through her body.

She was going to die! Right here at her own front door!

She kicked frantically, hoping to hit her assailant or the door, to make some noise! Wake the neighbors! Anything she could!

Her thoughts swirled, rapid images of her parents back home, unaware that they would never see her again, and her Nana in Santa Barbara, and then there was Kurt, her sometime boyfriend . . .

Her eyes rolled back in her head, her lungs screamed silently as the will to fight back drained from her body. Her arms were heavy, her legs leaden, her entire being centered on the overwhelming need for air. It was over. She couldn't fight, couldn't remain conscious.

Her hands fell to her sides and she was vaguely aware that who-ever was holding her was letting her fall onto the concrete stoop.

As the merciful blackness rolled over her, Lucy's last thought was of Laney . . . dear sweet, trusting, stupid Laney.

CHAPTER 11

"Bentz is back in town?" Russ Trinidad frowned into his drink, swirling the scotch and studying it as if it held the keys to the universe.

Hayes had asked Trinidad to meet him after work for a drink, which was unusual in and of itself. So Trinidad's normally suspicious nature was on high alert. "What the hell is he doing back here?"

"It's about his ex-wife."

"Jennifer?" Trinidad snorted as water ran through bamboo stalks in a small waterfall near the entrance and soft Japanese music played in the background. "Piece of work, that one. Though I never really knew her."

"Consider yourself lucky," Hayes said.

At six feet, Trinidad was shorter than Hayes, but kept up a military physique. In Trinidad's world black was beautiful and bald was sexy as any head of messy hair. They were seated in a corner booth in a bar in Little Tokyo, not too far from Parker Center, the building housing the Robbery-Homicide Division of the LAPD, yet far enough away not to be a cop hangout. Trinidad was into his second glass of scotch while Hayes worked his way through his first sake.

Hayes had decided to confide in Trinidad, Bentz's ex-partner, because the near-retiring detective was one of Bentz's few allies in the department. However at this point Bentz had been gone so long, even Trinidad was iffy.

"Okay, I'll bite." Trinidad took a sip from his drink, saw a fleck of something foreign floating in the scotch, and flicked it out with a practiced finger. He drank again, didn't bother complaining to the waitress. "Fill me in on our old friend Bentz."

Hayes did.

Told him about meeting with the former LAPD detective the night before, about the photos Bentz had received showing his dead wife out and about in L.A.

"So he thinks his ex-wife might still be alive?" Trinidad said, frowning and finishing his drink. "He IDed her."

"Yeah, but she was real busted up."

"You're buying into it?" Trinidad's eyebrows rose. "Sounds like bullshit to me."

"I'm not buying into anything, but I checked. The only person to request a death certificate on her was Bentz himself. No one else bothered." Unsettled, Hayes twisted his cup in his palms. "I mean it's possible he's gone off his nut. The guy nearly died in a freak accident. In a coma for a while."

"And comes out of it only to be visited by his long-deceased ex-wife," Trinidad scoffed. "How nice."

"Or nuts." Hayes took a swallow of the sake and watched a young Asian couple enter and take seats at the bar. "He gave me a copy of the envelope and death certificate that were sent to him. He's having 'em checked for fingerprints and to see if there's any DNA on the seal of the envelope through the New Orleans PD."

"So you're not stickin' your neck out for him, are you? Nothing you can do unless you've got the originals and even if he gave them to you, I'd say you'd be making a mistake getting involved with this."

"No problem since he didn't. But I thought you were supposed to be his friend."

Trinidad lifted a shoulder. "Friends don't help friends become paranoid." He leaned across the table and lowered his voice. "Rick Bentz is a loose cannon. Nearly lost it when he killed the Valdez kid, and, hey, that's understandable. But afterward, he never pulled himself together. I thought maybe he'd got a handle on everything when he settled in with the New Orleans PD. Rumor has it he's some kind of hero, solving difficult homicides. But, I'm telling you, there was a time he was this close"—he held up his thumb and forefinger so that they nearly touched—"to snapping. Looks like he finally did. My advice, even though you don't want it: You'd be smart to avoid whatever it is he's peddling."

"Haven't done anything yet."

"Yeah, well, it's the 'yet' part that's the problem, isn't it?" The edges of Trinidad's mouth tightened.

At the bar, the Asian girl laughed as she ordered her drink and her boyfriend rubbed the back of her neck gently, but firmly, never letting up. Hayes bet he was already getting a hard-on. Young love. He'd been there a couple of times.

Trinidad patted the pocket of his shirt and found his cigarettes. He took one out, fingered it, and signaled for the waitress, not bothering to fight Hayes for the tab. Together they walked into the early evening light where the hazy sunset was reflected on the glass wall of a new condominium building. Farther down the street, the domed tower of the Cathedral of St. Vibiana was visible, its ornate Spanish architecture a contrast to the geometric skyline of downtown Los Angeles.

Trinidad lit up, drawing smoke deep into his lungs as they walked along the crowded sidewalk. "Bentz was a good cop. The Valdez thing really fucked him up." Shaking his head, he added, "Then his wife messin' around with his brother. Hell. Who wouldn't go off the deep end?" They turned a corner to a spot on the street where Trinidad had wedged his Chevy Blazer. "But I'm about ready to retire." He let out a cloud of smoke. "Looking up old records? Exhuming a body when everybody knows who's in the casket? I don't need this shit."

"What if Jennifer Bentz didn't die?"

"She did. We don't need DNA to prove it. *Her* car. *Her* body identified by *her* husband. No other missing person who matches her description."

"We don't know that."

"I'm just sayin' that Bentz had a tendency to bend the rules until they broke, and I'm not that guy anymore. I've got less than a year until retirement. I don't want to fuck it up."

But his words didn't match his expression as he tossed his cigarette onto the street and stomped on the smoldering butt with a little more force that was necessary. "Shit." He looked up at the sky and shook his head. "Goddamned Bentz. Why the hell is he back now, seein' ghosts, makin' waves? That son of a bitch left me holding the bag, y'know. And other officers, too. Walked away from a couple of cases, some messy ones that never did get solved."

Hayes remembered one high-profile case, a double-murder investigation that went stone cold when Jennifer Bentz's accident derailed her ex-husband. The Caldwell twins . . . The killer had gotten away, leaving little evidence behind other than their mutilated bodies. At the time of the double homicide, Bentz had been a mess, a rabid drunk.

"Bentz would never ask you to do anything illegal," Hayes said as Trinidad opened the door of his Blazer.

"Yeah, right." He jabbed his key into the engine and looked up at Hayes. "You know the old saying: If you believe that, I've got some swampland I'd like to sell you in Florida."

"It worked for Disney."

Trinidad grinned, showing off a mouthful of big teeth. "You keep thinking that way. But be careful."

"So, you're not gonna help him."

"Help him find his dead ex-wife who faked her suicide and killed some woman in a car wreck?"

"Yeah."

Trinidad shook his head. "No way, man." With a roar of the engine, he was off.

Hayes climbed into his SUV, twisted on the ignition, and gunned it just as his cell phone chirped. Roaring into a sea of traffic, he glanced at the display.

Riva Martinez's name came onto the screen.

His partner.

"Hayes," he said. "What's up?"

"We've got a double. Two female bodies found in a storage unit in one of those facilities under the 110." She gave him the cross street and address of an on-ramp to the Harbor Freeway—the 110—then added, "Looks like the vics are twins."

"What? Wait a second." His mind raced ahead and he told himself to slow down. He was making connections that didn't exist. Seeing Bentz again had reminded him of the Caldwell case, the unsolved double murder that had occurred twelve years earlier.

"Got a problem?" Martinez asked.

"Twins?" Hayes spoke slowly as adrenaline rushed through his veins. "Identical?"

"I'd say so. We'll know for sure soon. You'd better get down here."

She hung up, leaving Hayes with an overwhelming sense of doom. He hit the gas.

Bentz had never solved the Caldwell murders. The killer of those twins had never been caught. Somehow he'd disappeared from the face of the earth, or at least left Southern California. Of course there had been hypotheses cast about. Some people thought that the guy was in prison, caught for some other crime, and had never been fingered for the Caldwell murders. Others believed that he'd died or moved on. There was speculation that the killer had just up and quit, but that didn't come from cops. No one in the department really believed a sadistic murderer had just given up his avocation for fly-fishing or golf.

"Damn." Ignoring the speed limit, Hayes set his lights on the dash and put in a quick call to Trinidad. His thoughts were dark and jumbled as he plunged through an intersection where the light was changing from amber to red.

How was it possible that within forty-eight hours of Rick Bentz returning to L.A., a killer had nearly duplicated the double murder that had led to the end of Bentz's career?

Coincidence?

Or diabolically calculated?

The last twenty-four hours had proved fruitless for Bentz. One dead end after another. He'd driven to Santa Monica again, parked, and walked the length of the boardwalk. At the end of the pier he stared out to sea and imagined Jennifer here. With him. With James. By herself.

He'd even driven by some of the places he and Jennifer had frequented when she'd been alive. A burger joint where they'd shared baskets of fries not far from West Los Angeles College. A bar on Sepulveda where she'd introduced him to martinis. A romantic Italian restaurant where they'd sat next to each other in a dark booth, Jennifer's hand on his thigh. Ernesto's was no longer. The building itself had gone through many transformations and now was a Thai place that specialized in "to go" orders. Out of some twisted sense of irony, he bought a bowl of gai yang that was heavy on the garlic.

He'd cruised past the pay phone on Wilshire knowing nothing would come of it and had even driven to the spot where he'd last seen the woman who looked like Jennifer waiting for the bus on Figueroa. He'd spent two hours at the stop, arriving an hour before the time he'd seen her the day before, and leaving an hour afterward. To no end. No woman in a lemon-colored sundress. No Jennifer. And though he'd determined the route that particular bus took each afternoon, it didn't cast any light on his investigation.

He'd grabbed a pizza to go, brought it back to his motel room, and ate a couple of slices as he went over his notes, focusing on the information he'd gathered from Shana McIntyre. She'd given up more than he'd expected, but still, he didn't get the sense that Jennifer had been in touch with her.

He'd tracked down the bus driver on the route where he'd seen Jennifer. The driver, a woman in her late forties with spiky gray hair and a bored attitude, didn't remember a woman who looked like Jennifer in a yellow dress. She hadn't been certain, of course, but she knew that the woman in the photos was not a regular bus rider on her route.

Another dead end.

He was racking up more than his fair share.

Bentz had placed calls to the others on his list but didn't reach anyone, and he didn't leave messages. He wondered about the rest of Jennifer's friends. Would they be any more help than Shana had been?

And what about Alan Gray? Where had that rich prick landed? The Internet told him little, but piecing together information from several magazine and newspaper articles, it seemed Gray had a place in Palm Desert and played a helluva lot of golf. Good golf, judging by scores from some recent amateur tournaments.

He'd phoned and left a message for Hayes, but Jonas hadn't returned the favor; probably didn't know anything. But then, who did, he wondered as the air conditioner blew the blackout drapes around. They were open, the blinds cracked to allow sharp lines of sunlight through the dusty window.

Nothing made any sense, Bentz thought, glancing through the window to watch a curvy woman in her mid-thirties adjust the sun shade over the dash of her ancient Cadillac. Satisfied that the unfolded sun protector was in perfect position, she grabbed a huge purse from the passenger seat, slung the strap over her shoulder, then locked the Caddy. Looking over her shoulder, she hurried through the breeze-way to an interior unit that faced the pool.

He wondered about the other occupants of the shabby motel. Every guest here had his or her secret, furtive truths to keep hidden within the identical units with worn carpeting, toilets that needed their handles jiggled, and mini-refrigerators that would barely hold a six-pack.

Snapping the blinds shut, Bentz tried to concentrate.

All in all, the day had been a dark walk down memory lane, which hadn't helped him determine whether or not Jennifer was alive or dead.

As he finished his third piece of pepperoni and olives, he wondered why the hell he'd ever come to L.A. Maybe everyone else was right. Maybe he was chasing after a ghost. Maybe whoever was behind the pictures and death certificate was just getting his or her jollies, knowing that Jennifer had been haunting him ever since he'd woken from the coma. Maybe now that perv was just trying to use that information to push him over the edge. To make sure he was really going out of his friggin' mind.

But who would have known that he'd seen the ghostly image of his wife upon waking? Just Kristi and a couple of nurses. Unless they'd said anything to someone who wanted to get at Bentz, nothing would have come of it.

"Hell." He closed the pizza box, wiped his fingers, and speed-dialed his wife, the woman he loved. The one waiting for him in their home outside New Orleans. The one who was trying her damnedest to trust him.

Olivia didn't answer and he didn't bother leaving a message. What would he say? That he loved her? She knew it already. That he missed her? Then why wasn't he on the next plane back to Louisiana? That he didn't know what the hell he was doing in L.A.? Then why was he still here?

He thought of his conversation with Shana. Tomorrow Tally White would be working at the middle school where she was a teacher. As for Lorraine, Jennifer's stepsister, he hadn't connected with her, either. There were other friends and acquaintances as well, of course, but Shana, Tally, and Lorraine were at the top of his list as confidantes of his ex-wife. Women who might just know what had happened to her. Not to mention Fortuna Esperanzo, Jennifer's friend at the gallery.

Of course he would have loved to have talked to Father James about her—James, his own damned brother—but that was impossible. There would be no rising from the dead for James; Father James would not be pulling a Lazarus. Bentz was sure the priest was dead, the victim of a serial killer, and nearly certain he was rotting in hell.

With Jennifer?

That was a question he couldn't answer.

His heartburn was acting up. He fished a half-used roll of Tums out of his pocket, popped a couple, and found the keys to his rental car.

He frowned at his cane propped against the wall, snatched the stick along with his jacket, and walked outside into the lingering heat of the day. After locking the unit he crossed the cement walkway to his Ford and passed the old man next door who was walking his dog. Spike looked up at Bentz, only to return to sniffing the potholes of the parking lot, either looking for discarded bits of food or a place to defecate. Bentz nodded at the man, then climbed into his rental.

He'd spent enough hours in the So-Cal motel with its four dingy walls closing in on him.

He twisted on the ignition, cranked up the air, and hit the gas. It was time to drive down to San Juan Capistrano. If he was lucky, he'd make it and still have a couple of hours before night fell.

Hayes squealed to a stop under the overpass of the Harbor Freeway. Roadblocks had been set up, changing the traffic pattern around the storage units. Flashing lights strobed the street and the sooty cement pilings holding up the cavernous structure of concrete and steel.

Onlookers, some with cell phones taking pictures, had gathered around the storage facility tucked beneath the on-ramp to the 110.

Two officers directed traffic, waving vehicles into the open lane as gawking drivers slowed, threatening to create major congestion. Other uniformed cops guarded the entrance to the storage units strung with yellow crime-scene tape. Orange traffic cones and barricades effectively forced the curious out.

Still, people gathered as vehicles rushed overhead, tires singing, engines rumbling, causing a deafening noise. A KMOL news van emblazoned in blue and sporting several satellite dishes was parked half a block up, two wheels over the curb to allow other cars to pass. The slim blond reporter Joanna Quince and a stocky cameraman lugging a shoulder cam headed toward the underpass. A helicopter for another local television station hovered overhead, the whir of its rotors silenced by the din of the freeway.

Hayes double-parked near the crime scene van and wended his way through the police cars, passing the SID van. The investigators from the Scientific Investigative Division were already at work. They'd search for footprints, handprints, hairs, or any kind of trace evidence that might provide clues to the identity of the killer. Photographs were being snapped, a videographer was filming, measurements taken. Hayes looked upward, searching for a security camera, but the one that was mounted over the units was obviously broken, the camera hanging at an awkward position from a rusted pole.

So much for any film of the storage units.

Martinez, a petite woman with fiery red hair and a razor-sharp tongue, stood at the door of Unit 8 and waved Hayes inside.

"Take a look," she said with the hint of a Hispanic accent. "But I gotta warn ya, it's not pretty."

Hayes braced himself, keeping his eyes away from the victims for a moment. He focused on the dusty cement floor, the jars of nails, and a broken lawn chair that had been pushed into the corner of the unit. After all this time, he still wasn't comfortable around dead bodies. The scent and look of death bothered him, got under his skin, cut into his brain, lingering there for days. He usually managed to hide it.

Not tonight.

Looking down at the defiled bodies of twin girls who seemed barely out of their teens, he couldn't mask the raw pain that cut him to the quick.

They had been laid out purposefully, bound and gagged, naked, curled into the fetal position. Bruises and ligature marks were visible on their necks. Facing each other, their eyes open under the glare of a single lightbulb, each girl stared sightlessly at her twin. Their skin was so pale it seemed blue. Each victim's blond hair had been pulled away from her face and tied with a long red ribbon. The same ribbon bound them. Posed as they were, identical twins, they resembled two macabre wraiths gazing into a mirror.

Staged to look like they were still in the womb. Just like the Caldwell twins.

Hayes's jaw tightened. "Any ID?"

"Yeah . . . their clothes and purses, even their jewelry and cell phones, all over there. Along with their birth certificates, times of birth highlighted in pink." Martinez hitched her chin to a corner. There on the floor, the clothing and personal effects of the two girls sat in neatly folded stacks.

A tidy, fastidious crime scene, Hayes thought as he leaned over the folded clothes. This was all too familiar. On top of each pile was a copy of the birth certificates, the date and time of their births highlighted with pink marker. Probably the same pink ink that would be found on the girls' bodies, Hayes suspected. Assuming, of course, this was the killer who'd torn through L.A. years ago.

"Lucille and Elaine Springer," Martinez said. "I already called Missing Persons. They're checking now."

Jonas thought of his own kid. Twelve years old and going on thirty, as they said, but still an innocent. It would kill him to lose Maren, but to have someone intentionally take her life . . . Bile rose in his throat and he turned his attention away from his personal life to the situation at hand.

The photographs had been taken, body temperatures recorded; the victims were ready to be moved. But Jonas knew, with chilling certainty, what they would find when the bodies were rolled over onto their backs.

Oh, sweet mother.

"Remind you of anything?" a gravelly voice asked. Hayes looked over his shoulder to see Detective Andrew Bledsoe in the doorway.

Jonas straightened and nodded. "The Caldwell case."

"And isn't that a coincidence with our friend Bentz back in town?" Somehow Bledsoe managed a smug smile, as if the twin girls had never been more than corpses, just another case to solve.

Martinez scowled, her lips tight. She glared up at Bledsoe, her eyes dark with a seething rage. "Is there a reason you're here?"

Though he was in his fifties, he was one of those guys who looked a decade younger. At five-ten and under two hundred pounds, Bledsoe cultivated a perpetual tan and kept his jet-black hair slicked back. His suits were usually tailor-made and his steely blue eyes didn't miss much. He was a good cop. And a pain in the ass. "I was on my way back from a scene in Watts, heard it on the scanner."

"Well, we're busy here." Martinez didn't conceal her disdain for Bledsoe. The guy had always bugged her. Hayes knew it; everyone in the department did. Riva Martinez wasn't one to hide her feelings.

Turning her back on Bledsoe, she knelt near one of the bodies while Hayes studied the other.

"Ligature marks around the neck," Martinez noted, almost to herself, "and numbers and letters scrawled across each torso, just under their breasts."

The message written heavily in neon pink on their torsos was clear. Each victim was marked with her time of birth twenty-one years ago, and her time of death this morning—which was exactly twenty-one-years later. To the minute. As if the killer found pleasure in snuffing out their lives the moment they became adults.

"Goddamn it." Hayes felt cold inside despite the stifling, suffocating heat of the small enclosure. These girls had been born fourteen minutes apart, so they had died precisely fourteen minutes apart.

Hayes didn't doubt that the younger of the two—Elaine, born at 1:01 AM—had witnessed the horror of Lucille being strangled at 12:47 AM. Probably strangled by the very ribbon that was now binding her hair, wrists, and ankles, as well as gagging her mouth. Hayes suspected that the ribbons in their hair would contain traces of skin from where the fabric had dug into the soft flesh of their throats. And he knew he would find other ligature marks on their necks. The victims were subdued by some kind of strap, then finally killed with a heavy ribbon woven with thin, sharp wire.

Each girl had lived exactly twenty-one years.

Just like the Caldwell twins, the last homicide Rick Bentz had worked here in L.A. That case had gone ice cold when he'd turned in his resignation.

Hayes hated to admit it, but this time Bledsoe had a point.

Why were these victims chosen to be killed now, only days after Rick Bentz had returned to Los Angeles?

CHAPTER 12

"Stupid!" Olivia glared at her cell phone. It was in her hand, but she hadn't punched in Bentz's number because she felt nervous about phoning him. Which was ridiculous! She'd never been one of those women who was timid or shy or the least bit lacking in confidence. Yet here she was seated in her living room, feet curled beneath her, a cup of tea long forgotten and cold on the coffee table, and she wasn't sure what to do. Hairy S perched on the other end of the cozy couch while one of Bentz's old Springsteen CDs played in the background, but the homey atmosphere was little comfort.

She was paralyzed.

Didn't know whether to call Rick or not.

Even though she'd seen that he'd called earlier but hadn't left a message.

"Oh, to hell with it," she said and hit the speed dial number that would connect him to her.

He picked up before it rang twice. "Hey," he said, and he did sound glad—or was it relieved?—to hear from her.

"Hey back at you."

"What's up?"

"Just checkin' in," she said. *Tell him. Tell him now. You don't have to wait until he returns. Let him know that you're going to have a baby. Insist that no matter what his reaction is, you're thrilled with the pregnancy, that you've already started looking at baby clothes and thinking of where to put a bassinette.* "What're you doing?"

"Driving down to San Juan Capistrano."

"The mission? Why? Searching for swallows?" she teased, reminding him of the phenomenon of the swallows returning to Capistrano each year. "Didn't know you were a bird-watcher."

"Too late for the swallows, I think. They come in the spring."

"Then?" she asked.

"I needed to get out of that fleabag of a motel."

"To find Jennifer?"

A pause. "Maybe."

"Seen her lately?" She couldn't hide the sarcasm in her voice. Who was he kidding?

"I don't know."

She wanted to tell him he was being foolish. Instead she bit back a sharp reply and moved to safer territory. "How're you feeling? Your leg."

"It's still attached."

"Doing your exercises?"

"Every day."

"Liar." She laughed and she heard him chuckle.

"What's new with you?"

She gathered her strength, told herself she was just going to blurt it out and let the chips fall where they may, when Harry S, hearing something outside, started barking like crazy. "Hey, you, hush!" she said and heard her husband laugh again.

"Great. You call me just to shut me up."

"I think I've told you, I'm one fabulous wife."

"I . . . know . . . Livvie . . . maybe a million times . . ." His voice was faint and spotty; she couldn't catch all the words.

"Hey, I can't hear you. You're breaking up." But she was too late with her message. The call was already lost and she said to the dead connection, "By the way, Hotshot, you're going to be a father again." But, of course, he wouldn't be able to hear her and she decided, once again, giving Bentz that kind of news over a spotty wireless connection was a bad idea.

Lately it seemed she didn't have any good ones. She carried her cup into the kitchen and left it in the sink while a quarter moon rose over the cypress and pine trees rimming the backyard. A few stars winked and when she cranked open the window she heard a chorus of bullfrogs loud enough to give the Boss a run for his money.

She fed Chia, talked to the bird, and then, still feeling antsy, decided to take a turn on the treadmill. She'd wait until Rick came back to Louisiana, or, if this wild goose chase of his took too long, she'd fly out there and give him the good word about her pregnancy face-to-face.

"Five days, Bentz," she said, tapping a finger against her chin. "Five days. That's all you've got. Then, California, here I come."

"Who found the bodies?" Hayes asked. Glad to be out of the tiny claustrophobic closet of a storage unit, he breathed the fresher air of the freeway system during rush hour. So what if their gas and diesel exhaust collected under the overpass? At least the smell of death wasn't filling his lungs.

"A college student." Riva Martinez pointed to a cruiser where a young girl stared out the window of the backseat. Her eyes were round with fear, her face pale behind the glass. "Felicia Katz. Goes to USC, but keeps some of her stuff here. She came down here this afternoon intending to take something out of her unit—an old chair, I think. Her unit is number seven." Martinez indicated the unit next to the one with the bodies. "She noticed the door of eight wasn't latched, saw the lock was broken. She thought someone had probably broken into it and stolen whatever was inside, so she took a peek."

"And got an eyeful," Bledsoe cut in.

Hayes's stomach twisted as he thought of the victims who were now being preliminarily examined before being hauled away in body bags to the morgue for autopsies. And twenty-four hours ago they were innocent young women, probably getting ready to celebrate their birthdays.

Martinez continued, "Anyway, Katz saw the vics, texted her boyfriend, then called 9-1-1."

Hayes glanced back at the car holding the witness. "Why the boyfriend first?"

"She claims she freaked."

"I'll bet," Bledsoe interjected.

"Who's the boyfriend?"

"Robert Finley. Goes by Robbie. Coffee barista by day, grunge band drummer by night. He showed up just after the first officer—that would be Rohrs—got here. We've got Finley in another squad car. Trying to keep him and Katz separate until we get each of their stories and compare them."

"You think they had anything to do with it?"

"Nah. You?"

"Probably not." Hayes shook his head.

"It's the Twenty-one killer," Bledsoe interrupted. He'd stuck around and was eyeing the scene.

"Who?" Riva asked. She was relatively new to the department and hadn't heard some of the old stories.

"That's what we called him. He killed another set of twins, Delta and Diana Caldwell, on their twenty-first birthday. They were reported missing two days earlier, so we figured he nabbed 'em, held 'em, and then killed 'em at the exact minute they turned twenty-one."

"So he knew them?" Riva guessed, her eyes narrowing.

"Or *of* them. But he was never caught." Bledsoe's expression turned hard. "The Caldwell parents called us every week for nearly six years. After that, I heard they split up."

"And no other cases like the Caldwell killings until now?" Riva asked, glancing back at the storage unit. "So this could be a copycat?"

Bledsoe shook his head. "Some of the details were never released to the press or the public. The red ribbon, the pink marker. The fact that their clothing was neatly folded, as if Mommy or the maid had taken care of them." Bledsoe glanced over Hayes's shoulder. "Speaking of the press."

Hayes turned to find Joanna Quince, the determined news reporter he'd seen earlier, talking with one of the uniforms guarding the barricade. He grimaced and turned away, but not before Quince caught sight of the detectives and recognized Bledsoe.

"Detective," she shouted. "Could I ask you a few questions? Is it true this is a double homicide? That two girls were found in one of the storage units?"

"I'll handle this," Bledsoe said. Bledsoe liked the press, that much was true, but he wouldn't give too much away. He would refer Joanna Quince to the public information officer, who would issue a statement and field questions once the next of kin were notified.

That job—telling the family—fell on Hayes's shoulders, and as far as he was concerned, talking to overwrought loved ones was almost as difficult as discovering the bodies.

Bentz pushed the speed limit as he drove south on "the Five," the interstate freeway that stretched from Canada to Mexico. The sun was low on the horizon and the traffic was thick and swift, a faster pace than he ever experienced in Louisiana. Bentz had expected to return to Los Angeles and feel at home, if not with the police, then with the area itself. He'd spent so many years of his life here.

But, no, he was a fish out of water now.

The phone call from Olivia had bothered him and he wondered, not for the first time, if he'd made a big mistake coming to L.A. Not only had he upset his wife, but if his boss in New Orleans found out that he was on the West Coast chasing after a dead woman, Jaskiel would have him back in psych evaluations in no time. Or she could put him out to pasture for good, thinking he'd gone round the bend. His career as a cop could be over.

So what? It's not like the NOPD isn't functioning without you. Who knows when or if you'll be allowed back on active duty.

His fingers tightened over the wheel as he switched lanes and a moving van roared past his Ford Escape as if he were standing still. He looked at his speedometer. He was going seventy.

His cell phone rang. He clicked off the radio and glanced at the LED screen. Montoya's number.

Good. Bentz had been brooding about Olivia ever since their last conversation. He needed a distraction.

He clicked on. "About time you called. You got something for me?"

"Not much. No fingerprints on the envelope or the death certificate, other than yours and mine."

Bentz swore under his breath.

"You didn't really expect any."

"No, but I thought maybe we'd get lucky. That maybe the guy was sloppy."

"Don't think so. DNA's not back, but I'll bet a year's salary that the perp didn't lick the flap of the envelope. These days everyone knows that shit if they watch any truTV or *CSI*, or *NCIS*, or *Law & Order*, or you name it."

"It was a long shot," Bentz admitted, spotting his exit.

"I've got the lab analyzing the type of ink on the doc, but it probably won't be something that will help."

"Doesn't hurt to try." Bentz eased up on the gas, flipped on his blinker, and slid into the exit lane.

"You know, this thing you're doing, you should just give it up."

"Oh, yeah?"

"I know you're going out of your mind not working, but hell, can't you do something else?"

"You mean something a little less insane?"

"Yeah. Golf would be good. Or fishing. Hell, we've got great fishing down in the Gulf."

"I'll think about it. I could buy me a new fancy pole and set of clubs in between my calligraphy and yoga classes."

"Wouldn't be a bad idea."

"Then you, too. Sign us both up. And add in ballroom dancing. You'd look fantastic in one of those sparkly gowns."

Montoya didn't so much as chuckle. "You think you're funny?"

"I know I'm funny."

Montoya wasn't laughing. He asked, "You see your ex-wife again?"

Bentz hesitated as he drove onto the ramp. "Maybe," he admitted, slowing for a red light. "Not sure."

"Really?"

"Really. She phoned, too. Called me by the pet name she'd given me."

"Right."

"I'm just telling ya."

"So what're you doing about it?"

Should he tell the skeptic? Hell, why not? "I talked with one of Jennifer's friends. She said James and Jennifer met in San Juan Capistrano, so I thought I'd drive down."

"Are you kidding me? What does that have to do with anything? You think your dead brother is involved?" Montoya muttered some oath in Spanish, before adding, "This is sounding crazier by the second. I've been to San Juan Capistrano. A couple of times. There's a history to it, man. The whole town is supposed to be rife with ghosts."

"Kinda like New Orleans."

"I mean it. That so-called friend of Jennifer is messin' with ya. San Juan Capistrano? Come *on*. You tell this friend you've been seeing ghosts and she sends you to Capistrano. Give me an effin' break."

"She's *not* a ghost," he said, though in truth he was feeling haunted. Exactly what whoever was behind this wanted.

"Look I gotta go." Bentz's ridicule capacity was on overflow.

"Great. Walk about the hallowed grounds, talk to the white lady or the faceless monk or the dead guy in his rocking chair. Or Jennifer, since you obviously think she's hanging out with them. Listen, if you ever get close enough to talk to her, give her my love."

"Screw you, Montoya," he said as the light turned green and he eased ahead toward the mission.

"You should get so lucky." His partner hung up and Bentz felt his lips twist upward a bit. He missed that cocky son of a bitch, just as he missed his job, but not quite as much as he missed Olivia.

"Check the cell phone records, include the texts and read what they say if anything," Hayes said as he and Martinez left the crime scene and walked toward their cars. "They should give us a window of time when the girls were abducted. If this is like the Caldwell case, then we can assume the vics were killed somewhere else and brought here to be staged and discovered. We need to find out who owns the facility and who rents units here, not just Unit 8 but all of them. See if there's any connection to the Springer twins. Or if anyone saw anything suspicious."

"I'll have all the traffic cameras checked as well, and some of the security cameras in nearby businesses."

They would canvass the area using uniformed police and detectives to try and locate anyone who had seen anything. A convenience store and gas station were in clear sight of the underpass and storage units. Maybe someone, an employee or customer, saw something that would give them a lead. Anything to go on. If the times of death on the bodies were accurate, the victims had already been dead over twelve hours, and each minute that passed was critical to the investigation.

"And we should contact those groups dedicated to twins in the area. The killer knows they're twins. He had to know when they were born to abduct them just before their birthday. That takes planning."

"Online groups, too," Martinez suggested, and the scope of the investigation just got a whole lot wider.

"Right."

"Our doer is organized," Martinez observed as she took in the scene. "Meticulous. Probably a neat freak."

"Who only kills once every twelve years," Hayes reminded her.

"We think. I'll check with other agencies, in other states, the F.B.I. He might be spreading his love around. See if there are any murders of twins in the surrounding states. Hell, make it the entire United States."

"And recent releases from the prisons. Maybe he's been incarcerated for the last twelve years. I'll run a check of prison records. We should look at the psychological profiles of anyone who's been released for a violent crime in the last year."

"Could be a long list."

"Amen." He hated to think how much time it would take.

They reached Martinez's car and she opened the door, then asked, "So tell me, what was the meaning of that crack by Bledsoe? What the hell does Rick Bentz have to do with this?"

"Nothing. Probably coincidence." Hayes reached into his pocket and slid his shades onto his face. "The connection is that Bledsoe worked with Bentz and Trinidad on the Caldwell twin case."

She was nodding. Getting it.

"Bledsoe always needs someone to blame."

"That's it? Not because Bledsoe was shut down by Bentz's wife?" she asked. "Detective Rankin said something about it when his name came up this morning."

"Rankin has her own ax to grind," Hayes said. He didn't want to get dragged into department gossip, especially not twelve- or fifteen-year-old rumors.

"Yeah, she said she dated Bentz, too."

"Along with others."

"Including Corinne O'Donnell," she pointed out.

"That's right." He nodded, leaning a hip against the car and feeling heat from the back panel through his pants. "And there were a few more. One was Bonita Unsel. Worked Vice before she came to Homicide. Others. I can't really remember. Ancient history."

"History that happened before Bentz left town." Little lines gathered between her eyebrows as an eighteen-wheeler rolled up the ramp to the freeway. "Maybe our guy isn't so much about killing twins as in putting another murder in Bentz's face. Maybe he knows Bentz is back in town."

"It's possible," he agreed.

"So how did it all go down back then—the Caldwell twins' murders?" Martinez asked. "Was it Bentz who dropped the ball on the case?"

Hayes shook his head. "Nah. The guy was a mess, believe me. But it wasn't his fault, at least not entirely, that the case went cold." Though he'd never admitted it, Hayes did think that Bentz should have resigned from the double homicide early on, leave it to Bledsoe or Trinidad. At the time Rick Bentz had been a pale version of his once sharp self, dulled to the point of not caring about his work. The LAPD had taken the position that Bentz, as lead investigator was responsible for finding the killer of two beautiful twenty-one-year-old college coeds. The case was in the public eye, which made the failure to make an arrest that much worse. "He became the scapegoat."

"Bledsoe still seems to blame him."

Hayes lifted a shoulder. "Bledsoe and Bentz never got along. They worked the case together, but, as I said, Bentz was the lead. When he left, Bledsoe took over, but always blamed his old partner."

"Ouch."

"Yeah, no love lost between those two."

Martinez's cell phone went off. "I'll call ya if I find out anything." She clicked on the phone. "Martinez."

Hayes glanced back at the scene, crossed an alley, and jogged to his car, thinking about the long list of calls to be made and records to be checked in this early process of tracking down a killer. With the mountain of work ahead of him, he'd be lucky to see his daughter again before she turned thirty.

CHAPTER 13

The night was muggy and the scent of the Mississippi River rolled through the streets of New Orleans. Tonight, driving through the French Quarter, Montoya felt as dark and disturbed as the slow-moving water, his conversation with Bentz echoing through his mind.

Bentz was being a damned fool, off chasing the ghost of his dead ex-wife when he could be home, here, with his real, living, flesh-and-blood spouse. It just didn't make sense. Bentz, usually pragmatic, was definitely not playing with a full deck. No doubt his near-death experience had messed with his mind. Big-time.

There wasn't much traffic this time of night, but the lights of the city, revitalized since the hurricane, blazed, as he pulled into his driveway.

Pocketing his keys, he walked up the sidewalk and into his house, a double-wide shotgun that he'd been renovating when Hurricane Katrina had struck with all the vengeance of hell. God, the place had been a mess, though not hit as severely as some of the homes that were nearly obliterated. Still, the damage was enough that he hated the thought of another hurricane. He'd rebuilt, like so many others. His renovation plans included retaining as much of the original charm of his shoebox of a house as he could, while updating to accommodate his new family. Not only had he gained a wife in Abby, but she'd come with a skittish gray tabby named Ansel who hid beneath the furniture, and a happy-go-lucky chocolate lab, Hershey. The dog now danced at his feet, his tail wagging so wildly it swiped precariously at everything on the coffee table.

"Hey, boy," he said while scratching behind the Lab's ears. "Wanna go outside?" With a deep bark, Hershey raced him down the long hallway that bisected the house and led to the enclosed backyard.

Following Hershey, Montoya put in a call to Abby. She was a photographer and tonight she'd scheduled a late-night photo shoot in her studio outside the city.

The dog was running back and forth, a bundle of energy. "I get it, man," Montoya told the dog, tossing a yellow tennis ball into the yard as he waited for Abby's voice mail to kick in. Hershey took off at a dead run and found the ball in the darkness while Montoya left his wife a message. The big lab then galloped back and dropped the ball at Montoya's feet. His tail wagged until Montoya snatched the ball up and tossed it so the dog could pounce on it again. Another throw and an equally quick retrieval, again and again. They played the game for nearly half an hour, the dog a bundle of energy, Montoya thinking about his ex-partner and Bentz's emotional suicide mission to L.A.

What was the guy doing? Bentz's first wife Jennifer had been no angel. And she was dead and buried. Fortunately. The way Montoya understood it, she'd been a bitch of a thing when she'd been alive. Bentz had divorced her, hadn't he? Montoya had never met Jennifer but he'd heard from Bentz himself that she'd cheated on him, over and over again, even with Bentz's damned half brother. A priest, no less.

"Bitch," he said, throwing the ball into the air and watching the dog take off, nearly flying.

Ironically, Olivia had been attracted to that same man once, Father James McLaren, before she'd married Bentz. But she'd come to her senses and they'd been happy together.

Until recently.

Ever since Bentz had awakened from the damned coma, the one his daughter had insisted would take his life, he'd been a changed man. Remote. Almost haunted.

Montoya had chalked it up to inactivity; not being able to work, not having the strength to fight or walk on his own. Now Montoya wasn't so certain. *Maybe when a guy brushes up with death that closely, he comes back to life with a new, dark attitude.* Because that was how it was. Rick Bentz had not returned to consciousness with a newfound appreciation for life, a revitalized *joie de vivre*. Nu-uh. None of that getting called to the light shit. No born-again Christian was Bentz.

Instead he'd awakened with an urgency to find his dead ex-wife, a bitch if there ever had been one.

Bentz was a good man who'd definitely gone around the bend.

It was all a flippin' mess.

In Montoya's opinion, Jennifer Bentz should bloody well stay dead.

Before driving to San Juan Capistrano, Bentz had done his homework. He'd searched the Internet as well as the public records of Orange County and the town of San Juan Capistrano, looking for anything relating to an inn or hotel dedicated to Saint Miguel or San Miguel. He'd thought Shana McIntyre might have been lying—jerking his chain. But no. He'd found reference and pictures of a small chapel that wasn't a part of the larger mission.

He'd also found that Saint Miguel's Church and grounds had been sold by the diocese in the early sixties and renovated into an inn. Over the past forty years it had been sold and resold. The latest transaction in the public records indicated that the inn had been purchased by a Japanese conglomerate eighteen months earlier and wasn't open for business.

Using his G.P.S., he navigated the streets of the quaint, famous city. Gardens flourished and red tile roofs capped stucco buildings throughout the town. Twilight was settling in as he drove through the historic district where people window-shopped or dined outside at umbrella-covered tables.

Across the railroad tracks, Bentz drove several miles, angling away from the heart of the town and into an area that hadn't flourished. He passed warehouses on the old San Miguel Boulevard and crossed a dry riverbed to a squalid dead-end street.

Although the rest of the town was charming and bustling with activity, this area felt tired and worn. FOR LEASE signs faded in empty storefront windows. He slowed as the old inn came up on his right, the lawn now thick with waist-high weeds, the stucco and brick exterior crumbled and tinged with soot. Apparently hard times had hit this part of the neighborhood.

Bentz turned his rental car around in an alley and parked in a pockmarked lot serving a strip mall that held a used bookstore, some kind of "gently used" clothing store, and a small mom-and-pop corner market going to seed. One of the shops, formerly a pizza joint, according to the signs, stood vacant. Now a FOR RENT sign with a local number was taped to the window.

The single business that seemed to be thriving was an adjacent tavern that advertised "Two For One" night on Tuesdays. A couple of beater pickups, a dirty van with the words WASH ME scraped into the dingy back panel, a dented red Saturn, and a silver Chevy with a faded parking pass were scattered sparsely on the broken, dusty asphalt. The aura of the neighborhood was gray, wrought with desolation and desperation, as if this little patch of the town were clinging to dreams of a bygone time.

From his car he viewed a few people on the street; a couple of kids were skateboarding on the cracked sidewalks and an older guy, in shorts and a broad-brimmed hat, was smoking a cigarette while walking his caramel-colored dog, a one-eyed pit bull mix who tugged on the leash. The dog lumbered along and sniffed the tufts of dry grass and wagged his stump of a tail any time the old guy so much as said a word.

Bentz climbed out, left his cane, but picked up a small flashlight and a pocket-sized kit of tools in case he needed to pick a lock. Hitting the remote to lock the Escape, Bentz walked back to the old inn where an ancient chain-link fence encircled the grounds. Barely legible, a NO TRESPASSING sign creaked in a slight breeze that kicked up the dust and pushed a torn plastic sack and a few dry leaves down the street.

He checked the gate.

Locked tight, of course.

Searching for a way inside, he hitched his way around the perimeter of the building while aiming the beam of his flashlight on the fence. He moved slowly, inching around the perimeter until he discovered a spot where the metal mesh had been torn. He slipped through. His arm brushed against the sharp broken links, his shirt tearing, his skin scraping. He barely noticed. His hip and knee were protesting as well, but he ignored the discomfort, intent on his mission.

Inside, he stared somberly at the crumbling, decrepit building.

The bell tower was one of the few sections still intact. Most of the windows had been boarded over and tall weeds choked what had once been a lush yard and manicured grounds. Some of the roof tiles had slid off and splintered on the overgrown pathways and gardens. A fountain in the heart of the circular drive had gone dry; the statue of an angel poised to pour water from a vessel into a large pool, now decapitated and missing one wing.

This was the location of their trysts?

Their romantic rendezvous?

Narrowing his eyes as he stared at the run-down buildings, Bentz had a hard time turning back the clock, thinking about the old mission as it once had been with manicured lawns and gardens, stained-glass windows, and flowing fountains.

He stepped over a pile of debris and worked his way through rubble and brush to the ornately carved front doors. A rusting chain snaked through the handles, its lock securely in place.

To keep out the curious, the homeless, or looters.

Or a cop with too much time on his hands who might be obsessed with his dead ex-wife.

Ignoring the voice in his brain, he picked the lock and found his way through an archway into what had once been a courtyard, a square surrounded on all sides by the two-storied inn. Each long side was divided into individual units, complete with doorways on the ground level and balconies with boarded over French doors on the second. The courtyard was already in shadow, the gloom of evening seeping around the chipped and broken statue of St. Miguel as the sun sank low behind the bell tower.

So far, so good, Bentz thought.

The place seemed empty.

Lonely.

Walking along the portico, peering through a few dirty panes of the remaining windows, he nearly stepped on a rat that scurried quickly through a crack in the mortar.

Not Bentz's idea of a romantic getaway.

At least not now, not in the inn's current condition. The place was downright creepy, a great setting for a horror film. Testing each of the doors along the covered walkway, he felt the prickle of apprehension on the back of his neck.

All rooms were locked firmly.

Number seven, a corner suite, was no different. The number dangled precariously from the frame and looked ready to drop into the debris collecting on the porch.

Using his set of picks, he sweated as he worked the lock and it finally sprang open, the old hinges creaking eerily.

Now or never, he told himself, but he felt as if he were walking upon Jennifer's grave as he stepped into the stuffy, stale suite. In an instant he was thrown back to a time he'd tried hard to forget.

A table was broken and cracked. A television stand was overturned, the floor scraped and filthy. Cobwebs collected in the corners and the dried corpses of dead insects littered the windowsills.

The entire place was near being condemned, Bentz guessed, his skin crawling. Stairs wound upward and creaked with each of his steps as he painfully climbed to the second floor, where a landing opened to a bedroom. There were two other doors. One led to a filthy bathroom, where dingy, cracked sinks had been pulled from the wall and a toilet was missing. The second door was closed, its latch broken, but when Bentz pushed on the old panels, he discovered it opened to an inside hallway. In one direction was the emergency exit stairs. In the other a long corridor stretched along the back wall of the building. He walked it and found the hall eventually funneled into a staircase that dropped into the area that had once been the lobby and office of the inn.

Handy, he thought. A secret entrance for a priest who didn't want to be seen going through the front door of unit seven to meet his mistress.

Bentz returned to the bedroom, dark and gloomy.

Their bedroom. Where the memories and despair and guilt still lingered.

The place Kristi may have been conceived, if Shana McIntyre could be believed. There was a chance Shana was lying, of course, that she knew of this place from her own romantic trysts. Shana had never made any bones about the fact that she didn't like him. She would thoroughly enjoy playing a sick joke on him, just to watch him squirm.

Almost smelling the odor of forgotten sex, he eyed a dusty bookcase that lined one wall. A few forgotten books were scattered on the shelf, their pages and covers yellowed. Other books had fallen to the floor, and from their mottled edges it appeared that something had been nibbling on them. He picked one up, a legal thriller from the nineties. A novel Jennifer had read. He remembered discussing it with her.

Her copy?

His throat went dry as he flipped through a few pages, then tossed the book aside, the ever-darkening room creeping into his soul.

Coincidence, nothing more.

And yet . . .

He *felt* as if she'd been here. Almost.

"Fool," he muttered as his gaze landed on a desk. It had been pushed in front of the closet and was missing a few drawers. On the scarred top was the base of an old telephone, the receiver dangling over one side.

Had Jennifer really spent hours here? Nights? With James? He crossed to the French doors, the glass boarded over on the outside, many of the panes cracked. The doors had once opened onto a small, private balcony overlooking the courtyard. Thinking they might open inward, he tried the levers.

Neither door budged.

It was getting darker by the second, the room musty, dragging the breath from his lungs. He ran the beam of his flashlight over a worn chaise. Foam stuffing bloomed crazily from the frayed velvet that had once been ice blue and now was a dingy, dirty gray.

Bentz's muscles tensed as he trained his small light on the bed, nothing more than a stained mattress on a rotting frame. It had been shoved into a corner beneath a broken stained-glass window, then forgotten.

Staring at the mess, cleaning it up in his brain, Bentz imagined what the room would have looked like nearly thirty years earlier. A time when Jennifer and James had first started their affair.

Don't even go there, he warned, but couldn't help imagining how the area would have looked. Surely a carpet would have covered the plank floors. The chaise, in a soft blue, would have been new and plump, the desk, a shiny rosewood antique. The bed would have been turned down and inviting, with smooth sheets and a cozy coverlet.

He thought there had been a desk chair, perhaps upholstered in the same blue as the chaise. He imagined a black cassock and clerical collar recklessly discarded over the chair's back.

One fist clenched.

He considered his half brother. Father James McClaren had been a handsome man with an altar-boy smile, strong jaw, and intense blue eyes that many women, not just Jennifer, had found seductive. There had been those, like his ex-wife, who loved the challenge of it all, the act of bringing a priest to his knees. Then there had been the frail or weak-willed who had turned to their priest in times of need only to be seduced by the unscrupulous James.

Self-righteous sinner.

Bentz could almost hear his half brother's deep laugh, imagined the whisper of his footsteps on the bare floor. In this room, alone with Jennifer, James had probably stripped naked, then with her giggling and backing away, had followed her, kissed her, and begun undressing her.

Or had it been the other way around?

Had she, dressed in scanty lingerie, waited in the bed for him, listening for his footsteps, eyeing the door until he stepped into the room?

It didn't matter. Either way, they'd ended up in bed, making love over and over again.

So much for the vow of chastity.

Odd, Bentz thought now as he played out the scene in his mind. Much of his anger and outrage had dissipated over time. That burning sense of betrayal had been reduced to dying embers.

It had been so many years.

And now there was Olivia.

His wife.

The woman he loved.

Dear God, why was he here when she was waiting for him in New Orleans?

There was nothing for him in California.

Jennifer was dead.

Yet, for just a split second, he smelled the scent of gardenias, a whiff of her perfume.

Yeah, right.

Then Jennifer's voice came to him. The barest of whispers. "Why?" she asked and he knew it was all in his head.

Dear God, maybe he really was going off his nut.

He turned toward the French doors and in his mind's eye he saw sunlight playing through the gauzy curtains. A bottle of champagne chilled in a bucket of ice on a bedside table while James and Jennifer rolled in the sheets and the bells of the chapel rang joyously . . .

Bong! Bong! Bong!

"Jesus!" Bentz jumped, snapped out of his reverie by the very real peal of church bells from a nearby parish.

Telling himself he was a dozen kinds of a fool, he shined the beam of his flashlight over the rubble and asked himself what he expected to accomplish by coming here. He'd found nothing concrete. Not one reason to believe that Jennifer was anything but dead.

Mentally berating himself, he walked to the French doors and peered through a slit in the boards covering the broken panes to the courtyard below.

His heart stopped.

Ice water slid through his veins.

Jennifer!

Or the spitting image of her.

Or her damned spirit, standing on the far side of the courtyard, caught in the long twilight shadow of the bell tower.

Disbelief coursing through his veins, Bentz hurried to the stairway and raced downward. He shoved open the door and dashed across the porch and into the courtyard, his damned leg throbbing painfully. Heart pounding, he flew across the uneven flagstones. The toe of his shoe caught on the edge of a stone. He didn't go down, but the twinge of pain slowed him.

He shot a glance to the edge of the courtyard, but it was empty.

No Jennifer.

Damn!

No woman, earthly or otherwise, stood in the silent, darkening enclosure. He turned, looking all around, cursing himself as he considered the fact that he'd conjured up her image, possibly caught a glimpse of the statue of St. Miguel. Had his willing mind transformed the broken statue into what he wanted to see? What he expected to witness?

Had it all been the power of suggestion?

No way!

His wildly pounding heart, accelerated pulse, and goose bumps on the back of his neck confirmed that the vision was very real. He dragged in deep breaths of the dry air and tried to think rationally, rein in his thoughts. Find sanity again.

Good God, he'd always been so rational . . . and now . . . now . . . Shit, what now? He shoved his hands through his hair, told himself to calm down. But as he did, he glanced up at the second story of the old inn. One of the balconies was different from the rest; its door hadn't been barricaded.

Why?

A shadow moved within.

His eyes narrowed.

Was it a play of light, or a dark figure lurking in the shadows, hiding behind the tattered, gauzy curtains?

"Oh, hell," he whispered. He took off again, forced his feet into a dead run. His bad leg was on fire, his breathing ragged as he leapt over the step and across the porch to the doorway of room twenty-one.

The door was ajar.

His heart nearly stopped.

He reached for his sidearm, but wasn't wearing his shoulder holster. His pistol was locked in the glove box of the rental car.

He didn't have time to run back for it. *Take it easy. Slow down. Think this through. It could be a trap!* Carefully, he pushed on the door.

Sweating crazily, he swung the beam of his flashlight over the rubble within. It was similar to the other room, squalid and neglected.

And smelling of gardenias.

What the hell?

Thud!

The sound of something falling in the room above reverberated through the living area.

He shot forward. Reminding himself that he might be walking into a trap, and that he should have brought his sidearm, he started up the stairs. He didn't bother to test for rotten wood or broken railings, just hurried upward.

The smell of her perfume was stronger here. His throat tightened. On the landing he paused, feeling exposed, an open target. Back to the wall, heart pumping wildly, he shined the beam of his small light over the empty bedroom, then inched toward the closed door of the closet. He braced himself. Then flung the door open.

Empty.

What had he expected?

Sweating, swallowing back an unsettling fear, he zeroed in on the bath. *One, two, three!* He kicked the door open.

With a shriek and flap of frantic wings, an owl flew from his roost on an old towel bar and soared out the broken window.

Bentz's knees nearly gave out. Jittery, he backed out of the room where feathers, dung, and pellets, the regurgitated undigested pieces of animals the owl coughed up, littered the floor.

Then he thought of the back stairs.

Damn!

Nerves tight, he backtracked to the upper hallway and heard the sounds of fast breathing and quick steps down on the first level.

Flinging himself over the rail, he half-stumbled down the stairs and cast his narrow light beam down the murky corridor.

Empty.

No one.

Dead or alive.

His leg on fire, he hitched his way to the nearest exit and found himself in what had been the lobby of the old inn, the main entrance to the small mission.

The air was stale and unused.

Except for the slight scent of Jennifer's perfume.

For the love of God, what was this?

He knew before he tried the front doors that they would be locked. He also knew that he could wander around this old structure, search the chapel and wine cellars, the individual rooms and reception hall and he wouldn't find her.

She was gone.

And he knew nothing more than he had when he'd left L.A. earlier today.

Perfect! I think with a smile. I peer through binoculars from a hiding spot in the upper story of an abandoned warehouse that reeks of must and oil. But the smells don't bother me. Not today. I focus on Bentz, who is still limping his way around the inn checking doors and flashing his light into the dark corners.

Go ahead, Bentz.

You'll find nothing.

It's getting darker, the shadows lengthening, but I can still see him studying the crumbling exterior of the mission. From here I'm safe to imagine him puzzling out the mystery of his first wife.

Good!

"Keep looking," I say in the barest of whispers, adrenaline pumping through my body. "But, uh-oh, be careful . . . who knows what you'll find."

I can feel my lips twist in satisfaction because I read him so perfectly. I know now that I can manipulate him however I want. And it feels good.

About time!

"Good boy, RJ," I coo softly, as if to a collie who's mastered a difficult trick. "Good, good boy."

God, how I love to see him squirm!

He's already walking away from the inn, so I step away from the window just in case an ancient, watery streetlight might reflect in my field glasses.

I can't afford to be careless.

Rick Bentz might be a lot of things, but a fool he is not.

I know that.

He's just a dogged, single-minded bastard of the lowest order. He deserves this and I can't wait to see him twist in the wind. Oh, yeah. How perfect will it be for him to know the sheer terror, the mind-numbing fear that overcomes you when you're haunted? He will get to experience the confusion and horror of thinking he's losing his sanity.

And there are ways to ratchet up his torment. Oh, yes.

It's time to add a little pressure on the home front.

Olivia . . . she is the key, I think, the coup de grâce. There is no better way to get to Bentz than through his damned wife.

I see him slip through the opening in the fence and head down the street to the parking lot. His shoulders are still broad, but his once purposeful gait is now uneven.

A coldness settles in my heart.

Do you feel me, you sick son of a bitch?

Do you have any idea what you did to me, the pain you put me through?

No?

Well, you will, Bentz, you damned well will.

In fact, and I promise you this, the pain and suffering and guilt will be so intense, so excruciating that you'll wish to heaven and hell that you were dead.

CHAPTER 14

Bentz found his car and made note of a few changes in the parking lot. One of the twin pickups had left and there was now an old Datsun with expired plates idling in front of the bookstore. A teenage girl was behind the wheel, gabbing on her cell phone. WASH ME was still in prime position in front of the tavern, but the silver Chevy with the stickers was no longer parked near the dirty van.

He wondered if one of the cars could belong to "Jennifer" or whoever she was. If so, she certainly was no ghost. As far as he knew the State of California only issued licenses to living people and, if folklore were to be believed, ghosts really didn't need wheels.

On a whim, he walked into the tavern, glanced at the waitstaff and few patrons huddled over a long bar or staring at a big screen in the corner. Satisfied that whoever he'd been chasing hadn't taken refuge in the establishment, Bentz ordered a zero-alcohol, made small talk with the waitress, and asked if she knew who owned the Chevy. She gave him a blank stare that was almost identical to the expression of the bartender when Bentz posed the same question to him. If they knew anything, they weren't going to give it up, but his gut told him they didn't have any idea of the answer and didn't really care.

Ignoring the beer and leaving some bills on his table, he left the tavern and headed to the bookstore, where a shopkeeper nearing eighty was waiting to close. Now the girl who had been in the Datsun had moved inside and was still talking on her cell as she cruised the aisles, concentrating on a wall of books in an area labeled "Vampires and Ghosts." Without a break in her conversation, she picked up various books, thumbed through them, then replaced them on the shelf.

The bookstore was nearly empty, one balding guy near thirty poring over computer texts and a woman with a little girl in pigtails perusing the children's books section.

No one here could have played the part of Jennifer.

The grocery, too, was devoid of customers. Bentz bought a sixteen-ounce Pepsi and checked the aisles. Two teenaged boys in long hair and baggy shorts were checking out the candy section while stealing peeks and whispering about the "hot" girl at the till. A harried young mother, toddler on one hip, eyebrows knit in concern, was shopping for disposable diapers and scowling at the price.

They were the only patrons.

No Jennifer.

Of course.

Outside, behind the strip mall, two men in their early twenties stood smoking near a Dumpster.

Nothing surprising there. Bentz drank his soda and wondered why the hell he'd come down here. What, if anything, had he learned?

Just that you're a gullible ass, willing to chase shadows.

He climbed into his rental and kicked himself for not having the presence of mind to take pictures of the woman he'd been chasing; even a dark image on his cell phone would have helped.

He twisted his key in the ignition, then looked at the empty spot in the lot where the silver Chevy had been parked. There was something about that car that had seemed out of place. His cop instincts were in overdrive, which happened whenever he experienced an anomaly—something that didn't seem to fit.

He tried to recall anything about the vehicle. It was an Impala, he thought, maybe a 2000. He tried to visualize the numbers on the license plate, but only remembered that it had current tags issued in California. There was something unique about the plates . . . two or three sixes in the number. He wasn't certain. But there was some kind of expired parking pass on the front windshield, a hospital permit of some kind, though part of the information had faded to the point that it hadn't been easily visible, and he'd been in a hurry. Yet he sensed there was something about the pass that was a little out of the ordinary . . . what the hell was it?

He tried to envision the damned thing. Failed and gave up. Whatever had caught his attention was now gone. It would come to him. Probably in the middle of the night.

Again, he should have taken pictures. With that thought he cut the engine and got out of his Ford to snap photos with his cell phone. He took shots of the license plates and makes and models of the cars parked but also in the lot and on the street leading to the old inn. All told there were only eight, and one of them was on blocks, the plates long expired. A no-counter.

Then there was that old parking pass thing.

Bentz decided to check out any hospitals in the area. There was a good chance that whoever owned the Chevy had some kind of hospital or medical facility connection. Unless the sticker belonged to a previous owner.

He was driving back through the quaint town when his cell phone rang and he picked up, barely registering that the screen read UNKNOWN CALLER. "Bentz."

"Hi, Rick," a woman said, her voice vaguely familiar and frosty as hell. "This is Lorraine. You called."

Lorraine Newell. Jennifer's stepsister.

"That's right. I'm in L.A. and wondered if we could get together."

"I can't imagine why."

"I have some questions about Jennifer's death."

"Oh, for the love of God. You have a helluva lot of nerve." She let out a long-suffering sigh. "I knew calling you back was a big mistake. What do you want?"

"I'll tell you when we meet."

"Come on, you're not going to try and be coy now, are you? It's so not you. Let's not mince words. I've always thought you were a straight shooter. A miserable son of a bitch, but a straight shooter."

"Can we meet tomorrow?"

"I'm busy most of the day. Work and appointments."

"Tomorrow night, then."

She hesitated. "Why do I know I'm going to regret this?" She paused as if second-guessing herself, then said, "Okay. Fine! Can you be at my place around . . . four-thirty? I've got a dinner meeting, but I suppose I can give you a few minutes. For Jennifer."

Big of you.

"I live in Torrance now."

"I've got the address," he admitted.

"Of course you do." There was a bitter sneer in her voice.

"See you then," he said, but she'd already hung up.

As he merged onto a highway, he let his mind sort through new information. He didn't have much to go on. A Chevy Impala with some kind of parking permit, a vehicle that might or might not be a part of this Jennifer fraud. A few other vehicles as well.

And then there was Shana. She was the only one in L.A. who knew about Saint Miguel. Either that or she fed him that information to direct him there, so that "Jennifer" could show up. What part was Shana really playing?

True, he still didn't have a lot to go on, but it was a little more than he'd had two hours earlier. Nothing might come of it, but then again, it was a start.

"You're telling me this new double is like the Caldwell twins all over again?" Corrine asked as Hayes hung his jacket on a hook near the door of her apartment. With two small bedrooms and a killer view of the mountains, the unit was compact but breathtaking, clean and neat. Just like its owner.

"Identical. Down to the way the clothes were folded, the ribbons in their hair, the damned way their bodies were positioned." He was tired and hungry and grouchy.

She shook her head. "You know the names?" she asked and her eyes had turned dark.

"Yeah, he left their ID. Elaine and Lucille Springer."

"Damn!" She let out a breath. "I remember seeing the missing persons' reports, from Glendale."

"Yep."

"Son of a bitch." Shoving her hair from her eyes, she glared out the window. "Both dead. Like before."

"Just like."

"You tell the next of kin?"

"Yeah. I talked to the parents," he said, remembering their denial, their worst fears confirmed, then the horror and grief. "Nice people. He's some kind of insurance salesman. She's a teacher."

Corrine nodded slightly, her jaw tight, her eyes shadowed as if she felt the pain of these people she'd never met. "I remember," she said softly.

"They came to the morgue, made the IDs, and you could see it killed them." He shook his head, wiped a hand over his face. "Killed them." He recalled the Springers: the father, Greg, dressed in khakis and an Izod golf shirt, his face pale beneath a tan. His wife, Cathy, the mother of the twins, had walked in quietly, like a zombie, face masked with an expression of denial. Oh, God, it had been bad.

Hayes slumped into the recliner positioned in front of the television. It sat near the high counter and stools that separated the compact kitchen from the living area. Corrine came up behind him and rubbed his shoulders.

"It's never easy," she said.

"Both kids. Gone." One minute they'd been parents, happy and secure in life, the next they were totally bereft. Hayes had tried and failed to erase the vision of Cathy Springer's face, the denial in her blue eyes giving way to horror, her knees buckling as she collapsed into her husband's shaking arms.

"Nooooo!" Cathy had wailed over and over again, her grief-stricken cries echoing down the long corridor. Her fists had curled, pounded frantically against her husband's chest as he'd tried to calm her.

And the father. Greg's demeanor had been riddled with defeat and pain, his gaze accusing as he'd stared at the detective. Hayes had known what he was thinking. *Why my girls? Why mine? Why not yours? Or anyone else's? Why my sweet innocent babies?*

It was exactly what Hayes would have thought if anything ever happened to his Maren.

"You'll catch the bastard who did this," Corrine reassured him.

"I hope so."

"Have faith, if not in divine intervention, then in the skill of the department. Forensics and technology are a whole new ball game. Twelve years ago we didn't have half the forensic tests that we have now. The perp is toast. And if he turns out to be the Twenty-one killer, then it's a two-for-one. Cause for celebration."

He wanted to believe it.

Corrine was massaging his shoulders, trying to ease out the knots of tension in his muscles. "How about a drink?" she suggested. "I've got pasta, those bowties—"

"Farfalle."

"Yeah, I guess. With pesto and an Italian sausage or two."

"This from the Irish girl?"

She laughed. "And I'm fresh out of corned beef and cabbage." Her fingers were strong and comforting, but his head was on the case. Why had the killer struck now? Why the Springer twins? Who the hell was he? Would he kill again soon or wait another twelve years?

"Talk to me," she said, still massaging him. It was a ritual they practiced when a particularly tough case was getting to either one of them. "You really believe the murders are connected."

"Have to be."

"Noooo. Don't close your mind."

"How would a copycat know the details of a twelve-year-old cold case that weren't released to the press?"

"Cops talk."

Hayes looked up at her. "To killers?"

"Unwittingly. Or maybe whoever was talking had one too many beers and was overheard."

"Long shot."

"Okay then, maybe conversation in prison. The Twenty-one is locked up for another crime but shoots his mouth off. Now his cellmate is on parole and thinking he'll take up where the Twenty-one left off."

"No."

"I'm just suggesting you keep your mind open. It could be a copycat." Still kneading the tension from his shoulders, Corrine leaned forward and kissed his forehead. "Or you might be right. Maybe the Twenty-one is back, from who knows where, ready to rock and roll. Maybe you should check recent parolees."

"Already doin' it."

"Of course you are." He looked up and she was grinning.

"Bentz is back in town," he said.

Corrine nodded. "I heard the news. It's all over the department." When Hayes lifted an eyebrow, she shrugged. "Trinidad put the word out, I think."

"Some people aren't thrilled." He looked pointedly at her and she smiled.

"You mean Bledsoe?" she teased.

"I was wondering about you."

"Well, I'm not exactly president of the Rick Bentz fan club, but I figure what happened is ancient history." She winked. "Besides, I got myself a new guy and he's lots cuter."

"You haven't seen Bentz."

"Okay, okay, you're right. The jury's still out on that one."

"He's still recuperating from an accident. Sometimes uses a cane."

"So now you want me to feel sorry for him since he and I both are gimps?"

"That's not what I meant. And you're no gimp. Not anymore!"

"Good." Corrine sighed and shook her head. "It's weird. Who would think it would matter? He's been gone what, ten years?"

"Twelve."

"Really? Oh, yeah, he left around the time of the Caldwell twins' murders . . . That *is* a coincidence." She pulled a face. "Gotta be a co-incidence." She looked at him and he could almost see the gears turning in her mind. "Right?"

"Has to be."

"I will admit this, though: Bentz's visit is causing a bit of a stir. While you were out at the scene, the gossip ran like wildfire through the department. Isn't that weird?"

"Who would care?" he asked.

"To start off with, Bledsoe. He's pissed as hell, though I don't know why. Give me a break. It's not like Bentz is coming back looking for a job."

"Bledsoe's always pissed."

"Yeah, and I think Trinidad is nervous . . . why, I don't know. Prob-ably because he was Bentz's partner and friend. Doesn't want any of his old stink to rub off."

"What about Rankin?" Hayes was thinking aloud.

"Who knows? It's been a long, long time."

"She had it bad for Bentz."

"Didn't we all?" she teased, then said, "Stick around for dinner. You know I make a mean pesto."

"I do know, but I'm not hungry. Sorry."

With a sigh she nodded. "Yeah, I know. I get it." And she did. Cor-rine O'Donnell had been a crack detective, the lead on several high-profile cases, until she'd broken her leg and blown out the ACL on her knee during a chase when she'd been hit by a car. Lucky to be alive, she was now reduced to pushing papers in the department. Active duty was out. Despite the fact that she worked out, was strong and otherwise healthy, the knee was still an issue. Though she tried to hide it, she sometimes, though rarely, walked with a bit of a limp. What really bugged her, Hayes knew, was the fact that she couldn't wear three-inch heels any longer.

"I'll get you the drink."

"I should go back to the station."

"Tomorrow's early enough," she said, rattling around in the freezer for ice cubes. "You're not going to bring those poor girls back."

That much was true, yet they both knew that the first hours after a murder were the most crucial. As the time between the commission of the homicide and the gathering of evidence lengthened, the chances of catching the killer diminished.

"It's so weird that the Twenty-one killer would show up after all these years." She appeared holding out a short glass with three fingers of whiskey, then handed him a cold can of ginger ale. "You can do your own mixing."

She winked at him and he smiled for the first time since seeing the bodies. Being with her was easy; she didn't make too many demands and understood him, far better than either of his wives had. And she was pretty. Trim and lithe, with the build of the long-distance runner she'd once been, Corrine O'Donnell was a force to be reckoned with. Her eyes were large and deep-set, a flinty gray that, when she was aroused, smoldered deep and dark. If he hadn't been so gun-shy, he might just let himself fall in love with her, not that she was asking for any commitment.

Yet.

"Look, Hayes, you're off duty. Have a drink . . . maybe nothing quite as strong as this, though, since you and I both know you're going back to the station." She plucked the glass from his hands, carried it back to the kitchen, and returned with a light beer. "Okay, so relax, have a little dinner, then go back and hit it again."

"You're okay with that?" he said, skeptical. Delilah would have had a fit; but then, Delilah had never been a cop.

"Okay with it? Well, I'm not thrilled, but yeah, I'm okay. However, the minute you catch the creep, you throw his ass in jail and you hightail it back here."

"It could take longer than a few hours," he said, but took a swallow from the long-necked bottle of Coors light.

"For a super-detective like you?" she mocked, walking around the chair and throwing her bad leg over his to sit on his lap. "Naaahh." Then she kissed him, hard, her lips warm and pliant.

His body, racked with tension, responded instantly. He kissed her back, felt her tongue join his just as his cock came to life. She was already working at his tie and buttons and his hands were all over her ass, ripping off her jeans.

For the next twenty minutes, Jonas Hayes forgot all about the double homicide.

Bentz stopped at a take-out deli in Culver City that was only a few blocks from the motel. He ordered pastrami on rye with a side of coleslaw and a Pepsi from a kid who looked to be all of sixteen. The kid, ROBBIE according to the tag pinned on his shirt, had a severe case of acne and an expression that said he would rather be anywhere but behind the counter at the Corner Deli. The place was almost empty, with any luck because of the late hour and not lack of quality. Another kid swabbed the floors while Robbie put together Bentz's order.

Fifteen minutes later, Bentz was back in his motel and eating at his desk. Between bites of his sandwich, he sat at his laptop and made a list of the car descriptions and plate numbers he'd photographed in the shopping center and near the inn. He kicked himself for not paying attention to the Impala, but he was able to get the other cars' plates from the pictures he'd taken.

He didn't have a printer, so he sent an e-mail to himself that he could print later. Then he'd see if Hayes could run the plates and find out who owned the cars parked near the abandoned inn.

He finished the sandwich and wiped his fingers on a napkin before running a search of medical facilities in the area, just in case the silver Impala was somehow connected to his sighting of Jennifer. His search, which included the greater L.A. area, came up with hundreds of names.

There had to be a way of narrowing it.

He finished his soda, rattled the ice in the cup, and thought about the cars in the parking lot, a fixation, he decided, but something to work with.

He doubted the driver of the Impala was from San Juan Capistrano, so he centered his search in L.A. Culver City was an obvious choice, but too obvious. Again, the list was long.

Frowning, he leaned back in his desk chair and stared at the screen. What was it about that permit on the Chevy that bugged him?

Something unique. It had been faded and sun-bleached, the numbers nearly impossible to read, as if whomever had used the permit hadn't updated it in a long while. Maybe a hospital worker who had retired, or moved to another job, or sold the car?

Tapping a pen on the desk, he closed his eyes, drawing up the image. There had been numbers and a date, and the name of the hospital, and something else . . . a logo or picture of . . . what? Some familiar symbol that scurried around in the dark, murky corners of his brain but wouldn't come to the fore. Crap! He concentrated to no end. The symbol eluded him and he gave up. Sooner or later, he knew he'd remember something important about it.

He hoped.

He wadded up the trash from his meal, tossed it into a wastebasket. After cranking up the A/C a few notches cooler, he did some exercises on a towel stretched over the thin carpet. His leg already hurt, but he kept at it until his muscles ached and he was sweating. Finally he gave up on the repetitions and hit the shower.

With his tiny, complimentary bar of soap and a thimbleful of generic shampoo, he washed off the grime, dust, and sweat of the day. The spray was weak, but warm, and he let the water run over his hip and knee, both of which were beginning to throb and remind him that he was getting old, hadn't yet recovered. He couldn't go chasing ghosts upstairs and across courtyards and through dirty, dark corridors and expect not to pay the price.

He managed to dry himself with another impossibly thin towel, then flopped onto the bed and used the remote to turn on the TV.

He found a station with "breaking news."

Video of a crime scene. The camera panned an overpass of the freeway, police officers worked a roped-off area, a warehouse behind a reporter in a blue jacket. Holding a microphone and staring soberly into the camera, she said, "Today, here in a storage unit beneath the 110 freeway, officers discovered a grisly scene. The bodies of two girls, whom sources have revealed are sisters—twins—were discovered, victims of a tragic double murder."

"What?" Bentz froze, his hand still holding the remote, his gaze riveted to the tiny screen.

"The names of the victims have been withheld pending notification of next of kin. A source close to the investigation, speaking on the condition of anonymity, told us that the girls had been reported missing early this morning, the day of their twenty-first birthdays." The reporter paused meaningfully, then added, "Unfortunately, they never made it to their party, the one they had planned to celebrate with family and close friends."

"Jesus, Mary, and Joseph!" Bentz sat bolt upright and stared at the TV. Déjà vu cast a stranglehold on his throat. *Twins? On their twenty-first birthday?* The footage changed to a different camera angle and Bentz watched as Detective Andrew Bledsoe, a few pounds heavier than Bentz remembered, flecks of gray showing in his black hair, talked to the reporter. Bledsoe, appearing serious and troubled, offered her nothing concrete, but Bentz knew the truth.

He fell back on his cheap pillow and felt sick inside.

The cops weren't saying much, but Bentz could read between the lines.

The Los Angeles Police Department feared that the Twenty-one killer, the madman who had taken lives in the past and gotten away with it, was back.

And back with a vengeance.

CHAPTER 15

"I'm sorry!" Bentz said, his voice echoing as it reached her from the other side of the tunnel, "This is something I have to do."

"No! Don't go! Rick, don't leave me! Don't leave us!" Olivia ran after him through the darkness, her legs pumping but feeling wooden, her feet tripping on the rails and gravel of the track. She pushed forward, her heart pumping. He wasn't that far ahead of her, but he was backing up, still facing her, but running away.

"Rick!" she screamed. "Stop!"

"I can't."

"But the baby. Rick, we're going to have a baby!"

Another noise, loud and fierce. The thunder of a heavy engine, the clack of wheels against rails.

Bentz turned away as if he hadn't heard her and continued moving through the cavernous tunnel, leaving Olivia gasping, racing, trying to outrun the huge engine with its ominous light bearing down on her.

No!

A whistle blasted, shrieking so loudly she thought her eardrums would shatter.

No! Oh, God, no!

"Rick! Help!" she cried as the end of the tunnel seemed to shrink, becoming smaller and farther away.

Her heart drummed and her legs were heavy, so heavy.

"Bentz!" she tried to scream, but her throat was strangled, her voice a whisper.

He turned back toward her for a second and she saw his badge, catching in the bright sunlight. "I can't," he said as the day turned to night and suddenly he wasn't alone. A woman was with him, a beautiful woman with long dark hair and crimson lips. She took his hand, linked her fingers through his, and smiled with malice and glee as she pulled him away.

"No! Wait! Rick—"

The train thundered ever closer, the tracks quaking. She stumbled, barely able to right herself.

A horrific whistle shrieked while brakes squealed. The sound of metal screeching against metal was deafening, the smell of burning diesel acrid in her nostrils.

Steam swirled all around her.

Help me! Help my baby!

But her prayer fell on deaf ears as steam and shrill noise reverberated through the tunnel.

"No!" she yelled, startling herself awake.

Her heart was pounding, her body drenched in sweat, the sheets of her bed twisted. *Dear God. It was a dream. Only a flippin' dream.* Taking in deep breaths, she glanced at the clock. Three-fifteen. Still a few hours before she had to get up and dressed for a day at the shop.

She sat upright, pushed her hair from her eyes, and realized her fingers were trembling, the residual effect from the nightmare.

From his dog bed on the floor, Hairy S lifted his scruffy head. His ears pricked forward and his little tail beat against his bed hopefully. "Oh, sure," she said. "Come on, jump up!"

He didn't need a second more of encouragement. The dog hopped from his bed, made a running leap, and landed near Olivia's pillows. After washing her face enthusiastically, he burrowed under the covers and she stretched out again. With one hand she scratched Hairy behind his ears. His warm body curled close to hers.

A far cry from her husband's embrace, but it would have to do for now. *Her husband.* What the hell was he doing in L.A.? Chasing after a ghost, or a dream? She tried not to think that he was still harboring feelings for his dead ex-wife, but she knew better. His guilt, she thought, was swallowing him whole and someone was preying upon him.

Who?

The same nagging question that had been with her since he'd shown her the mutilated death certificate kept poking at her brain relentlessly. It's not that she didn't believe in ghosts; she just wasn't certain. She'd had her fair share of dealing with unexplained, if not paranormal, activity. Hadn't she, herself, seen through the eyes of a twisted, sadistic serial killer?

Oh, for some of that insight now.

She glanced at the clock. It was only one-twenty in the morning in L.A. Was Bentz still awake? Was he thinking about her? Chasing down a dream? She touched her still-flat abdomen and wondered if she and Bentz and the baby would ever have a normal life.

Yeah, well, what's that? You knew what you signed up for when you married a workaholic.

Sighing, she closed her eyes, determined to relax and find sleep again. She was just starting to doze when the phone rang. Smiling, she said to the dog. "I guess he can't sleep, either."

She picked up the receiver and said, "Hey," a smile audible in her voice.

"Do you know what your husband's doing in California?" a woman's hoarse voice whispered.

"What?" Olivia was suddenly wide awake, the hairs on the back of her neck prickling in fear. "Who is this?"

"He's looking for *her*. And do you know why? She's his true love, not you. Jennifer. He's never forgotten her."

"Who is this?" she demanded again.

But the phone went dead.

"Bitch!" Olivia hissed into the receiver. Of course Bentz was in L.A. She knew that. She also knew that he was looking for Jennifer or a woman who was impersonating his ex-wife. She looked at caller ID; the display flashed UNKNOWN CALLER. "Great." No name. No number. No area code. No way to figure out who had called her. *It's no one, just a crank call, someone who knows Bentz went to L.A. to determine what happened to Jennifer.*

But there weren't many people who knew that fact. At least not here in New Orleans. Only Montoya and herself. So the call must've come from somewhere else, and she'd bet her life savings that it had originated in Southern California.

Bentz, it seemed, was rattling a cage or two. Which was what he'd hoped to do.

As she set the phone onto the nightstand, she thought about calling her husband and explaining what had happened, but decided to let it go.

For tonight.

Instead, she tossed back the covers and padded to the kitchen, where she poured herself a glass of water and drank it down. She stared out the window over the sink to the backyard, watching the play of moonlight through the cypress trees.

Afterward, she set her glass in the sink and double-checked that all the doors were locked and the windows latched.

Only then, did she return to bed.

She glanced at the digital read out one last time and decided that in five hours she'd call her husband and find out what the hell was going on.

Bentz stayed up listening to news reports, soaking up any information he could find on the Internet. Why the hell had the Twenty-one killer or some damned copycat decided to strike again, after all these years? It was too late to call Olivia, so he spent several restless hours thinking about the case surrounding Delta and Diana Caldwell's murder. It had been a travesty, a horror for the shell-shocked, grief-ridden parents and older brother, another D name . . . Donny or Danny, no. Donovan! That was it. The girls' brother had been eight years older and at the time of the tragedy had been forced to hold his shattered family together. Apparently it was an effort destined to fail, as years later Bentz had learned through the grapevine that the kid's parents had divorced.

When Bentz closed his eyes he could still see how the victims had been posed: naked, facing each other, bound in a red ribbon that reminded him of blood. Bentz had nearly thrown up at first look.

Whenever he thought back on the Caldwell murders he worried that he hadn't given the investigation 100 percent of his focus. He had worked the case as best he could, considering his own mental state, but it wasn't enough. Bledsoe was right. Bentz had left Trinidad holding the bag. And now, it seemed, two other girls had lost their lives to the same maniac.

Maybe if he'd been more on his game with the Caldwell twins, the new double homicide wouldn't have happened and two innocent girls would still be alive today.

*   *   *

After a sleepless night Bentz decided to offer up his help on the new double homicide investigation. He knew he wouldn't really be a part of the LAPD, but certainly he could help, "consult," as it were, as he'd been the lead at one time in the Caldwell twins' murder.

He said as much when he called his old partner for information.

"Shit, Bentz. You know I can't talk about this," Trinidad said. "As for the reasons you came back to L.A.—I heard some of it from Hayes— I can't be a part of it. I got to think about my retirement. I can't do anything to screw it up, and I'm not talking about the new murder case. Not with you. Not with my wife. Not with the press. Not with any-damned-body."

"I worked the first case."

"That's assuming they're related."

"They are."

"You know this because of a news bulletin, a thirty-second sound bite at eleven? Give it a rest, Bentz. I gotta be straight with you. No one here wants your help."

Bentz didn't give up. Remembering the Caldwell twins' tragedy spurred him into making another call. This time to Hayes.

"I figured you'd call," the detective said. "This is police business, Bentz. Got nothing to do with you. I'm already sticking my neck out for you as it is. So, don't even ask. We'll all be a lot better off."

Bentz hung up, but he wasn't able to leave it alone. So he phoned Andrew Bledsoe.

He wasn't pleased to get a call.

"Jesus, Bentz, you've got a lotta nerve calling here after how you left me and everyone in the damned department hangin'. Now, you want information? Are you out of your frickin' mind? You know I can't talk to you. Shit, didn't you do enough damage back when you were on the force? You remember that time, don't you? When it was legal for me to talk to you? I didn't like it then, and I don't like it any more now. What is this? You calling me? Why? No one else will talk to you?" Bledsoe raged. "Shit, you're really scraping the bottom of the barrel, aren't you? Don't forget, dickhead, you almost got canned, so you can damned well read about this one in the papers like everybody else!"

Bledsoe hung up, still muttering under his breath.

Bentz hadn't expected anyone to bend over backward for him. Nonetheless he was frustrated as hell that he wasn't allowed any information about a double homicide that in all probability was linked to his last case with the department, the murder investigation he wasn't able to solve.

He was stewing about it when Olivia called. On her way into the shop late, she had decided to phone him around nine West Coast time. At first, his wife was evasive about the reason for the early morning call. But Bentz suspected something was up and said as much.

"Can't I just phone to say I miss you?" she asked.

"Any time." But it really wasn't her style.

"I'm just hoping that you'll wrap this up soon. How's it going?"

"Not as fast as I'd hoped," he admitted. He didn't tell her about seeing Jennifer at the old inn; he didn't want to discuss it with anyone until he knew what he was dealing with, had some concrete evidence that she'd been there. However, he did fill her in on the case of the murdered twins and how it seemed to mirror the last case he'd worked on in L.A. twelve years ago.

"And you think because you returned to California this sicko is on the hunt again?" she asked, skeptically.

"I don't know what to think," he admitted.

"Does the LAPD want your help?"

He laughed. "What do you think?"

"That bad?"

"Worse. They want me to get out of Dodge, I think."

"Are you considering it?"

"Well, yeah, I'm thinking about it, being as you miss me so badly."

"Hey. Don't put this on me. You're on some kind of mission out there, so you stick it out until you've done whatever it is you have to do. I'm fine here. I'm not going to have it on my head that you returned for me and left unfinished business. Uh-uh. No way."

"I'll wrap it up as soon as I can," he promised. And then they hung up and he was left with the feeling that Olivia was holding out on him. He sensed that something more was going on and with all that was happening here in L.A., he was concerned. New Orleans was nearly two thousand miles away, but he'd seen "Jennifer" in Louisiana more than once, and the death certificate had been sent to the NOPD, so whoever was behind this knew him inside out and probably realized that he was married.

Although Bentz knew he was the primary target of this head game, whatever it was, the easiest way to hurt him was through those he loved, which only added to the worry gnawing a deep hole in his gut.

Like it or not, he had the feeling that Olivia or Kristi could be at risk.

By noon he'd drunk several cups of the coffee brewed in the motel's office and bought a copy of every paper he could find in the boxes on the street. He had spent hours reading news accounts of the double homicide and had learned the names of the victims and some of the details of the crime. Of course some information was missing, kept under wraps by the LAPD so that they could flush out the true killer when the time came. Sick as it was, attention-seekers looking for their fifteen minutes of fame sometimes claimed responsibility for vile acts. They lived off the attention, the media frenzy, or were deranged enough to believe they had actually performed the crime, no matter how horrendous. A double homicide of this nature got a lot of press and therefore attracted a lot of false claims.

It was all a pain in the ass.

Montoya had spent his morning finishing the paperwork on a homicide. The night before there had been a knifing at the waterfront just off the river walk, not far from the New Orleans Convention Center. The victim had died, but with the help of witnesses the killer had been apprehended. Montoya was finishing the crime report when Ralph Lee called from the lab. Despite being ankle-deep in forensic evidence attached to real cases, Lee had taken the time to examine and test the death certificates and pictures that had been sent to Bentz.

"There's not a lot you can work with," he said as Montoya leaned back in his chair, stretching out his neck and shoulder muscles. "It looks like the photographs haven't been tampered with. I haven't been able to see any evidence of alteration."

Montoya didn't know if that was good or bad.

"What we were able to determine was that the car the subject was getting into was a GM product, probably a Chevy Impala. You said you thought the shots were taken in California and that's consistent with the vegetation, license plate numbers, and street signs. The one we saw was for Colorado Boulevard. I enlarged the photos so that I could read the headlines on the newspapers and then I double-checked. The *USA Today* and *L.A. Times* were dated two weeks ago on Thursday, and the headlines are consistent for that date. We tried to get a reflection of the photographer from some of the shots, but couldn't get any images. I have a few partial license plates for cars parked in the area and I listed them along with make and model in case your shutterbug inadvertently caught his own car on film, assuming it wasn't the Impala.

"As for the death certificate, no DNA was found on the envelope flap. We ran the fingerprints through the national database. No matches on AFIS. The red ink is consistent with ink found in a Write Plus pen, and they're sold all over the country and into Canada, but are more popular in the western states. The document—the death certificate—is authentic and over ten years old; we can tell by the paper. That's it." Lee sounded almost apologetic. "I don't know if that helps you or not."

"You guys went above and beyond," Montoya said. "This will definitely help."

"Good. I've got the report. I can e-mail it to you or you can pick up a hard copy when you swing by to retrieve the original documents, since this isn't an active investigation."

"I'll get them this afternoon," Montoya promised and hung up. He'd done all he could for Bentz and his damned ghost hunt. Montoya would call and pass the information on. Then, maybe Bentz would wise up and come home to his real flesh-and-blood wife.

Time to give up looking for a woman who no longer existed.

CHAPTER 16

Lorraine Newell lived in an aging tri-level home on a cul-de-sac in Torrance, south of the heart of L.A. The apricot-colored paint was blistering and peeling in the sun, and the lawn was patchy, the green grass bleached in spots where the sprinklers hadn't quite reached. A far cry from the palace Lorraine, a would-be princess, had hoped for.

Although Bentz was fifteen minutes early, the minute he punched the doorbell the door flew open. It was as if Lorraine had been perched on the steps off the entryway, waiting for the sound of the melodic chimes to announce his arrival.

"Rick Bentz," she said, shaking her head, dark hair brushing her chin. Jennifer's stepsister hadn't aged a day since he'd last seen her. Like minor royalty, she still carried herself imperiously despite the fact that she was barely five-five in heels. Lorraine had never liked him and had never made any bones about the fact. Today she didn't bother with a fake smile or hug, which was fine by Bentz. No reason for pretense.

"You're the last person I'd ever expect to show up here," she said.

"Things change."

"Do they?" She moved out of the doorway and led him into a living room that was straight out of the late eighties, when her husband Earl, a car dealer, had been alive. Bentz remembered the plaid chairs clustered around a long forest green couch, a marble-faced fireplace surrounded by a wall covered in mirrored panes that gave the room a weird funhouse feel. Fake plants gathered dust, the coffee table books of California and wines were the same ones he remembered from nearly a quarter of a century earlier.

"Sit," she said, waving him into a chair while she took a seat on the arm of the couch. She was dressed in tight fitting jeans, a black tank top, and ballet slippers. Not exactly what Bentz would call business attire, appropriate for a dinner with a client, but then again he never had understood the studied casualness of Southern Californians.

Lorraine got right to the point. "What is this about Jennifer's death?" Using finger quotes to emphasize her point, she said, "You know her *accident* never set well with me. And I never bought the whole suicide angle. You know that. She was a drama queen, but a car accident?" She shook her head. "Not Jen's style. Pills, maybe . . . but I think even that is a stretch. Though she was a little self-destructive, I grant you, I couldn't see her actually taking her own life." She looked up at Bentz. "Jennifer was the sort of person who might have attempted suicide as an attempt to grab attention. But to actually drive into a tree? Let her body be thrown through glass? Mangle herself? No way. She didn't have the guts for a stunt like that. She could have survived, been scarred, or crippled." Lorraine shook her head emphatically as she folded her arms around her midriff. "Uh-uh."

He showed her copies of the pictures, but held back on the death certificate.

"Oh dear God." She was shaking her head as she eyed the photographs of her stepsister. "These . . . these really do look like Jen. I mean, yeah. But it has to be an imposter; someone who looks so much like her that one of your enemies, maybe someone you sent to prison, decided to play a practical joke on you." She looked up. "Seems as if it worked."

If you only knew. He thought about the woman in his backyard, the dreams he'd had of Jennifer. "I'm just trying to figure it out."

"A few pictures of a look-alike do not a case make. They wouldn't bring you all this way." She frowned. "There's something else, isn't there? Something that drove you to come back to California."

"I have a little time off."

"Another department trying to get rid of dead wood?"

"It's not just the photos, Lorraine. I think I've seen her."

"Oh, Jesus." She pressed a slender hand to her forehead. "This is really getting nuts. So, what? You want to know if *I've* come into contact with her? Maybe gone out for a drink? Had her over for dinner?"

He didn't say anything; he often found it was best to let people rant and rave. He frequently learned more from silence than from a series of direct questions. "Well, you've really lost it this time. This is just plain nuts." She paced over to the plate-glass window that dominated the living room. Outside, a hummingbird was flitting along the deep purple blooms of a climbing vine that wound its way to the eaves.

"You know, Rick," she said. "You've lost it. Really. If Jennifer were really alive, I would know it. She would have contacted me. Where has she been hiding all these years? And if she wasn't the woman in the car, who was? Why did *you* identify the wrong woman? Don't tell me you were drunk."

"Of course not! I thought . . . I still think she was behind the wheel."

"But now you're not sure? Because of photos of a woman who looks like her? Because you *think* you saw her?"

Bentz ignored the question. "What do you remember about the last time *you* saw her?"

"Oh, God, do you really want to go into all that?" she asked, retracting into her hard shell.

"Sure, Lorraine. Why mince words?"

Her lips pulled into a knot of dislike and her nostrils flared. "Okay, she did call me a few days before the accident. She was obviously troubled, maybe drunk, I don't know. But not right. When I asked her what was wrong, she blamed you. Said you didn't believe that she loved you, and it was eating away at her. I knew about the infidelity, of course, but for some reason she had it bad for you. Well . . . you, *and* the priest. Your half brother, was it?"

Bentz's guts twisted, but he kept his expression bland. "Anything else?"

"Nothing that involves you. Sometime I think back and wish she'd stayed with Gray. If she would have stuck it out with Alan Gray, she'd still be alive today. Alive and rich. Instead . . ." She shrugged. "I told her she was making a mistake when she broke it off with Alan, but she wouldn't listen."

Getting to his feet, he tried not to wince, didn't want to let on to Lorraine that he felt any pain whatsoever.

As she walked him to the door, she said, "You know, even if Jennifer is alive, why the hell are you doing this? Give it up, already. Let sleeping dogs, or dead ex-wives, lie. If you're really bothered, you should leave it to the professionals. Tell the police what you know. Let them handle it. You're married again. Go home. Pay attention to your new wife." Lorraine opened the door and waited for him to walk onto the cracked cement porch. Spying a dying petunia blossom, she deadheaded the shriveling pink bloom and added, "Don't make the same mistake twice. If you give your new wife some attention, maybe she won't stray the way Jennifer did."

Bentz ignored that last bit of advice. "If you think of anything else or hear from her—"

"For the love of God, Bentz, she's dead. *D-E-A-D*. And I haven't heard of anyone coming back since J.C. did it oh, what was it? A few thousand years ago!" She closed the door but before it latched tossed out, "Say hi to Crystal for me."

He didn't bother correcting her. Kristi had only vague memories of her mother's stepsister. Not once since Jennifer's death had Lorraine called or sent a card or tried to contact Kristi in any way. Bentz saw no reason to change that now.

He drove away from Torrance without much new information. Lorraine had been insufferable in the past and she hadn't mellowed much with age, but the key question was, had she been honest with him?

He wasn't sure. She, like Shana, had wanted to get her licks in and she had. But she certainly hadn't seen Jennifer. He kept his eyes on the road as he headed north toward Culver City. Traffic on the freeway was moving at a good clip despite the yellow haze that had settled over the area. In the west, the orb of the sun glowed in the dingy smog. He cracked the window and fiddled with the air, still thinking about what Lorraine had told him, which was essentially, "Take your ball and go home." But then, they'd never gotten along. And what were all the references to Alan Gray? He was someone Bentz hadn't thought of for decades. But Lorraine hadn't forgotten.

As he spied signs for his exit Bentz realized he was making great time. Just a few more miles. The phone rang as he was moving onto the ramp. Catching site of Montoya's cell number, he answered. "Bentz."

Montoya gave him a quick rundown of everything he knew, which wasn't a lot. Except for the silver Chevy. An Impala, in fact. Just like the car that had caught his attention in the parking lot in San Juan Capistrano. He explained as much to Montoya. "So what I'm looking for is a six- or seven-year-old car, California plates, with an expired parking pass to a hospital."

"You didn't happen to get which hospital?"

"No. But there was a symbol on it . . ." What the hell was that image? He couldn't remember. Just flat out couldn't remember.

"I saw on the news that there's another double homicide. Twins," Montoya said. "Same doer?"

"Looks like." Bentz's hand clenched hard over the wheel, so tightly his knuckles blanched as a black BMW crawled up his ass. Montoya knew the story behind the Caldwell twins' murders twelve years earlier. Bentz had confided in him long ago.

"Copycat?"

"Not buying it." Bentz switched lanes to the exit ramp, sliding in behind an old pickup filled with gardening tools. He let the bastard in the black BMW fly by. The car had to be pushing ninety.

Another car was in its wake. Keeping up.

A streak of silver.

Bentz saw the taillights and recognized an older model Chevy Impala. A dark-haired woman was behind the wheel . . . a sticker on the windshield.

Holy crap!

Jennifer!

He dropped the phone. "Son of a bitch." Signaling as a red Volkswagen beetle's blinker started, indicating the driver wanted to edge toward the exit ramp, Bentz gunned his engine. With inches to spare, he swerved out of the lane marked exit only and accelerated.

"Come on, come on," he urged his rental. The silver car, a quarter of a mile ahead, was darting between lanes.

Could it be?

No way.

Jaw set, he drove as fast as he dared, cutting through cars and trucks and vans, keeping the silver car in his sights. As if the driver knew she was being followed, she began even more evasive moves, slipping between cars, passing on the left or right. She didn't seem to care, just as long as she was putting distance and vehicles between her car and his.

But Bentz bore down on her, gaining ground.

Suddenly, she cut to the right, skidding and nearly missing the Sunset Boulevard exit. Brake lights flashed. Horns blasted.

The Impala disappeared down the ramp. Jaw set, Bentz tried to follow, cutting over to the right, but a minivan blocked his way. A woman wearing a cell phone headset, oblivious to everything around her, drove her minivan right on the bumper of a lumbering flatbed that was taking the off-ramp. There was no time to speed around both vehicles, so Bentz was stuck.

He slammed a fist into the steering wheel.

God, what he wouldn't do for lights and a siren right now!

To make the exit, he was forced to slow down and drop behind the minivan. Once off the freeway, he had to stop for a red light that the Chevy slipped through on amber and red. While Bentz gripped his steering wheel in frustration, Minivan Mom sat gabbing into the mouthpiece of her phone.

Bentz looked down the road and saw the Impala speed under another yellow light. He'd never catch her.

So close, but so far away . . .

California plates . . . He squinted. The last two numbers looked like 66, but he couldn't make out the rest.

By the time the light changed and Bentz was able to pass the boxy minivan, the silver car was gone, out of sight.

Adrenaline racing, nerves stretched to the breaking point, Bentz prowled the area. As he waited at a red light, his cell phone rang.

"What the hell happened to you?" Montoya demanded and Bentz explained.

"You think you saw the same woman on the freeway? Come on. What're the chances of that?"

"She knew I was at Lorraine Newell's."

"How?"

"I don't know. She probably followed me. Second guessed what I would do."

"L.A.'s a big city. Lots of dark-haired women. It wasn't Jennifer or the woman who looks like her."

"I'm telling you—"

"What? You're telling me what? That in a city of millions of people you just ran across the one you were looking for on the freeway? You're talking needle in a haystack."

"It was the same car, damn it. And a dark-haired woman driving, but no, I didn't see her face. I did catch a glimpse of that parking pass. It had a cross on it, like the hospital was affiliated with some Christian church."

"If you say so."

"The license plate ended in 66, but I didn't catch any of the other letters or numbers."

"You're sure that wasn't 666?"

"I'm not in the mood for jokes."

"That's the problem, Bentz. This whole thing is some lame-ass joke this woman is pulling on you. When are you going to wise up and get back here? Look, I got work to do here. Real work. Call me when you come to your senses." Montoya hung up, leaving Bentz to cruise the side streets for nearly an hour.

He checked parking lots and streets and traffic, searching out the silver Chevy. There were lots of silver or gray cars, all catching light in the sunny, hazy day, but none of them were the Impala.

Giving up, he stayed off the freeway to wend his way back to Culver City through Westwood and Beverly Hills. He was nearly back at the inn when his phone rang again. This time no caller was listed.

"Bentz," he said.

"Catch me if you can, RJ," a breathy female voice whispered.

His heart leapt to his throat. "What?"

"You heard me."

"Who is this?" he demanded.

"Oh, I think you know." She laughed, a deep, naughty chuckle that caused his blood to run cold. "You just have trouble believing what is right in front of your face. I'm back RJ, and the good news is that you still want me."

I glance in the rearview mirror, catching my own smile. "Good job," I tell myself. Rick Bentz is running around in circles, chasing down all of his ex-wife's old acquaintances, digging up the past. Which is just damned perfect.

It's a good feeling, knowing I finally got to him. "You bastard," I say, thinking of his chiseled face. "You deserve it." Still driving, I kick off my high heels and drive barefoot, my toes curling over the accelerator. I sensed his frustration through the wireless connection and it was a rush. Following him at a distance, watching him tear after a ghost.

I'm still on an adrenaline high, one I plan to keep going.

Approaching the freeway overpass I toss the phone into the passenger seat and roll down my window. Yes, it's a little smoggy, but it's L.A. Of course there's haze. It doesn't stop the wind from rushing through my hair as I wind my way toward the ramp.

The prepaid cell phone is perfect.

No way to trace a call.

Poor Bentz. He won't be able to find me; not until I want him to.

He fell right into the trap that I laid for him. Maybe he's losing his edge.

Good.

He never knew that I watched him; followed him. I knew exactly when he was visiting Shana McIntyre and, today, that bitch Lorraine Newell. Jesus, she's a miserable human being.

And as for Bentz?

Dear God, the man is predictable.

Always has been. These people never change.

I punch the throttle, then check my speed and ease up a bit. This wouldn't be a good time for a ticket.

But my heart pounds wildly.

It's time to ramp things up a bit.

I warm inside at the thought. My reflection winks at me. "Smart girl," I say into the wind as I consider my next move.

Bentz will never know what hit him.

CHAPTER 17

Hayes slapped the files shut and leaned back in his desk chair. It squeaked in protest, adding to the cacophony of sounds— computer keys clicking, phones ringing, conversations buzzing. And beneath it all was the ever-present rumble of the ancient air conditioning system.

Someone laughed as a printer clicked out pages a few desks over. Trinidad was taking a statement from a long-legged black woman, most likely a witness in one of the open cases. They had more than their share of homicides to solve, but the buzz in the department was about the Springer twins' murders. This was a crime that had captured the attention of the media as well as the horrified public. Reporters had been calling, keeping the Public Information Officer as busy as the detectives solving the case.

And time was sliding by without any serious leads.

Hayes picked up the remainder of his iced tea, a drink that had been ignored, the ice melting since lunch. He took a long swallow and felt the paper cup getting weak.

He'd spent the day rereading the cold case file on the Caldwell twins' homicides, trying to find some bit of evidence that had been overlooked twelve years earlier.

He'd come up dry.

After Bentz had bailed, Trinidad had been assigned another partner, a female detective named Bonita Unsel, who had since left the department. She and Trinidad, with Bledsoe's help, had handled the case by the book, but the Twenty-one killer had literally gotten away with murder. Twice.

Absently, his mind on the case, Hayes finished the drink as he scrolled through the crime scene photos on the computer. A box of evidence had been pulled, and as he'd combed through it he'd noted that the ribbon used in the first killings appeared identical to the ribbons that had bound and gagged the Springer twins.

The son of a bitch had kept his killing kit intact, down to the heavy red ribbon with wire running through it, the kind used to wrap fancy, expensive Christmas presents. Years ago the department had hunted down the manufacturer of the ribbon, checked with distributors and local stores, only to come up with a big goose egg.

Nor had they been able to find any fingerprints or trace evidence to link the suspects. They'd spent hours interviewing friends and acquaintances of the victims. Boyfriends, girlfriends, family members, classmates. Lots of interviews leading nowhere.

The primary suspect had been a boy named Chad Emerson who had dated both girls at one time or another, but his alibi had been solid and he'd seem genuinely devastated by the Caldwell twins' deaths. Same with the older brother, Donovan, whom Bledsoe had been certain was involved. Nothing concrete. So he'd been envious of the attention his sisters received; jealousy itself wasn't a crime, and it wasn't unusual. Nonetheless Hayes intended to check out both suspects and see if they had any connection whatsoever to the Springer twins.

"Hey!"

He looked up to see Dawn Rankin, one of the other detectives in the department, walking toward his desk. She dropped a report into his in basket. "I sent this to you via e-mail, but thought you'd like a hard copy. The shooting in West Hollywood. Witness statements."

"Not an accident?"

She shook her head. "Looks like we'll get an indictment. Weird, huh? Best friends and one ends up killing the other over a woman."

"Stupidity has no bounds."

"I guess." She flashed him a wicked little grin. "Hey, I heard that Rick Bentz is back, digging into his wife's death."

"Ex-wife, but yeah."

"What's that all about?" Dawn's eyebrows drew together. She was a pretty woman. Petite, smart, with a smooth complexion that required little or no makeup, she forced a smile that didn't reach her eyes.

"Not sure. Thinks he's being gaslit, that someone's manipulating him into thinking Jennifer is still alive."

"He made the ID."

"Yeah, he knows." Hayes felt a twinge of a headache coming on. "He never struck me as the kind who would fall into this kind of trap. I mean if someone was messin' with him, he'd blow them off."

"Unless he wants to believe she's still alive." She threw up a hand. "Not that I could ever figure him out."

Hayes remembered now: back in his younger days Bentz had hooked up with Dawn. Aside from a passing interest, she seemed long over him, though at the time of the breakup, according to rumors, it had been messy.

"Anyway, I spent the afternoon talking to people who knew the vics in the Springer case. I even tracked down the boyfriends of both the Springer girls. They both, conveniently, have alibis, but the one who dated Lucy, Kurt Jones, has a record. Nothing serious or violent, but drug charges. The word on the street is he's a dealer." She shook her head. "Small-time stuff. I don't think he's our guy."

"Not likely to be linked to the Caldwell twins."

"He's old enough, just not the right kind of nut job."

Bledsoe overheard the tail end of the conversation as he walked into the squad room. "Don't tell me, you're talking about my favorite ex-dick Bentz." He pulled a face. "Wouldn't you know he'd show up when the Twenty-one comes out of the woodwork? I'm thinking the killer came out because he knows Bentz is here, just to rub it in his face and piss him off."

"Oh, yeah, that's how serial killers work," Dawn said, obviously irritated at the intrusion. Bledsoe had that way about him, an ability to aggravate without trying. "Next you'll be saying Bentz killed the Springer girls."

"Nah. He's a bastard, but not a killer . . . but then again, there was the Valdez kid. Bentz nailed him."

"Accident," Dawn said. "That's low, even for you."

"I'm just not a big fan of coincidence," Bledsoe said, holding up his hands as if in surrender. "I'm just sayin'." His phone rang, and he left, walking smartly away, cell jammed to his ear.

"Jerk," Dawn said, watching the other detective leave while scroung-
ing in her purse for her pack of Marlboro Lights.

"I didn't know you were a Bentz fan."

Her eyes slid back to Hayes. "A fan? No. He's another son of a
bitch. But Bledsoe?" She said, retrieving her new pack. "They have
special spots in hell for his kind."

An hour before dusk Bentz drove to Santa Monica, a place that
kept coming up in conversation and had been a part of his life with
Jennifer. A pretty damned important part, considering they'd first
made love here, before they'd been married. Had that memory been
Jennifer's fascination with this quaint seaside town? Or was he kidding
himself? He found a parking spot on the street and was about to lock
up when he noticed his cane in the backseat. Since the nagging pain
in his leg had intensified after chasing "Jennifer" through Saint
Miguel's Inn at San Juan Capistrano he grabbed the damn thing and
headed toward the sea.

He passed under the archway spanning the approach to the long
pier. Though it wasn't yet dark, the neon lights of the amusement
park already glowed over the water. A roller coaster climbed high
above the arcades and other rides. Passengers' screams rose over the
rattle of cars on steel tracks. Larger still, the gigantic Pacific Wheel
turned more slowly, rotating high above the water, giving patrons a
bird's-eye view of the beaches and storefronts as it spun over the
ever-darkening ocean.

Rick stared at the brilliant display looming above the beach and
water. How many times had he and Jennifer brought Kristi here? How
often had they taken her to the aquarium? Eaten hotdogs? Walked
barefoot in the sand?

His gut clenched.

He remembered several nights when he and his wife had come
here alone, without their daughter. They'd walked along the pier,
feeling the salt spray of the ocean after stopping for a drink at one of
the hotels near the beach.

And still she'd found time to meet James here.

Now, he twisted the kinks from his neck and decided against
strolling along the beach while mentally walking down memory lane.
The pain running down his leg wouldn't allow him to tromp through

the sand and reminisce. He settled for dinner in a noisy Cuban restaurant decorated in brilliant primary colors, as it had been for years. The square tables were angled throughout a main dining area separated by half walls and potted palms while the up-tempo melody of a Caribbean-flavored song swept through the rooms. Although the restaurant was crowded, he lucked out and was led to a table near the windows where he watched what remained of the sunset through the glass.

The setting sun wasn't one of the Pacific's best displays as the fog was rolling in, blurring the horizon, distorting sea and sky, causing most of the pedestrians along the beach and pier to disperse.

He and Jennifer had been in a couple of times, even celebrated one of her birthdays here, but the memory was fuzzy and he didn't work too hard at calling it up. He wondered if she'd dared dine here with James, not that it mattered. Not anymore. Long ago, he'd been wounded by her affair. The second time around, the pain had been much less. He'd half-expected it and he'd been prepared, enclosed in his own emotional armor or some such crap.

So what about the woman driving the silver Impala? How the hell had she found him? Or had she? Was he making more of it than it was?

Maybe the erratic driver was little more than a figment of his imagination, an image incited by this whole damned mess. It could be the woman just resembled Jennifer and his freaked-out psyche had morphed her into the real thing.

You're losing it, his conscience taunted, and that pissed him off because he was certain it was just what the person behind this elaborate fraud wanted.

He ordered a cup of black bean soup and pork adobo, both of which were as good or better than he remembered. The pork was succulent, the soup spicy, the memories bittersweet.

As night descended and the lights came up, he walked along the pier, using his damned cane. He peered at the carousel without much interest, not really seeing it through the fog. His thoughts churned about the woman in the silver car, the murder of the twins, the crank calls, and the "ghost" he'd seen outside the crumbling building in Mission San Capistrano.

This was personal.

Whoever was behind the hoax knew just how to get to him and had spent a long while pulling the scheme together. He doubted the mastermind was anyone he'd arrested and sent to prison. If one of the thugs he'd collared had a hard-on to get back at him, the jerk would have just done it. Taken a potshot at Bentz, knifed him in the street, blown up his car. Something deadly and finite.

This was different. Someone wanted to play psychological games with him. Someone he'd wronged personally.

Jennifer.

She was the one person he'd never forgiven and had let her know it. Even when they'd tried to get together a second time, Bentz had been guarded. Untrusting. Ready for the other shoe to drop. And drop it had.

Big time.

He passed a store selling sunglasses and beach paraphernalia, but barely paid attention as he reached the part of the pier that jutted out over the water, an arm that stretched into the Pacific and the thickening mist. Though there were streetlights offering illumination, the fog swirled and rose, creating an eerie luminous veil. One he couldn't see beyond.

Only a handful of other pedestrians were around. One young couple, a guy in a stocking cap and baggy shorts was all over a blond girl whose hair was clipped to the top of her head. Entangled on the park bench, the two kids seemed oblivious to the rest of the world.

Young love, Bentz thought and flashed on Olivia and the way she made him feel whenever they were alone. As if he were the only man in the universe. *Older love.* He pulled out his phone to give her a call and noticed an old man smoking a cigar and resting against the rails. Sporting a trimmed goatee and shaved head, the man nearly drowned in a jacket that was several sizes too large for him. A slim runner in a baseball cap was leaning forward, his hands on his knees as he caught his breath from a workout. Farther west, closer to the end of the pier, shrouded in haze was a solitary woman.

Bentz stopped short.

In a red dress with long dark hair falling down her back, she faced away from him, staring out to sea.

Jennifer! She has a dress like that.

Bentz's heart skipped a beat.

Had, he reminded himself. *She* had *a dress like the one this woman was wearing, a knee-length shimmery thing with a nipped-in waist and no sleeves . . . Holy shit, it was identical to his ex-wife's.* He remembered Jennifer showing it to him after a day of shopping. "What do you think?" she'd asked, twirling in front of him, allowing the candlelight to play upon the soft folds of red silk.

"It's nice."

"Oh, come on RJ," she'd cooed. "It's way more than 'nice.'"

"If you say so."

She'd laughed then, throwing back her head. "Yeah, well, I do say so. I think it's probably sexy. Or damned gorgeous." With a lift of one dark eyebrow she'd backed her way down the hallway and into the bedroom and he, like a fish to a lure, had followed.

Now, his fingers curled over the handle of his cane.

Don't go there, he told himself as he noticed the woman on the pier was barefoot. *Jennifer always went barefoot at the beach. Oh, hell, don't assume every shoeless slim woman with coffee-colored hair is Jennifer . . . no!* He corrected himself. *Don't assume she's the woman impersonating your ex-wife.*

Nonetheless, drawn to the vision, he started walking west, toward the sea. His eyes were trained on her, searching for something that would expose her as a fraud, but she was too far away, the mist too dense. He walked faster. As if she sensed him following, she backed away from the rail and started walking quickly toward the end of the pier, where heavy fog rolled in, masking her image.

Bentz swallowed hard, tried to figure out what he would say to her. His pulse was pounding, thudding in his brain as he followed. This time, damn it, she wasn't going to get away. There was no place to run.

And yet she seemed intent on escape.

He felt it.

Faster and faster he hurried, his cane hitting the planks of the boardwalk in a staccato beat, his leg throbbing.

He had no time for the pain.

Hurry, hurry, hurry, his brain screamed, *catch her.*

And what would he do when he tapped her on the shoulder and she wasn't his ex-wife?

For Christ's sake, don't worry about that. Be more concerned if she is. What then, Bentz? What if she's the damned look-alike or worse yet, Jennifer herself in the damned flesh? No ghost. Your ex-wife!

She, too, was hurrying, running barefoot toward the end of the pier, her legs flashing beneath her red hemline.

His leg was screaming in pain, thigh muscles on fire, hip aching, but he went into a dead run as he saw her, plunging into wisps of hanging fog.

Where was she going? She was running straight into the darkness, headed for the black night at the end of the pier.

Bentz's lungs burned, his leg aching as she finally paused and braced the rail. At last! Now, finally he would have a chance to confront her.

But a moment later her hands reached out to the railing, bracing against it.

What the hell?

Without hesitation, she climbed onto the top bar, then over.

Oh, for God's sake, she wouldn't jump. Or would she? This was Jennifer. Daring crazy Jennifer.

"No!" he yelled.

For a heartbeat she balanced on the tiny edge, teetering. In that instant she glanced back, and Bentz drank in her beautiful face, her gaze locking with his. A split second later, she looked at the black water swirling around the pilings, gauging the distance, the depth. *Oh, God, she was really going to jump!*

"Stop! Jennifer!" he yelled.

One minute she was standing there, caught in a swirl of fog.

Then, before his eyes, she disappeared.

As if she'd actually leapt over the edge.

"No! Jen!" He rushed forward, running with dread prodding him on. "Oh, God!"

What the hell had happened? His eyes searched the gloom.

Did he hear a splash over the lapping tide?

Yes?

No?

God, where was she?

Confused, convinced he'd find her hanging from the railing, he grit his teeth and hurried to the rail to the very spot where she'd climbed over. Below the shifting water was dark as ink, no swimmer or body visible.

No Jennifer.

He yelled. Called her name.

He had nothing but a penlight. Still, he had to look. Moving gingerly, Bentz climbed over the rail and planted his feet on the thin ledge. The fingers of his left hand gripped the rail as he shined the small beam downward, but it did little to pierce the damned fog or illuminate much of the black water.

"Jennifer! Jesus, God! Jennifer!" he screamed at the dark swirling tide.

"Hey you!" some guy shouted frantically.

But Bentz didn't look up, his eyes on the black churning waters below. Was she there? Hiding? Caught under water?

Or had it all been a vision of his willing mind? Had there even been a woman on the pier at all?

He didn't know, but he couldn't let her drown, whoever she was. "Son of a bitch!"

He let go. The sea air rushing up at him, swift and furious.

He hit the water hard, the jolt of landing rattling his aching body. The cold began to seep through his skin as he sank fast, downward into the stark black depths.

Down, down, down. Into the night-black sea. Salt water closed around him as he kicked off his shoes and jacket, his eyes open and burning as he tried to penetrate the infinite darkness of the vast Pacific.

Nothing!

He searched the inky water, holding his breath, knowing she had to be here, somewhere. Close. *Where are you? For the love of God, Jennifer!*

His lungs were near bursting as he kicked, propelling himself upward, letting out a stream of air as he broke the surface. He gulped in air and cursed as he hunted for her.

Where the hell had she gone?

Where, damn it?

He shook his hair from his eyes, willing her to appear.

Come on. Come on!

Give it up, Bentz, his mind taunted. *She doesn't exist. You know it. You're chasing a damned figment of your imagination.*

Fear, cold as the ocean, slid through him. He was cracking up. That was it. Oh, sweet Jesus . . .

Don't give up! You saw her!

Treading water, he scoured the surroundings with his gaze—under the pier, along the pilings, near the shore, and beneath the shifty surface of the murky depths.

There was no sign of a woman in a red dress.

Or anyone at all. He spun around in the water, his bad leg dragging, his lungs tight as he eyed the undulating sea to no avail. Where was she? Where had she gone?

As people shouted above, he let the tide push him under the pier and through the supports. He swam, head above water, looking for any sign of her, any clue to where she'd been. He scanned the entire area. The beach was empty here. No one clung to the pier overhead, and he didn't see anything bobbing in the water.

"Jennifer!" he yelled, cupping his hands around his mouth, his voice echoing crazily over the water and rush of the tide. He held fast to a barnacle-laden piling, searching again and again, breathing hard, willing her to appear. *Come on, come on! Where are you?*

"Jennifer!" he shouted again, spitting salt water. The smell of brine stung his nostrils as waves slapped over him, his wet clothes moving with the tide. He didn't see anything or hear a response other than voices high overhead, feet pounding on the boardwalk. Still he tried to find her, or any evidence that she'd been here. He kept searching, releasing the piling and treading water as he squinted through the fog, straining to see any sign of movement along the long stretch of darkness beneath the pier.

Nothing but darkness . . . the play of shifting shadows beneath the pier, but further out, beyond the overhang, streetlights cast an ethereal glow. The thin light was caught in the shifting fog while the neon glow of the amusement park rose like a blazing specter in the mist.

All unworldly.

All surreal.

Jennifer, or whoever she really was, had disappeared. He searched around each support post, eyeing the shadows and feeling as if cold

death were lurking nearby. He held fast to one of the supports and
called her name again and again, but it came back to him, his own
voice, echoing hollowly over the rumble of the sea.

Shivering, he felt a fish glide past as he released the piling and
swam toward the shore.

His heart thudded at the prospect of finding her, dead from the
leap into the water, dead because she'd been running from him.

*After luring you onto the pier . . . this is all part of her plan. Don't
go into the blame game; not yet.*

And she's not here. You're alone.

The voices overhead were louder now, more of them, though, from
down here they seemed disembodied, muted by fog and tide.

*She's not here. She was never here. You imagined her again. The
red dress . . . it's symbolic.* Jennifer casting herself into the vast darkness of the water punctuated by the skeletal pier . . .

Dear God, what had happened to her?

Now the shouts on the boardwalk overhead were audible.

"I saw him, I tell you. Some guy jumped into the water."

"You saw him? In this fog?"

"Yes! Damn it, some lunatic did a swan dive off the railing."

"So now it's a dive. Barney, you've been drinkin' bad tequila
again."

"For the love of Christ, I'm tellin' ya, a guy in a suit jumped off the
goddamned pier!"

"There's nothin' down there."

"How can ya tell? It's so hard to see with the fog," Barney insisted.
"I called 9-1-1. The police should be here any minute."

Good, Bentz thought. He could use a little help. He swam from
under the pier, toward the shore, rolling with incoming waves. He
was relieved to see the flickering lights of emergency vehicles on the
ridge above the beach. As he clambered through the shallow surf a
flashlight beam caught him from above.

"There he is!"

"I told ya!" Barney again, and other voices joined in as a crowd
gathered overhead on the pier. Over it all, the sound of a siren screamed
through the night, getting closer. Bentz dragged himself out of the
water and up the beach. Cold to the bone, he slogged his way up the
wet sand and turned back toward the water.

The lights of the city were blazing, the Ferris wheel casting an eerie reflection on the shimmering waters. He wondered about Jennifer in that cold dark bay. Was she hiding in the shadows, laughing at him, pleased that she'd goaded him into leaping from the railing? Or was she caught beneath the surface, entangled in seaweed, staring sightlessly upward as the red shroud of her dress billowed against her deathly white skin?

For the love of God, get a grip! He swiped a shaking hand over his face as several people ran up to greet him.

The couple he'd seen on the pier was the first to arrive.

"Hey, dude, are you okay?" The guy was in his twenties, his stocking cap pulled low over curls that sprang from the edges. He seemed genuinely concerned and called over his shoulder, "Hey, anyone got a blanket or something?"

"I'm fine." *Just cold, tired, and afraid I'm going out of my friggin' mind!* Bentz coughed. He couldn't stop shaking. "There was a woman on the pier—she jumped into the water and I went in after her."

The blond girlfriend shook her head. "I didn't see a woman."

"She was there at the end of the dock."

"Is that why you were running?" Girlfriend asked. "I saw you throw away your cane."

Bentz nodded as the sirens screamed closer.

"Where is she now?"

"I don't know, but we need a search."

Bentz's teeth began to chatter and he was shivering. The police cruiser, lights flashing, screeched to a halt at the end of the beach and two officers climbed out.

"He's going into shock," the older man who'd been smoking his cigar said.

Bentz shook his head and held up a hand to stop further nonsense. "No. Really. Just cold. I'm serious about a woman leaping off the pier, damn it! I saw her. She jumped in."

"Let's go!" Several guys took off running to the waterline, though Bentz had little hope they would find anyone. Jennifer, or whoever she was, had disappeared.

Again.

The old guy ripped off his too-large jacket that smelled of burned tobacco. "Here. You need this."

Grateful, Bentz thrust his arms into the warm sleeves of the jacket, never taking his eyes off the shoreline, where the men were beginning their search.

"Sir?" called a low voice.

Bentz turned to see two officers from the police cruiser striding across the expanse of sand as a fire truck and rescue vehicle arrived.

"We have some paramedics here to assist you," one of the uniforms said.

"It's all right. I'm a cop." Bentz dug into his pocket and found, thankfully, his waterlogged wallet and badge. He handed it to the officer. "I don't need the ambulance. I'm okay, really, but you might want to get your search and rescue team in. I saw a woman jump from the pier."

The cop nodded, his eyes assessing Bentz. "But, sir, you need to get checked out."

"All I need is a smoke and someone to call Detective Jonas Hayes. LAPD Homicide."

"Someone dead?"

Bentz shook his head. "Hayes is a friend of mine." He forced a smile as the young kid came up with a Camel and a light, the first cigarette Bentz had smoked in a long, long while. He drew hard on the cigarette, felt the warm smoke curl in his lungs. Exhaled. "I used to work for the LAPD."

CHAPTER 18

"Hell, Bentz, I've got better things to do than babysit you." Hayes was pissed and didn't try for a second to hide his irritation. It had been Hayes's idea to meet in the bar half a block away from the So-Cal Inn in Culver City.

Bentz stared sullenly over the bar into the huge mirror that reflected the entire length of the long, narrow establishment. The bar top was tile with pendant lights straight out of the sixties hanging over it. He asked, "How's the Springer double homicide coming?"

"You know I can't talk to you about it." Hayes nursed a Manhattan while Bentz ignored his nonalcoholic beer. "But . . . we haven't got any really good leads. Lots of bad ones." He waved away the topic of the double homicide. "So you still think Jennifer is alive, haunting you? And she took a flying leap into Santa Monica Bay."

"I don't think it's Jennifer, but I can't be sure. Not unless there's an exhumation. I'm going forward with it."

"Whatever." Hayes was still steamed, his forehead lined with wrinkles of worry, his lips pulled into a frown. "Your gun get wet?"

"Wasn't wearing it. Locked in the glove box. But my cell phone's deader than a doornail." Bentz counted himself lucky that his pistol and the envelope with the photos and death certificate had been locked in the car, safe and dry. Even his cane had survived, but his jacket and good shoes were somewhere on the bottom of Santa Monica Bay. Now he was wearing his battered old Nikes.

He was also grateful that Jonas had smoothed things over with the cops. Although the search team had not found a body or evidence of a female swimmer, Jonas had been able to convince the Santa Monica Police that things were "cool."

Even if he hadn't believed it himself.

After a peripheral search of the area, the fire truck and ambulance had been sent off and the officers had taken Bentz's statement without any citations being issued. Hayes had even given him the time to shower and change clothes at the motel before they'd met at this dive.

Now, though, Hayes was pissed. "Your obsession with your dead wife isn't gonna be my problem, okay?"

"I get it."

"And you can't go callin' me, pulling in favors if you're gonna keep dragging the police into your own weird fantasies." Bentz was about to protest, but Hayes held up a hand. "I know why you're here, Bentz. Someone's fuckin' with you. But until some law has been broken in my jurisdiction—no, make that until some *homicide* has been committed in my jurisdiction, I don't want to be involved." He looked across the table, dark eyes deep with concern. "Sane people don't go jumping off piers in the middle of the night. Or breaking into old inns and nosing around for ghosts. And they don't chase after people getting onto a bus or driving down the freeway, regardless of how many crank calls they get in the middle of the night.

"As for looking up a dead ex-wife's family and friends? Or calling old partners at the department who think you bagged out and left them holding the bag? That's not investigation, Bentz. It's masochism."

Bentz couldn't argue that point. Trinidad and Bledsoe had let him know what they thought of him when he'd called offering help.

Hayes, some of his anger spent, finished his Manhattan, draining the liquid slowly. He set his glass on the table and shook his head. "Take my advice, Bentz. Go back to New Orleans, to your wife. Remember her? The one who's still alive? Do that and forget all this."

If only I could, Bentz thought.

"Thanks for the drink." Hayes left and Bentz took a long draw on his zero-alcohol beer.

Leaving L.A. wasn't an option.

At least, not yet.

* * *

The shower feels good. Hot water streaming down my body as I think about what happened on the pier. I knew Bentz would take the bait, and it was heartwarming to watch him as he struggled to catch up with "Jennifer."

"Fool," I whisper. I scrub my hair, lather, and rinse it. Then once more I grin as I recall the tortured expression on his face.

Perfect!

I turn off the spray and wrap a towel around my body, all the while thinking of my next move. God, how I'd love to hurry things along. But I'll be patient, I think, squeezing my hair with the cotton towel.

Naked, I lean over and dry my hair with the blow dryer, its high-pitched hum drowning out the music I've had blasting for hours. A mixed set of sounds from the eighties—Journey, Bruce Springsteen, Bon Jovi, The Pointer Sisters, Madonna, and Michael Jackson—have been playing, the volume cranked up and the window cracked open. The neighbors must have heard my tunes, as well as anyone passing by. Anyone would swear that I was home all night. My car, parked outside, would only convince them further. Smart of me to leave my vehicle. I walked to the bus stop, then rode the bus as far as I could before switching to a cab that took me to Santa Monica.

I returned the same way.

My plan had been on hold until Bentz finally decided to return to Santa Monica, as I'd suspected he would. I had to wait for the right moment and thankfully tonight it happened. I smile thinking about how well I executed my scheme.

I waited, knowing he would eventually show up at the pier. I made certain everything was in place. I watched as he went into the restaurant. While he ate dinner I had just enough time to put my plan into action.

Sure enough, after dinner Bentz decided to stroll down the boardwalk. Leaning on his cane, no doubt remembering Jennifer.

I dangled the bait. He snapped at it. He chased after Jennifer like a wolf after a lamb. Only things didn't turn out his way, now, did they?

I stretch, wipe off the glass, and then check out my reflection in the damp mirror. My head moves in time to the beat of a Fleetwood Mac song, one of Jennifer's favorites.

Bentz would appreciate the irony, I think.

What an idiot.

Trying to resurrect a dream.

Feeding on his own damned guilt.

Serves him right.

"Just you wait, Ricky-Boy," I say into the mirror. "You ain't seen nothin' yet!"

Bentz slid closer to Olivia, pulling her close, feeling her naked body against him in their bed. "I love you," he whispered, but she didn't respond, didn't open her eyes, wouldn't give him the satisfaction of a response.

It was there again, that secret she kept, the one that forced her into silence.

But, with her eyes closed, she instinctively tilted her chin up and he couldn't resist. Just being this close to her caused his blood to fire, his heart to pound. Desire made him hard. Hot and wanting, he kissed her with a passion that fired his blood and consumed him.

She responded. Moaned into his open mouth, her hands scraping away his clothes, her fingers running down his arms.

"I love you," he said again and was met with silence once more. Though her body was trembling, her skin hot, her lips wet, she didn't speak.

Beneath her passion he felt something more, something intense and longing but so distant. She was a million miles away.

He was losing her.

Somehow, despite their lovemaking, she was sliding way.

The smell of her filled his nostrils. He ran his tongue along her neck and lower still, tasting perfume and the salt of her body.

He kissed every inch of her, feeling her response, noticing her quiver. Inside he was burning, his cock already hard, so damned hard.

He told himself to take it slow, to pleasure her, but she was as frantic as he, her lips full and warm, her fingers insistent as she kneaded his muscles.

Skimming his thumbs over her ribs, he kissed the tips of her breasts, and then drank in a full view of her. She finally opened her eyes, the gold irises nearly invisible, her pupils black and round as they dilated.

He breathed across her abdomen, his head sliding down her body to the red lace of her panties—a tiny thong that barely covered any of her.

Her muscles had tightened. "You really can be a bastard," she whispered and her voice was off . . . not quite right, even though she'd finally spoken. He caught the whiff of gardenias, the faintest scent in the air.

"Just for you," he replied, his breath hot over her panties—that little bit of naughty lace. She writhed beneath him as he took the scrap of lace in his teeth and pulled it off.

"Really?" And her skin turned cold. "Seriously. Just for me?"

"Who else?" he asked, sliding up her body as her fingers dug deep into his head, adding a pinch of pain to the pleasure. God, he wanted her and she was quivering with her own desire, moving beneath him.

"Livvie," he whispered and parted her legs with his knees.

In a breathless moment he thrust deep into her and lost himself, body and soul, in the magic of his wife. His blood was thundering in his ears and he breathed in short, fast gasps. Faster and faster he moved, but she was no longer responding and the flesh he'd felt cooling was now stone cold.

When he looked down at her, she'd changed, her features having morphed into Jennifer. White skin, dark hair, the scrap of a red thong now a tattered bloody dress.

"I love you," Jennifer said, but her mouth didn't move. She smelled of brackish water and death. Her glassy eyes shifted to zero in on him.

His skin goose-pimpled and his blood ran cold as the sea. He tried to roll off her, but her hands came up and held him tight. Held him in place like a vise.

"It's your fault, RJ," she said with lips that didn't move. "Yours!"

Bentz bucked, trying to break her hold as his eyes flew open.

He was in the bed at the motel.

Alone.

No Olivia. No Jennifer.

Just his guilt. His damned guilt.

Letting out a long breath, he realized he was saturated in cold sweat. The dream had been so real. So evocative and terrifying. He wanted to call Olivia but glanced at the clock. 12:47. Nearly 3 A.M. in Louisiana. He would wait.

Climbing out of bed, he walked to the window and opened the blinds to look at the night-washed parking lot.

It was empty aside from the usual vehicles.

Quiet.

Still unnerved, he went into the bathroom and threw water over his face. Telling himself he'd been through a lot worse in his life than bad dreams, he popped a couple of ibuprofen for the pain in his leg before returning to bed. He clicked on the television and searched for any inane show to occupy his mind. But he didn't believe for an instant that some late-night talk show host would dispel the dream.

He figured nothing would.

He'd just have to live with it.

The next morning, after a fitful night, Bentz found a place where he could replace his cell phone on his current plan. He was the first customer to enter the strip mall for the day and he looked like hell. But he ended up with a new phone.

Two doors down there was a casual-wear store, so he picked up a new pair of khakis and a cheap sports jacket.

He'd have to wait on shoes.

He returned to the motel, showered, shaved, called and left a message for Olivia, then spent the next few hours spinning his wheels, thinking, and reentering numbers into the new cell. He pieced together the events of the last few days and wondered how the woman—"Jennifer"—had known where he would be. As far as he could tell, his room wasn't bugged. He didn't find any listening devices tucked into hidden niches. Not that it mattered. To his recollection he hadn't mentioned his plans while talking on the phone here. He did a second peripheral check of the rental car and couldn't find any tracking device in the undercarriage or wheel wells.

But somehow, "Jennifer" had known where he was going, where he had been.

How?

And why was she doing this?

In the motel room with the television tuned to an all-news channel, the blinds open so that he didn't feel completely cut off from the world, he sipped his tepid coffee, his mind turning back to the night before. What the hell had happened on the pier? She'd been there. He'd seen her, but Hayes had said that the cops had questioned the people on the pier, the old man who'd been smoking a cigar and the kids who had been so into each other. When Hayes had asked about the runner, he hadn't been found and no one remembered him.

Bentz made a note of it, though most likely the missing jogger wasn't any big deal.

Great.

Using his laptop computer he Googled images of the Santa Monica pier and found the webcam, a camera that photographed the entrance to the pier every four seconds. Maybe he could get photos of the pier from last night, as well as from traffic cams. Though he was no longer a cop in L.A., he still had a badge and some pull. He was certain he could talk his way into getting the information.

By eleven he'd talked to the security company that ran the camera on the pier and been promised that they would review the images from the night before. Afterward Bentz had made his way through a pot of coffee while searching the Internet for a hospital or clinic that might have issued the outdated parking pass he'd noticed on the gray Chevy. Then he used his new phone to leave messages with Fortuna Esperanzo and Tally White, two of Jennifer's close friends who hadn't bothered calling him back.

Tally was a schoolteacher and Fortuna still worked in an art gallery in Venice. Neither woman was a fan of his.

A motorcycle backfired on the street. Through the thin motel walls Benz heard Spike get off a round of quick, sharp barks before he was shushed by his owner. Bentz stretched, felt his spine pop, then stood and tested his leg.

Picking up his keys, Bentz wondered how long the old guy next door was staying. He grabbed his damp wallet and slipped his sidearm into its shoulder holster beneath the cover of his new jacket. Then, because his leg was still aching, he snagged his cane from its spot by the door.

Outside, he felt the heat of the day though it was barely noon. He eyed the dusty parking lot, recognizing four cars other than his own that seemed to be regulars. Besides his rental and the older guy in the driving cap's Pontiac, there was a bronze Buick parked at the far end of the lot. A white MINI Cooper was often gone all day, but returned every night. The older navy blue Jeep Cherokee never budged. The rest of the vehicles came and went, but these four always returned. Just like the damned swallows of San Juan Capistrano, he thought, remembering the legend and his own trip to the mission town. He'd already made note of the license plates and talked to Montoya about them. Since the woman impersonating Jennifer seemed to know his whereabouts, he wondered if she'd been following him from here each day. He was going to make certain that these cars were legit.

He also took a good long look at the area.

As far as he could see, no one was watching him. No one loitered. There was a gas station and convenience store next to another motel across the wide boulevard. A little farther down sat a three-story building that looked like it had shops on the street level and offices above. Then came the bar where he and Hayes had met last night.

But no silver Impala anywhere in sight.

Restless, itching for something to do after spending hours on his laptop at the battered desk in his motel room, Bentz walked to the car.

So Hayes thought he should pack it all in and return to New Orleans.

No damned way. Someone was baiting him, impersonating his dead wife, and following him.

He intended to find out who.

With the help of Montoya and his cell phone company, he tried to track down the owner of the phone who had called him, the woman impersonating Jennifer. It appeared to be one of those untraceable prepaid phones that criminals were so fond of.

So he was left to his own devices and hungry as hell. He bought a few newspapers, then stopped at a local diner that served breakfast all day. Over the clatter of silverware, sizzle of the fryer, and buzz of conversation, Patsy Cline was singing "Crazy."

Perfect, Bentz thought as he used his cane to help lower himself into a booth with a table straight out of the fifties: Slick green plastic top rimmed with chrome, matching napkin holder, and bottles of ketchup and mustard at the ready. He scanned a faded menu, ordered from a tall woman with a pile of red hair adding three inches to her height, then spread the newspapers on the table.

While reading the most recent accounts of the Springer girls' mur-

ders he dived into his "All-American-All-Day-Breaker" which consisted of two eggs, five sausage links, a heap of hash browns, and a
mountain of toast. His coffee cup was never empty, though he had to
ask for ice water.

The food was substantial and filling, if not gourmet.

Once he'd forked up the last bit of potatoes, he flipped the newspaper closed and caught a glimpse of an ad that stopped him short.
It was for a thrift shop, a Catholic thrift shop, and the symbol in the
corner of the page, a cross with the letter A attached, was sickeningly
familiar.

It was the same symbol from the sticker on the Impala he'd seen
at San Juan Capistrano. A symbol for St. Augustine's.

He stared at the information for a second, then asked the waitress
if they offered wi-fi service here. She looked at him as if he were nuts,
so he paid quickly, then drove to a nearby coffee shop where he
knew there was free Internet access.

After ordering another cup of coffee he really didn't need, he sat
in a worn couch and fired up his laptop.

Over the sounds of soft jazz, grinding coffee, and the hiss of the
steamer, he connected to the Internet where he searched for any
mention of St. Augustine's hospital or clinic in the L.A. area. For the
first time since coming to L.A., he felt a ray of hope that he might
have a way to discover who was tormenting him.

He found a parish in West L.A. on Figueroa Street, a school in Culver City, and several other institutions, but no hospital or clinic.

The fact that one of the schools was on Figueroa and the other in
Culver City bothered him. Jennifer had lived with him in Culver City
and supposedly, according to her friend Shana McIntyre, had met
with James in a little motel somewhere near the USC campus on
Figueroa St. It was the same major street where he'd thought he'd
seen her at the bus stop.

Possible? Had he seen her? He clicked his pen, wondering.

There were too many connections. Too many coincidences. Too
many possibilities.

Doggedly he kept at it, searching the Internet until he came to the
mention of St. Augustine's Hospital, which had closed five years earlier. Bingo! He stared at the information for a second, then jotted
down the address, and was out the door.

He had several stops on his agenda. First, he planned to drive to the old hospital, just to get a closer look. Then he would try to catch Fortuna Esperanzo at work in the gallery in Venice. Afterward he planned on heading to Hoover Middle School, where Tally White was a teacher. He remembered Tally had befriended Jennifer when her daughter Melody had been in the same first-grade class as Kristi.

He punched in the address, headed for the freeway, and barely moved. The 10 was jammed in the middle of the day, but he kept at it, inching past an accident, then picking up speed.

As he headed east he checked his mirrors, on the lookout for a tail, watching to see if he was being followed, particularly by a silver Chevy.

Using his cell, cognizant that he might get pulled over as he wasn't using a hands-free device, he left a message with Montoya, asking him to look up more on St. Augustine's Hospital and see if there was some way he could get personnel records from the archdiocese or whatever institution or attorneys or board oversaw the hiring or firing of the staff. There *had* to be records somewhere. True, there would be a lot of staff to sift through, but only for a couple of years. He explained that the Impala was seven or eight years old and the hospital was closed five years earlier, so even if the car was bought new, the window of time when the sticker could have been issued was relatively short.

A plus.

He also left the license plate numbers and hoped that somehow there would be a match. If Montoya used the police department's computers, databases, and DMV records, they might be able to find some shred of evidence to help him sort out the mystery.

Bentz knew he didn't have a lot to go on, but he figured it was a start. Tedious work, but a slight inroad. His cell rang. Bentz saw it was Montoya and grinned.

"Got an answer for me already?"

"Up yours, Bentz. It's not like I don't have a job to do here."

"Just see what you can do."

"Great. Anything else?" he mocked.

"Not yet." No reason to tell him about last night's leap into Santa Monica Bay. Yet.

"Well, just let me know because it's my mission in life to be your bitch."

"Fulfilling, isn't it?"

"You owe me, man."

"Always have, Montoya." He hung up just before taking his exit off the freeway, then wound his way around the surface streets to the site of the old hospital.

It wasn't a large piece of property. The crumbling stucco building that had once housed St. Augustine's Hospital was now surrounded by mesh fencing and warning signs that trespassers would be prosecuted "to the full extent of the law."

Fine.

Ignoring the warnings, Bentz climbed over a gate and jumped onto the packed dirt inside the enclosure. Pain jolted his hip as he landed, reminding him that he still wasn't a hundred percent. But he kept on, making his way toward the abandoned hospital.

The stucco exterior was just a shell. Limping a bit, he walked around the rubble and ducked into a gaping doorway. Inside, the building was skeletal, torn down to the studs. Tired floorboards creaked beneath his sneakers, and he saw evidence of bats in the rafters. Some of the old plumbing was intact, rusted pipes running up and down between aging two-by-fours and beams. Whoever had started this renovation had stopped suddenly. Because of the failure of the economy?

Outside again, he paused by a huge sign that faced the road and advertised a strip mall that was to be built. But the intended date for opening had already passed and it was obvious whoever was backing the project had pulled out. So here sat the remnants of St. Augustine's Hospital, a sad ruin of a building.

Using his cell phone, he took a few photos of the sign, of the crumbling building and the surrounding area. He saved them, then text-messaged them to Montoya.

He wished he could bring Hayes in on this. It would make a lot more sense to work with the cops in California rather than depend upon Montoya in New Orleans. But he just couldn't count on the LAPD.

Yet.

Slipping his phone into his pocket, he returned to his car, his leg aching as he slid inside and pulled away from the desolate construction site.

CHAPTER 19

Olivia didn't feel pregnant. Her body hadn't changed at all, at least on the outside. She wasn't suffering nausea, wasn't tired, and wouldn't have had a clue that she was carrying a baby other than the pregnancy test. Or tests. She'd taken the same test three different times, each kit made by a different manufacturer. Every one of them had confirmed that yes, she was pregnant. Which she'd already known after the first strip had turned a brilliant hue. But, she figured, better safe than sorry. Or in her case, better sure rather than uncertain.

The only difference Olivia felt was the weight of her secret. Not telling Bentz was killing her. She didn't like secrets or, for that matter, surprises, so as she drove to the Third Eye she made a definitive decision. Today she would make arrangements to take a week or two off and fly to California.

Though Rick had only been gone a few days, Olivia knew he wouldn't be back for a while. It was as if he were running away. From her. From their life.

Oh, yeah, he had an explanation. He had this sudden obsession with his first wife and he was out chasing ghosts in California. On top of that, a gruesome double murder had taken place in L.A., a killing that was nearly identical to the Caldwell twins' double homicide. He'd never felt right about leaving Southern California with that case still wide open, and he'd taken a lot of heat about it. She knew her husband well enough to realize that he saw the possibility of solving this new crime as a chance to redeem himself, an opportunity to catch the killer and put him behind bars once and for all. Not that the LAPD would appreciate his efforts.

But he was still running away and it was time to find out why. He'd been acting weird ever since he'd come out of the coma, and unfortunately she was never able to call him on it. At first, she'd been relieved he was alive. While he was recovering she'd forced herself to remain patient, understanding that he was not only suffering pain but also dealing with loss of purpose. She had been encouraging, tolerant, supportive.

But she was sick of it.

It was time he bucked up.

Beneath his distracted, distant exterior was the man she had fallen in love with, and she was determined to find him again.

What he needed, she decided, was what her grandmother referred to as "the two-by-four by the back door. Sometimes ya need it to get their attention." To Olivia's knowledge, Grannie Gin had never kept a piece of lumber propped on the sun porch. It was just her way of saying "a kick in the pants" or a large dose of reality.

And that was just what Olivia planned to hit Rick with. The truth.

She parked her beat-up truck in a lot, then walked toward the Third Eye. On her way down the street she passed a baby boutique and paused to look at the window display. There was a quaint assortment of layette sets, cute little one-piece sleepers, and bibs decorated with all kinds of animals. One bib, decorated à la New Orleans, was embroidered with a grinning baby alligator with a bow around its neck. It was surprisingly adorable.

Her own reflection, a watery image, superimposed itself upon the window. She was going to be a mother! Her husband needed to know.

What the hell was she waiting for?

Why in the world was she scared?

She put her hand over her flat stomach, walked into the shop, and, on a ridiculous whim, bought the alligator bib.

It was the first thing she'd bought for the new little Bentz—well, unless she counted the multiple pregnancy tests. Her appointment with her doctor wasn't for another couple of weeks. That didn't matter. She was going to quit being a wimp and tell Bentz that he was going to be a father again.

And he'd damned well better like it.

*   *   *

Unlike its Italian namesake, the city of Venice, California, still had just a few of its original canals. Most of the waterways built back in 1905 had since been paved over when the city of Los Angeles decided it needed more real streets for cars. However, the remaining canals and stretch of sandy beach were enough to lend character to the seaside community, which was packed on this sunny, warm day. Mild weather had brought out the bicyclers and skaters, along with an array of street performers who reminded Bentz of the musicians who peddled their talents in the squares of New Orleans. Like his home, this town boasted a carnival atmosphere, a sense of "anything goes."

The art gallery where Fortuna Esperanzo worked was only a few blocks from the beach, tucked between a tourist shop that sold everything from T-shirts to cameras and an "authentic" Mexican restaurant with a sprinkling of outside tables. The panorama was much the same as it had been a dozen years earlier.

Bentz parked the rental, eyed his cane, left it on the floor of the backseat, and jaywalked across the wide street. The salty scent of the ocean wafted to him, reminding him of his dunk in Santa Monica Bay the previous night. When he'd lost Jennifer. Again.

He stepped under an awning and through the open door of a gallery filled with abstract and modern sculpture and seemed empty. Bentz hitched his way up a wide wooden staircase which led to an open second-floor loft. It was filled with paintings, mosaic work, and tapestries by local artists.

In one corner Fortuna Esperanzo stood on a ladder, replacing the bulb of a light that was trained on a huge, unframed canvas. Wild black strokes slashed across a field of orange and red. The painting was called simply *Rage*.

"Nice," Bentz remarked sarcastically.

Startled, Fortuna dropped the lightbulb and it shattered. "Oh shit!" She glared down, eyeing him over the top of the ladder with small, dark eyes framed by perfectly plucked, pencil-thin eyebrows.

Her pink glazed lips pursing into a tight knot of dislike. "I figured you would take the hint when I didn't call you back, Bentz." Slowly she descended the rungs to stand on the floor, carefully avoiding the shards of thin glass. "What the hell are you doing here?"

"I just wanted to talk to you."

"Oh, yeah, right." She skewered him with a stare of disbelief. She was thin to the point of being bony, her taupe size-practically-nothing skirt and sweater hanging off her thin frame. "You really expect me to believe that after twelve or so years you're just dropping by for a chat? Give me a flippin' break. Where the hell is my broom?" She walked to an alcove and retrieved a push broom and dustpan. "You want to talk?" she muttered as she began cleaning up the mess. "About what?"

"Jennifer."

"Oh, God, why?" She stood suddenly and stared at Bentz as if he'd just flown in from Jupiter. "What good will it do now? That poor woman."

Downstairs another patron wandered into the gallery. Bentz saw her through the open railing. A silver-haired woman with red reading glasses perched on the end of her tiny nose, she wore a perpetual scowl along with white capri pants and a sleeveless top, She wandered through the displays only to stop and contemplate a glass mosaic cat that might have been the ugliest piece of so-called art Bentz had ever seen.

Jesus, was she serious? A piece of crap with a price tag that probably exceeded what Bentz made in a week?

Fortuna leaned over the railing and called cheerfully, "Hello, Mrs. Fielding! I'll be right down." She left her broom and dustpan propped against the ladder and glanced at Bentz. "You know, I really don't have anything to tell you."

"I'll wait."

Rolling her eyes as if to say "whatever" she headed down the stairs at a quick clip. Once on the main floor, she began showing the dour Mrs. Fielding pieces of colored glass that resembled African beasts. Ugly lions and gazelles and elephants. At least, that was his interpretation. Who knew what the artist really had in mind?

Bentz took it upon himself to clean up the mess, hauled the broom and dustpan back to the little closet, and even found another lightbulb. He'd just screwed it in so that it showcased the black and red mess of a painting when Fortuna walked up the stairs.

"Oh, don't think you're getting on my good side just because you played janitor," she said.

"You're welcome."

"I could have done it myself." She spied a piece of glass he'd missed and picked it up before folding her arms over her chest. "Just what the hell is it you want to know?"

"Jennifer's state of mind before she died."

"Are you kidding me? I don't know."

"You were one of her closest friends."

"What does it matter now?"

"Someone's been calling me, saying she's Jennifer."

"Oh, so what? Someone's just having a little fun at your expense."

He hauled out the copies of the photographs and Fortuna eyed them. "These were sent to me."

"And? The woman looks like Jennifer, yeah. So what? Oh, God, you don't think? I mean you wouldn't believe? Oh, no, I mean, that's rich." She laughed, though there was no mirth in her tone. "You actually think Jennifer might still be alive."

"I didn't say that."

"Then who the hell is in her grave?" She shook her head. "This is too much. Someone's really screwing with your mind. And you know who would have loved this? Jennifer. You're finally getting yours."

More than you know, he thought, but didn't say it. "I just thought you might remember something she did or said that was out of character for her in the week or so before she died."

"Nothing that I can think of." Fortuna sighed. Ran red-tipped fingers through her thick hair. "She did everything she normally did, well, I think. You know, the regular stuff. A haircut, I think. I was there the same day and she had gone shopping and visited her astrologer."

He felt the muscles between his shoulders tighten. "Astrologer?"

"Oh, yeah, you remember . . . Phyllis Something-Or-Other." She was staring at him. "You didn't know?"

"That my ex-wife went to a psychic? No."

"I said *astrologer*. There's a fine line."

He knew all about it. Olivia's grandmother had read tarot cards during her lifetime. "Okay, Phyllis the astrologer. Who checks star signs. Moons rising and retrograde and all that stuff."

"I think it's a little more involved than that, but personally I never got into it too much."

"Just Jennifer?"

"Yeah, near as I can tell she went alone, but at least once a month, sometimes twice."

"For how long?"

"Years. Since college I think." Fortuna nodded as she tried to remember. "Yeah, I recall her saying something to that effect."

Bentz was thunderstruck. In all the years he'd known his first wife, all the secrets they'd shared, never had she said a word about consulting an astrologer. Not that it was a big deal, but he wondered what other secrets Jennifer had held so tight. "What did she learn from Dr. Phyllis?"

"Oh, God . . . I can't remember," she said, then snapped her fingers. "Oh, wait! I do remember Jennifer mentioning that Phyllis told her she'd only have one child and . . ." Her voice trailed off.

"What?"

"Well, I don't know if the astrologer had anything to do with it, but for some reason Jennifer always thought that she'd die young."

"What?" His heart stilled. Jennifer had never mentioned any such fear to him.

"She'd make throwaway comments. Like, 'I know I'll never see Kristi graduate.' Or 'I know I'll never go to Europe, there's not enough time.' And one time . . . Jeez, it gives me chills just to remember it, she told me, 'You know, I'm glad I'm never going to grow old.'" Fortuna's voice dropped and she looked away from Bentz. "God, I hadn't thought about that in a long, long time." She cleared her throat. "I really can't tell you anything else." She headed down the stairs just as two men who looked to be in their thirties entered the gallery below.

A genial smile pasted onto her face, Fortuna went into salesperson mode. The finest Hollywood actress had nothing on her.

Resigned that Fortuna had revealed everything she could remember, Bentz followed her down the stairs and left a business card with his cell number at the register, then walked out of the gallery.

Outside, the sun was intense. Pedestrians strolled along the sidewalk, peering into shop windows. Next door, a few patrons of the restaurant sat at the outdoor tables where umbrellas shaded drinks and platters of spicy Mexican food. Two laughing kids on roller skates nearly knocked over a slim woman walking a kinky-haired dog that probably outweighed her. They whisked by without a second thought even though the dog took off after them.

Bentz lunged forward to help, but the slight woman caught herself and managed to pull her frantic dog back into the "heel" position.

Life went on.

Except for Jennifer.

Something was definitely off there.

Rick clicked on the remote lock for his car as he crossed the street. He was bothered by what he'd learned, about things he hadn't known, things important to Jennifer. Her friends all seemed to know her much better than he had, even, perhaps, better than she'd known herself.

Did it matter?

So what if Jennifer had kept her visits to the astrologer to herself? Big deal.

Nothing he found out about her surprised him any more, but he couldn't help but wonder as he slid into the hot interior of the Ford what other secrets he would uncover. Lost in thought, last night's nightmare still chaffing at his subconscious, he nosed the vehicle out of the parking space, then made a quick U-turn. He realized she probably kept a lot of her life tucked away, hidden from his scrutiny. Just because she'd told him the truth about Kristi's paternity, didn't mean she'd been honest about other facets of her life. The damning truth of the matter was that he hadn't really known his first wife at all.

CHAPTER 20

"No way he's going to have his wife's body exhumed." Bledsoe barked out a laugh at the ridiculousness of the situation. "Bentz has really lost it."

"He could petition as a family member," Jonas Hayes said while pouring himself another cup of coffee from the pot in the kitchen area of the squad room. Why he was defending a man who had yanked him all the way down to Santa Monica at night to work things out with their PD, Hayes didn't understand. He must really hate himself.

"*Ex*-family member," Bledsoe reminded him, rankling Hayes even further.

Hayes had always thought Bentz got a raw deal way back when, blamed for not solving the Caldwell case and shooting a kid while protecting his partner. Yeah, the guy got jammed up with the department. But those mistakes didn't add up to making him the scapegoat for everything bad that had happened in homicide twelve years earlier.

Hayes stared down into his inky coffee. "If he finds out it's not his ex-wife in that grave—"

"It's her, for chrissakes! He fuckin' identified her. Why the hell are you playing fuckin' devil's advocate?" From his chair at a table with the *L.A. Times* spread across it, Bledsoe pointed at the carafe in Hayes's hands. "Any more in that?"

"Empty."

"Shit."

"You could make some more," Martinez suggested as she walked into the kitchen and rinsed out her cup.

"Yeah, right." Bledsoe snorted at the idea.

"Have you ever made the coffee?" she demanded.

"Yeah, I think so . . . back in ninety-seven," Bledsoe said with a snicker.

Paula Sweet, a detective who sometimes worked with the K-9 Division, swept into the lunchroom. "I remember that." In her mid-thirties, Sweet had been divorced twice, seemed content to be on her own, and was known to take in stray dogs and cats. She glanced at Martinez. "Believe me, you don't want Bledsoe anywhere near the coffeepot."

"Hey! It wasn't that bad."

Sweet gave him the you-are-so-full-of-it stare. "No, it was worse. You got the crossword in there?" She was already pushing pages aside, searching for a section of the newspaper.

"Somewhere." Bledsoe shrugged and turned his attention back to Hayes. "Maybe an exhumation wouldn't be such a bad idea. We pop the coffin, take some DNA samples, and find out the corpse inside is really his ex-old lady. Then Bentz can crawl back under the rock he came from."

"*If* it's her," Hayes said.

"Don't tell me you're buying his crap now." Bledsoe snorted in disgust. "Of course it's her. As I said, he positively identified her. Him." He pushed his chair back so hard it scraped against the floor. "Once a bad cop, always a bad cop."

"Ouch." Sweet found the section of the paper she wanted and swept it off Bledsoe's table. "Didn't mean to tick him off," she said to the room as a whole.

Bledsoe scowled, obviously disgusted that no one was jumping on his let's-all-blame-Rick Bentz bandwagon.

"Don't worry about it." Martinez grabbed the empty pot and began rinsing it. "He's always in a bad mood."

"And you're always a bitch."

Martinez swallowed a smile, pleased that she'd goaded him. "Don't ever want to disappoint," she mocked.

"I'm outta here. I have work to do." The senior detective left the table in a mess and strode out.

"And good riddance," Sweet whispered, glancing conspiratorially at Martinez, who grinned even more widely.

Hayes rubbed the back of his neck. He understood the tension in the air.

It was late in the day. Everyone in the homicide area of the Robbery-Homicide Division had been logging in overtime. The detectives' nerves were strung tight as bowstrings, their tempers pushed to the limit. Because the truth of the matter was that they were getting nowhere fast solving the Springer twins' homicides.

Yeah, it hadn't been long since the murders had been committed, but not one solid lead had developed. No one had seen anything, heard anything out of the ordinary, or sensed anything was wrong. Interviews with friends, family, and neighbors had produced zero suspects. They had zippo to go on. The press was squeezing their public information officer, and in the meantime they'd dragged the old Caldwell twins case back to page one.

All the attention to the Springer twins' double homicide didn't change the fact that it was just one of many as yet unsolved homicides. Some were older, others fresh. A domestic violence homicide had happened just last night while Hayes had been in Santa Monica, saving Rick Bentz's ass, as well as trying to convince him to go home.

In the domestic case, the husband was the primary suspect, his wife of three years the victim. Then there was the nineteen-year-old kid in the morgue who'd taken five to the chest in the early hours of the morning.

All those were just the tip of the iceberg.

Everyone's caseload was getting heavier by the second.

Hayes walked back to his desk, glanced at the clock, and inwardly groaned. He wouldn't be home early tonight, and he'd probably have to cancel his plans with Corrine.

She would understand, of course, but that didn't mean she wouldn't be a little pissed.

He settled into his desk chair and started clicking through pictures of the Springer crime scene, trying to see something new. He flipped to the statements of the people closest to the girls, including the last people to see them alive. In Elaine's case, it was her roommate, Trisha Lamont, who had caught a glimpse of Elaine, or "Laney," as Trisha called her, cutting across the quad after their last class together. Trisha had assumed she'd gone straight home, and no other evidence or statements discounted that.

He checked the statement from Cody Wyatt, who, according to Trisha, was the closest thing to a boyfriend Laney had. But Wyatt hadn't
seen Laney since early morning when they'd met for coffee at the
student union the day she'd been abducted.

The person who'd found the bodies, Felicia Katz, was a blank;
seemed like the girl was just unlucky enough to have her storage unit
next door to the crime scene.

There was one guy, Phillip Armes, who had been walking his dog
in the park near Lucille Springer's apartment. He claimed to have
seen a tall man whose race was undetermined walk across the street
toward Lucille's apartment house. But it had been far away, dark, and
old Phillip was pushing eighty with thick glasses. Not much of a witness. Lucille's neighbors hadn't heard or seen anything, but scuff
marks on the porch of the girl's apartment might be consistent with
an attack.

The only sure thing was that Lucille and Elaine had been text-
messaging that night. Around the time Phillip Armes said he'd seen
Lucille with the guy following her, she'd been busily sending messages to her sister. Both cell phones had been discovered at the kill
site, their messages intact, messages that corresponded to the records obtained from the cell phone company.

The bastard who had abducted Elaine had sent a picture of her,
trussed and terrified, to Lucille just before the attack.

Twelve years ago, during the Caldwell investigation, the victims
didn't have cell phones. It was one deviation from the current crime,
but you could chalk it up to recent changes in technology, availability,
and pop culture. That one factor was about the only difference in the
crimes, though the Caldwell twins had been left in an abandoned
warehouse, and the Springer girls were found in a storage unit.

Hayes was eyeing the reports, tapping the eraser end of a pencil
against his lips, only vaguely aware of people coming and going. He
felt, rather than saw, Dawn Rankin stop by his desk. Her purse was in
one hand, a sweater tossed over her arm, as if she intended to leave
for the day. "Guess who I got a call from?" she asked, her tone serious.

"I give."

"Donovan Caldwell. Remember? The brother of the victims?"

"Yeah?"

She had his attention now and she knew it. Her big smile showed a bit of a gap between her front teeth. "He's calling up with the same old story his family used to peddle; that we haven't done enough. Now two more innocent lives have been lost because we're inept and blah, blah, blah."

"After twelve years."

"Yeah." She nodded.

"Just like Bentz."

"What?"

"He shows up and the killer strikes again. What's that all about?"

"Two separate instances."

"Maybe."

She bit her lip as she thought. "I'm not sure. As Bledsoe pointed out—only if you believe in coincidence. Me?" She frowned darkly as she walked away. "I'm betting there's a connection."

Hayes watched her go and reminded himself she had a personal ax to grind with Bentz, as did Bledsoe and a few others. Could it be that Hayes's faith in the guy was unfounded? Even his old partner, Russ Trinidad, wanted nothing to do with Bentz. "I hate to say it," Trinidad had confided in Hayes just this morning, "but the guy's bad news. I already told you I'm too damned close to retirement to get caught up in his mess. He wants to dig up his ex-wife? Fine. But leave me out of it."

Maybe Bledsoe had a point, Hayes thought, tossing his pencil onto the desk. It might be best if Bentz dug up Jennifer's corpse, had a DNA test done, and settled the matter once and for all.

If Jennifer Bentz was buried in that casket, all well and good. And if she wasn't?

He figured it was nothing short of the damned gates of hell opening.

The school was a long, low brick structure that could have been a county building in the Midwest except for the shady row of royal palms lining the drive. Also, one of the two flags gave the location away. Alongside the stars and stripes of Old Glory waved the flag for the state of California with its field of white and large grizzly bear in the foreground.

Bentz drove slowly past the main doors of the school. He avoided the bus-only lane and passed a long porch designated as the student pickup and drop-off area. On the far side of the drive he located a parking lot marked FACULTY ONLY.

Ignoring the sign, he pulled into an empty spot, cut the engine, and waited. From his vantage point he viewed one long wing of the school and beyond it caught a glimpse of the curved end of a track.

He had a hankering for a smoke. Maybe it because of the butt he'd smoked last night on the beach. Or maybe it was because he was so close to a middle school, where, at twelve, he had coughed his way through his first cigarette.

School was out, the area devoid of any but a few kids with backpacks or skateboards making their way across the adjoining lots and sidewalks.

Bentz figured most of the teachers and administrators were still inside finishing up, making lesson plans for the next day, correcting papers, or whatever it was that teachers did.

In groups of two or three, or even singles, members of the staff filtered out. They were chatting, laughing, rattling keys, and putting on sunglasses. A few looked at him quizzically, probably making note of his license plate and features . . . a lone guy hanging around near a school.

One prim woman dressed in a red skirt, white shirt, and blue over-blouse seemed ready to accost him. Even her sandals had the patriotic theme down, straps of red, white, and blue surrounding her feet. However instead of confronting him, she gave him an icy glare reserved for the likes of a pedophile, then climbed into her green Honda and roared off. She was adjusting the earbud of her cell phone, ready to make a call. Bentz figured she might be dialing 9-1-1 and the police might show up to question or arrest him at any second.

Have at, he thought watching a scrap of paper kick up in her wake.

Before the cavalry arrived, though, Bentz noticed Tally White emerge through the glass doors. She was walking alongside another teacher and they were engrossed in their conversation. Tally was tall, nearly five-ten, and had put on a few pounds over the years. She'd always been a little too thin, runner-lean, but now curves were evident beneath her peach slacks and matching shell. Her brown hair showed bits of gray and was cut into one of those wedge hairdos, where the back is shorter than the sides.

Her friend was a good five inches shorter than she, a square-bodied black woman whose oversized sunglasses hid half her face. Wild corkscrew curls were untamed by the headband that forced them away from her forehead. The two teachers were laughing and talking, lugging book bags and heading toward cars parked a few spaces from him.

"Showtime," he told himself as he stepped out of the car and said, "Hi, Tally."

She looked away from her companion, and upon spying Bentz, nearly tripped.

"Oh, God. Rick?" She wasn't sure and squinted, as if she needed glasses. "Rick Bentz?"

"Good to see you."

"But why are you . . . ? I mean I know you called and I should have phoned you back, but I didn't know you were here, in California." She glanced nervously around the parking lot, as if looking for an escape route, or that she was afraid someone might see her speaking with him. She visibly squared her shoulders as if ready to take on the world. Or at least Bentz's part of it. "Wow. I . . . I never thought I'd see you again."

"I wanted to talk to you," he said. "About Jennifer."

Beneath her tan she seemed to pale and she glanced around the emptying parking lot. A minivan with two men in the front seat slid out the gate. "Here?"

"I'd buy you a cup of coffee. Or a glass of wine?"

"Uh, no . . ." She suddenly remembered her coworker. "Oh. Sherilou," Tally said, motioning toward Rick with the fingers of the hand holding onto the book bag. "This is Rick Bentz, an old . . . the husband of one of my friends. Rick—Sherilou. She and I both teach English."

Sherilou shifted her purse and books, then shook hands with Bentz. "Glad to meet you," she said, though it was a patent lie. Her eyes were filled with suspicion and her handshake was weak. Unsure.

"I'd better scoot," Sherilou said with a false smile at Rick.

"Nice to meet you," Bentz said as sun glinted off the hood of Tally's VW.

"You, too." To Tally, she added, "Look, I've got to get going."

"See you tomorrow," Tally said and Sherilou hurried off, easing her book bag into the back of a blue Prius before sliding behind the wheel. Tally watched her go, then turned to Bentz and squinted up at him. "How's Kristi?" she asked. "She and Melody lost touch."

"Good. Getting married later this year."

"I'll pass that along to Melody. She's married, too. Has a three-year-old and expecting another." Tally rolled her eyes as she pulled pictures out of her wallet and proudly showed Bentz two snapshots of a towheaded little girl. The smiling imp posed with a stuffed animal, a white rabbit, in front of a blue backdrop.

"Cute," he said and meant it.

"Yeah. Who would have ever thought of me being a grandma?" She stuffed the wallet back into her purse, but her eyes twinkled. "It's so weird. I love it."

"I'll bet."

She caught his sober tone and let out a long sigh. "So. Tell me. What do you want to know and why?" As she loaded her book bag and purse into her Volkswagen Beetle, Bentz told her. While the sun lowered and a few straggling kids hurried from the school, he explained everything. Except about the fact that he thought he was actually seeing his dead ex-wife again; he kept that little detail to himself.

She was quiet. Stunned as he passed her the copies of the pictures he'd received as well as a copy of the marred death certificate.

"For the love of St. Peter." Shaking her head in disbelief, Tally held the photograph of Jennifer sliding into her car up for closer inspection. "It—it can't be Jennifer," she said, slightly unsure, squinting up at Bentz for confirmation. "You and I both know that. We were there . . . at the funeral. She was in the coffin." The picture in her hands began to tremble as Tally stood at the open door of her car. "I mean, it's just not possible." But her voice was faint, a whisper. She cleared her throat; squared her shoulders, took control again. "This woman in the picture, she, um . . . she's a dead ringer."

"It appears."

"But not Jen." Tally didn't sound convinced. "Someone . . . someone's playing a game with you. Yeah, I get that, but honestly, I don't know what you want from me, what I can tell you." She glanced down at the picture again. Visibly shivered.

"Just anything in the last few weeks of her life that you thought was incongruous. Out of character. Any confidences."

"Oh, God . . . this is so weird. Surreal, you know?"

"Yeah, I do know, but is there anything you remember about Jennifer that I might not, anything that happened the week before she died?"

"Oh, Lord, it's been so long . . . " She let her voice trail away and he thought for a second she might not answer, but she finally said, "Jennifer was nothing if not incongruous. You know that. One day she was this way, the next, another, and the third something different still. I'm not sure she was happy," Tally added wincing.

"I figured."

"Those days when the kids were still in school were difficult, to say the least."

"She didn't do or say anything out of the ordinary?"

"Oh, gee." Looking down at the open toes of her shoes, she frowned, deep in thought. "As I said, it was a long time ago. She was struggling, I guess, because she'd . . . um . . . she'd taken a lover." She glanced up at him, her cheeks burning, but Bentz didn't react except to nod, encourage her as she seemed to be having second thoughts.

"James."

"I . . . I'm not sure. She never said his name, but I think so."

"My brother, the priest."

Licking her lips nervously, looking away, Tally seemed reticent to say any more, so he helped her along. "I know that James was Kristi's biological father." Even after all these years, that admission stuck in his craw. The betrayal had been deep, two pronged, coming at him from both his brother and his wife. Hell. "I know that they met at San Juan Capistrano, an inn down there."

"Mission Saint Miguel, yeah. That and somewhere in Santa Monica."

Shana had mentioned the pier before and it burned in his gut as he thought about how many times Jennifer had suggested they spend the day at the beach. How they'd taken Kristi to the famous amusement park located on the pier, the restaurants they'd frequented as the sun had blazed before settling into the horizon.

"She was big on the beach," he offered.

"Oh, yeah." Tally's eyebrows quirked up for an instant. "Jennifer was never cut out to be a cop's wife. She was frustrated, I think, as she gave up her aspirations as an artist to raise Kristi. Not that she was a bad mother . . ."

Oh, right. Saint Jennifer.

Tally went on, "She loved Kristi, I know that. But she hated the fact that she wasn't your kid, Rick. She'd said that time and time again. Guilt ate at her."

"Not enough to change her behavior."

"No," Tally said with a sigh. She was still squinting as two girls half ran by and yelled, "Hi, Mrs. White."

"Hey, Brinn. Marcy." Tally rained a smile on them before turning back to Bentz. "No, the guilt was bad, but it wasn't enough to change anything, I suppose. Maybe nothing would have been. She loved you, but she was obsessed with James, if that makes any sense."

Not on a dare, but he didn't say as much.

"I'm sorry but there's not a whole lot more I can tell you. You knew her as well as anyone."

"I don't feel like I knew her at all." And that was the understatement of the century.

"Then you're no different from anyone else." She touched his arm, thought better of it, and drew her hand back. With a sigh, she added, "This has nothing to do with you, I know, but Jennifer once told me that the reason she married you was to get away from some other guy."

"James?" he asked.

She shook her head. "Someone she knew before you."

"Alan Gray?" Bentz wondered why his name kept coming up.

"I don't remember . . ." She hesitated, leaned a shoulder against the doorjamb of her car. "No, you're right. I think maybe that's the name. One time when we were together Jennifer had a few too many martinis and she said that the reason she married you was that Alan had a cruel streak. That he was obsessive and even handcuffed her to the bed once, wouldn't let her go. After he'd sobered up, he'd apologized, but she never forgave him or forgot it."

Bentz didn't move. Rage burned through him. At Gray. At his damned ex-wife.

Jennifer had never confided this story to him.

Was it the truth? Or a quickly fabricated lie to gain sympathy, come up with a reason why she threw over a millionaire for a cop?

He didn't know. Trying to understand Jennifer was like trying to walk on quicksand; his footing was never secure.

"She said she suspected him—Alan—of being into more than real estate. She thought he might be into illegal stuff. What, I don't know, but that's the impression I got. Of course with Jennifer, I was never sure. She made a big deal of it, swore me to secrecy. Lord, I thought she was going to make me cross my heart and wish to die."

Bentz was irritated that he'd never heard this before. "You didn't think of saying anything when she died."

Tally snapped her head up, suddenly worried. "No. Why would I?" And then she caught on. "It was a suicide, right? That's what everyone thought. There was a note." She was suddenly anxious, as if she realized she'd said far too much. "Look, I really don't know what difference it makes now. And I've really got to get going. I don't know anything else, really. And I don't know how this could help you."

He didn't either. But it was something.

"Thanks," he said and slipped a card from his wallet. On the back he slashed out the digits of his cell phone. "If you think of anything else." He handed her the card and she nearly crushed it in her fist.

"Of course," she promised, but they both knew it was a lie.

Tally White wanted nothing more to do with him, nor the memories of his dead ex-wife.

He stepped away from her car as she pulled the driver's door closed and jabbed her keys into the ignition. A moment later Tally gunned the Volkswagen out of the faculty lot, putting as much distance as she could between herself and Bentz.

So what else was new?

He had that effect on people.

CHAPTER 21

I'm alone in the elevator.

Slowly, with a loud grinding noise, the large car ascends. When I reach the second floor, no one is there to meet me.

Good.

The stark hallway is empty as well.

Perfect.

Quickly, on noiseless footsteps I make my way down the pressboard corridor to my private room, the windowless space where I am totally alone. The place that no one knows about, that no one would link to me. The walls and floor are pressboard and a single bulb gives off a harsh, unshaded glow.

I close the door.

Lock it.

Test the lock to make certain it's solid.

Then I let out a deep breath and survey my surroundings in this, a place many would see as a cell. But in here, by myself, I'm free. I usually hate being alone, but not here. Not in this one place that is my sanctuary. Here, I'm finally at peace.

On a previous trip to this quiet place, I hung a full-length mirror on one wall—just so I would have company. Across from the reflective glass, I stacked big plastic tubs of clothes and makeup. I also assembled a short rod, screwed it into the walls so that I could hang plastic garment bags of nicer clothes, the dresses and jackets and pants that I kept for my special purpose. I even have a computer in here, a laptop that I can use while sitting on my faux leopard beanbag. The chair sits in one corner with a small battery-powered lamp on a TV tray. All the comforts of home.

There's a small bookcase, one I put together unassisted. The only books on the shelves are photo albums and scrapbooks, collections I've been keeping for years.

After rechecking the lock one more time, I find my iPod and plug in. Today, I'll listen to R.E.M. and feel the thrum of music run through my body. As I hum along, I drag the heavy tomes from their resting place, plop myself into the chair and open the pages. Some of the pictures and articles have yellowed with age, but they are all in perfect order, as I have so carefully placed them. Photographs of Bentz. Articles about him. His entire life as a police officer captured.

There is one of a crime scene where Detective Bentz, standing just on the other side of the yellow tape, is talking with two other officers. In the background sits the house where the victim was found. But I'm not interested in the little bungalow with a blooming wisteria running over the front porch. Nor do I pay any attention to the blood still visible on the front steps.

No.

I focus on Bentz.

The good-looking prick.

In this shot, his face is in profile. His features are harsh and rugged, his stern jaw set, his razor-thin lips flat in anger. Always the tough cop.

Yeah, right. "Bastard," I say, keeping my voice low.

I spy another photograph of him on the Ferris wheel at an amusement park. Kristi is at his side. She is all of seven in the photo, and Bentz's lips are wide in a grin—a rare shot of him having fun.

The photograph, not clear to begin with, is around twenty years old. I run my fingers over the images. As I have done hundreds of times.

Twenty years!

Twenty effin' years.

The child a grown woman.

It's true, I think ruefully, *time flies.*

But no more. Time is about to stand still.

These pages with their clear plastic covers are filled with his life.

Old wedding photos of his first marriage are fading, washing out, the fashions worn by the happy couple evidence of another era.

As the music runs through my brain I flip forward quickly, my fingers urging the years to spin past, faster and faster. Until I stop at the present. Here the more recent pictures of his new wife, Olivia, are fresh and clear.

New wife.

New life.

We'll see about that.

One picture of the bitch, a photograph where she's looking straight into the camera, catches my eye. In the shot, Olivia is serene and smiles slightly, as if she knows a secret, as if *she* can read my mind.

What a nut case!

And to think that Bentz actually believes he's happy with a woman who has several screws loose!

A psychic?

If so, then she should be worried.

Really worried.

But then, of course, she's a fraud.

Do she and Bentz believe her "visions?"

Well, then how about this, Olivia? Tune into what's happening to you, will you? What do you think about lying six feet under, huh?

Rick Bentz won't be able to save you.

And he'll know what real mental anguish is.

I glare at the woman staring up at me. So smug. So self-satisfied. As if she really thinks she can see the future.

Oh, like, sure.

"No way," I whisper to her. "No damned way." But her curved lips get to me and I remember that somewhere in her past she had a twisted ability to see murders committed as they happened.

How will she feel about her own? I wonder.

The thought is thrilling, brings a zing into my veins, not so much for her pain and suffering but for Bentz's.

He'll be the one who will have to deal with the torment, the pure, soul-sick torture of knowing that, because of him, the woman he loves will be subjected to excruciating, mind-shattering fear and deep, abysmal pain.

But I can't get ahead of myself.

Everything is falling into place, but my mission is far from over. Still undone.

There are those who need to be destroyed, those who have served their purpose by leaking information about Jennifer to Bentz, those who knew her well and now are of no further use. I take a deep breath.

To remind myself of my mission, to stay on target, I reach into my pocket and pull out my Pomeroy 2550, a sweet little multipurpose tool that disguises its sharp blades in an innocuous plastic shell. Designed to look like a pink manicure kit, the tool can become lethal with the flick of a tiny lever. It boasts a corkscrew, screwdriver, nail clipper, a pair of petite scissors, and a tiny little knife as sharp as a surgeon's scalpel.

My favorite.

The razor-thin blade is perfect.

Grinning at this newfound ritual that solidifies my determination, I hum along to the refrain of "Losing My Religion" as I slowly draw the blade across my inner wrist.

A sharp sting.

I suck in my breath in a hiss, losing track of the words to the song. But it's a bittersweet pain and I locate the melody again, catching up to the band.

With eager eyes, I watch the blood bloom. *My* blood rise against my skin.

Reverently, almost mesmerized by the image I'm creating, I drizzle the thick red drops onto the photograph of Olivia.

She smiles up at me through a nearly opaque sheen of red.

Unknowing.

Fearless.

I smear the blood over the plastic that protects her image and yet she grins.

Poor, dumb bitch.

"Don't tell me you need another favor," Montoya said when Bentz phoned him as he drove with the pack on the clogged L.A. freeway. He had the window cracked but closed it and cranked up the A/C.

"You're off work anyway."

"And I thought I'd go home, spend some time with my wife, and relax. This is your deal, Bentz, not mine." Despite his complaints, Montoya didn't sound pissed off.

"Okay, okay, but I could use some help."

"What?"

"Some more searches of Internet and police records."

"Great."

"I need the name of an astrologer who may or may not still be alive or practicing. All I have is a first name: Phyllis."

"No last name. Nothing else?"

"She was somewhere in the Los Angeles area. And then, if you can, find out if Alan Gray is still in business. He's a developer in Southern California. At least he was twenty-five years ago."

"Alan Gray?" Montoya repeated "Have I heard of him?"

"Probably. I might have mentioned him. He's a big shot. Multimillionaire, owned a house in Malibu, I think, and maybe had an apartment in New York, and a place somewhere in Italy, too. Even a yacht that he kept moored down at Marina del Rey, if I remember right. He was involved with Jennifer before she and I became an item, and I'd like to see if he's still around."

"You don't ask for much."

"Only what I need," he said and hung up.

It was late in the afternoon, the sun sitting low in the sky, the heat of the day settling into the pavement. Bentz decided to grab some dinner at Oscar's, a restaurant he and Jennifer had often frequented in their old neighborhood. He needed a quiet place where he could find some vestiges of the past and try to put together everything he knew about his ex-wife. Which changed day to day, as if Jennifer really had been a chameleon. Bentz hoped to mesh the old with the new to get some idea of the woman who, with each passing day, was becoming more of a stranger to him.

Even in death, Jennifer Nichols Bentz was the ultimate enigma.

Shana McIntyre was pissed as hell as she walked into her cedar-lined closet and yanked the headband from her hair.

She should never have talked with Bentz, never have confided in him, never have told him one solitary thing about Jennifer. The woman was dead, damn it. She had driven herself into a damned tree and, thankfully, was at rest.

In the dressing area of her massive closet and connecting bath, Shana stripped off her tennis skirt and sleeveless tee to stand naked in front of the floor to ceiling mirror. Not too bad for a woman on the north end of forty, she thought, though she'd have to consider some boob work and a full face-lift in the next five years to add to her tummy tuck and lipo. She pulled her breasts up to a spot where they were perky again and thought she could use another cup size as well. B to C. That would be nice. Then she drew back the skin around her chin and mouth. The lines there weren't too bad yet, but there was a bit of sag that would only get worse. At least Jennifer Bentz would never have to worry about laugh lines, age spots, or cellulite. Early death, though scary, in some ways was seductive.

Shana believed that Jennifer was dead and had been for twelve years. Whoever had sent Bentz those photos was just mind-fucking him.

So why had Shana thought it necessary to play with Bentz? True, she'd had her own doubts about Jen's death, but come on, there was no way the woman was alive today.

It's because you were attracted to him, her mind silently accused, though she would never admit as much. A cop? Come *on.* But, then, Bentz always had been and was still undeniably sexy, and lately Shana had been more than a little denied in the sex department. Leland had once been a wild man, insatiable, but with advancing age and a few health issues his interest in sex, along with his ability, had diminished.

No amount of talking would get him to go to a doctor and inquire about Viagra. It was as if even suggesting the idea were an affront to his manhood.

What manhood, she thought unkindly because, truth be told, she was losing interest in the man she once would have killed to marry. Hadn't she seduced him away from his first wife, that imbecile Isabella?

And Rick Bentz, even with his uneven walk, oozed virility. He caused her mind to wander down twisted and darkly seductive paths she didn't dare follow. Jennifer had hinted that he was a great lover. She'd insisted that she hadn't strayed for sex so much as for forbidden sex, with a priest, no less. Her husband's half brother.

But then Jen had been one messed-up woman. Shana had thought so when they'd hung out together.

God, that seemed like another lifetime.

It *was* ancient history, long before she noticed the strands of gray in her hair and the evidence of sagging in certain areas of her body that had once been firm.

Christ, it was hell growing old . . . old*er*, she reminded herself. She wasn't yet fifty and she knew a lot of women who were over sixty and looked fabulous, though they had to work at it.

"Ugh." She eyed her figure again and told herself to buck up. She was told over and over how beautiful she was, how great she looked, and so far no one had dared tacked on the "for your age" line that diminished the compliment.

She threw a cover-up over her body, though there was no reason. The maid had left long ago, the gardener wasn't scheduled for a few more days, Leland was out of town *again* wooing some big client in Palm Springs.

Hurrying down the marble stairs, she cut through the sunroom and out to the yard, where Dirk was barking loudly at the neighbor's Chihuahuas, who were yipping from the other side of the hedge and fence. "Enough," Shana said and dragged Dirk into the house. She stuffed him into the laundry room and closed the door.

She just needed some time alone, without the aggravation of Leland's dog giving her a headache. These days she spent more time with the damned animal than she did her husband.

She eyed the refrigerator and thought of the chocolate mousse pie within. It was a ritual she allowed herself. Each week she bought a different decadent dessert and left it calling to her on the third shelf of the refrigerator. She allowed herself one bite of pure heaven, then left the rest to slowly dehydrate and turn dark. Lemon meringue or key lime pie, coconut or Boston cream or fudge cake or eclairs. They all rented space on the glass shelf at eye level, then were evicted on the next Saturday night.

Her ritual of self-deprivation and control.

Today she wouldn't even bother opening the door but hurried back outside and crossed the patio to the pool. It was twilight, the pool light glowing at the far end, the aquamarine water smooth and welcoming.

She dropped her cover-up and kicked off her flip-flops near the edge of the pool. Descending the mosaic tiled steps, she slid into the warm water and relaxed as it surrounded her calves, then her hips, and finally embraced her waist.

Vaguely aware that those nasty little Chihuahuas had quit their incessant yapping, she began her nightly ritual, her second workout today, with even strokes. Freestyle to the far end, breaststroke back, sidestroke for two laps. That was one set. She'd do five sets and then, only then, would she allow herself a drink. For next to the white box containing the chocolate mousse was a pitcher of martinis, already made and chilling.

It was another test of her willpower, waiting until after her exercise regimen before allowing herself a tall drink with exactly three olives. She'd suck the pimento out of each. God, Jennifer had loved martinis.

Stroke, stroke, breathe, stroke, stroke, breathe, turn.

She headed back, changing her rhythm as her body movements altered for the breaststroke. Night was closing in, the moon high. The subdued outdoor lighting cast small pools of light near the walkways. Brighter beams washed up the trunks of the palms, and the huge arched windows of the house were illuminated from within.

It was a gorgeous place to live.

Even if her life had become lonely.

Stroke, stroke, stroke.

She lost herself in her routine, silently counting off the turns, knowing instinctively from the way her muscles strained when she was coming to the end of her self-imposed exercise regimen.

She could almost taste the martinis as she completed the final lap. Letting water drip from her body, she started up the steps. She was reaching for her cover-up when she heard something.

A footstep?

A chorus of barking arose from the other side of the fence as the Chihuahuas started up again. Inside the house, Dirk responded with a low, warning growl.

"Great," Shana said, intent on marching into the house and giving the dog a piece of her mind. What the hell was wrong with him? He never engaged the yappy rat-dogs from inside the house. It would serve the neighbors right if Dirk ever got loose and attacked those ankle biters. God, she hated them.

From the corner of her eye, she saw movement.

What?

Something dark.

A shadow in the side yard.

Or was it?

Her skin crawled as fear slithered through her.

She peered, staring at the side of the house, telling herself that nothing was out of the ordinary, there was nothing to be concerned about. And yet . . .

Just beyond a circle of decorative light, she caught a glimpse of movement again, something slinking near the undergrowth.

Heart hammering, she peered through the darkness, told herself she was being a ninny, one of those frightened little women she detested and then she saw it again. Something or someone creeping closer.

Something was definitely wrong.

"What the hell—?"

In a flash, a dark figure lunged, running, footsteps slapping across the cement.

Shana started to scream, as the sprinter rushed forward, eyes dark and glittering.

The attacker hit her mid-section, ramming her hard enough that she tripped, fell backward into the pool, her assailant pushing firmly.

Bam!

Shana's head hit the side of the pool.

Pain exploded behind her eyes. She nearly passed out, but tried to hang onto consciousness. To fight.

Still the maniac was on her, in the water with her as she flailed. Gloved hands circled her throat. Held her under. She saw the features of an angry face through the curtain of water. Features twisted in hatred. Oh, God, she should recognize the monster but she couldn't think, couldn't draw a breath.

Dear God, help me. Someone, please help me, this psycho wants to kill me!

She struggled and tried to roll in the water, to twist so that the attacker was under the surface. Shana was strong, a swimmer, but she was already tired and she couldn't battle the fierce determination of this would-be killer.

No! Sweet Jesus, no!!!

She was already coughing. Trying to keep her wits. Find a way to survive.

But she was losing ground. Sputtering. Her strength drained even as she tried to pry the steely hands from her throat, hoping to land a blow with her feet. *Kick him, Shana, kick! Or bite. Do something, anything!*

But the water was heavy.

Her assailant was agile, even in the water.

Her lungs and nose were burning. Her throat on fire. She was trying to cough again, but couldn't expel the air trapped inside. Her throat was raw, her lungs screaming.

Oh, God, oh, God . . . no, no, no!

Everything was going black, swirling above her, the stars and moon circling her head as a jet cut across the inky sky. *I'm going to die,* she thought with sudden understanding and surrender. Her arms moved more slowly, her legs stopped kicking.

She was floating on her back, staring upward as the blackness consumed her and she finally caught a glimpse of the person who had fought so hard to kill her.

Why? she wondered. *Why me?*

Far in the distance she heard someone yell. "Rico!" her neighbor screamed at the dogs. "Daisy! Little Bit! You all hush!"

But the Chihuahuas were rabid and kept up their high-pitched barking and wails as the night closed in on Shana. She struggled for a breath, then finally blackness took away her pain.

CHAPTER 22

The day was warm. Despite the breeze blowing off the Pacific.
Bentz was back in Santa Monica, walking on the pier, slowing at
the very spot where he knew he'd seen "Jennifer" jump into the bay.
Here, he felt a chill and as he looked downward into the water, imagined he saw her ghostly image in the inky depths, her skin pale and
blue, veins visible, her red dress diaphanous and floating around her
like a scarlet shroud.

He blinked. Of course she wasn't there, the water once again a
clear aquamarine shimmering as it caught the sunlight.

His cell phone rang.

According to caller ID, it was Jonas Hayes's private cell.

"Bentz," he said, still scanning the sea and feeling the pain in his
leg. Worse since his midnight swim. Age was creeping up on him,
though he was loath to admit it, except to Olivia who thought he was
still young enough to father another kid. If she could see him now,
limping along the boardwalk, conjuring up wraiths in the water . . .

"We need to talk." Hayes's voice was tight, all-business. He obviously hadn't warmed up since their last conversation.

"When?" Bentz squinted as he looked downward to the shadowy
area under the pier where a fisherman was casting out a line and
where, if he figured right, Jennifer would have landed when she
plunged into the water and disappeared. As far as he knew, the Coast
Guard had not recovered the body of a woman in a red dress, so he
had to assume the woman impersonating his ex-wife was still very
much alive. Ready to haunt him again.

Just as she'd disturbed his dreams.

After doing some work on the Internet, searching for information regarding Alan Gray, he had called Olivia, then watched some mindless television. He'd dozed off with the television on, falling into a restless sleep full of disjointed images of his ex-wife . . . Jennifer reaching for him from the water in a sopping wet red dress. Jennifer at the wheel of a silver car with smudged plates.

Wanting some closure, some hint of how a woman could leap from such a high vantage point and completely disappear, he had returned to Santa Monica today in search of answers. Today the sky was clear, the sun so bright he was wearing shades against the glare. A soft breeze ruffled the huge fronds of the palm trees near the beach. He checked his watch—his new watch, as his old one had given up the ghost after his swim. "What time do you want to meet?"

"Now would be good," Hayes said. "Actually, give me thirty or forty minutes. Can you meet me somewhere near the Center? I'm at the office."

"Sure." Bentz understood that "the Center" meant Parker Center, LAPD's headquarters building that housed the Robbery-Homicide Division. What he didn't get was Hayes's turnaround. The last he'd heard Hayes would have liked nothing better than to shove him onto the next eastbound 737 headed for New Orleans. Then again, from the professional, nearly distant tone of Hayes's voice, Bentz was guessing this wasn't just a friendly lunch date. Hayes wasn't calling to patch up their relationship.

"How about Thai Blossom on Broadway? It's not far. Good food. Reasonable."

"I'll find it. What's up?"

"I'll tell you when you get there." Hayes hung up and Bentz was left with a bad feeling.

It wasn't like Hayes to be cryptic or curt. Something was definitely going on. And definitely not something good. Bentz turned and, using his cane, headed to his car. He was still suffering from his late-night swan dive and swim. His leg was definitely acting up, and he'd already downed double the dosage of ibuprofen this morning, washing the pills down with a large cup of coffee.

Of course, all this walking and trudging through sand hadn't helped. But he had wanted to explore the underbelly of the pier by daylight, hoping to find an escape method the woman might have used. A ladder, a rope, a catwalk. Unfortunately, when he'd hitched along the beach, he'd looked up and seen only the guts of the massive dock, pillars covered with creosote and tar. No means of escape.

By light of day Santa Monica Bay was a different animal. The other night the whole area around the pier had been eerie with the lights of the amusement park muted and fuzzy in the fog, but bright enough to reflect in the black waters. This morning the pier wore an entirely different face. Yes, there was a carnival atmosphere, but it seemed far less sinister. The amusement park bustled with noise and the shouts of delighted riders. There were lots of people walking, riding bikes, jogging, or window-shopping on and around the beach. Men fished off the pier, people strolled on the beach, kids played in the sand. Nothing menacing or dark.

Almost as if he'd dreamed the horrid situation. He'd checked with the webcam people twice, and there was some hitch in locating the film. "Just give me another day," the technician had told him. Bentz wasn't sure if the holdup was about authorization or technical issues, but he was skeptical that he'd ever get access to the webcam records.

He looked out to sea one last time.

How does a woman plunge into the water and disappear?

Maybe Hayes would help answer that question.

"Yeah, right," he muttered, climbing into the warm interior of his rental car. After a quick U-turn, he stepped on it and was lucky enough to stay ahead of a few yellow lights. Traffic, for once, was light and he didn't spot a tail or catch one glimpse of Jennifer.

As he drove he toyed with the notion that Hayes might want to talk to him about the old Caldwell case, to pick his brain to see if there was something the files didn't hold. Maybe Hayes was hoping Bentz had a forgotten piece of information that might be the key to unmasking the Twenty-one killer and solving the new case with the Springer twins as the vics.

He thought of the grief-stricken parents, the hell they must be going through. A few times in his life he'd almost lost his daughter and the horror of it was branded in his memory, even though she'd pulled through. And now Olivia wanted another child. Of course she did. He didn't blame her; she was younger than he and had never been a parent.

Maybe . . .

If he survived whatever was going down here on the coast.

He ended up at the restaurant five minutes before they were supposed to meet, but Hayes was already inside, waiting at a booth with vinyl seats, a plastic-topped table. Fake bamboo screens separated tables. The restaurant smelled of jasmine, tea, ginger, and curry and from the kitchen came the sound of rattling pans and voices speaking in some Asian tongue.

Hayes looked up from his small, steaming cup of tea. He didn't bother smiling, just nodded as Bentz slid onto the bench across from him and slid his cane beneath his feet. They were nearly the only people in the restaurant, which had just opened for the day.

Hayes eyed the cane. "You feelin' okay?"

Bentz lifted a shoulder and kept his face impassive as the waitress, a petite Asian woman with a friendly smile and long black hair wound onto her head, brought another cup of tea and two plastic menus. Hayes ordered without looking at what was offered. Sensing the other man's intensity, Bentz said, "I'll have the same."

As soon as the waitress left, Bentz eyed a somber-faced Hayes. His gut clenched. "Something happened."

"Where were you last night?"

"What?"

Hayes didn't respond. Just waited. Dark eyes assessing, lines showing near the corners of his mouth and around his eyes. His big hands rotated the tiny porcelain cup around and around, steam rising in fragrant swirls.

"I was here in L.A. Culver City, to be exact. At the motel." What the hell was going on here?

"Anyone able to confirm that?"

"What?" Bentz asked, not liking where this conversation was leading. He waited as a busboy delivered soy sauce to their table, then said, "I don't know, but I got in around . . . seven maybe, or eight? I didn't check with the desk." He stopped short and eyed the man he'd counted on as a friend. "What the hell happened, Hayes?"

"You know Shana McIntyre, right?"

"Jennifer's friend. Yeah. You know I do."

"You visited her?"

"A few days ago. What? She complain that I was harassing her?"

Hayes shook his head. "It's more serious than that, Bentz. Shana McIntyre was killed last night."

Bentz was stunned. He tried to soak it all in as the waitress returned with steaming platters of spicy vegetables, meat, and rice. She placed them on the table, then smiled expectantly. "Can I get you anything else?" she asked as if from a distance.

Shana was dead? But he'd just seen her . . .

"We're fine," Hayes said.

Bentz sat back, having lost his appetite. A feeling of doom settled like lead in his gut. He couldn't believe it. As the waitress disappeared, clicking off on high heels to another booth, Bentz pushed his platter aside and lowered his voice. "Wait a second." He was still trying to wrap his mind around what Hayes was saying. "Killed?"

"Murdered." Dark eyes drilled into him. Silent questions—accusations—in their dark depths.

Jennifer. This has to do with Jennifer. The dark idea snaked through his brain as he understood the unspoken accusations in Hayes's eyes. *What?*

"Holy Christ. You think I did it?" he asked, shocked all over again. "No." Bentz shook his head, feeling for the first time in his life like a damned suspect. "Wait a second."

"Look," Hayes said seriously. "This is a courtesy, okay? One cop to another. Your name was found on her computer. She keeps a calendar there."

"I told you I saw her."

"And you never went back?"

"No." Bentz's gut wrenched. This was madness. He couldn't believe for a second that anyone who knew him, who had worked with him, for God's sake, would think him capable of killing someone.

What about Mario Valdez? You killed him, didn't you? An accident, yes, but the kid died. At your hand. You are capable, Bentz. Everyone here in L.A. knows it.

"Tell me what you discussed with her."

"Jennifer, of course." He told himself not to be paranoid. Hayes wasn't trying to nail him. He was just doing his job. The hostess was leading two men in business suits to a booth nearby. Bentz watched them pass before settling his gaze on Hayes again.

A dark eyebrow raised. "That's all?"

"Yeah." Bentz recounted their discussion, explaining about the conversation from the time he was met at the door by Shana and her mammoth dog to his departure. He even recounted that shortly thereafter he'd spied "Jennifer" at the bus stop on Figueroa.

Hayes's face didn't change expression. "Did Shana buy it that your ex-wife might be alive?"

"Nah. She thought Jennifer was dead, though she always had her doubts that she committed suicide."

"She thinks Jennifer was killed?" Hayes's underlying message was clear: She was killed and you were involved.

"I get where you're going with this, but I wouldn't be here, looking for the truth, if I had any connection to Jennifer's death. And I have no motive to kill Shana McIntyre."

Hayes was unmoved. "You have to admit, these are strange coincidences. The Twenty-one killer strikes again, and now Shana McIntyre is dead . . . all within a week of your return to L.A. Any detective worth his salt would be making some connections."

Bentz's jaw tightened. A storm roiled inside him and it was all he could do to hang onto his temper. "When I left Shana, she was alive. That was a few days ago . . . check her calendar. I never went back and never saw her on the street and never so much as talked with her on the phone. You can check my cell records."

"We will."

"Good. Then you'll see that last night I was on the phone with my wife in New Orleans. The cell tower in the area should have caught the signal. Jesus, listen to me. I don't have to explain myself to you or anyone else."

Hayes held up a hand defensively. "I just thought you'd rather hear it from me first."

Bentz bit back a comment, trying to restrain his anger. No need to shoot the messenger. "First and last. I wasn't at Shana's place last night. But you would know that if you checked her security system," Bentz said. "The place is gated like she's a celebrity. Anyone think to get into the system, see what those cameras all over her house picked up?"

"We're looking into it."

"Well, do, because I wasn't there. And while you're at it, you might check out some of the information I sent you about that silver car and the license plates. Someone's fuckin' with me, Jonas, and that person's playing the LAPD for a fool. I didn't kill Shana McIntyre, but someone wants to fuck me over. Someone orchestrated this whole thing. They're probably watching us now."

The waitress came by with more tea and her ever-present smile, but Hayes shook his head and she moved on as three middle-aged women were seated at a table not far from them.

"You're paranoid," Hayes said, his voice still low as the women scraped their chairs back, his accusations echoing Bentz's own very private fears.

"That's right, but I've got a good reason."

"I'm here as your friend."

"You know the old line about, 'with friends like you, who needs enemies?'"

"Just watchin' your back." Hayes's dark eyes flashed and his lips drew tight. "More than a few people in the PD would like to see you go down, Bentz."

"So what else is new?"

"As I said, I've got your back."

"Prove it. Get me that information. We're done here." Bentz stood up, grabbed his cane, and shoved his plate toward Hayes. "You might want to put this in a 'to go' bag."

Bentz had a point, Hayes thought grudgingly as the clock ticked toward five and he still a stack of paperwork looming on his desk. The air-conditioning system was working overtime, the cold office emptying as detectives signed out and the night shift dribbled in. For the third time Hayes scanned the statements collected from the neighbors and friends of Shana McIntyre, trying to make some sense of the events surrounding her death. An impossible task, he thought, clicking his pen nervously.

Although he didn't see enough evidence to string together any kind of case, all factors did point to one thing: someone had lured Bentz here and, once he'd landed on West Coast soil, a homicidal rampage had begun.

Were the Springer girls part of it?

He didn't know. His frown deepened as he clicked his pen even more rapidly.

Thinking he was missing something, he flipped through the reports one more time. The neighbor to the north of the McIntyre property owned dogs that had gone nuts around ten-thirty the night before, an event consistent with the time of death. But, of course, that neighbor had seen nothing out of the ordinary. No surprise, as the hedges and fences made it impossible to peek into the abutting yard.

Another neighbor three doors down had spotted a dark pickup on the road, but that vehicle belonged to one of the lawn care companies who serviced the neighborhood. The truck had broken down and was later towed—all legit.

Hayes stretched his neck and rotated his shoulders in an attempt to dispel some of the tension mounting in his upper back. Between his caseload and his ex-wife's most recent custody demands, he needed a break. He used to have time to run or play pickup ball, but lately he'd been too busy to squeeze in a workout.

He reviewed the information he knew about the McIntyre murder. The department had gotten the call around eight in the morning, when the maid had found a very dead Shana McIntyre face up in the pool. The maid had dialed 9-1-1; a uniformed cop had responded, then called in RHD.

Hayes and Bledsoe had caught the case and arrived about the same time as SID, the Scientific Investigation Division, rolled up. Of course a T.V. camera crew showed up shortly thereafter.

Shana McIntyre hadn't just hit her head on the side of the pool, though there was blood on the tile near the stairs. The bruising at her throat and other evidence suggested that she'd been attacked.

Later, while searching the place, they'd found his-and-hers laptop computers in the den. The pink Mac had been logged onto Shana's calendar, where Bentz's name had appeared in capital letters.

"Interesting," Bledsoe had remarked. "The guy's in town less than a week and three people are dead. Two vics of the Twenty-one and now this woman has him on her calendar. Bentz is batting a thousand."

Hayes hadn't been so quick to judge. "You don't think he had anything to do with the Springer twins' murders."

Bledsoe had glowered at Shana McIntyre's monitor. "Didn't think so. But this one . . ." He'd scratched at his chin and looked up over the rims of his reading glasses. "I don't know. Look, I've never pegged Bentz as a killer. But something's off, Hayes. You and I both know it, and somehow it's connected to the fact that good ol' Ricky Boy is back in L.A."

On that point, Hayes didn't disagree.

The husband, Leland McIntyre, who drove back from Palm Springs, had seemed genuinely upset. He had an alibi, but then murder-for-hire wasn't an impossibility. An insurance broker, Leland McIntyre had taken out a whopper of a policy on his wife, over two million dollars. Then there was the list of her ex-husbands and the previous Mrs. McIntyre, Isabella, who, if you could believe the neighbors, had held a grudge against Shana for stealing her husband. It was hard to tell. There were so many ex-wives and husbands in the mix, it nearly took a flowchart to keep them all straight.

And all the suspects from dysfunctional relationships didn't change the fact that Rick Bentz had visited Shana only days before her death. *He's in town less than a week, and she ends up dead.*

The last person to see Shana alive was the gardener, earlier in the afternoon. The final call on her cell phone had been to her husband in Palm Springs. The phone records for her cell, the husband's cell, and the home phone were already being checked.

No signs of forced entry at the house, but the killer had probably climbed the gate and walked around the house. Of course there were four security cameras in and around the house, but they had been inoperable for years.

No break there.

The McIntyre homicide was a tough one, Hayes thought, even if you pulled Bentz from the pool of suspects.

Damned Bentz. He was proving to be a real pain in the ass. Still, Hayes would give Bentz the benefit of the doubt and track down some of the information Bentz wanted. There was a chance it might even help with the case.

Just as soon as he fought his way through the statements and evidence of this latest crime.

He glanced at the clock again and figured it would be a long one. If he was lucky, he'd be home at midnight. Great. He glanced down and a note on his calendar caught his eye: Recital. Oh, hell, Maren was singing tonight at some church near Griffith Park in Hollywood. Hayes had promised his daughter he would attend and he couldn't stand facing her disappointment or Delilah's scowl of disgust. He had to show up. Somehow he'd take off an hour for the kid.

It was, as Delilah was always delighted to remind him, his responsibility.

Montoya was sweating, his muscles aching from running on the indoor track for half an hour, then working out on the weight machines—a new exercise regimen his wife had initiated by giving him a membership to a gym for his birthday. Yeah, it was a great stress reliever, and yeah, he was more toned, but this new "healthy" lifestyle was about to kill him. After all, what was wrong with a smoke and a beer?

On the way to the locker room he waved to a couple of guys he knew, then showered, letting the hot water run over his body before he toweled off. He dressed in khakis and a polo shirt, then slipped his arms through his leather jacket and headed out.

Into the warm Louisiana rain.

Fat drops pounded the parking lot as he dashed to his Mustang, unlocking it with his keyless remote on the fly. Nearly soaked again, he considered driving straight home, where Abby was waiting, but decided to detour to the office to check on the information he'd requested for Bentz. Having seen the press release about the latest L.A. murder, he didn't want to delay.

"Damn," he said, flipping on his wipers. Bentz was in trouble. Montoya could feel it. People were dying. People somehow connected to his partner.

Streetlights glowed, casting shimmering blue pools of illumination on the pavement as he nosed his car into the street and pushed the speed limit, running amber lights, thinking about Bentz in California.

The guy was stirring up trouble.

But then, that wasn't exactly a news flash.

Though Montoya had thought Bentz was out of his mind, the events of the last few days had proved him wrong. Bentz might be stirring the pot, but something was hiding just beneath the surface, something murky and decidedly evil. It was all Montoya could do not to buy an airline ticket and fly out. He had some vacation time he could use. Abby would understand. She always did. But he hadn't been invited. This mess in California was Bentz's private deal. He was figuring out his own past, exorcising his own damned demons. If he wanted his partner's help, Bentz wouldn't be shy about asking.

And yet, what if Bentz needed help and didn't realize it? What if he were getting in over his head. Jesus, the man was an idiot where women were concerned.

Taking a corner fast enough to make his tires squeal, Montoya slowed a bit to call Abby.

"How's my favorite detective?" she asked.

"Fine as ever," he lied.

"Still have a tiny ego, I see."

"It just needs a little stroking."

"Your ego? That's what you're talking about?"

"Naughty woman."

"And you love it."

She was right. They both knew it. "Look, I'm gonna be running a little late," he said as he drove past the Superdome and had to stop for a red light. People with umbrellas dashed across the crosswalk and splashed through puddles.

"Let me guess, Hotshot. You're officially off the clock, so now you're going to work for nothing for Bentz."

"Something like that."

"Should I wait up?" she'd said with a trace of sarcasm.

"Might be a good idea."

"Oh yeah?"

"Oh, yeah." The light turned green. He hung up chuckling. She was the first woman who'd been able to give as well as she got, and he loved that about her. As the police band crackled and the wipers slapped the rain from the windshield, he drove through the city to the station. Easing into an available parking slot, he cut the engine. Turning his collar against the downpour, he raced into the building and up the stairs.

The squad room was quiet, only a few detectives were still working, most having already called it a day. Montoya sat at his desk, fired up his computer, and searched his e-mail for the documents he'd requested.

Sure enough, a few answers had come in, answers he hoped would help Bentz. He checked the wall clock: 8:47, not even 7 P.M. on the West Coast. He dialed quickly and Bentz picked up on the third ring.

"Bentz."

"Yeah, I know." They both had caller ID. "How's it going?"

"Not good. Shana McIntyre was murdered."

"I heard."

"Yeah, well, the LAPD isn't happy." Bentz's voice was tense.

"No one is. Look, I might have some information for you. I'll send it via e-mail, but thought you might want to hear it directly."

"Shoot."

"The long and the short of it is that Elliot, our resident computer whiz, went to town with the information you gave me on the parking pass, partial license plate numbers, and car description."

"Did he get any hits?"

"Bingo. The god of all things technical just sent me the information. Says he sifted through federal, state, and private records to find it."

"Lay it on me."

Montoya scanned the monitor. "So the silver Chevy that's been dogging you could be a vehicle once owned by an employee of Saint Augustine's Hospital. Her name was Ramona Salazar."

"Was?"

"Yeah, that's the kicker. She died about a year ago."

A beat. Then Bentz asked, "What happened to the car?"

"Still registered to her."

"Got an address?"

"Yeah, but it's the old one where she lived when she was still alive. The car could have been sold, but whoever bought it never bothered registering it."

"I wonder why."

"Me too. Someone might be using her ID, or some family member could be driving the vehicle even though it's still in her name."

"I'll find out."

"Good. And I've got some info on a few astrologers named Phyllis, nothing concrete. There's a Phyllis Mandabi who reads tarot cards in Long Beach," Montoya said, checking his notes. "And there was an astrologer who practiced in Hollywood about fifteen years ago—Phyllis Terrapin. She left there for Tucson, got married, and doesn't have her shingle, if that's what you want to call it, out any longer."

"Got it."

"And you shouldn't have any problem finding Alan Gray. He's still a big shot in the Los Angeles area. Got a new firm though, named ACG Investments. He's the CEO."

"Thanks." Bentz said. "I already tracked him to ACG, but haven't figured out what he's into."

"I'll see what I can find out."

"Great. You did good."

"I know," Montoya said, and with a few clicks of his mouse, forwarded all of the information to Bentz's personal e-mail address. He was about to hang up, but said, "Hey, Bentz?"

"Yeah?"

"Watch your ass."

CHAPTER 23

She's dead!

As I shake a fresh pitcher of martinis, I give myself a pat on the back for how neatly the killing went off. Without a goddamned hitch. Despite those miserable yapping little dogs.

That bitch Shana never knew what hit her.

Her reaction, a look of surprise melding into a mask of sheer horror, was priceless. Our eyes met for a heartbeat, then I sent her reeling and fumbling and splashing into the water.

Perfect!

I hum to myself as I add a little vermouth, very dry, just a whiff, then pour myself a drink.

Bentz is sweating now, I know. He's wondering about the trap he's fallen into, searching for a way out. What a joke. His little stunt at the pier followed up by Shana's unexpected, and oh, so unfortunate, death.

"Boo-hoo," I whisper aloud.

Smiling to myself, I dig in the refrigerator, find a jar of olives, and drop two into my glass. Drab green, stuffed with pimento, they dance in the clear liquid and slide to the side. Like little eyeballs staring at me.

"Proud of me?" I ask the drink, then take a sip. "Ummm. De-lish!"

I pluck one olive from the glass and suck the pimento from it, savoring the taste and smell of gin as I walk into the living room and drop into my favorite chair.

I taped the news coverage of Shana McIntyre's death and I play it over and over, listening to that imbecilic reporter, Joanna Quince from KMOL, trying to stutter her way through the story.

"Idiot," I say to the TV, dangling the other olive over my mouth as Joanna tries to pronounce McIntyre. "It's Mac-En-Tire," I say, irritated. I've watched it three times before, waiting for the on-camera flub and it grates on my nerves. "Shana would be soooo upset if she heard you screwing up," I say to Joanna, and that's the truth. Shana was so proud of stealing Leland away from his first wife. It seemed that getting him down the aisle was payback for the same thing happening to her.

"What goes around, comes around," I say, then click off the moronic reporter and think about the next one who will have to suffer a similar fate to Shana's.

It should happen soon, I think, to make my point.

Yes, sooner better than later.

So that everyone understands that the latest spate of killings are not coincidence, that they are directly tied to Rick Bentz.

I already know who will be the next traitor to be sacrificed, and this one will be child's play. It could happen as quickly as tonight.

That's an appealing thought, and it could work. After all, I've planned it for so long. Another long sip of the cool martini. But I'll just have one. For now. Later, I can have another for my next celebration.

I'm tingling inside, anticipation sliding through my body. How long I've waited, but oh, it was worth it. That old quote about revenge being best served up cold was right on the money.

So, so true.

I finish my drink, savoring the last drop. Bottoms up! Lowering the glass, I get to work. I'll need to make a phone call before I leave and then . . . oh, yeah, and then . . .

The fun is just beginning.

Ramona Salazar.

The name rang no bells for Bentz, none whatsoever.

Using his damned cane and feeling his knee twinge, he walked the short distance from the sandwich shop to his motel in the new shoes he'd picked up at a store in Marina del Rey. Like everything else in this part of the world, the loafers were outrageously expensive. He could easily go broke trying to find out if his ex-wife was dead or alive.

At least he had a name to start with, a lead, if a very shaky one. He had spent the afternoon staked out in his motel room between the television and his laptop, taking notes as information about Shana McIntyre was released. Old footage of her wealthy husband had flashed across the screen, and Bentz had taken note, knowing that the husband was always at the top of a suspect list.

But real detective work entailed more than watching news reports on KMOL or Googling Leland McIntyre, and frustration was beginning to burn in his gut. He hated having his hands tied like this. When Montoya had called, he'd been relieved to have another venue to investigate.

Ramona Salazar.

It was already twilight, the sun setting in the west, the noise of the San Diego Freeway resounding off the hills as he reached the parking lot of the So-Cal. Closer he heard the sound of water splashing. He guessed more than a couple kids were in the interior pool judging from the cacophony of the whoops, hollers, and laughter reaching him.

Vaguely he registered that the car belonging to the old man who owned Spike was missing. He hitched his way along the porch, unlocked the door to his room, and walked inside. It was just as uninviting as ever.

"Home," he said sarcastically as he placed his cane near the door and dropped his food onto the desk. According to Montoya, Ramona Salazar had died about a year earlier. Bentz powered up his laptop and opened up some kind of wrap sandwich he'd picked up just before Montoya called. The "Californian," as it was so imaginatively named—a green tortilla slathered in some kind of lemon/Dijon sauce and filled with free-range smoked turkey, whatever the hell that really meant, a slice of pepper-jack cheese, avocados, tomatoes, and sprouts. It was all pretty damned bland, but he barely noticed as he clicked onto his e-mail and found the information Montoya had forwarded.

Sure enough, Romana Salazar was connected to the car, at least he'd hoped this was the right woman and the right car. Otherwise he was back to square one.

He didn't have a printer, but figured he might be able to use the "business office," which was really just a small PC for guests shoved to the side of the registration desk in the So-Cal office. Rebecca would be on duty, and she'd told him he could use the ancient desktop and printer any time. As long as she was around and her son Tony wasn't online playing computer games behind his mother's back.

First up, he thought, connecting with a search engine and typing in Ramona Salazar's name, he'd collect any and all information he could find on the woman, including her obituary.

If he was barking up the wrong tree, so be it.

At least he finally had a scent to follow.

Maren sang like the proverbial lark, her mezzo voice rising to the rafters of the little church in Hollywood. Hayes focused on his daughter's shiny face in the rows of Miss Bette's students as they sang as an ensemble for several songs, harmonizing on an old spiritual, then rocking out with songs from the eighties and nineties. Hayes recognized a few Michael Jackson numbers and a couple by Elton John.

After the group sang and harmonized, each of the students individually sang solos on the small, old-fashioned stage that looked like it had come right off the set of *Little House on the Prairie.*

Hayes had slipped into the little church in Hollywood late, caught a disapproving glare from Delilah, then turned his cell phone to "silent." From that moment on, he'd listened raptly while his daughter, at least in his opinion, outshined everyone.

The singers were all were coached by the same statuesque African-American woman who accompanied each either at the piano or on an acoustic guitar. Hayes suffered through the individual performances. All of the kids could carry a tune alright, but none of them could hope to make it past the first round of an *American Idol* competition no matter what their proud, smiling, nearly smug parents who filled the pews thought. Well, except Maren, of course. She was the star. Hayes figured he was as bad as the other proud mamas and papas, except, his daughter really was talented.

Three boys and four girls each were spotlighted before Maren took on a Toni Braxton song. Hayes watched her, his little girl, only twelve years old, belting out a number like a pro. She'd barely developed, still wore braces, but she was as beautiful as her mother and a helluva lot more talented.

Maren moved to the music, her mocha-colored skin shimmering under the lights. Her straightened hair streamed down her back, and her dark brown eyes seemed impossibly large and expressive in her sweet face. She was tall and thin, like both her parents, her newfound curves in proportion, her dimples "cute" rather than sexy. At least he hoped so.

She sang a soulful rendition of "Unbreak My Heart" that nearly brought down the house, then finished with the upbeat Whitney Houston song "How Will I Know?"

Hayes jumped to his feet and clapped wildly. After the bows and brief words of thanks from Miss Bette, Hayes carried some flowers he'd picked up at Safeway to the stage and handed them to his daughter. Maren's gasp of delight and Delilah's cool look of surprise said it all.

"Good job, honey! You were incredible. Move over, Mariah Carey."

"Oh, yeah, right," one of the other mothers muttered.

"Oh, Dad." Maren rolled her eyes, but she couldn't stop that infectious grin from stealing across her lips. "I thought you were working."

"I was."

"Mom said you wouldn't come."

Hayes shot his ex a quick don't-do-this glare. "Mom was wrong." He hugged his daughter.

"I just didn't want her to be disappointed again," Delilah said.

Hayes wasn't going to be pulled into it. Not here. Not now. "Well, she wasn't. What do you say I take you out for pizza?"

He expected Delilah to argue that it was too late, or that Maren had homework, but instead she stiffly agreed. There was no doubt that she could be a bitch sometimes, but Hayes believed her motives were all about protecting Maren. She might've turned into a grumbling, unhappy, never-satisfied wife, but Delilah was still a damned good mother.

For that, he supposed, he should be thankful.

Once they were outside, he flipped his phone on and saw that he had messages. He was about to answer them when he caught Delilah's meaningful glare. "I just have to listen to these," he said, walking to his car and leaning against the hood. "I'll meet you at Dino's."

"Sure," she said tightly, obviously disbelieving as she ushered Maren to her white Lexus SUV.

The calls were from Riva Martinez. Donovan Caldwell had been phoning the station demanding information on the Springer twins' homicides, insisting that he should be privy to everything the LAPD had on file as they'd "royally screwed" the case of his sisters' murders twelve years earlier.

Hayes called her back on the way to Dino's. "I think you should refer Mr. Caldwell to the Public Information Officer," he suggested.

"Already did, and he told me to go scratch," Martinez informed him. "He's figured out that Bentz is in town again. Caught some write-up online about Bentz's stunt on the Santa Monica Pier. Anyway, this Caldwell guy is out for blood. He wants to talk to Bentz, to Bledsoe, to Trinidad, or anyone associated with his sisters' case. If you ask me, he's a damned psycho."

"He lost his whole family over the bungled case."

"Hell, Hayes, listen to you. We didn't *bungle* it; we just haven't solved it. Yet."

She had a point. Hayes checked his watch. "I'll talk to him. I just can't do it right now."

"Don't worry about it. I can handle him, but I thought you'd want to know."

"I do. Thanks." Hayes hung up and tried to push all the thorny pressures of the job aside. He had more pressing matters to worry about. Pepperoni or sausage pizza . . . and how to step carefully through the verbal minefield of the next hour or two with Delilah.

Bentz hit a dead end.

Ramona Salazar, whoever she was, meant nothing to him, and he couldn't find any association between Salazar and Jennifer. He stretched out on the ugly bed, pointed the remote at the TV, and watched an all-news channel. Again they replayed footage from Shana's house: the ambulance parked inside the gated driveway, the swimming pool from an aerial shot, the McIntyres in happier times. Bentz sank into the mattress with a pang of guilt. If he hadn't come to L.A. would she still be alive? Or was this a random act of violence?

He didn't believe that for a second.

He called his daughter, left a message, and Kristi phoned back within five minutes.

"Hey, Dad, what's up?" she asked.

Bentz couldn't help but smile as he conjured up her face, as beautiful as her mother's. Rolling off the bed, he walked to the window. "Just hanging out." He peered through the blinds to the parking lot where darkness had settled in, the big neon sign for the So-Cal Inn glowing brightly over the asphalt.

"Still in L.A., right? Working on an old case that doesn't involve Mom. Right?" He heard the sarcasm in her voice. "You know, Dad, it's really weird that you can't confide in me. I don't like it."

There was no way out of this. She was too smart and he didn't like trying to deceive her. "Fine, you're right. I'm looking into her death." He picked up the remote and muted the sports report. The basketball players still jumped, but they did it all in silence.

"Why?" Kristi asked. "Why are you doing this?"

"Because I'm not sure your mother committed suicide. I think she might have been murdered."

There was a beat, a pause. Kristi, who was usually quick to rush in, even finish his sentences for him, was uncharacteristically silent. "And why do you think that?"

"It's a long story."

"Five minutes long or five hours long?" she asked as the television flickered noiselessly. "Come on, Dad, give."

"Okay, I guess you deserve to know."

"Duh."

"The truth is, I'm not even sure it's your mom in her grave."

"What! Are you serious?" There was an edge of panic to her voice. "Now you're freaking me out."

No surprise there. It was the reason he hadn't wanted to confide in his daughter in the first place.

"Holy God, not in her grave? What the hell is going on?"

He told her. Starting with the death certificate and the photos he'd received, including the "sightings" of Jennifer or her impersonator, ending up with his jump off the pier and Shana McIntyre's murder. "So that's what I'm doing in Southern California."

"I can't believe this," she said, obviously upset. "I mean, Mom's not alive. You know that, right? We went through all this. I thought you were just tripping on the meds. Come on! If she were alive, she would have contacted us, or at least me. And if you think you're seeing her ghost . . . I guess I can get that," she grudgingly admitted. "It's not like you, but I've seen things I can't explain. I still see images of people in black-and-white and then they die. That's pretty damned eerie. And Olivia, she saw through the eyes of a killer, so . . . just because you saw Mom or thought you saw her, doesn't mean she's alive." She took in a deep breath and he imagined her pushing the hair from her eyes. "I can't believe this."

"I'm just sorting it out. Obviously someone wants me here in L.A. Whoever it is lured me in."

"Why?"

"That's what I'm trying to unravel."

"Well, I don't like it."

He snorted. "That makes two of us."

"You're not like the Lone Ranger, are you? Tell me there are people helping you."

He'd never felt so alone in his life, but he wouldn't admit that. He'd already burdened her with enough difficult information. To worry her further wasn't necessary. "Yep. Montoya in New Orleans and I've still got a few friends in LAPD." He sat on the edge of the bed, ignoring the television and the fact that he was beginning to hate this place. The four walls of the little motel room were closing in on him and he missed his daughter. Missed his wife.

"Who? Who are your friends there?" she demanded, because she'd been old enough to remember when they'd lived in Los Angeles. She knew her father did not leave on good terms by any stretch of the imagination.

"Jonas Hayes, to start with. You remember him?"

"No."

"Well, he's got my back."

"I don't know if I believe you. I assume Olivia knows all this."

He squeezed the back of his neck. "Uh-huh."

"So the daughter is last to know."

"I wouldn't say that."

"I would," she said, steamed.

She was really pissed off. Nothing Bentz could do about it now.

"Is that why you called?" Kristi demanded. "Something about this case?"

He felt the anger radiating through the connection. "I thought you might remember if your mom ever mentioned a woman by the name of Ramona Salazar?"

"Ramona who? Salazar?" she repeated. "No. No Ramonas."

"What about Phyllis?"

"Just the astrologer."

"You knew about her?" Bentz's muscles stiffened.

"Sure. I even called her once for a reading, but Mom hit the roof, thought you wouldn't approve, so I never got the reading and Mom told me to keep it on the down low, that it was 'just our little secret' or some other melodramatic phrase. You know how she was."

Apparently not.

"Jeez, I'd nearly forgotten all about her."

Bentz mentally kicked himself. Of course Kristi would know things about Jennifer that he didn't. Montoya had already mentioned a woman named Phyllis Terrapin. "So, how into this astrologer was she?"

"Oh, it wasn't that big of a deal. Just something Mom did. Like her hair and her nails. I only saw her a couple of times when Mom had picked me up." Kristi laughed. "I called her 'the Turtle' behind her back because of her name and she kinda looked like one, short neck, big glasses. Mom didn't think it was funny, which I thought was weird. She usually had a pretty wicked sense of humor, but not when I teased her about the whole astrology thing."

"Of course she didn't," he said. How many other secrets had mother and daughter shared, secrets he'd been totally oblivious to?

They talked for a while longer, but Kristi had nothing more to add about Phyllis "the Turtle" or anything else he'd been investigating out here. "I'll call you in a few days," he promised, and they hung up. "Phyllis the Turtle," he muttered under his breath. Probably nothing, but he'd check her out.

He stood, stretched out his back, and noticed the remains of his Californian wrap drying out on the desk. He scooped the wilting let-tuce and soggy tomatoes into the white sack, wadded it into a ball, and tossed it into the trash. Then he settled into his desk chair again, placing the laptop on his thighs and turning so that his heels were propped on the bed. This way he could catch the latest TV news and scores as he did his thousandth Internet search.

He'd just typed in Phyllis's name when his cell phone rang again.

Caller ID showed that the phone was registered to L. Newell. Lorraine? Jennifer's stepsister?

He answered before the damned thing rang twice. "Bentz."

"Oh. Hi. It's Lorraine." She sounded tense. Breathless. What was this all about? "I . . . thought you should know . . . Oh, God . . ."

"What?" he asked, his senses on alert, an eerie feeling crawling along his skin.

"I saw her. I saw Jennifer."

Bentz's feet dropped to the floor. He slid his laptop onto the desk. "What?"

"I said I saw—"

"I know, but where? When?" He couldn't believe it. His heart was thudding, adrenaline spurting through his veins, his hands clutching the phone as if it were a lifeline.

"Just a few minutes ago. Here. On my street. In Torrance," she said, her voice quavering. She sounded scared as hell. "In . . . in a gray car."

Really? Bentz was already grabbing his keys and wallet with his free hand.

"I don't think she expected me to be looking out the window."

"Did she see you?"

"I don't think so."

"Wait a minute. You saw a woman who looked like Jennifer in a gray car?" Again, he glanced through the blinds to the dark parking lot illuminated by the motel sign. Something felt wrong about this.

"Yes!"

"How could you see her?"

"Uh . . . the streetlight. The car stopped under the streetlight and she looked right at the house. Right at me."

"Is she there now?"

"I don't know. She drove past slowly, around the cul-de-sac, only three or four minutes ago. I'm frightened. She's dead, Rick. She's supposed to be dead." Lorraine's voice was hoarse with panic. "I didn't know what to do. I thought I should call you."

"I'll be there in half an hour. Sit tight."

He hung up and threw on his shoulder holster, new jacket, and shoes. His cell phone was just about out of juice, but he pocketed it along with his badge. Ignoring the ache in his leg Bentz flew out of the room and into the parking lot. Inside his car, he snapped on the ignition and drove out of the lot, squealing onto the street.

Someone else had seen Jennifer, or the woman who looked like her. Finally.

Once he was on the side street heading toward the 405, he phoned Jonas Hayes.

The call went directly to voice mail and he explained what he was doing.

Then he hit the freeway heading south, weaving through taillights to move ahead, pushing the speed limit. The night was clear and somewhere above the lights of the city the stars shone. He saw the moon and the blink of airplanes cutting across the sky, but his mind was on the phone conversation with Lorraine.

Was it possible?

Was "Jennifer" showing herself? Or casing Lorraine's house?

Or was Lorraine just freaking out?

Imagining things?

Like you? His mind teased while the speedometer inched past eighty.

As he maneuvered around a shiny red BMW another theory struck him. "Damn." Shana was already dead. Could "Jennifer" be looking for her next victim? That thought hit him hard. Was the woman he'd been looking for a murderess? His stomach twisted into a painful knot and he stepped on it, flying past a semi hauling milk and smelling of diesel, just as an idiot on a motorcycle blew by him and the eighteen-wheeler as if they were standing still. The biker had to be doing a hundred, maybe more, cutting through traffic. *Idiot!*

Minutes ticked by and Bentz willed his cell phone to ring. He needed to talk to Hayes, or someone from the department, he thought just as he saw his exit ramp and some girl driving a Honda sped around him while texting. He barely noticed.

Bentz couldn't take any chances with Lorraine's life. There was no way of telling what this "Jennifer" was up to, but his gut told him it wasn't good. As he neared his exit ramp, he slowed and put another message to Hayes's voice mail, asking the L.A. detective to return the call immediately.

Bentz needed this confirmation. That he wasn't going out of his mind. That he wasn't conjuring up and fantasizing about a dead woman. Lorraine's sighting of Jennifer could do just that. At least now, if nothing else, by the time he left Lorraine's place tonight, the LAPD would know that Lorraine had been frightened, maybe even threatened by a woman who resembled Jennifer Bentz.

"Son of a bitch," he muttered, easing down the ramp into a clog of traffic at the stop light. A small man wearing an overcoat, camouflage pants, and a hat with a long feather slowly pushed an overflowing grocery store cart across all the lanes of traffic while Bentz felt time slipping by. Precious time.

At last the man rolled past, the light changed, and the idling vehicles were able to move again. Bentz gunned it, his heart hammering crazily. Fueled at the prospect of coming face to face with Jennifer.

Lorraine Newell knew she was a dead woman.

Shaking, she watched as her assailant, the woman who had held the phone to her ear and a gun to her temple, hung up the phone in her living room. All the shades were drawn. They were alone. And she'd lied to Rick Bentz, begged him to come over. She should have warned him, told him the truth, but she'd been afraid, so damned afraid. Either way this witch was going to kill her.

Trembling inside, she looked at the woman holding the gun on her, the dark, deadly muzzle only inches from her forehead.

"He's coming," she whispered and thought she might pee all over herself. How had she been so foolish to open the door to this woman, to agree to let her use her phone? She was just being a Good Samaritan. She'd wanted to help. When she'd opened the door, handing her phone through the crack, the woman who had pleaded that she'd needed to call a tow truck and that her cell was out of batteries had turned into a demon. She'd slammed the door in Lorraine's face, pulled a black gun from her jacket, and rammed the steely muzzle deep into Lorraine's ribs.

Once in the house, she'd bound Lorraine's hands behind her back, then held the phone to her ear and forced Lorraine to read from a careful script, only improvising when she had to.

And she had.

Oh, God forgive her, she would have done anything to save her life. But it was for nothing. She knew it now.

"You . . . you can leave me out of it," she said, in a desperate plea, sweat running down her back, her insides quivering. "I won't say anything to anyone. I promise. When Bentz gets here I'll . . . I'll tell him it was all part of a joke."

"It is," the woman said cryptically.

"Please."

"Shut up!"

If only she could run. Could knock the gun away. But it was too late. She didn't doubt for a second that this fiend would blow her to kingdom come.

Without a modicum of mercy her captor snatched the paper away—the script she'd forced Lorraine to read. Lorraine had searched the woman's face for a shred of compassion, a crack in her icy veneer. But the woman's expression was stone cold as she then prodded Lorraine forward, down a short hallway, and into the kitchen.

Where it was dark.

Oh, God.

There had to be a way to save herself. Had to!

"Move!" she ordered, the unforgiving nose of the pistol hard against Lorraine's back.

Tears ran down Lorraine's face. Her heart, beating so rapidly, so erratically, felt as if it would explode. She said a silent prayer, begging God for mercy.

"Please. Don't do this," she whispered, physically quaking with fear. She didn't want to die. Not now. Not this way. She was too young, had too much to live for. "Please," she begged, desperation cracking her voice. "I won't tell a soul. I swear. You can trust me."

"Shhhh. It's going to be all right." Slowly her attacker ran the cold muzzle of the pistol up Lorraine's spine, from the small of her back to the base of her skull.

Where it stopped.

Oh, sweet Jesus!

In that horrifying second Lorraine knew it was over.

Nothing she could do or say would change this demented criminal's mind.

She closed her eyes just as the gun blasted.

CHAPTER 24

Something was off.

Way out of kilter.

Bentz felt it in the air, in the silence of the night. When he pulled up in front of Lorraine's home the street was empty—no silver Chevy prowling the neighborhood. A few lights glowed from the tri-level house, but the curtains were drawn. Hadn't Lorraine said she'd seen Jennifer from her window? Worse yet, as he approached he noticed the front door was ajar.

Had she left it open for him?

No way. When he'd talked to her, Lorraine had been scared out of her mind. Every muscle in his body tensed. "Lorraine," he called, slowly and silently withdrawing his weapon from his shoulder holster. "Lorraine? It's Rick Bentz."

Silence.

Carefully, sensing danger, he nudged the door further open with his weapon, and hearing no sound from within, slipped into the house. Lights were on in the living room, and he stiffened at a subtle movement across from him until he realized that it was his own reflection in the mirrored wall. The room was empty, a book facedown on the worn green sofa.

"Lorraine?" He listened but heard nothing.

Moving silently through the hallway toward the back of the house, Bentz passed an empty dining room with mail piled on the table. As he approached the darkened kitchen he smelled it.

The distinctive, metallic odor of blood.

His stomach dropped to the floor.

Bracing himself, he stepped into the kitchen doorway and caught a glimpse of feet, one slipper kicked off, poking out from behind a cabinet. He stepped closer. Her body lay facedown, blood matting the back of her head.

Lorraine.

Bile crawled up his throat. Bentz flicked on the light and quickly checked to make sure the room was empty before kneeling at her side. But he knew she was dead. He felt for a pulse.

Nothing.

"Holy Christ." This was his fault. He knew it. "Son of a bitch." Yanking his phone from his pocket, he dialed 9-1-1, identified himself, and gave the dispatcher the pertinent information.

Who had done this to Lorraine?

No doubt the same person who had offed Shana McIntyre. The connection was obvious: Rick Bentz.

And Bentz knew he was the cause. The catalyst. "Jennifer" had shown herself to Lorraine, knowing full well that Lorraine would phone him. Then, after Lorraine had reported the sighting, "Jennifer" had killed her with flawless dispatch. Even now she could be watching, enjoying the show.

Twisted bitch.

Though he sensed that the house was empty, the murderer long gone, he couldn't be certain. He hung up and checked the rest of the house. Moving carefully, trying not to touch anything or disturb any fingerprints or evidence the killer may have left behind, he searched closets and did a perfunctory check of the back deck, but the perp had fled the scene. Of course. Bentz put in another call to Hayes and left his third message within an hour, then returned to the living room. A loud, unworldly screech reverberated through the room.

Bentz ducked behind the hallway wall, then peered out in time to see a gray cat streak from the back of the couch and bolt behind a plaid upholstered chair. From behind the worn cushions it hissed, glaring at him with glittering gold eyes.

Bentz's skyrocketing pulse slowed a bit. He'd forgotten Lorraine had always kept cats, having seen no evidence of the animal when he'd visited.

Shaking inside, craving a cigarette, he waited outside on the porch near a grapefruit tree. His leg throbbed and he tried to maintain calm by focusing on the sounds of the night. Over the buzz of insects and the barking of a dog a few streets over, the wails of sirens split the night air. Good. He shoved his hair away from his face, noticing a nervous neighbor peeking out at him through blinds.

The show's about to begin, he thought while a jogger ran past the entrance to the cul-de-sac. His eyes followed the movement. The runner was a slim woman—or was it a man?—in a baseball cap and dark clothes. No reflective gear. She glanced toward him, but she was too far away to see her features.

Yet, there was something about her that seemed familiar.

What? The thought stopped him cold. *Familiar? Are you out of your mind? You can't even make out the runner's gender. Get a grip, Bentz, and figure this thing out before another one of the people you interviewed winds up dead. Think, for God's sake. You're going to have to answer a lot of questions.*

As he watched, she turned down a side street. Maybe she'd seen a silver car cruising the neighborhood. "Hey!" he called after her, but she was too far away. He'd never catch her on foot, and he couldn't leave in the car. Not after calling the cops, who, by the sound of screaming sirens, would arrive within the next thirty seconds.

Forget the runner for now.

Bentz turned off the voice in his head and, still longing for a cigarette or a stiff drink or both, walked toward the curb.

Why had Lorraine phoned him?

Had she really seen Jennifer?

Or was it all a ruse?

He stared down the dark street where the runner had disappeared just as flashing lights strobed the night and a police cruiser screamed around the corner.

Who had killed Lorraine?

Jennifer?

Bentz knew in his gut that Lorraine's murder had everything to do with the death of Shana McIntyre. Both women were dead because of their relationship to his ex-wife. Both women were dead because of him. Because they'd spoken to him. Guilt squeezed the breath from his lungs. If he hadn't called them, hadn't shown up on their doorsteps, would Shana and Lorraine be alive today?

Bentz rose as the police car screeched to a stop at the curb. Two

Torrance police officers exploded from their vehicle and wheeled toward him.

"You Bentz?" the driver asked, a young buck with his weapon drawn. His lips were tight, his eyes narrowed, suspicion giving him an edgy appearance.

"Yeah. I'm a cop. New Orleans PD. My firearm is in my shoulder holster. Badge in my wallet."

"What happened here?" the second cop asked, a woman as intense as her partner, her gun pointed dead center at Bentz's chest.

"Shooting. Looks like a homicide." The words rolled off his tongue, business as usual. So cold and routine, Bentz thought. But you knew her. You knew this woman. "She called me . . . was scared by something she saw. I came right over, found her dead."

"The vic inside?"

"Yeah. In the kitchen. Back of the house. It's clear, aside from a cat."

"I'm on it," the woman cop said as the wail of another siren cut through the night. She took off for the house.

Across the cul-de-sac a neighbor, a fat man in a tight sweatsuit, drifted onto his front porch, to eye what was happening while the male cop still kept his weapon at ready.

"Don't move," the first cop ordered Bentz. The muzzle of his pistol didn't waver. "'Til we sort this all out, I don't want you to friggin' breathe."

Olivia clicked off the television, stretched on the parlor sofa, and whistled to the dog. She'd stayed up later than usual, watching the end of a sappy movie she'd seen twenty years earlier.

Upstairs she changed into her nightgown, noting in the bathroom mirror that her body showed no signs of pregnancy. She was just turning down the bed, wishing Bentz were home, when the phone rang. "Speak of the devil," she said to Hairy S, who was poised to jump onto the mattress. "Only someone on the West Coast would call after midnight. Right?"

But caller ID told her it was a restricted call and her insides tensed a bit as she said, "Hello?"

For a second no one responded, and Olivia felt that same drip of fear that was always with her when Bentz was on a dangerous case. "Hello?"

"He's getting himself into trouble," a woman's voice rasped in her ear.

Olivia's scalp prickled. For a second she couldn't speak.

"People are dying," the voice informed her.

"Excuse me? What?" Her heart was suddenly racing, her palms damp. She knew this was the same crank caller who had phoned a few days earlier. The woman intent on rattling her.

"There's been another murder." The voice was little more than a hiss.

"No!" Her stomach hit the floor. Rick? Had something happened to Rick? For the love of God, what was this woman saying? No, no . . . of course the caller had to be talking about Shana McIntyre. Right? "Who is this?" Olivia demanded, some of her fear bleeding into anger.

"Take a wild guess," the sandpapery voice suggested. "Or ask RJ. He'll know."

"Ask whom?"

She heard a hollow, sultry laugh.

Jennifer. Bentz's first love.

"Why are you doing this?"

Click.

The phone went dead in her hand. Olivia felt herself shaking inside, not from fear, but from rage, white hot and seething. A fury so deep it nearly blinded her. To think that someone would dare mess with her husband, then try to intimidate her in her own home. "You sicko," she hissed, wishing she could confront the bitch, then slammed down the receiver.

Incensed, she wanted to punch out Rick's number, then thought better of it. Whoever had called her expected her to go crying to *RJ,* as Jennifer used to call him. The caller wanted Olivia to play the role of the frightened little female.

No way.

Olivia wasn't going to give the bitch the satisfaction.

For now she'd sit tight. But in the morning she would dial her own phone company and see if they could give her any information about this pathetic call. Until then, if the coward called back, Olivia was ready to tear into her.

"Get over it," she muttered, either to herself or her tormentor, she didn't know which.

To cool off, she headed downstairs and double-checked all the locks on the doors and windows. A little obsessive, but it helped her feel safe. Reassured that everything was in order, she climbed the steep steps back to her room, the bedroom she shared with Rick.

She hated to do it, but for the first time in a long, long while, Olivia shut her bedroom window. Somehow it felt like giving in and that really pissed her off, but she flipped the latch, wanting to play it safe. No longer was there a cooling breeze off the bayou slipping into the room, no rustle of the cottonwood leaves, no scent of magnolia drifting inside. Nor could she hear the soothing sounds of chirping crickets and croaking frogs.

Irritated that she had to change her routine for some whacko, she slid between the sheets and patted the mattress. Hairy S didn't need a second invitation. He hopped onto the bed and burrowed deep under the covers to lie unperturbed next to Olivia. "Good boy," she said absently as she scratched his furry little head. He let out a soft grunt of pleasure, but Olivia didn't even smile. She was too aggravated, too frustrated. She thought again of flying to California to tell Bentz about her pregnancy.

She was tired of this separation.

Sick of the secrets.

Maybe she should leave tomorrow. Or at least in the next few days . . .

Plumping her pillow, she decided that first thing in the morning she'd go online and buy herself a damned airline ticket. She'd fly to L.A. and reconnect with her husband. Whether he wanted to or not. That was what marriage was all about, wasn't it? Connection. Communication. Trust. Oh, God . . . she was losing him; she could feel it in the emptiness of their dark bedroom.

But not without a fight, damn it. She wasn't going to give up on him.

She closed her eyes, willing herself to sleep, and was about to drop off when the phone blasted again.

"Son of a . . ."

Before the second ring, she steeled herself for another creepy on-

slaught and yanked the phone from its cradle. "Now what?" she
snapped.

"And I love you, too," Bentz said.

Her heart softened instantly and her throat grew thick at the
sound of his deep voice. God, she missed him. "Hey," she whispered,
tears burning her eyes. Good Lord, she was acting crazy. Tears? It had
to be her hormones, right? But it was just so damned good to hear
his voice. Clearing her throat and pushing herself to a sitting position, she asked, "What's going on?"

"Nothing good."

Her heart turned to stone.

"I'm at the Torrance Police Department."

"Torrance?"

"Yeah. I thought you should know. Hear it from me."

"Hear what?" she asked, suddenly frightened.

"Oh, Jesus, Livvie, it's a mess," he said and she heard the weari-
ness in his voice. "I got a call from Lorraine, Jennifer's stepsister, saying she'd spotted Jennifer outside her house. I drove down there
and when I got to the house, Lorraine was dead. Homicide."

"Oh dear God," Olivia whispered, holding the phone against her
head in one hand, twisting the covers with her other. This couldn't
be happening. Couldn't! "Jennifer?" she asked, but felt the truth hit
her deep inside. Jennifer Bentz, real or imagined, ghost or person,
was behind the carnage.

"Who knows?" He explained the events of the night while Olivia,
feeling cold as death inside, listened, trying to concentrate while
feeling as if a vise were tightening around her chest. Though she no
longer had visions of murders from the victim's eyes, she still felt the
mind-numbing dread run through her as she thought of the dead
women and the torture they'd gone through.

Bentz was saying that his friend Jonas Hayes had driven down
from L.A. He'd been sympathetic when Bentz had complained about
having his firearm confiscated and being forced to endure questioning in the interrogation room. For the first time in his life, Bentz had
been questioned on the other side of the mirrored window.

The Torrance police had believed his story, though there were still
a lot of questions in the air because Bentz had visited both Shana and

Lorraine in the past week and since then both women had been murdered. Bentz was, without too many doubts, under suspicion.

Olivia felt sick inside.

". . . it took hours," he said, his voice tense with a hardly-restrained anger, "to explain about the whole Jennifer-thing and how someone wanted me in the L.A. area, the murderer most likely, so he could start his rampage. The long and the short of it is, I'm being used as the excuse, or even motive, for the killer to strike."

"Wait a minute. You're saying you think Jennifer or whoever is impersonating her is killing people and trying to make you look like you're involved?"

"That's about it."

"Good Lord, Bentz. That's not only far-fetched. It's just plain nuts."

"And would take incredible planning, as well as luck." He paused as if thinking things over. "Look, as I said, I just wanted you to hear it from me, rather than from someone else or on the news. Once the media ties Shana to Lorraine to me and Jennifer, things are really going to heat up." He hesitated and she imagined him running one hand in frustration through his thick hair, his eyebrows drawn together, his jaw set.

"I'm glad you called. I've been worried."

"Is that why you answered like you did?"

"Wait? What? How did I answer?" she asked.

"Like you were all pissed off. What was that all about?"

She hadn't wanted to confide in him, to worry him, but since he asked, she saw no read to lie or sugar coat what was going on. "Well, Hotshot, you weren't the first call I had tonight."

"No?"

She wanted to lie to him. The last thing he needed was any more stress, but she already felt guilty enough about keeping the news of the baby a secret. They couldn't have any more secrets between them. Their relationship was fragile enough already. "My favorite prank caller phoned earlier tonight."

"Who?" His voice was low. Hard.

"I don't know."

"The same woman who called before?"

"I think so. No caller ID and she didn't say who she was."

"Damn it, Livvie. You can't stay there. Not alone."

"This is my home. And besides Hairy S—"

"Is useless. We've had this conversation. I'm coming home now . . . Or tomorrow. With everything that's going on here, people being killed, I don't like the fact that you're alone."

"It's all happening in California, which is, what? Fifteen hundred miles away? Someone committing murders in L.A. isn't dangerous to me."

"It's a plane ride."

"But you're in L.A. She won't leave."

"Humph." He hesitated, as if tossing that over in his mind.

Olivia finally reached over and flipped on the bedside light, and the dog crawled upward, his wet nose peeking out of the covers.

Bentz asked, "So what did she say when she called?"

"That 'he's getting himself into trouble.' I figured she meant you, since she called you RJ. And then she said there was another murder. I thought she was talking about Shana."

"Not likely. She was probably patting herself on the back for Lorraine. Damn it, I just don't understand what she's doing."

"No one does, but you will. You're like a dog with a bone when you go after something."

"What time did the call come in?"

"After midnight, maybe a quarter to one. I'd stayed up watching a movie. Just a minute, let me check." She hit a few keys on the phone pad, read the display for the restricted call, then clicked back to him. "Yeah, twelve fifty-two, I was just going to bed. The call was short. Twenty-eight seconds. I plan to call the phone company in the morning to find the source of the call even if the number is restricted."

"Good idea, but I still think you should leave."

"It's the middle of the night. I've locked up, double-checked the windows. Besides, the murderer is in California. You have more to worry about than I do."

"There's a pistol in our room. Locked in the closet."

"I know."

"Get it out and keep it in the nightstand."

"Rick—" she protested. Now he was beginning to sound crazy. "I don't even know how to shoot it."

"It's easy. Aim. Pull the trigger."

"After I load it and flip off the safety."

"You lied; you do know how."

"But—"

"Humor me. Just until I get home, okay?"

"And when will that be?"

"Soon," he vowed, conviction ringing in his voice.

"Okay. Good. We have a lot to talk about."

"I know." He hesitated a second. "Be safe, Livvie. I love you."

A pang of emotion tightened in her chest. Stupid tears again stung her eyes. "Love you, too. *You* be careful."

She hung up and stared at the ceiling. Maybe she should have begged him to give up his damned quest and come home. Not that he could now, with those women he'd talked to now murder victims. Unfortunately, he needed to stay there. She wanted him to finish whatever it was that had drawn him to L.A. Then he could come home for good and she'd tell him about the baby. Not before. She knew that if she had mentioned her pregnancy he would have been on the next plane home. If that were the case, he would always regret that he hadn't been able to find out what the hell had happened to Jennifer.

She switched off the light.

Olivia wanted this murderous, heart-wrenching rampage over. Forever. Never did she want Bentz to have regrets, to think he'd abandoned someone who needed him, to wonder if he'd left a part of him, his heart and dreams, in sunny California.

She needed all of him, or none of him. She wasn't willing to settle for second best to his ex-wife.

Jennifer.

"Damn you," Olivia whispered to the empty, dark room. How the hell did Bentz's ex-wife figure into all of this?

She rolled over and stared through the window to the inky Louisiana night.

Bentz needed to finish this. Put Jennifer's damned ghost to rest.

Before anyone else died.

Before Olivia lost him forever.

CHAPTER 25

"I already told all this to the Torrance police," Bentz said as he drove Hayes back to Parker Center, where Hayes had left his SUV.

It was pushing 3 A.M. Bentz, tired as hell, drove along Sepulveda, then eased onto the 110 heading north. Despite the late hour the freeway was still busy, red taillights glowing on the gently sloping lanes ahead.

Hayes had come with Riva Martinez, who had joked that Hayes picked the absolute worst time to turn his cell phone off. "Better late than never," Bentz had told the LAPD detectives, grateful that they'd responded at all. If they hadn't shown up, Bentz would probably still be at the Torrance Police Station, shifting uncomfortably on the wooden chair in that damned interrogation room.

At least they hadn't cuffed him. After handing over his gun to the first-responding officers, Bentz had been detained at the crime scene, where he watched as the cops had put up barriers, roped off Lorraine's home, and interviewed the neighbors who had drifted onto the sidewalks.

Once the neighbors had emerged, the cul-de-sac's glum mood had taken on a surreal note, a carnival atmosphere colorful enough to rival the amusements on the Santa Monica Pier. Gathered under a streetlight, decked in bathrobes and sweat suits, flip-flops, and fluffy slippers, residents gossiped among themselves. Smoking and shaking their heads, they eyed the emergency vehicles with wry speculation and offered to give statements to the cops.

Bentz had overheard many of their comments about Lorraine.

"A lovely woman," an elderly woman had intoned.

"A good neighbor," a man who lived next door had said. The Owl, Bentz dubbed him, with his round glasses, a thin beard, and a dour expression. "I just can't believe that someone broke into her home. This is a nice neighborhood. Safe." The Owl paused as the gurney and body bag rolled past. "I mean, it always has been."

Another woman had put in her two cents' worth. "Don't know a lot about her. I think she was married once." With a cloud of white hair and a matching bathrobe, she'd introduced herself as Gilda Mills, had lived in the neighborhood twenty-seven years. Nervously, she'd stared at Lorraine's home as if it were the den of the devil. "But I'm not sure." Gilda's bony fingers were forever at the side of her mouth as she said, "No kids, at least none that she ever spoke of. She had a half sister. No, I think it was a stepsister who died. Committed suicide or something . . . oh, dear, I really can't remember." She had taken two steps away from the curb, seemingly afraid that whatever evil lurked within might ooze over the lawn and onto the toes of her pink slippers.

Bentz had inwardly groaned when the news van had arrived. Fortunately Hayes and Martinez had pulled onto the cul-de-sac a few seconds later. A lanky twenty-something reporter for the television station had taken notice, smelling a story as he recognized the cops from L.A. outside their regular jurisdiction. Watching as the reporter tried and failed to get a statement from Hayes, Bentz had realized he was just too damned tired and shell-shocked to find it amusing.

Soon thereafter Bentz had been escorted to the station in Torrance, where he'd spent three hours answering questions and waiting in the interrogation room. The lieutenant had explained that they needed to do a quick background check on Bentz, verify that he was an officer in good standing with NOPD and that he had permission to carry a firearm. Although the cops had treated him with respect and professionalism, Bentz had not liked spending time in the perp's seat. Not even for one minute.

Hours later, the lieutenant finally had told Bentz he was free to go. About damned time, Bentz had thought as he holstered his firearm and signed the receipt for his possessions. By the time Bentz had climbed behind the wheel with Hayes in the passenger seat, it was after 2 A.M.

"Just humor me by going over it one more time," Hayes said, bringing Bentz back to the here and now as they sped along the freeway in the darkness. Bentz had cracked the windows so that the night air rushed in, cool and bracing. Something to keep him awake. "Tell me what happened tonight. Start with the facts. Then your take on it."

"First I got a call from Lorraine Newell, Jennifer's stepsister." Bentz was sick to death of going over the same information, but now that Hayes was ready to listen to him he would churn through it one more time. One more round to enlist Hayes's help.

Staring through the bug-spattered windshield, Bentz recounted the night blow by blow, from the minute he got Lorraine's call to the nightmare of finding her body on the kitchen floor. He even added in the fact that Olivia had been the victim of harassing phone calls since he'd traveled to the West Coast. "It's a female caller and she refers to me," Bentz said. "Calls me RJ just like Jennifer did. It's meant to spook Olivia."

"Does it?"

"Not much. Mainly pisses her off."

"Sounds like your kind of woman."

"She is," Bentz agreed. "But it worries me. I'm going to call Montoya and have him keep an eye on her until I get home."

"She probably won't like having a keeper."

"Doesn't matter." It was the best he could do for now, though it didn't seem like enough. He'd never forgive himself if Olivia got dragged into this mess. He couldn't have his wife in danger. Spying the sign for his exit, Bentz pulled into the right lane.

"You saw a jogger." Hayes stared out the window to the lights of downtown Los Angeles, where skyscrapers rose into the blue-black sky. "Same guy you saw the night you jumped off the pier?"

"One was a man; the other a woman."

"You sure? You said they were both slim and athletic. Both wore baseball caps, no hair showing."

That much was true. And he had questioned the gender both nights. "Could go either way, I guess."

"I got the tapes from the Santa Monica Pier webcam."

Bentz, easing down the ramp, slid Hayes a glance. "*You* got them? And I didn't? When I was the one who requested them?"

"The company that owns them wanted to go through the local police and the Santa Monica PD called me."

Burned, Bentz asked, "See anything interesting?"

"No woman in a red dress, not for two hours before or after. No woman matching Jennifer's description, but all the other players were in place. The old man smoking his cigar, the guy and the girl sucking tonsils, and a jogger. The runner didn't just pass by, but stopped and stared the length of the pier about the time you were running along the boardwalk. That, in and of itself, isn't a big deal. I didn't make anything of it until you mentioned seeing a jogger tonight."

"Could be a coincidence."

"Could be, but something's going on."

"That's the understatement of the year."

"Okay. Something *big's* going on. And I don't put much stock in coincidence."

"Me, neither."

"So it all seems to be about you and your first wife." Hayes rubbed at his jaw, pinching his lip as he thought. "Why now? Why would someone wait twelve damned years to get back at you?"

"I wish I knew." Bentz slowed for a red light at the end of the ramp.

"I'll want all the info you have. Everything."

"It's yours."

"And you'll have to stand down."

"Don't know if I can do that."

"Look, let's get real. The department's still gonna consider you a person of interest and really, you can't blame them. You can't compromise our investigation, Bentz. You know that. No detective works his own case. And as it is Bledsoe wants to rip you a new one."

"He's always ready to rip someone a new one. May as well be me," Bentz said philosophically, though there was an edge in his voice.

"Be that as it may, everyone in the department agrees that you showing up in L.A. triggered some of these homicides. We need to sort everything out."

"It's about time," Bentz said, thinking that finally, with the help of the department, he'd get some answers. Hopefully before another person ended up dead.

"So you talked to Shana McIntyre and Lorraine Newell since you've been in town. Anyone else?"

Bentz nodded, one step ahead of him. "I also spoke with Tally White, an old friend of Jennifer's. A schoolteacher. They met through the kids. Tally's daughter Melody is the same age as Kristi. I also got in touch with Fortuna Esperanzo, who used to be Jennifer's friend. They worked together in an art gallery in Venice. Fortuna is still employed there."

"And that's it?"

"Yeah," Bentz said, fighting off a feeling of foreboding. "I've got information on them at the motel. We could swing by and I'll give it to you."

"Let's do it."

Bentz moved into the next lane so that he could take the 405 toward Culver City. Despite his exhaustion, adrenaline fired his blood and he knew that he wouldn't be able to sleep. Nor would he really stand down. He would continue to pursue his investigation, steady and low key. He wouldn't impede the LAPD's work, but he intended to stay abreast of their progress. It would be easy enough to do. He still had Montoya and a few other friends back in the New Orleans Police Department, people who were willing to check files and run facts for him, stay on top of what was happening here. Hell, Montoya lived and breathed for this kind of shit.

Hayes could tell him to back off all he wanted, but Bentz wasn't stopping now. Not when the stakes were rising, lives were being brutally ended, all because of Bentz.

Two women were dead and now his wife had been harassed. Threatened. His grip clenched hard over the wheel. The truth of the matter was, Bentz was scared to death, and the only way he knew to shatter that fear was to cut to the source.

Find the killer.

But, for now, he'd at least appear to play by the rules. He turned onto the street that led to the So-Cal Inn. The lights of the motel blazed bright in the night, casting a glow over the cars parked in the lot. Bentz scanned the cars parked there, noting that all the regulars were present as he pulled into his slot and cut the engine. "So looks like you just caught a new case," Bentz said, pocketing his keys. "What are you going to do first?"

"Eat some crow." Hayes threw Bentz a dark look. "I hate to say it, but looks like you were right. I think the first step is to exhume your ex-wife's body. Let's see who's in that casket."

Fortuna Esperanzo was an insomniac. Sleep forever eluded her. Her mind would never slow down enough, was forever spinning. Even with a deluxe personalized mattress, the ambient sound of a tiny waterfall trying to soothe her, and heavy draperies that completely blocked out all traces of the Southern California sun, she never slept well. Tonight she'd given up the fight after a few hours of restlessness and taken the sleep medication her doctor had prescribed. Now she was drifting off at last, falling to a level of sleep so relaxing that she didn't hear the sounds of her own snoring. But she felt her cat, Princess Kitty, move on the bed beside her.

Groggily, not even bothering to check the clock, Fortuna rolled over, unconcerned by the white Angora's antics. Nocturnal by nature, Princess Kitty had been skittish ever since Fortuna had found her wandering the streets of Venice, her long hair matted, her tiny body thin as a rail. That had been twenty-one years ago and the cat was still going strong, jittery and nervous as ever.

Suddenly Princess Kitty hissed.

What? Fortuna pulled herself from the thick veil of sleep.

A growl and another hiss.

"Shh," Fortuna said, forcing one eye open just as the cat jumped off the bed. What the hell was the matter with Princess? "I'm not letting you out."

She caught a whiff of something sweet and cloying, and her skin goose-pimpled.

"Kitty?" she said, her voice trembling, fear clutching her heart.

That awful smell! What was it? Gas? Oh, Lord, was there a gas leak in the house?

Was there someone in the room with her? Oh, God no! She strained to see, but she wasn't wearing her contacts and the room was nearly stygian, pitch black. She couldn't make out anything but darkness, black on inky black.

Did something move by the closet?

The hairs on the back of her arms lifted. She reached for her cell phone, which sat charging on the night table.

At that second, she felt rather than saw movement. Whatever was there leapt across the short span of tiled floor to the bed.

Fortuna started to scream. To move.

But she was pinned face up on her bed, a body in black holding her down, a cloth that reeked of that horrid smell forced over her nose and eyes. She gasped, dragging more of the foul stuff in.

Ether!

Panicked, she flailed her arms and legs, trying to rid herself of the weight straddling her. Her heart was racing, beating a thousand times a minute as terror gripped her entire body. She had to fight this! But the hand over her face wouldn't budge and Fortuna was out of breath, the insidious gas flowing into her lungs with every gasp. Scared out of her mind, she dragged in a long breath of the sickly sweet fumes and, oh . . . It made her mind swim, made her limbs feel so heavy.

She couldn't black out now. Wouldn't!

Frantic, she kept fighting, trying to roll away from her assailant's viselike grip. To no avail. The person, strong and lean, didn't budge, just kept applying pressure.

The fumes were horrible, burning down her windpipe and into her lungs, searing her throat.

Why? Fortuna wanted to scream. *Why are you doing this to me?* But she knew deep down this attack had to do with Rick Bentz's visit and all his questions about Jennifer. Nothing good ever came from that woman, even though she was long dead.

Supposed to be dead.

Fortuna had known she shouldn't confide in Bentz. Some secrets are better left unspoken. *Fool!* Fortuna's arms moved more sluggishly. Her legs felt like lead, and blackness pulled at the corners of her subconscious.

Move! Fight! Don't give in! her brain screamed at her, but her muscles refused to listen, her arms barely twitched. It was all she could do to keep her damned eyes open despite the terror that invaded her body and soul.

"Nighty-night, bitch," her attacker whispered.

Fortuna felt the sting of a needle pierce her bare arm. *Oh, God, please . . . no . . .*

But it was too late.

Fortuna sensed her body sink into the mattress as her attacker sighed. A sigh of contentment. Fortuna imagined her assailant was smiling, though she couldn't see anything, her eyelids were so heavy, so damned heavy.

Her languid mind swirled slowly with bits of thoughts, fragments of fear as she stared up in the darkness, trying to get a glimpse of this person pinning her to the mattress.

But it was too dark. Too hard to stay awake. She needed to sleep. Fortuna gave in to the overwhelming desire and let her eyelids ease shut as her assailant slid off the bed.

Fortuna tried to move.

Couldn't.

Not even when she felt her skimpy nightgown being slid over her head. *Oh God, I'm going to be raped*, she thought, but found she really didn't care. Her pulse was slowing . . . the drug oozing through her blood. The prayers of her youth came to her, prayers she hadn't uttered in twenty years . . .

Our Father, who art in heaven, hallowed—

And then she felt herself being dressed. As if God had already responded.

From the red pain in her eyelids she knew there was light in the room now as the intruder slid a garment over her head, pulled her arms through sleeve holes.

Why?

This is crazy.

Or maybe she was hallucinating, feeling the effects of the drugs flowing through her bloodstream.

She felt a slim ray of hope pierce her heart. Perhaps there was a chance she wouldn't die after all, she thought, fighting to stay awake. Her attacker might not want to do her ill. Surely this person who was lifting her off the bed and carrying her through the house was an angel of mercy.

Yes, that had to be it.

Surely she wasn't going to be trussed like this if the intent was to kill her. If death were the objective, certainly she'd already be dead.

There are worse fates than a quick death, her mind warned, but the thought was fleeting.

In a heartbeat she slid completely under the welcoming blanket of unconsciousness.

CHAPTER 26

Bentz woke up with a bitter taste in his mouth and a strong re-solve to get home in his gut. What the hell was he doing in Los Angeles when Olivia was being threatened in New Orleans?

He'd only gotten a few hours' sleep, but in the light of day the cheap motel room looked more alien and inhospitable than ever. Why was he still here, chasing some impersonator when his wife needed him back home, was possibly in jeopardy?

Still in bed, Bentz reached for his cell phone on the nightstand and called Jonas Hayes. The call switched to voice mail, and he left a message that he was out of here, headed home. Easing out of bed, Bentz knew it was the right thing to do, the only thing to do.

He dragged himself into the shower and stood in the hot stream of water, ignoring the razor. Then, feeling almost alive, he wrapped a towel around his waist and started slamming clothes into his bag. He knew leaving L.A. wasn't a great idea. It would look suspicious if, after all his protests about being innocent, he took a jet out of California the day after Lorraine's body had been discovered.

Too bad.

He'd spent most of the night and the early morning hours laying out his notes at Hayes's office in the Center. So now LAPD was offi-cially in charge of the investigation of Jennifer's death. Jonas had made a copy of everything, including his photographs, his list of Jennifer's acquaintances, plate numbers, addresses, and phone contacts. Bentz had given them a blow-by-blow of the events that had happened since he'd landed in Los Angeles less than a week earlier.

"You sure cut a big swath," Bledsoe had observed, his smile

twisted when he'd arrived for the morning shift. "Anyone who talks to you ends up dead."

"Up yours, Bledsoe," Bentz had said, his hackles up. "Do you honestly think I'm stupid enough to kill Lorraine, then call the police?"

"I just think you bring a string of bad luck, that's all." Bledsoe had backed down a bit.

Dawn Rankin had showed up at the station just as Bentz had been leaving. She'd managed a cool smile that didn't quite touch her eyes. But that was expected. She and Bentz had been lovers and their breakup years before hadn't gone well.

At all.

Their affair had been hot, stormy, and cut short because of Jennifer. Dawn had never forgiven him and made no bones about it. That she had smiled at all was something.

While at the station he'd also passed on the name of Jennifer's dentist, in case Hayes could manage to get the body exhumed. Finally, some progress. Now, rubbing a towel over his wet hair, Bentz wondered if Jennifer's X-rays would match the teeth of the remains buried in that coffin. One way or the other at least one question would finally be resolved . . .

Before crashing this morning Bentz had called Montoya and left a message asking his partner to check on Olivia until he returned. Then Bentz had put in a call to Melinda Jaskiel, his superior, asking for home surveillance. Though he and Olivia lived outside the city of New Orleans' limits, he had enough friends in the department that someone would check on her.

Olivia would be mad, of course. She thought she could handle herself, but things were getting dangerous and he didn't like the thought of her being alone, even if she was nearly two thousand miles away from the recent killings. Before falling asleep early this morning Bentz had thought that would cover things, take care of Olivia.

But no, after a few hours he realized he needed to get home, needed to make sure Olivia was safe. It wasn't that he wouldn't return to California, but for now he needed to physically reassure himself of her safety. Who knew what this psycho had in mind? The psycho who'd reached out to Olivia over the phone . . .

He wasn't going to take any chances.

He would fly home and see his wife in the flesh. Make love to her.

Reaffirm his life with her. He even thought fleetingly of her need to have a child and did the mental calculations all over again. Hell, he'd be over sixty when the kid graduated from college.

So what? You can retire in ten or fifteen years and enjoy watching the kid grow up. Would that be so bad?

No. But the truth was he couldn't imagine retiring any more than he could wrap his mind around starting all over again with a baby.

He finished packing up his gear, placed his shoulder holster and pistol inside the bag with his clothes, then unhooked his computer and slid it into its case. The last thing, of course, was the damned cane. He wanted to throw it into the trash, but instead hauled it with him. With one last cursory glance around the shabby room, he closed the door.

After checking out of the motel, he drove to LAX through traffic that slowed and stalled while the Pacific sun battled through the smog to beat through the windshield. Time seemed to stand still and he was crawling out of his skin.

Now that he'd made the decision to return home, he found himself impatient, anxious to get there. Some of his irritability could be attributed to lack of sleep, he supposed, and the fear that two women had just died because he had come to Los Angeles. But truth to tell, his underlying sense of urgency was all about seeing that Olivia was safe.

The minutes dragged, but he finally saw the airport tower, then Encounters restaurant, the landmark for LAX. "It's about time," he muttered under his breath.

He turned in the rental car and hauled his things into the terminal to buy his ticket. Inside, the terminal was crawling with travelers, the lines to the counter snaking around to the door. *Serves you right for not buying a ticket online,* he thought.

Bentz told himself to hold on, be patient. He'd get on the next plane, though the only daily nonstop flight had already departed. He chose the airline on which he'd flown west, getting into what had seemed a short line. But, of course, there was a holdup. Slowly he inched forward behind a woman in tight jeans and a short jacket, a cell phone glued to her ear, a designer bag at her feet. Every so often she would nudge the carry-on forward with the pointed toe of a boot. The protest from inside the bag came in the form of a nasty little yip. "Just a sec," Tight Jeans would say into the phone. Then she'd look down at the bag and coo, "It's okay, Sherman."

Sherman didn't think so and yapped all the louder. Through mesh in the top of the bag, Bentz watched the dog spin crazily within his confines as Tight Jeans went back to her phone conversation. It would be just his luck if dog and owner ended up flying to New Orleans in the seat next to him. Not that it really mattered, as long as he got home.

The woman in front of him reached the ticket counter and clicked off her phone. "*We've* got a big problem," she began, her tone already a challenge. "This ticket is all wrong. If I connect through Cincinnati, I won't get to Savannah in time for my cousin's rehearsal dinner. I need a direct flight."

"I don't think we have any directs to Savannah, but let me see what I can do," the rep for the airline said and began typing on her keyboard.

Bentz shifted from one leg to the other and glanced down the length of the crowded terminal, past knots of people lugging backpacks, roller bags, or suitcases. A teenager toted an odd-sized guitar case while three men pulled what appeared to be golf bags. Near the doors, an attendant pushed an older man in a wheelchair past a solitary woman standing before the departure and arrival information board. Her face was tipped up as she searched the monitors. A beautiful familiar face.

Bentz froze.

She was the spitting image of Jennifer.

Don't even think it!

But she stood there, eyeing the large screen through her sunglasses.

No way. Not now.

"No, that won't work, either," Tight Jeans was whining as if from a distance as Bentz squinted, trying to control his thundering pulse.

He told himself he was imagining things, conjuring up her image because he was leaving town. But as he stared the tanned woman with her coppery-brown hair pulled into a ponytail glanced toward him, the hint of a smile on her lips.

His felt as if a ghost had walked across his soul.

Then she turned and walked briskly in the opposite direction. White shorts, pink, tight, sleeveless T-shirt, shimmery flip-flops.

It could be anyone. A tourist on her way to Disneyland. Someone picking up family members. A woman waiting for a delayed flight.

Or someone pretending to be Jennifer. His long-dead ex-wife.

"Son of a bitch," he said under his breath and broke away from the line to follow her. He couldn't let her get away now—this imposter who'd been playing with him. Especially now that she was linked to the deaths of at least Shana McIntyre and Lorraine Newell, maybe even the Springer twins.

She looked over her shoulder again and his heart nearly stopped. If she wasn't Jennifer, she was his ex-wife's long-lost twin.

He dropped his cane near a trash receptacle and walked even faster, keeping up with her long strides as she disappeared amid a cluster of travelers. Faster and faster, pulling his damned roller bag with the computer case balanced atop it as she headed for an outside door. He wanted to drop his luggage, but couldn't. His gun was tucked into his bag and he couldn't risk leaving it.

She slipped through a group of Asian tourists moving down another terminal.

"Oh, no you don't," he whispered, keeping her in his sights. Adrenaline surging through his blood, he wended through the throng of travelers, cutting between a handful of Goth teenagers and a matronly woman with cheetah-print bags.

What the hell was "Jennifer" doing here?

Reeling you in, you moron. It's no coincidence that she's here at the airport, waiting in the same terminal. She had it planned.

But how had she known he'd come? What was this ridiculous cat-and-mouse game? The bait. The tease. Never letting him get too close, always lingering just out of his reach.

Murder, Bentz. She's up to her beautiful eyeballs in murder.

She made it to the exterior doors, but Bentz was gaining on her, breathing hard. He was nearly jogging now, his heart pumping, his eyes trained on her. Without a word he swept past an airport police officer. He didn't want to draw any attention to himself. He couldn't risk being hauled in and questioned all the while knowing "Jennifer" was slipping away.

Nu-uh.

This time he was going to catch up with her.

Come hell or high water.

His damned leg was beginning to throb, but he gritted his teeth. As soon as the door closed behind her, he stepped through and dragged his luggage over the rough cement of the passenger pickup area.

Where the hell did she go? He stared past the smokers, the weary travelers sitting on benches, the people talking on cell phones and waiting for their rides. Airport security attendants waved cars on, trying to keep the traffic moving.

Then he spotted her, crossing to the short-term parking lot. She moved out of the shade and into the bright sunlight. Bentz hurried after her, nearly tripping as his bag caught on the edge of the curb.

"Hey!" he shouted. But she strode on, cutting through the parked cars baking in the sun, not once looking over her shoulder. "Hey! Jennifer!"

She sped up, digging inside her purse. A moment later keys flashed in her hand.

Bentz scanned the parking lot ahead and spotted the car—the silver Chevy Impala with a faded parking permit.

Ignoring the pain in his leg, he sprinted now, his luggage jerking along beside him. "Stop!"

Frantically, she was unlocking the door.

Dropping his luggage beside the Impala's bumper, Bentz lunged and stripped the keys from her hand. "Not a chance." Breathing hard, he stared at her through sweat beading between his brows.

Who was this woman, this younger version of his ex-wife? Flesh and blood; no unearthly wraith.

She tried to get by him, but he blocked her exit by filling the space between her car and the minivan parked next to it. "Who the hell are you?" The smell of her perfume, gardenias, permeated the air and messed with his mind, but he refused to be seduced by the past. He was putting an end to this game, here and now.

She turned her beautiful face toward him and his insides turned to jelly. She looked so much like his ex-wife, she could have been Jennifer's identical twin. Except that she was too young.

"I need my keys back," she said firmly, without fear.

"Not yet, lady." He grabbed her arm and held on tight, wanting to shake the truth from her.

"What's your problem?" she asked.

"You are."

"Me?" Her eyes narrowed in a scowl as she deliberately pulled her arm from his grasp.

For a millisecond he wondered if he'd made a mistake, if she really had no idea that she resembled Jennifer so closely. Except that she was in the same damned car he'd spotted in San Juan Capistrano and on the freeway. This woman had been dogging him.

"Give me back my keys," she demanded as a man walking toward his car, jacket tossed over one shoulder, eyed them suspiciously.

Realizing that he might appear to be assaulting her, Bentz released her arm but stood his ground. "You're not going anywhere." He pushed her keys into his pants pocket.

"Do I have to call the police?" she said, and the man in the distance slowed down to watch.

"Great idea." He pulled out his badge, flipped it open. "I *am* the police."

That seemed to satisfy the man, who slung his jacket under one arm and kept walking. "But then you know that, don't you?" Bentz pressed her.

Her glossy lips turned into a pouty frown.

"Hey, if this badge isn't good enough, then we'll talk to someone from L.A. Fine with me. We've all been looking for you."

"Then you already know who I am?" she asked, one eyebrow lifting over the frames of her sunglasses.

"I know that you're trying to play some sick mind game with me."

"Is that so?"

"You've been taunting me, trying to make me think you're my dead ex-wife."

"You sound like a lunatic. Give me back my keys."

"Not on your life."

He flipped up her sunglasses and found himself staring into eyes as green and vibrant as Jennifer's. And yet something was off, something not quite right.

His heart was pounding in his eardrums, a million questions sizzling through his mind. Who was she? Why was she doing this? Where had she come from? "Two women are dead because of you."

Something flickered in her eyes and she pulled back slightly. "What? Dead? No."

"Shana McIntyre, killed in her pool. You heard about it, right?"

She seemed genuinely shocked. "You think that I . . . ? Oh, God, no. I had nothing to do with that."

"And Lorraine Newell. You remember her?"

The look she gave him was blank, as if she'd never heard of the woman.

"She's dead, too. Took a bullet to the head last night. Just after she called me about you. She spotted you last night, right before you killed her."

She seemed slightly unnerved. "I don't know anything about that."

The faint trembling of her lower lip was convincing. But then he'd had a taste of her acting ability. "You and I, we need to go downtown."

"What?"

"There are some people you need to talk to. Detectives who have some questions for you."

She closed her eyes a second. "Listen RJ, I—".

"Why do you call me that?"

Her smile faded, and for a second she became Jennifer again. "Because it's what I always called you. Don't you remember?"

He almost bought her act. Almost. But he couldn't believe her gall. "Are you really still trying to make me think you're her?" he asked, dumbfounded that she would try to keep up the ruse. "Why the hell are you doing this? Why are you haunting me? What do you want? Why did you show up at my house?" Although Bentz was usually taciturn, preferring to let a suspect ramble on and on while he sat quietly, he couldn't keep the questions that had been plaguing him from tumbling out of his mouth.

"At your house?"

"You remember—the cottage outside New Orleans?"

"What?"

"And the hospital . . . You were there, too. In the doorway. When I was waking up from the coma. And then again on the pier in Santa Monica. Oh, and yeah, at the old inn in San Juan Capistrano."

She remained silent as a flock of pigeons scuttled to a landing on the pavement beyond her car. In his peripheral vision Bentz noticed them pecking at the street, then scattering as a car cruised by.

When she didn't respond, he felt his fists clench in frustration. "You've been calling me, harassing my wife, and you're a person of interest in two murder investigations. So that's it. We're taking a ride down to police headquarters." He reached into his pocket for the Impala's keys. "Get in. I'll drive."

"Wait a minute."

"Not comfortable with that, *Jennifer?*"

"I, uh—" She looked away, across the tops of the vehicles, their windshields reflecting the bright glare as travelers scuttled in and out of the terminal.

Could he trust her? *No way!* But there were so many questions . . .

"All right. We do need to talk."

"No shit." He held the keys fast in his hand. His heart pounded like a drum and his thoughts spun in wild circles, nerve synapses jangling. Jesus, she looked like Jennifer. So much. She smelled like her and walked like her and teased like her. "So talk."

A jet thundered overhead, its roar receding as it cut upward through the blue sky.

"Not here."

"Here's fine. Or, better yet, at the station."

"I was thinking somewhere a little more . . . private."

"You've got to be kidding."

"How about Point Fermin?" she asked, and one corner of her mouth lifted in a way that cut straight to his heart.

As it always had.

"Why there?" he asked, but he knew the answer. He and Jennifer used to take road trips past the old lighthouse. There'd been so many lazy afternoons strolling the acres of shaded lawns, finding secluded spots beyond the colorful gardens.

"Because, RJ, it's special for us, isn't it?" she said, her grin widening. "You must remember all the times we drove there, working our way down the coast. The picnics. The sunshine. The lovemaking."

It was true . . . but how did she know? How could she recount the most intimate details of his life?

He squeezed her car keys so hard, the jagged metal edges cut into his palm. Now that he'd met this woman Bentz had more questions than answers.

But that was going to change. Starting now.

"So Bentz is gettin' out of Dodge," Bledsoe said, catching up with Hayes in the stairwell of the stationhouse. "I don't like it."

"You didn't like it when he was in town, either. Face it, Bledsoe, nothing makes you happy."

"The guy's a prick and I wish he'd never shown up. But that was before he was connected to all these homicides. Now, I think he should stick around." They reached the ground level of the station house and Hayes pushed open the door, the warmth of the afternoon a change from the air-conditioned interior of Parker Center. Outside, Bledsoe adjusted the waistband of his pants, hiking them up. Then he shook out a cigarette and offered the pack to Hayes, who declined.

"I quit, remember? When I married Delilah."

"She's history, isn't she? Corrine won't mind."

He let that pass. For some reason Bledsoe seemed jealous of his relationship with Corrine. Why, Hayes couldn't fathom, but Bledsoe's enigmatic motives were usually best left unexplored.

Bledsoe lit up as they walked to the parking lot. "I just don't get Bentz. He flies in here all whacked out about seeing ghosts, hangs out and stirs up trouble, and people start dying. Then, after he's found at a murder scene, he decides to take off. Make sense to you?" he asked, drawing hard on his cigarette. "Or is it just a tad suspicious?"

"It's not like he's skipping the country."

"Nah. Just L.A. And you didn't answer my question."

"I can't." Hayes called over to Bledsoe, who had reached his convertible. Older BMW. The top was down, black leather interior baking in the sun. "You go over any of his notes?" Hayes asked.

"Yeah," Bledsoe said grudgingly. "Saw what he got out of McIntyre and Newell. Looks like they didn't think much of him, either. Our boy Bentz isn't winning many popularity contests, but then he does seem to have more than one screw loose, if you know what I mean."

"Anything else?"

"Just the same info he gave us before. The photographs, doctored death certificate, notes about a silver Chevy with an old parking tag for St. Augustine's, and questions about Ramona Salazar, another dead woman." He took another drag and let out a stream of smoke. "A whole lotta nothing, if you ask me. Unfortunately there wasn't anything linking his being in town to the Springer twins' homicides. At least nothing I've found so far." Bledsoe crushed out the rest of his Marlboro on the pavement, then found a pair of sunglasses in his jacket pocket. He slid them onto his nose. "What I want to know is, if Bentz isn't our killer, then who the hell is? This chick running around the city, chasing after him?"

"Could be."

"The one helpful thing Bentz supplied was the plates and reg on the mystery woman's car. Silver Impala registered to Ramona Salazar."

"I'd like to find that car," Hayes said.

"I'd like to find the driver," Bledsoe amended. "Since the owner's dead. See how Bentz's mystery woman shakes out. Bentz said Lorraine Newell called him last night, claiming she spotted the Jennifer imposter. We're checking the phone records now, but he's too smart to lie about that. So, how did the murderer anticipate that?"

"Maybe the killer was there. Maybe it was a ploy to set up Bentz."

"Have Newell call him, then off her?"

"He claims someone's playing head games with him."

"Head games my ass. They're fuckin' with him big-time."

Hayes couldn't agree more. He loosened his tie and squinted at the passing traffic. "You know we're having him followed."

"A lotta good that'll do. So he goes to the damned airport. Turns in his car." Bledsoe shook his head. "Talk about a waste of department funds. Better call our guys back." Bledsoe opened the door to his car and slid inside. "You know, Hayes, this is all off. Nothin' seems to fit. I talked to Alan Gray, another name on Bentz's list. He's in Vegas this week, had a hard time even remembering Jennifer Nichols Bentz." He glanced up Hayes. "But then, a guy like that, with all his money, probably has more women than he knows what to do with."

"Maybe."

"Can't expect him to remember them all."

"Sure you can."

Bledsoe fired up the BMW's engine. "I should be so lucky."

"Sometimes more women means more trouble."

But Bledsoe didn't hear his words of wisdom. He was already backing up to head out of the parking lot.

Hayes unlocked his 4Runner remotely, then climbed inside. He folded the sun visor and tossed it into the back, started the engine and adjusted the temperature as he drove out of the lot. He'd already phoned Fortuna Esperanzo, gotten no answer, and left a message, then contacted Tally White. He had set up a meeting with her later this afternoon.

Afterward, if things went well, he would be back in Culver City at the cemetery.

All the paperwork had been filed, the red tape cut. Jennifer Bentz's former dentist was sending her records over. It looked like Bentz was finally going to get his wish of having his ex-wife's body exhumed.

God only knew what they'd find.

CHAPTER 27

Through the window, Olivia noticed a patrol car rolling slowly along the country road that ran past her home.

Out here. In the middle of no-damned-where. The road was quite a distance from the house, barely visible through the trees, yet she recognized that the cruiser belonged to the City of New Orleans.

Great. So Bentz was running a security patrol clear out here. While he was looking for his damned ex-wife in California.

After she'd told him she'd be fine. She grabbed the phone and placed a call, but, as expected, he didn't pick up. *Typical.* Whenever he was on a case, he was hard to reach. That part she understood. His whole fascination with the ghostly Jennifer was the thing that bugged her.

Yet he'd obviously called in a few favors to have the police drive by the house. He was just such a control freak when it came to security. No doubt because of his line of work. He'd seen the worst of human nature and cruelty time and time again. Not to mention the times that danger had hit close to home, when she and Kristi each had been victims of madmen.

She sighed, releasing some of her indignation.

Maybe the security detail wasn't such a bad idea.

After all, she *had* received some harassing calls.

She poured herself a cup of tea, walked into the den, and logged on to the computer. She'd already scouted out the best deals on flights to the West Coast and had found one that would be perfect. It left this afternoon, putting her in L.A. around 7 P.M. Just in time to take Bentz to dinner and give him the news that he was going to be a daddy again.

She clicked on the Web site and found the reservation that she'd placed on hold. With another click of the mouse, she purchased the ticket. One more click and the e-ticket was printed and in her hand. She had about four hours to pack and get herself to the airport, and then she was off to Los Angeles.

She'd already asked Tawilda, who knew where the spare key was hidden, to stay at the house for a couple of days and look after Hairy and Chia. The only loose end was letting her husband know she was coming, and that was proving difficult. She'd tried to reach Bentz this morning and had come up dry. He hadn't answered his cell phone and when she'd called the motel, she'd been a little alarmed when the clerk told her that he'd checked out.

Why?

Was he switching to another motel?

Was he coming home?

Or flying off somewhere else?

She didn't want to travel all the way to L.A. only to find out he'd flown to Seattle, or Boston, or Timbuktu. The fact that he'd checked out of his motel bothered her.

She tried him again and the call switched immediately to voice mail.

It was time they had a heart-to-heart. Before he got into too much trouble.

"Oh, Rick," she sighed, carrying her cooling tea onto the veranda. The dog was on her heels, the smell of the bayou thick in the mist rising between the cottonwoods and cypress. A mockingbird was trilling softly, a heavy breeze fluttering the leaves and teasing at her hair.

She loved it here and, damn it, so did her husband.

So it was time he quit chasing after ghosts and come home where he belonged.

Before some other innocent woman was killed.

Montoya couldn't believe his eyes. He stared at the computer screen on his desk and whispered, "Gotcha."

"Got who?" Brinkman asked on his way to the kitchen with his empty coffee mug. He paused at Montoya's desk, his interest piqued.

"Nothing." Montoya wasn't going to confide in the one detective he despised—Brinkman, with his thick glasses and a horseshoe of dark hair around his freckled pate. The guy did his job, but he was a pain in the butt know-it-all. One of those guys who had all the answers. Montoya couldn't stand him. "It's personal."

"Yeah, right. Probably has to do with Bentz getting himself into trouble in L.A." Brinkman's eyebrows arched above the rims of his glasses. "Oh, you didn't think I knew about it? It's all over the department." He snorted in his irritatingly supercilious way, then took the hint and strolled toward the kitchen. No doubt to bug the living shit out of the next person he ran into.

Montoya watched him leave, then cooled off slightly as he looked back at his monitor. There it was, the answer to the puzzle, or at least the start of the answer. Hopefully this was the tiny thread that, if tugged gently, would cause the whole carefully knotted mystery to unravel.

After days of fruitless research, following up on the information Bentz had gathered and looking for a lead, he had caught a break. Court records indicated that Ramona Salazar's next of kin was her brother Carlos.

Carlos Salazar . . . now Montoya just had to find the guy. He checked Salazar's address of record and, when that didn't work, he started sifting through phone and address records. After five calls to people who told him he had the wrong number, he hit pay dirt.

"This is Carlos," a man answered in a thick Spanish accent.

"Do you know a Ramona Maria Salazar?"

"Yes, I was the brother of Ramona, rest her soul," Carlos said without a second's hesitation. "Who wants to know?"

Montoya almost came out of his desk chair. He identified himself, then spoke in Spanish for a few seconds, assuring the man he was a police officer with the New Orleans Police Department. He told Salazar that he was working with the LAPD on a case involving a 1999 silver four-door Chevrolet Impala. That was a bit of a stretch, but the old man seemed to buy it, especially when he gave him the license number. "So, what I need to know is, did you inherit this car from your sister?"

"Sí, I did."

"And do you have that car with you now?"

"Oh, no, I sold it to my cousin's son, Sebastian. For his wife," the old man said.

"Does she still have it?"

"I think so." But he didn't sound sure, as if he were second-guessing the strange caller, worried about giving out so much information over the phone.

"The car is still registered to your sister?"

"I . . . I never bothered with the paperwork. I thought Sebastian would take care of it, but he's very busy . . ." Carlos's voice faded and he sounded even more uncertain now, as if he'd realized he was making a mistake and was going to stonewall any more questions from Montoya.

"It's okay. I'm just trying to locate the vehicle. We think it was used in a crime."

"*Dios,*" Carlos whispered, then turned his head away from the phone and rattled something off in Spanish. It was muffled; Montoya only caught a few words that indicated he was worried. Another voice responded—a woman's voice—but he couldn't make out what she was saying.

After the rapid-fire conversation, Carlos returned to the phone. "I think it is still with Yolanda."

"That's her name? Yolanda?" Montoya quickly wrote down the information.

"Yes, yes, Sebastian's wife."

"Do they live near you?"

"No . . . they own a place in Encino. Look, if there is a problem, you need to talk to them. I have a bill of sale for the car. I have done nothing wrong."

"No problem," Montoya assured him. "Just give me their phone number and address."

Carlos balked. "I don't think I should be talking to you."

"Does your cousin's boy have a problem with the police?"

"No. They are good people. Leave them alone. The deal was legal. I will see that the car is registered." He hung up before Montoya could get any more information from him.

Still, it was a start. Montoya tried to call Bentz with the information, but once again he couldn't reach his partner. Montoya left a short message on Bentz's voice mail and said he'd keep digging. He felt the same adrenaline rush that surged through his blood any time he made progress on a particularly vexing case. Damn if he wasn't getting closer.

For his next trick, he was going to locate Yolanda Salazar.

Could she be the woman who was haunting Bentz by pretending to be his ex-wife?

If so, the jig was just about up.

Make the call, Bentz told himself as he studied the woman who resembled his ex-wife. He should have dialed the police ten minutes ago when he first spotted her. Let them lock her up and end the ruse now.

But he didn't want to let her out of her sight until he had what he'd come for . . .

Answers.

Answers she promised to give him, if he would just indulge her in a short ride.

"If you want the truth, I'll tell you on the way to Point Fermin," she said, folding her arms. "After that, after you and I talk alone, then I'll go with you to the police station. But if you call the police now, I'll lawyer up and you'll never know the truth."

He didn't like it, didn't trust her. "I don't think so." He pulled his cell from his pocket. "I'm calling the cops now. I've got a friend in Homicide who wants to talk to you."

"He can talk all he wants, but I won't tell him anything. Stop the call now, RJ, or else you'll never know." Her lips twisted in that Jennifer way as she pointed at his cell phone. "You'll never know the truth. And it will eat you alive."

God, she knew how to play him.

But then she always had.

Reluctantly, he agreed. After all, he had the gun. She couldn't get away. However, that didn't mean he wasn't anxious, that he didn't hear the nagging voice in his head scolding him for being a fool.

"I'll drive," he said, unlocking her car. "You can ride shotgun." He retrieved his gun and shoulder holster from his bag, strapped it on, then tossed his luggage into the back. As he slid into the driver's seat of her car, he tried not to think of all the things that could go wrong. This was not the way a suspect was transported, but then, here in L.A., he was not a cop working a case. Just a man playing out some surreal nightmare.

She gazed at his weapon and pursed her full lips. "Nice." Her voice dripped sarcasm, but she didn't seem particularly rattled. In fact, he thought as he drove toward the airport exit, she sat beside him with the assurance of a woman who knew exactly what she wanted.

And that made all the more wary. Was she was leading him into some kind of trap?

He had to stay on alert. Ready.

But it was weird as hell. Her profile was so like Jennifer's—straight nose, deep-set eyes, high cheekbones, and sharp chin. She was the right size, too, but she looked as if she was closer to thirty-five than forty-five, and he would have bet that it wasn't due to any kind of plastic surgery.

For the thousandth time he wondered if this whole scenario had been planned, an intricately molded ruse to get him into the car and to Point Fermin. Either way, he wasn't scared. Intrigued, yes. Concerned, definitely. But not in fear for his life, which might have been just plain stupid.

He knew the route from memory, from the many times he and Jennifer had ventured this way. He didn't bother with the freeway, instead driving south on the surface streets to the Palos Verdes peninsula that rose high over the sea.

Beside him, she rolled down her window and released her ponytail, letting the wind rush through her hair. "Remember the lighthouse?" she asked, casting him a knowing look.

His throat turned to sand as he recalled the way Jennifer had stripped off her blouse near the white Victorian house with its distinctive cupola and red roof. It had been twilight in winter, the park nearly empty. She'd laughed at his reaction, then had turned and run barefoot through the trees of the grassy park. By the time he had caught up with her, he had been breathless with exertion and anticipation. There in the shade of a spreading tree they had made love just after the sun had set over the Pacific.

"Yeah, I thought you would," she said with a naughty grin.

How did she know these things? he wondered as he guided the

Chevy up the steep road that wound over the cliffs overlooking the ocean. To the west was the vast Pacific. To the east, huge houses with sparkling stucco facades and swimming pools crowded the hillside.

She kept the window down, letting the soft breeze over the Pacific Ocean seep into the warm car, the wind tangling her auburn tresses.

The ocean was a valley of blue stretching forever west. Sunlight sparkled on the surface, waves rolling and crashing to the shore far below. A few vessels were visible on the horizon.

Bentz told himself to snap out of it; he refused to be a part of her twisted fantasy. He was here to get answers.

"So really, who are you?" he asked, his elbow pressing against his ribs, subconsciously checking the weight of the weapon stowed there.

Over the rush of wind she flashed him a smug look.

"You're *not* Jennifer."

One of her dark eyebrows lifted, silently disagreeing. "Is that what you think?"

"She's dead. About to be exhumed."

She shrugged. "Then you'll know," she said in that breathy voice that could well be his ex-wife's.

Know what? That you're a fraud? He wanted to snap at her, but the salt from the ocean spray and the scent of her perfume gave him pause, brought back vivid memories of a time he'd tried so hard to forget.

"So talk," he said, trying to focus on his purpose. "Who killed Shana McIntyre and Lorraine Newell?"

"I don't know."

"Sure."

"Really," she insisted.

"You're saying their deaths are unrelated to your . . . reappearance?"

"I don't know."

"Well, then, what do you know?"

"That this is getting more complicated than I thought. More dangerous."

"Tell me something I don't already know."

He watched as she swallowed hard, her fingers curling tight over the seat belt. She was finally nervous. Good. Bentz kept his hands steady on the wheel, determined to pin her down.

"How did you know Ramona Salazar?" he asked.

"Who?"

"The last registered owner of this car. How do you know her? How did you get this damned vehicle?"

"It was a gift."

"From whom?"

"A friend."

He snapped out of the fantasy. "Don't do this, okay? No more games. I only agreed to come here with you if you'd talk to me, tell me what was going on, and now you're talking in circles and riddles. Oh, hell, forget it." He dug out his cell phone and speed-dialed Hayes.

"No, don't!" she cried.

"Too late."

Her lips twisted and she shook her head. "Who are you calling?"

"Who do you think?"

"The police."

"Bingo!"

"You shouldn't."

"Yeah, right." He put the phone to his ear and waited.

Hayes answered on the third ring. "Hayes."

"It's Bentz. I've got our girl."

"What?" Hayes asked. "Who?"

"Jennifer. She and I are heading down the coast. To Point Fermin."

"Why the hell are you going there?"

"Just meet us there."

"Wait a second, what is this? What the hell's going on?"

But Bentz clicked off and smiled coldly at the woman. "Better get your story straight, *Jennifer*. You've got a helluva lot of explaining to do."

CHAPTER 28

"Hold on!" Hayes said, pressing on the earbud of his cell phone. He'd been on his way to interview Tally White when he'd caught the call. "Meet you at Point Fermin? You mean on the peninsula?" But Bentz had already hung up. Hayes tried to call him back, but the son of a bitch wouldn't answer.

"Jerk!" Sometimes he wondered why he still had Bentz's back. Bledsoe was right; the guy was a loose cannon.

Hayes made a quick U-turn and received a horn blast from a woman in a gold Mercedes, followed by a quick middle finger from a kid in baseball cap driving a lowrider pickup.

He threaded through traffic on his way to the 110 and San Pedro near Point Fermin, far to the south of the city.

What was Bentz up to, calling in with such disjointed information? Bentz thought he was with *Jennifer?* That was just plain nuts.

Which would be proved in just a few hours when her remains were exhumed.

But maybe Bentz hadn't been able to say what he'd really meant, Hayes thought, running an amber light as he maneuvered his Toyota toward the freeway entrance. He called for backup, though he wasn't sure it was necessary.

"Martinez," she answered.

"Hey. I might need assistance. Not sure yet." He filled her in and his partner let out a low whistle.

"Jesus, Mary, and Joseph. I'm starting to think that Bledsoe's right. Bentz has gone loco."

"I was just thinking the same thing. Just be ready for another wild goose chase."

"Just the kind of thing I love."

Olivia took her seat on the jet, tucked between a bulky man who spilled over into her space and a mother with a squirmy toddler on her lap. The little girl, a dark-haired cutie with big eyes and pigtails, stared at Olivia intently as the mother dug into the diaper bag tucked under the seat in front of them. The guy near the window gazed out the glass while baggage thumped and bumped as it was being loaded beneath them.

Olivia tried calling Bentz one last time, left a message that she was on her way to Los Angeles, and turned off her phone. No use worrying. So he wasn't answering? So what? Nothing new there.

She'd left a message with the motel and with Jonas Hayes, the detective who was Bentz's friend in LAPD. She'd even put in a call to Montoya to tell him what her plans were, just in case Bentz talked to him before Olivia landed on the West Coast. A few minutes later, the plane was pushed back from the terminal. The little girl beside her started to cry, and the big guy by the window held tight to his iPod so he could plug in the second it was allowed.

Olivia leaned back and closed her eyes, felt the little girl brush up against her. She smiled at the thought that in less than two years, she would be in the same position as the somewhat harried mom, searching for pacifiers and diapers, trying to keep the attention of an active pre-toddler.

A little girl?

A boy?

It didn't matter.

In a few hours she'd see Bentz again and give him the news.

Smiling, she found she couldn't wait.

Yes, he might be taken aback, even shocked, but he'd get over it. In the end he would love the idea. And yes, when she saw him he'd fill her in and bring her up to date on what had happened to his ex-wife. Olivia might feel a ridiculous pang of jealousy that he'd spent nearly a week of his life reliving his past with a woman he'd once loved passionately, but she would get over it.

At least they would finally be together again.

And then they waited.

While the big guy next to her sweated and the little girl fussed, the captain announced that there would be a delay. A mechanical difficulty needed to be addressed. Twenty minutes, or maybe a half an hour.

Olivia found her book and opened it. She was anxious, ready to get this trip behind her. Now that she'd decided to fly to Los Angeles to see her husband, she found waiting excruciating.

It's no big deal, she told herself. *Not like an omen or anything. Relax. A few minutes won't make any difference. You'll be with Bentz soon.*

And for that she could suffer the noise and discomfort of a few hours on a plane.

"How's Kristi?" asked the woman who resembled Jennifer.

Leave my daughter alone, Bentz wanted to snarl as his hands tightened on the steering wheel. The Chevy's engine whined as the car sped up the sharp hills rimming the ocean. "I don't think you should bring her up."

"I miss her so—"

"Bull-fucking-shit!" he growled. His voice was low. A warning. "Don't go there. Got it? Do *not* go there. As if you're her long-lost mother." He was beyond disgusted. "Just leave my daughter out of this, you goddamned imposter! Now, tell me why the hell you've been 'haunting' me; what's the point? Who are you and what do you want?"

She wasn't rattled in the least, no sweat on her forehead, no death grip on the arm rest. One side of her mouth lifted in that damnable Jennifer way and she cooed, "Oh, RJ, get over yourself."

He was raging inside, his blood boiling. This fraud had promised him answers, and he was through waiting. "We're done," he said with a finality that must have finally gotten to her. "Hear me. This is over. Now."

"Okay, okay . . . I get it. You want answers. Just . . . just pull over up here. There's a place where you and I went down to the beach, up ahead at Devil's Caldron. Remember."

Jesus, God, how did she know that? He remembered the time, on their way to Point Fermin. Jennifer had teased him by touching him in the car. Hot and bothered, he'd pulled over.

Now this woman was sending him a coy look, as if she knew what he was thinking. Dear God, she was so damned much like Jennifer it chilled him to the marrow of his bones.

"There . . ." She pointed to the sign near the corner. Hands sweating on the wheel, heart thudding, he drove into the turnout perched high over the ocean.

Only one other car was in the lot, an empty white Datsun with a surfboard strapped to its roof. He pulled the Impala beside it, pushed the gear shift lever into park, and cut the engine.

Dust swirled over the hood of the car as, before she realized what he had planned, he reached down and scooped her bag from the floor beneath her.

"Hey!" she protested.

"Just checking your driver's license, Jennifer." He rifled through the purse, his hand closing over a slender wallet. Driven with urgency he flipped the wallet open, only to find it empty. No ID. Not even a credit card. "What the hell?"

She laughed. Raised a teasing eyebrow. "Come on, RJ. You of all people should know that a dead woman doesn't carry identification."

"Son of a bitch," he muttered, tossing the purse at her. Gritting his teeth, he leaned forward and flipped open the glove box at her knees. There had to be a registration for the car. Maybe she'd stashed her license there, too.

But the compartment was empty, skeletal metal and plastic lit by a small bulb.

"Give it up," she advised. "You'll never find what you're looking for." She laughed, deep and sexy and naughty. "You'll never find it because you don't want to face the truth. You don't want to believe that I'm Jennifer."

"I don't believe in ghosts." He slammed the glove box closed. "And I don't fall for cons."

"You did twelve years ago."

In the distance waves crashed, punctuating the sickening feeling in his gut.

"I staged my own death, RJ. I left the suicide note, the whole thing. My life was unraveling and I wanted . . . I needed a way out."

Bentz couldn't believe her. He *wouldn't* believe her. "Then who was driving the car, huh?" he demanded. "Who was wearing your rings? Who am I going to find in *your* coffin? You mean to tell me you found another woman who looked like you, put her in your car, and made her crash?" He shook his head. "Your story is a tough sell." He wasn't buying a single word of her fairy tale.

"But I *am* Jennifer," she said in that tone that sounded so like his ex-wife. "And I can prove it."

"This is gonna be good," Bentz said, shaking his head. "How?"

"You and I first made love on the beach in Santa Monica."

He didn't move as her words rolled over him.

"That's why I jumped off there. I . . . I thought you'd get it. I know you probably thought it had something to do with James . . . but it was because of us."

The temperature in the car seemed to heat ten degrees. No one knew about that first time, long before they were married.

"Face it, RJ," she whispered. "I'm back."

"What?" With a click her seat belt was unhooked and she leaned over, her lips hesitating for just a second, hovering, until she kissed him. Filled with ardor and the desire of youth, she grabbed his head and held him fast.

Images blazed inside him. Wild. Erotic. Sexy. In his mind's eye he flashed on Jennifer's naughty smile, her smooth, fiery skin, the curve of her neck. With the memories came the pain, reminiscences of the nasty way she cut him down, her secret, haughty way of diminishing him, the way she'd so brazenly taken lovers . . .

God, he'd loved her.

And he'd hated her.

But this woman wasn't Jennifer.

With that realization his erotic fantasies turned hollow and cold.

What was he thinking? Who was this fake?

In a split second he thought of Olivia, the woman who fired his blood and interlaced his dreams. It was Olivia's face he saw in his mind, an image of blond curls, sexy pink lips, whiskey-colored eyes that could gaze deep into his soul. A simple brush of her finger against his nape could make him hard and wanting.

Disgusted, he pushed the imposter away.

"Something wrong?" she asked.

"Everything."

She smiled then. "You are so right."

With a click, her door popped open and she was outside in a heartbeat.

"Hell," Bentz growled, unbuckling his seat belt. After fumbling with the handle he threw the door open and burst out of the car.

"Wait!" he yelled.

But she was already running toward the brush, disappearing down a path.

"Shit!" He took off after her, his leg throbbing as the soles of his shoes slid over the sandy pavement.

"Wait!"

Damn it all to hell! He ran after her as she disappeared over the edge of the cliff, her feet kicking up dust.

"Son of a bitch!" Bentz was on her heels, but slipped at the first turn, his new shoes giving him no traction on the steep gravel and dirt trail cut into the hillside.

He caught himself, but felt something pop in his bad knee. Pain exploded up his leg.

Great.

He kept running, agony searing his muscles.

Gritting his teeth, he pursued her, wincing and limping and cursing as he half ran, half slid down the path with its sharp switchbacks.

Somehow, he kept her head in his sights, her coppery hair glinting in the sunlight.

"Stop!" he yelled into the wind, but she ignored his order and continued to descend the hillside, down the treacherous trail.

Cursing himself for being a dozen kinds of fool, he followed. Bentz knew he was losing ground, but he would catch her on the beach. The strip of sand at the base of the cliff was a small crescent, one end cut off by the point where tidal waters swirled and crashed, the other end a wall of rock leading up to the cliff. The only land access to the beach was via this slippery path.

Once she got down there, there was no escape. No exit. She would be trapped and he would haul her ass into the nearest police station.

Ignoring the pain in his leg, he scrambled down, following until she was nearly out of sight. "What the hell is your game?" he wondered aloud, his jaw tight.

He caught a glimpse of her approaching one of the lower switchbacks on the trail. The precipice at that turn was so dangerous that a platform had been constructed, complete with safety railing. From that point tourists were able to look down to a spectacular view of the roiling sea in the cove known as Devil's Caldron.

He was gaining again.

Saw her reach the platform.

Panting, pushing himself, he hurried faster.

Ahead of him, she paused, waiting at the platform. For a second he thought she was waiting for him. Then, to his horror, she swung one leg over the railing.

Oh, God, what was she thinking?

But he knew.

Holy Christ, he knew.

"No!"

His heart clutched as she climbed onto the railing and perched on the edge, high above Devil's Caldron.

Oh, no. Please. He skidded to a halt, watching in horror. "Don't!"

She looked over her shoulder and blew him a kiss. Then she turned back to the ocean and lifted her arms over her head, poised like a ballerina. A moment later she jumped, her body a tiny needle of a woman soaring down past the cliffs. Bentz forced himself to watch as she disappeared from view and fell into the roiling furious tide far, far below.

CHAPTER 29

It was like watching Jennifer die all over again. Bentz stared into the churning waters, feeling sick as he clutched the railing. His heart was pounding, his mind screaming. Why had she jumped? Why?

His gaze scraped every inch of the shoreline and water, trying to locate a trace of her—a scrap of pink or white bobbing on the angry swirling surf so far below.

No. For the love of God . . .

"Hey!" he heard from somewhere, as if through a long tunnel. "Hey!"

Blinking, trying to focus, he turned and saw someone running down the hillside. No, two people. A long-haired boy in his twenties and a leggy girl chasing after him.

"I saw her jump. Jesus Christ, she jumped!" the boy said, his face red from the run, his eyes round with fear. "Is she okay?"

"She couldn't be," his companion said. "I mean, it's got to be fifty feet."

"More. Maybe seventy-five!" The kid was emphatic and ran to the railing, even if he was a poor judge of height. Then he noticed Bentz's gun. "Oh, whoa . . ." He stopped abruptly, raising his hands. "Easy, man."

"I'm a cop," Bentz said, digging out his badge and flipping it open. Something he'd done hundreds, maybe thousands of times, but today it felt awkward, surreal, as if he were watching himself. "Rick Bentz. New Orleans Police Department." His own voice sounded disembodied. He kept looking down at the surf. Surely she would surface. She had to. But his gaze scoured the raging tide, rocky shoals, and sweep of beach.

Nothing.

The boy said, "Oh, so . . . like you were chasing her. She was a criminal?" Obviously the kid wasn't buying it.

"From New Orleans?" his girlfriend said as she stepped behind her boyfriend and peeked coyly around his shoulder.

If you only knew, Bentz thought wearily and reached for his cell, his gaze still on the ocean. *Where the hell are you? Come on!* Silently he willed her to surface, to live, this woman he'd already buried.

"No service down here, dude," the kid said eyeing Bentz's cell. "You have to go up top to connect to a tower."

Bentz nodded, but he couldn't drag his eyes from the sea and the surging waves pounding the shore, sending up clouds of spray. Holy God.

There was no sign of anyone in the surf.

Once again, like the night in Santa Monica, "Jennifer" had disappeared. "Damn it all," he muttered between clenched teeth, then turned to the boy and girl and tried to concentrate.

"What's your name?" he asked the kid.

"Travis."

"Good. Here, Travis, take the phone, climb up to the top, and call 9-1-1." He slapped his cell phone into the kid's hand. "Tell them what happened, that a woman jumped into Devil's Caldron, then if they want to keep you on the line, stay. If not, hang up and speed-dial number 9. It'll connect you to Detective Jonas Hayes, a friend of mine and a detective for the LAPD. Tell him what happened here and that I won't be making it to Point Fermin. Tell him we need a search-and-rescue team. ASAP!"

Travis nodded, obviously relieved to have something to do, anything to help.

"But where are you going?" the girlfriend asked Bentz.

He nodded toward the swirling sea below. He knew it would be fruitless, but he had to try and find her. She couldn't have just vanished. No way!

Montoya's diligence was finally rewarded.

He'd spent so much time on the Internet and phone to California that his shoulders ached from inactivity. But it had paid off. He glanced to the window and saw that it was dark, most of the detectives from the day shift long gone.

But the long tedious hours had been worth it, he thought now, twisting the kinks from his neck.

Earlier, through the California DMV, he'd located several Yolanda Salazars who resided in Encino.

He'd weeded through them and zeroed in on the woman he was looking for. Just like Carlos had told him on the phone, Yolanda was married to his cousin's boy, Sebastian. He'd pulled all the records he could on her, found her to be clean, a student at a junior college, studying accounting while she paid the bills as a hairdresser.

But the bit of information on Yolanda that caught Montoya's attention was her maiden name. According to her marriage license she was born Yolanda Filipa Valdez.

Valdez? His heart skipped a beat as he made the connections. He leaned back in his chair and clicked the pen he was holding as a copy of her California driver's license appeared on the screen.

A pretty woman. Thirty-two, according to the driver's license. A model citizen.

Nothing to make her suspicious whatsoever.

Aside from not registering her car, which wasn't that big of a deal. But there was another piece to the puzzle, a factor that made the lack of registration more interesting.

Yolanda just happened to be the older sister of Mario Valdez, the boy Bentz accidentally shot while he was still working for the Los Angeles Police Department.

Montoya clicked his pen again, put in another unanswered call to Bentz and Jonas Hayes, the one detective Bentz felt was on his side in L.A.

Montoya considered flying out to the West Coast to help, then discarded the idea. Bentz was a grown man, able to handle his own problems, even if people were dropping like flies around him. He'd figure it out.

If he needed help, he'd call. Right?

He stared at the picture of Yolanda Valdez Salazar. "What's your deal?" he asked the image. Did she look enough like Bentz's wife to fake him out? Had she been involved with the deaths of Shana McIntyre and Lorraine Newell? He clicked his pen again and eyed the screen.

And what about those twins who were killed? Was she the master-mind behind the double homicide that looked, on the surface, iden-tical to the murders twelve years earlier? She would have been around twenty when Mario was killed, and the same age when the first dou-ble homicide was committed. *Younger* than her victims.

"Nah," he said aloud, leaning even further back in his chair and frowning. That didn't add up.

The picture on the screen just stared at him blankly. A killer? The mastermind behind the entire Jennifer Bentz haunting?

If so, she would have had to have made a trip or two to New Or-leans to "appear." He figured he'd help the L.A. cops out and check her credit card statements, find out if she'd taken a trip to the Big Easy any time in the last year. And then he'd e-mail all the information he'd gathered about the woman to Detective Jonas Hayes of the Los Angeles Police Department.

He smiled, imagining that he was tugging on her string a bit, un-raveling her master game. "It's over," he told the image on the com-puter monitor. "You screwed with the wrong guy."

"So what the hell happened here?" Hayes demanded over the rush of the surf and wind and the steady whomp, whomp, whomp of the Coast Guard helicopter hovering high overhead.

"I wish I knew." Bentz felt numb inside, disbelieving. They stood on the sand, the afternoon sun warm and bright as a crowd of rescue workers scoured the roiling waters of Devil's Caldron. The California Highway Patrol was coordinating the search with the Coast Guard.

"But you're saying that this woman jumped into the water from up there?" Hayes pointed at the platform some forty feet above the water swirling in the cove.

"Yes." Bentz eyed the decking with its railing from below, seeing the posts and beams that supported the platform as it jutted over the cove.

"No one could have survived that."

A muscle in Bentz's jaw worked. He wanted to protest, to think that the woman was alive, that her leap into the churning waters wouldn't have taken her life.

He'd already explained his conversation with her, but of course he would have to make a formal statement to that effect. Hayes had asked him the reasoning behind the aborted drive to Point Fermin. He'd questioned how Bentz had been fool enough to get into the car with her.

A good question.

Bentz had thought about everything that had happened in the last few hours, turning the events over and over again in his mind. But he had no answers as to why the woman had finally let him approach her, only to elude him here. For the past two hours he'd scoured the rocky shoals, beach, and tidewaters hoping against hope that the woman who'd sworn she was Jennifer had survived the horrifying descent to the cove. But so far no one had found any sign of her.

"So where's the body?" Hayes was saying, staring out to sea. "Shit, we'll have to send divers down if the Coast Guard doesn't come up with anything. *If* they can even get down there. Shit."

Bentz reached down and cupped a handful of sand, thinking that she could not have disappeared without a trace, without leaving behind a patch of clothing, a trace of hair or skin. How was it that this woman defied all laws of forensic science?

"Nothing more we can do," Hayes said, shaking his head. "Okay, let's get out of here."

As they headed to the trail, Hayes couldn't help lecturing Bentz. "So you get into a car with her. Taking a little afternoon drive? God almighty, Bentz. I guess we're lucky she didn't take you over that cliff with her. But I don't get this woman trailing you, then disappearing. And why is it that this ghost of yours is so hell-bent into diving into water?"

"She's not a ghost," Bentz said as they started up the steep incline to the parking lot. "And I don't know." He was hobbling as he climbed the path, his knee and thigh on fire. No doubt he'd reinjured himself.

"When we get to the top, I'll need your weapon," Hayes said. "Just to make sure it wasn't fired."

"It wasn't."

"Just the same."

"Yeah, I know."

It took nearly fifteen minutes to reach the parking lot. Bentz was sweating, his leg throbbing. He eyed the silver car that Jennifer had driven, the one "Jennifer" had said was a gift. Everything about her story was all smoke and mirrors, nothing being what it seemed. The police had already roped the vehicle off, a tow truck on its way to take the Chevy to the police garage where it would be examined thoroughly.

His cell phone beeped, and he realized he had several messages. Mostly from Olivia, the last stating she was on a plane to Los Angeles. "Damn."

"Bad news?"

"Olivia's on her way. Her flight lands in a couple of hours. I need to pick her up at LAX."

"I don't think that we'll be done in a few hours," Hayes said. "There's a lot to go over. And I know she's coming in. She called me, too, when she couldn't get hold of you. We're sending a cop to pick her up. She can meet you at the Center, if you want. Afterward, I'll take you to rent a vehicle."

"Or she could rent one herself."

Hayes waved off the idea. "No, her pickup is all arranged. And I left her a message. You might want to call her and explain."

Bentz started to dial just as he heard shouts rising from the beach below. Turning, they saw the Coast Guard helicopter hovering over one spot in the ocean where a diver bobbed in the water. Bentz's stomach turned over.

Hayes's gaze was fixed on the basket that was slowly being lowered from the chopper to the ocean's surface. Squinting, his jaw tight, he stated the obvious: "Looks like they found Jennifer."

Sherry Petrocelli answered the phone and confirmed that she would pick up Rick Bentz's wife from LAX. She was off duty, but hey, she owed Jonas Hayes a favor or two. Not that she gave a damn about Rick Bentz. She didn't know the guy, but she'd heard the rumors, and now that he was back in Los Angeles, all hell seemed to be breaking loose.

The truth of the matter was that she wanted to be transferred to RHD, and Jonas was her "in." Her friend and fellow officer Paula Sweet had assured her that Jonas had the keys to the kingdom; he was well respected in that division, and his input and recommendation would help her land the transfer. She also knew Corrine O'Donnell, who was dating Jonas, and Corrine had agreed that Hayes could help. So if hauling Bentz's wife around was a way to get closer to homicide, so be it.

But first, she was going to dinner. Olivia Bentz's plane was delayed, so Sherry figured it was fine to meet her friend at Bruno's, an Italian spot in Marina del Rey, not too far from the airport.

They split a fried calamari appetizer, then Sherry ordered spaghetti with clam sauce. Throughout the meal, she ducked outside to make a couple of phone calls, checking in with the sitter and tracking the progress of Olivia Bentz's delayed flight. She didn't even have a sip of wine, opting for sparkling water, just to make certain she didn't mess up. If this was a step to improve her career, she was taking no chances.

So it really pissed her off when she started to feel sick.

Surely not the clam sauce or the fried squid. She'd never had a reaction to seafood in her life.

But her stomach was acting up, her head a little light.

"Wow," she said. "I feel like crap." She drank more of the sparkling water, hoping to settle her stomach.

"Let's get out of here," her friend said, then tossed back the remains of her martini. "Come on. I'll buy." She flashed Sherry a smile and dropped some cash onto the table. "But next time, you're on."

"Okay." When Sherry stood up, her legs were wobbly, her head spinning. Almost as if she were drunk. Which was crazy. And then there was the stomachache. She walked out of the restaurant unaided, but when she reached her car, she knew she couldn't get behind the wheel. "Oh, man, I can't drive," she said, pissed as hell.

"I can take you home."

"But I'm supposed to be at the airport in less than an hour."

"You want me to do it?"

"Oh, God, no." They were outside and even the fresh air coming off the ocean didn't help. That salty, fishy smell . . . If anything she felt more nauseated, her legs more unsteady.

"How about if I drive you?" her friend offered.

At first Sherry thought the whole idea was odd. "You would do that?"

"Why not?"

"I don't even know if I'll be able to go in and get her."

"Don't worry. I'll take care of it."

Sherry, sweating now, didn't argue as she fell into the passenger seat. God, she felt awful. "Maybe you should just take me home." She even thought about a hospital, but that seemed extreme.

"I will, just as soon as we ferry Bentz's wife around." For the first time, Sherry noticed the sound of disgust in her friend's voice as they pulled out of the parking lot and the first real doubts about her friend pricked at her consciousness.

They headed not in the direction of the airport, but north, away from the city.

"Hey what are you doing?" she demanded and caught an icy glare. *Oh God, this is a setup!* Sherry fumbled in her pocket for her cell phone, but it was too late. She couldn't think fast enough to get it; her reactions were already off. "You," she said sluggishly, her tongue thick. "You slipped me a mickey . . ." *Oh, shit.* The interior of the car spun.

"More than one, Sherry," her friend said with a calm, nearly serene smile. Her hands gripped the steering wheel so hard her knuckles were white as twilight fell and the dark night rushed past.

In that second Sherry Petrocelli felt a chill as cold as an Arctic wind blow through her soul. Her gun was locked securely in a safe at home, but even if it had been with her, she wouldn't have been able to reach for it, to fire. She was too far gone, her reactions all off.

If there were a way to stop this madness, she would. But it was too late.

Scared out of her mind, with no way out, she thought of her seven-year-old son, Hank, and her husband, Jerry, a goofball she'd loved for fifteen of her thirty-two years. Jerry and Sherry; they'd thought their rhyming names were so funny, so corny. Who would take care of them if she were gone? Who would raise her boy? Love silly Jerry?

"Please," she said, suddenly desperate, but it was far too late. Her mind was swimming away from reality.

"Please, what?" asked her friend, and the woman had the audacity to laugh at her. "Good night, Sherry," she said, sounding so pleased.

Sherry felt a tear slide down her cheek. *Oh, Jerry, I'm sooo sorry.*

In the next second, Sherry Petrocelli's heart quit beating.

CHAPTER 30

Once the jet touched down at LAX, Olivia couldn't get off the plane fast enough. The flight had been delayed by nearly two hours, making everyone onboard nervous while they repaired some kind of temperature gauge. Then the ride had been bumpy and loud. As the minutes had ticked away, she'd experienced a steadily increasing feeling of dread.

What if Bentz had already left Los Angeles?

What if he'd connected with this person posing as Jennifer?

What if another friend of his ex-wife's had been killed?

She pulled her carry-on from the overhead bin and shuffled her way behind the mother and toddler along the narrow aisle of the 737. Things didn't move much faster along the jetway, but by the time she reached the gate she'd dug out her cell phone, turned it on, and was listening to a bevy of messages, one of which was from Bentz. He was the most recent caller and his message confirmed Hayes's offer of a ride to the police station, telling her to look for an officer who would be waiting for her with a sign at baggage claim.

A little odd, she thought, trying not to press the panic button. No one had told her why she was being escorted by an officer rather than renting a car or taking a taxi herself. Or, since Bentz knew her flight number and arrival time, why wasn't he picking her up himself? Why meet at the police station?

Because there's trouble. Serious trouble.

She tried Bentz's cell and wanted to scream in frustration when he didn't pick up. Then she dialed Hayes's phone and again was sent directly to voice mail.

So much for the convenience of cell phones, of always being in touch. She slammed hers back into her purse and pulled her roller bag behind her as she followed the signs to baggage claim. Something felt off about this and if she hadn't heard her husband's request herself, she would have rented a car.

And gone where? He already checked out of the So-Cal Inn, right? You probably would have met him at the station anyway. Just be thankful that he's still in L.A. You'll see him soon. Less than an hour, probably.

Good!

Her cell phone rang and she saw it was Bentz's number. Thank God! "Hi."

"God, it's good to hear your voice. I was worried."

Her heart squeezed. "Yeah, I know." She felt tears against the back of her eyes and ridiculously her throat thickened. "The, uh, the flight was delayed, a mechanical problem that took a couple of hours to fix. But I finally made it."

"Good."

She could barely hear him with the sounds of the airport filling her ears, announcements for flights over the loudspeakers, the squeak of wheels on roller bags, and the excited hum of conversation as throngs of people moved through the wide concourse.

"Why are we meeting at the station house? I thought you would pick me up."

"Yeah, I wish, but I've got to make a statement. Some loose ends to tie up."

"Oh, God, someone else died," she said, knowing it was true. She stopped dead in her tracks and a woman pushing a stroller nearly ran into her.

"Sorry," the woman said, diverting around Olivia, who moved to the side of the wide hallway to stop by a T-shirt shop. "Am I right?" she asked, her heart drumming with dread. "Was someone else killed?"

"I think so. It's the person who impersonated Jennifer." He sounded weary and distracted. "It's a long story, but I saw her jump from an observation platform into the ocean, a good thirty or forty feet below."

"She jumped?"

"She was running away from me."

"Oh, God," she whispered, the cacophony of the airport turning into the rush of the sea, the people fading as, in her mind's eye, she witnessed a woman leaping to her death in the water below.

"A few hours later, the Coast Guard found a body."

Olivia leaned against the wall and closed her eyes for a second. "So she's dead? The person who's been gaslighting you?" Olivia couldn't believe it.

"Yeah. I think so. I'm going to have to ID the body in the morgue, which is kind of a joke. I mean, I only met her up close once. I don't even know her real name."

"You spoke with her. Had a conversation?"

"Yeah."

"Face-to-face, not one of those midnight prank calls."

"I was with her earlier today," he said. "I caught up with her and she was going to tell me the truth, or so she claimed, but . . . oh, hell . . . listen, I've got to go."

"No, wait! You met with this 'Jennifer?'"

"Yes. Look, Livvie, I'll tell you everything soon. Once I ID the body, I'll probably have to answer some more questions, but that will be at RHD, at Parker Center, so we'll hook up there. It's not far from the morgue. I'll meet you as soon as I can."

Someone was calling her, a number she didn't recognize, trying to cut in. She ignored the interruption and watched as two parents shepherded their bags and stair-step children wearing Mickey Mouse ears toward the main terminal.

"A police officer is picking you up," Bentz was saying. "Name's Sherry Petrocelli. She's a friend of Hayes's. She'll drive you to Parker Center. That's where the LAPD has their Robbery-Homicide Division."

"I *know* that."

"Good. I'll meet you. Hayes gave Petrocelli your cell number, so she'll be calling."

"I think she just did," Olivia said.

"Good. I'll see you soon."

"I can't wait. Love you."

"If you only knew."

Those damned hot tears touched her eyes again. Her throat was thick, choked with emotion. She whispered, "Maybe it'll be over now."

There was a pause on the other end of the connection. "I don't know if it will ever be over." And he hung up.

"Rick—" But it was too late. She stood there with the phone in her hand, feeling like an idiot. On the verge of a crying jag again.

That just wouldn't do. Her emotions and hormones be damned. She couldn't function in such an overwrought emotional state, near tears. She was a grown woman, soon to be a mother. Setting her jaw, she started walking again.

For the first time since touching down on California soil, she felt a measure of renewed determination to see this through. She told herself she was up for the challenge, whatever it was.

Bring it on, she thought, slipping her phone into her purse and sliding a pair of sunglasses onto the bridge of her nose. *I'm ready.*

Come on, come on, answer the damned phone.

I watch the passengers as they stream into the baggage claim area, hustling, herding, searching for their luggage. Loud and oblivious to me, they corral the children and guard their laptops as they wait for the carousel to spin, delivering their bags to them.

Where is she?

For a second I panic. Maybe she didn't make the flight. Perhaps I got the information wrong.

Or worse yet, I'm a suspect and they're waiting for me. Because Sherry Petrocelli didn't call the office to check in. My heart races at the thought that I could be caught before I'm finished, before I complete my task of utterly destroying Rick Bentz.

But a quick scan of the area assures me no cops are loitering on the chairs or hiding behind an open newspaper. These business travelers and families are not undercover detectives.

No, the baggage claim area looks clean.

I take a deep breath. I have to remain calm. Appear sincere. Make certain she believes that I'm Petrocelli. With that in mind, I force a smile that feels as false as plastic. But it will have to do.

It's essential that Olivia Bentz trust me, buy into the fact that I'm chauffeuring her to her beloved husband.

God, that thought makes me want to puke.

I study the entrance to the baggage claim area, eyeing the faces of the travelers, hunting for the one that is forever burned into my brain.

For the love of God, where is she? I start to pace, then stop. I don't want to attract attention; as it is I've been carefully avoiding the security cameras, keeping my back to them and my face covered. The wig and glasses help, but I can't take too many chances.

My palms are beginning to sweat.

Where the hell is she?

Damn it, could the bitch just show up?

I called her, left a message from Petrocelli's phone . . .

The cell phone jangles.

Finally!

I answer quickly, forcing the name off my lips. "Officer Petrocelli."

"Hi, this is Olivia Bentz. I think you tried to call me. My husband said you were going to pick me up at the airport, somewhere in Baggage Claim?" She sounds harried and tired.

Perfect.

My own tight nerves relax a bit. "That's right," I say.

"I'm here near the United carousel." Then I spy her approaching the area. Wearing sunglasses, her hair pulled away from her face, she's carrying a purse and pulling a single overnight bag.

She packed light.

Smart girl.

We both smile and hang up our respective phones.

"Olivia Bentz?" I call out as I flag her down. "How was your flight?"

She shrugs. "Delayed."

"I'm Sherry, a friend of Jonas Hayes. He asked me to pick you up."

"So I heard."

She eyes my uniform and I say, "You know I'm with the LAPD. Right?" She nods politely when I flip open Petrocelli's wallet with her badge. With my wig, I look enough like Sherry to satisfy her.

"I appreciate the lift, Officer Petrocelli," she says. So well-mannered and polite.

"Call me Sherry. The car's right outside," I tell her, and we walk through the doors to the parking area where the police cruiser awaits. I open the back door.

"You can put your things back here," I say, and she does, even her purse, which, I assume holds her phone. While she moves toward the front seat I spy her phone in a pocket of her purse. I remove my hat, and while I'm stowing it on the backseat I pick up her cell phone, click it to off, then tuck it back into the purse as I straighten. She's already slipping into the passenger seat.

Perfect.

Unafraid, she doesn't hesitate for a second and I feel a sense of well-being. How long I've waited for just this moment. But I can't get too cocky. Not yet. I've got a narrow window of time, so I hurry to the driver's side. The sooner I drive away from the airport with all its damned security cameras and wannabe cops, the better. I can't foul up now. Not when I'm so close, so damned close.

"How far is it to the Center?" she asks as she straps on her seat belt and I climb behind the wheel.

"Not far." I flash her a warm smile. "It's after rush hour, so it shouldn't take long. Half an hour at most."

"Good."

"Ever been to L.A. before?" I ask.

"Once, a long time ago. In my early twenties. I lived in Arizona—Tucson—for a while. While I was there I drove to San Diego a couple of times, and once I made it to Los Angeles. As I said, it's been a while."

Perfect. So she won't have any real sense of direction. Because she's not going anywhere near Parker Center.

She just doesn't know it yet.

How long had they been in this sterile interrogation room? Bentz shifted in the wooden chair, thinking it had been an eternity since he'd talked to Olivia on the phone.

The coffee in front of him had gone cold, but Bentz wasn't interested. Hayes, who'd been conducting the interview, had stepped out to see if Olivia had arrived. Bentz imagined her sitting in the squad room, waiting patiently. It wasn't fair to drag her into this, but he was glad she had come. Couldn't wait to see her. Touch her.

Bentz stood up and stretched, sick of the small, airless interrogation room. So typical; there was at least one in every precinct. A camera mounted high in the corner near the ceiling had recorded the entire conversation. Bentz could have asked for a lawyer or kept his mouth shut, but he had nothing to hide.

He knew it.

He sensed Hayes knew it. His account of the events at Devil's Caldron had been confirmed by Travis and his girlfriend. This was an exercise in futility, but one that ensured Hayes didn't make any mistakes.

He glanced at his reflection on the wall. God only knew who was standing behind the two-way mirror. Andrew Bledsoe and Riva Martinez were probably there, waiting for him to slip up and make a mistake. Maybe the DA was there, along with other detectives. Hell, maybe even Dawn Rankin was watching.

It was ridiculous, but Bentz understood procedure. Rake Rick Bentz over the coals. Prove that he's a good cop gone bad, someone insane enough to show up in Los Angeles and start killing people who had known his ex-wife.

Even though he'd talked things through with Hayes earlier, this was official, "for the record." So he'd suffered through the questions about his marriage to Jennifer, her betrayal, the divorce, the fact that while they'd been living together a second time, trying to see if it would work, she'd cheated on him all over again. And around that time, the accident that had taken her life. He understood that it was necessary to rehash this dark period in his life, though that hadn't made it any easier.

Then Hayes had segued to Jennifer the ghost, and Bentz had recalled how he'd seen her in his hospital room back in Louisiana. How he'd determined that the woman "haunting" him was actually a real flesh-and-blood imposter, one he'd stupidly driven along the coast. They'd stopped at Devil's Caldron, the park overlooking the sea, where she'd made the tragic leap into the ocean that had killed her.

"Well, tomorrow morning we should have some answers about your ghost. Or at least, your ex-wife," Hayes had said. The detective had cut through bureaucratic red tape and arranged for the exhumation of Jennifer's body, scheduled for the next morning. A step in the right direction.

Bentz was questioned about Shana McIntyre and Lorraine Newell. Hayes brought up the Caldwell twins, asked what he knew about the double homicide so similar to the Springer twins' case. "We've been through this before," Bentz had said, knowing that Olivia was waiting for him. He was tired, hungry and could offer them nothing more than the truth.

"Look, I can say all this a million ways," he'd said, "but it won't change what happened. I had nothing to do with Shana's murder or Lorraine's, and I don't have a clue what happened to those twins. It sounds like the Twenty-one or a copycat. That they were killed after I returned to Los Angeles . . . I agree, there seems to be a connection. Am I a catalyst? I hope to hell not, but I don't know. It would be quite a coincidence, and I don't have a lot of faith in those."

Bentz looked up as the door opened and Hayes stepped in. "Is she out there?" Bentz asked.

"Not yet," Hayes said.

An icy dread chilled Bentz. "What do you mean? They should be here by now. Would you give me my damned cell phone back?"

"Procedure, man." Hayes held up his hands defensively. "You'll get it back just as soon as we're done here. Martinez is tracking down Petrocelli right now." Across the table, his tie loosened, Hayes looked as bone weary as Bentz felt. "I just need to get a few more things on the record."

Bentz raked one hand through his hair. "And that would be?"

"At Devil's Caldron today, did the victim know you were armed?"

"She saw my gun. Made some comment about it earlier in the car."

"So you were chasing her with a gun."

"Yeah, but I didn't take it out of my holster. She knew I wouldn't fire at her."

"How would she know that?"

Good question. "Because she knows me. She knows things about me only Jennifer knew." His guts ground as he admitted, "It seems like every time I learned something I didn't know about Jennifer from one of her friends, that friend ended up dead. Almost . . . I know this sounds crazy, but it's almost as if they were expendable and had served their purpose." He looked at Hayes and shook his head. "It's pretty damned freaky. Like she was one step ahead of me. She seemed to figure out my next move before I even made it. Damn it, Hayes, she *knew* I'd be at the airport." And as he said the words, a new horror crawled through him. "Oh, God," he whispered, "Olivia."

"What?"

His mind was racing ahead, fueled by adrenaline and stark, gut-churning terror. If "Jennifer" knew his whereabouts, would she have been tracking Olivia's, too? "My wife. I told you about the menacing calls she's been getting. What if this psycho's after her, too?"

"But Jennifer or whoever she is, is dead now, right? You witnessed her jump into the sea."

"I know." But he couldn't shake the feeling of dread that clung to him.

"We've been over this," Hayes reminded him. "Petrocelli met her at the airport."

"Then where the hell are they?" He couldn't help the terror pulsing through his veins, pounding in his ears. He glanced at his watch. "They should be here by now."

"Maybe Olivia decided to check into a hotel? Get settled in somewhere instead of waiting around here."

"No way." Olivia had been as desperate to see him as he was to see her. He'd heard it in her voice.

Hayes sat back in the chair and slung his loose tie over one shoulder. "Look, you saw this Jennifer jump off the cliffs into Devil's Caldron, right? So your wife is safe."

Bentz wasn't certain. Nothing made sense anymore. Everything he believed in had gone sideways or turned upside down. He rubbed a hand over the stubble covering his jaw and tried to think clearly. Logically. Find the nugget of truth woven into so many lies. "Let's just get this interview over."

"We're done here." Hayes rose, straightening his tie. "But I'll need you to ID the woman we found at Devil's Caldron. The morgue isn't far." He opened the door and nodded toward the squad room. "Martinez will help you get your vouchered possessions, and then we can go."

While Hayes went over to his desk, Riva Martinez led Bentz down the hall to the property desk.

"Hey, my wife didn't show up yet, did she?" Bentz asked her, trying to keep a cordial tone. "Olivia Bentz?"

"Not yet. I called Petrocelli's cell, but she didn't pick up." Riva Martinez smiled at the property clerk, then started filling out the paperwork. As she handed him his gun, the look she sent Bentz could have cut through granite.

Bentz slung the holster over one shoulder, wondering what he ever did to piss off Riva Martinez. Maybe it was just the fact that her caseload had doubled since he'd returned to L.A.

"They should be here by now," he said, concern mounting. "It's not that far."

With a shrug, she handed him the bin containing his cell phone, wallet, house keys. "Probably traffic. Last week there was an accident on the 405, made me forty minutes late for my shift."

She nodded toward the paperwork. "Sign here to verify that you got everything back." After he signed, she gave him a copy of the receipt, then turned and walked briskly down the corridor.

Bentz watched her leave, the bad feeling in his gut worsening as she disappeared behind a tall rubber tree. Something was wrong.

As he headed back to the squad room, Bentz powered up his phone. No messages from Olivia. "Damn it." He dialed her. Got nowhere. "Come on, come on," he whispered as uniformed cops and detectives passed by. His call went to Olivia's voice mail box and he asked her to call him ASAP, then hung up.

This wasn't like her.

Relax. She's with a cop. Who knows what's holding them up? Maybe a problem with her luggage, or they stopped to get something to eat. Maybe her cell phone battery is dead . . . But he couldn't shake the feeling that something was wrong. He speed-dialed Montoya, who picked up before the second ring.

"Montoya."

"Got your call," Bentz said.

"Yeah, I just talked to Hayes. I sent him information on the owner of the Chevy, Yolanda Salazar. A relative sold it to her for cash. She never changed the title, which isn't a big deal, but the kicker is this: Her name is Yolanda *Valdez* Salazar. She's the older sister of Mario."

"What? Are you kidding me? Mario Valdez's sister," Bentz repeated, stunned. But he knew from the tone of Montoya's voice this was no joke. In a second he was back in the dark alley, a person aiming a gun at Trinidad . . .

A silver glint of moonlight on the black gun barrel.

Panic tearing through his heart.
"Police. Drop it!" he yelled in warning.
But in the next instant, the gun didn't fall away.
He's going to shoot! He's going to shoot Trinidad!
As the realization throbbed in his brain, Bentz pulled the trigger.
And the gunman went down . . .

Now, a dozen years later, that fatal moment was still emblazoned in Bentz's memory. The rush of relief that he'd saved his partner's life had quickly given way to horror when he saw that the gunman was just a kid, a boy with a toy pistol. It was a nightmare Bentz would never be able to put completely behind him. "Sweet Jesus," Bentz said, half to Montoya, half to himself.

"She lives in Encino," Montoya went on. "I e-mailed and faxed all the info to Jonas Hayes. It should be there by now."

"Good. Thanks."

Yolanda Valdez. He clicked off, saw that Hayes was still on the phone. Pacing the corridor, he tried to remember the older sister. There had been three kids in the family, right? Mario was the youngest and Yolanda quite a bit older, maybe twenty when the accident had occurred. And there had been a brother, too . . . what the hell was his name? Franco? Or Frederico? Or . . . no, wait . . . Fernando, that was it. But he didn't remember Yolanda looking like Jennifer . . . no, this wasn't making any sense.

Salazar? That didn't sound right. Hadn't she already been married? And the name had been different. He tried to come up with it, but her surname eluded him. Now she was Salazar? He rolled that around in his mind, tried to make some connections. Something didn't make sense.

He called Montoya back. When his partner answered, Bentz told him his concern. "I think she was married to someone else. Not Salazar. I think the name was Anglo . . . something like Johns, no that's not right. Can you double-check?"

"You got it, but everything I found only mentioned her maiden name, Valdez, and Salazar. But I'll dig further."

"Thanks."

Bentz hung up, disturbed.

He stepped around two cops talking in the hallway, then found Hayes at his desk, papers spread around him. Montoya's e-mail had gotten through. "Take a look." Hayes showed Bentz the driver's license photo of Yolanda Salazar. "You think that she's your Jennifer?"

"Not on a dare." Bentz rubbed the stubble on his jaw as he shook his head. "I don't know how this woman is connected to the Jennifer who's been trailing me."

"We'll have to dig deeper, but right now they're waiting for us over at the morgue." He motioned to the papers. "Bring those with you. We need to get over and ID our jumper."

Bentz tried to read the information Montoya had sent as he followed Hayes to the parking lot, where security lamps were already raining down soft blue light. "Anyone hear from Petrocelli?" Bentz asked as they reached Hayes's 4Runner.

"Not yet."

"I don't like this," Bentz said as he climbed into the passenger seat.

Hayes dialed his cell phone with one hand and started the engine with another. "Hey, Sherry. Hayes here. Just wondering what's the holdup. Give a call. I'm on my cell." Then he hung up. "I don't know, man. She's not answering."

Bentz glared at him. "LAPD's finest?"

"She'll be here when we get back."

"She'd better be. With my wife." Bentz stared out the windshield as Jonas eased out of the parking lot and pulled into moving traffic. Olivia. Where the hell was she?

Safe. With a trusted police officer. Relax.

He tried her number again, but the call went straight to voice mail. *Damn it, Olivia, where are you?*

A slow groaning terror thrummed through his bloodstream and it was all he could do to stay calm.

At the morgue, while Jonas Hayes had the coroner set up the body for viewing, Bentz paced, steeling himself. He'd never gotten comfortable around corpses, always felt a little nauseated when faced with death, a character flaw he'd attempted to hide from his peers. If other cops had gotten wind of it, he would have suffered years of razzing. Still, he'd been through this procedure enough to know how it went. Right now one of the attendants was wheeling a sheet-draped gurney into the viewing area, checking the toe tag to make sure they had the right Jane Doe.

"You ready?" Jonas asked.

Bentz steadied himself. "Yeah." It was a lie, of course. The last time he'd seen Jennifer she'd been so vibrant; naughty and teasing and running like a gazelle. So alive. And in a few short hours she'd been reduced to a draped, dead body on a cold slab.

"I don't know her name, you know," he reminded Hayes.

"Doesn't matter. Just let me know if this is the same woman."

Bentz nodded and Hayes motioned for the attendant to pull the sheet away.

Slowly the woman's face was uncovered. She lay staring upward, unmoving, her skin cast in a bluish hue.

Bentz felt bile climb up his throat as he gaped in disbelief.

Jennifer wasn't on the slab.

Instead he found himself staring into the decidedly dead face of Fortuna Esperanzo.

CHAPTER 31

"It's not Jennifer," Bentz said, forcing the words out, his fear and confusion mounting. What the hell was this? Fortuna? Dead? Oh, hell!

Hayes's head snapped around as he stared at Bentz. "What?"

"It's not the woman I was chasing. This is Fortuna Esperanzo. Jennifer worked with her in an art gallery in Venice."

"This woman?" Hayes pointed at the body. "Esperanzo?"

"Yes!" Bentz leaned against the wall and closed his eyes for a second, only to open them again and still find himself in the middle of this nightmare.

Hayes rubbed his forehead, frustration and exhaustion evident. "No wonder I couldn't reach her."

"Are you certain this is the woman they fished out of the ocean?" Bentz asked.

"Yep. She still smells of salt water," the attendant said. "Don't know how she died yet. Not until the autopsy."

Frustrated, Bentz shoved a hand through his hair. "What was she wearing?" He looked at the attendant. "You have the clothes?"

"I think . . . let's see." She checked a clipboard. "T-shirt, size small, sleeveless. Pink. Shorts. Size two. White. White panties, and a nude colored bra. Thirty-two B. No shoes. No jewelry."

"Son of a bitch," Bentz said.

"What?"

"The outfit. Exactly what the woman I was chasing had on. I mean, I don't know about the underclothes, but she definitely had on a pink sleeveless tee and white shorts. Someone knew. The killer. He or she knew."

"You don't think Jennifer's the killer?"

"How could she be?"

"Who else?"

"Damned if I know." As a wave of sickness roiled inside him, Bentz turned away. "Let's go talk to Yolanda Salazar and see what she knows. Maybe she can make the connection between Fortuna Esperanzo and the woman who jumped off the cliff." He was already walking toward the exit, a deep soul-numbing fear holding him in its icy grasp. Olivia, oh for the love of God, where was she? God help him if she was dead. To Hayes he said, "But first, we need to stop at the Center and find my wife."

As I stand on deck of my boat with my precious cargo below, I can't help the tremor of excitement that skims through my blood. So far, so good. Everything is going perfectly.

No thanks to that Olivia.

When we drove away from the airport, "Livvie" was checking out the road signs, a cause for some worry. What if she was more familiar with the city than she'd let on? She pressed me to do this sooner than later. I just couldn't take a chance that she would get wise and ask to make a call. I needed to have the element of surprise on my side.

As soon as the airport was in the distance, I slowed for an amber light and sneezed. "Oh, Jeez, could you get me a tissue?" I asked her as the light turned red and I braked to a stop. "There in the box?"

"Sure." She opened the glove box and began searching through the maps and napkins stuffed in there, not realizing that I had pulled out my trusty little Pomeroy Taser 2550. I had bought it on Craig's List, under an assumed name, of course. "Oh, here we go," she said as I hit the automatic door locks.

I struck quickly, placing the electrodes against her neck and pulling the trigger. Her mouth was open, her eyes bulging. Then her body reacted and she lost control of her appendages. Her breathing went wild, her eyes round in horror.

This was where it got tricky. I had to do this all while I was driving the car. Reaching into my purse, I pulled out a piece of pre-cut duct tape and slapped it over her startled mouth. Then I grabbed Sherry's cuffs and placed them over her wrists. I had to work fast, so there was no time to try and wrestle her arms behind her back. So Livvie got cuffed in the front.

That was when the asshole driver behind me laid on the horn of his Porsche and I realized the light had turned green.

"Take a chill pill, bastard!" I mumbled, too busy to care. I had my hands full, Olivia staring at me, her mouth working behind the tape, and that jerk wants me to peel out.

Blasting his horn again, the newest Dale Earnhardt wannabe screeched around me. Yelling filth, he flipped me off and burned rubber. Much as I would have loved to bash in the sleek car's rear end and take out the driver at the same time, I tamped down the urge. Right then I had a full plate.

Once Olivia—oh, excuse me, "Livvie"—was subdued, I stepped on it and headed to the marina. With her delayed plane, I had lost a lot of time. People would be calling. I had to give her another shock so I could shackle her. Then I loaded her onto the boat, which was no easy task. She weighs a helluva lot more than I had imagined.

Now, on the deck, Olivia secured in the hold below, I can breathe a little easier. I feel a little thrill and wonder if Rick Bentz has any idea that his precious wife isn't going to meet up with him. In fact, she's never going to see him again.

"Take that," I say under my breath and hope to hell that he's sweating bullets.

Olivia wasn't answering.

Bentz told himself not to panic, but even Hayes was starting to worry. He'd called Bledsoe from the car and asked him to get a unit down to Venice to cordon off and search Fortuna Esperanzo's house. They would check with the gallery where she worked as soon as they opened their doors in the morning. He'd also called Tally White, who was very much alive and scared to death. Tally was so freaked out by the pattern of killings that she'd booked a morning flight to Portland, Oregon, for a visit with her sister.

Hurrying inside the Center, Bentz eyed Riva Martinez, who was still working at her desk. "Bledsoe and Trinidad are going to Venice," she told Hayes as she twisted her red hair into a knot at the back of her head and secured it with a long-toothed tortoise shell comb. "Uniforms have already secured the scene."

"If it is a scene."

Bentz's jaw was rock hard. Three women dead since he'd arrived in Los Angeles, and that didn't include the Springer twins.

And now . . . Olivia?

Fear gnawed a hole in his gut.

But he couldn't, wouldn't let it get the better of him.

"My wife still didn't get here?" he asked.

Martinez shrugged. This time her dark eyes revealed a shred of concern. "I've been calling Petrocelli, but she doesn't pick up." Martinez's eyebrows pulled together as she stared at her computer monitor, where a picture of Shana McIntyre's body filled the screen.

Bentz had to look away. It had been bad enough seeing the dead corpse, worse yet to think his wife might be in the hands of the maniac who had killed Shana, Lorraine, and now Fortuna.

"I talked to Petrocelli a few hours ago," Hayes said, checking his watch. "Maybe four hours ago? She knew the flight was late, but said she'd get to the airport in plenty of time."

"It's been too long." Martinez reached for the jacket slung over the back of her chair. "I've already put a BLOF out for Petrocelli's vehicle; I figure I'd rather err on the side of caution."

"Good idea," Hayes agreed.

Bentz felt time slipping by, precious seconds that could be the difference between life and death for Olivia. "We have to find her."

"We will," Hayes assured him.

But Bentz wasn't satisfied. He felt restless, needed to do something, *any*thing other than wait around. God, if Olivia was in danger because of him, because of this Jennifer fiasco . . .

He put in a call to his daughter and felt his knees go weak when Kristi answered. "Hey, Dad, are you home?"

"Not yet." *Oh, God, Kristi, I wish I was. Back in Louisiana with Olivia. Christ, what was I thinking?*

"Still out chasing ghosts?"

"I guess." He didn't tell her about Olivia, didn't want to worry her. In truth he had only called to assure himself that someone he loved was safe, that he hadn't put his whole damned family in jeopardy.

Just Olivia.

Dear God, the thought that she might even now be in the hands of a murderer . . . Fear gnawed at his gut but somehow he was able to keep up the conversation with his daughter. After hanging up, he made another quick call. This time to the airlines. He was connected to a representative and, after arguing about legalities, the rep told him that Olivia had been on the flight and that the plane had touched down hours ago, which only confirmed what he'd already known as he talked to her. The airline had no more information for him.

She'd gone missing between LAX and here.

"The airport has security cameras," Bentz told the other detectives. "Cameras at the door and at baggage claim. I want to see the tapes."

"We'll get 'em. If we don't locate Petrocelli," Hayes agreed.

Bentz didn't know if he could stand the waiting. He didn't like this, didn't like the feeling. He'd experienced it too many times in his life before, when someone he loved was in danger. This wasn't the first time he'd been worried sick over Olivia's fate. He couldn't let anything happen to her. *Couldn't.*

And he couldn't sit around here, waiting for other people to call the shots. "Come on," he told Hayes. "We need to have a chat with Yolanda Salazar."

"I'm way ahead of you. Already working on a warrant. But you're not talking to anyone. This is our case, and you have a personal ax to grind."

"You bet I do. My wife is missing!"

"I'm talking about the shooting, Bentz. The department settled with the Valdez family, but I don't think it would be wise for you to get into it with them. In fact, I don't want them to know you're a part of this. At least until we know where we stand. If you go on the interview, you're a bystander. Lucky to be going along. You know the rules; you just need to play by them."

"Your rules."

"Shit, man, I'm glad to have you ride along, but it's my jurisdiction. My case. You're right. My rules." He stared long and hard at Bentz. "Now, are you going to ride with me or not?"

"Wouldn't miss it for the world," Bentz said sarcastically.

He tried like hell to stay calm, not go to the worst case scenario, but he was worried as he climbed into the backseat of the 4Runner, with Hayes driving and Martinez riding shotgun.

He checked again: No phone call. No text. Nothing. He tried to make sense of the events of the afternoon and failed. "Any prints or evidence found in the silver Chevy?" he asked.

"We don't know yet," Martinez admitted.

How the hell had Fortuna Esperanzo ended up in the Pacific Ocean, so close to Devil's Caldron? In his mind's eye he witnessed Jennifer jump. And then again. And again. Leaping from the railing, soaring into the air, vanishing from view. How was that possible?

He tried to imagine scenarios that might solve that mystery, if only to distract himself from the one question that thrummed through his body with every beat of his heart.

Where the hell was Olivia?

Exhausted, Olivia could barely move.

And she was scared to death as she lay in a dark, smelly enclosure, a cage deep inside a boat of some kind.

This madwoman Petrocelli, or whatever her name was, intended to kill her. Because she was married to Rick. That's why the other women were dead; because they'd known her husband.

No. That wasn't quite right. All of the dead women had known *Jennifer,* a woman Olivia had never met.

And they were killed. Murdered. Just like you will be if you don't find a way out of this.

Her limbs were useless, her head spinning. Though she was awake, her eyes wide open, her body still wouldn't do what she wanted. It was as if her brain were completely disengaged from her muscles, her nerve synapses misfiring.

Oh, God, how had she been so stupid to have trusted the woman? Why hadn't she checked her ID more carefully? Surely her captor, this lunatic, wasn't a real police officer with LAPD.

How do you know that? Cops can go crazy, and Petrocelli might just be the psycho.

It didn't matter. Whoever her abductor was, she was deadly.

Earlier, as she'd been yanked from the car and slipped into the sleeping bag, Olivia had gotten a glimpse of a dark street and loom-

ing buildings in an area that smelled of the sea. She had heard her attacker grunting and puffing with exertion as she had lifted Olivia into
what seemed to be a cart of some kind. A cart with at least one creaky
wheel.

Olivia had tried to yell, to scream, to flail her arms and legs, hoping to either hit her assailant or to attract the attention of anyone
who passed by.

But her brain hadn't been able to force her body to move, hadn't
been able to issue any commands her muscles would obey. The stun
gun's jolt had knocked her senseless, rendered her useless. She'd
thought of the baby inside her . . . Oh, dear God, had it survived the
surge of voltage that had rendered her helpless? *I'm sorry,* she
thought, *Oh, I'm so, so sorry.*

The cart bumped and jangled, her attacker breathing hard as she
was rolled over a rough surface. Listening, she heard a jet rumble
overhead and then the blast of a foghorn from a boat.

Trying to think, working to pull together her shattered thoughts,
Olivia attempted to figure out her surroundings, but it was so dark,
so claustrophobic, so damned hot in the sleeping bag, she was having trouble breathing.

*Think, Olivia. Don't give up. You've been in tight spots before
and when the shock to your system wears off, you can use your
hands; at least they're cuffed in front of you. Don't give up. Don't let
fear paralyze you. Think of the baby, of Rick. You can't stop fighting.*

Pull it together. There has to be a way!

The surface under the wheels changed, and the cart rolled more
smoothly. Then she was hauled upward and, still in the sleeping bag,
dropped to a hard surface before being dragged downstairs. It took
all her willpower to curl slightly, protecting her abdomen with her
flimsy arms. Protecting her baby . . .

"You could stand to lose a few pounds, you know," her captor
muttered.

At the bottom of the steps, Olivia was dragged for a short distance, then released onto the floor. Through the thick fibers of the
sleeping bag she smelled something acrid and foul . . . urine?

"Welcome home," the woman taunted with a smug tone in her
voice. She was breathing hard from the exertion.

Olivia heard metal jangling. Keys? She strained to listen, all the while flailing wildly as she worked her way to the top of the sleeping bag. Her wrists were still bound, her mouth taped. Frantically, breathing with difficulty, she was able to reach upward in the bag, her fingers slowly and unwillingly tracing the trail of closed zipper teeth to the top, where she found the inside tab and started tugging downward. Time and time again her fingers slipped, her body still not responding to her brain's commands, her nerves jangled and jumpy, closing in on a full blown panic.

Don't stop. Work at it. The taser won't last much longer.

Finally, she pulled hard, lowering her body, dragging the tab, forcing the clenched teeth of the zipper to part.

The woman laughed as she observed Olivia's pathetic attempts at escape.

Tough!

Olivia wasn't giving up without a fight.

She kept tugging, pulling on the tab until a rush of urine-tinged air stung her nostrils. The bag opened to reveal the hold of a boat. One lamp gave the room a weird yellow aura, showing Olivia that she was trapped inside a cage with steel bars from ceiling to floor. A cage for animals, judging from the smell and bits of straw wedged into the floorboards. An empty bucket was pushed into one corner near a jug of water. Obviously for her, she thought, her insides turning to ice.

A barred gate was the only access into the cage. As Olivia watched in dull horror the woman who had abducted her inserted a key and locked her inside.

Click!

To Olivia, it sounded like the very knell of death.

"Fool," the woman said and pulled off a blond wig.

"Make yourself comfortable. You're going to be here for a while."

Good. Olivia would rather be alone to plot her escape.

As if reading her thoughts, her captor said, "Oh, and you can work like the devil to take off your gag so you can scream at the top of your lungs, but it doesn't matter. No one will ever hear you down here."

She smiled almost beatifically, and fear clamored in Olivia's chest.

How long did the madwoman plan to keep her here? A day? Two? A week? Forever?

And what then? Surely this wasn't an elaborate kidnapping. No. Olivia knew the harsh truth; her abductor planned to kill her. And her baby. Oh, dear Lord. It was only a matter of time.

"I wonder what your husband is doing, Olivia? If he's figured out that you're missing." The woman seemed to extract a deep-rooted satisfaction from that thought.

Olivia wanted to rip her to shreds. Now, she forced herself to deal with the maniac.

"Oh, I see." the nut case was saying, "You think he's a hero. Made a name for himself in New Orleans as some kind of ace detective, didn't he? Fooled everyone. Every-damned-one." She was getting agitated now, her eyes glittering with hatred. "I don't want to burst your bubble about that fantasy of living happily ever after with your hero. But the truth of the matter is that Rick Bentz is a prick. A has-been cop and not even a good one at that. He killed a kid, did he tell you that?" Her eyebrows lifted as she practically oozed satisfaction over the chance to rant about Bentz to a rapt, captive audience.

"Your husband is a loser, Olivia. And you? It's just your dumb luck that you married him. Wanna know why? Because your husband is such a major fuck-up, you get to pay the price. You and the others."

Then, glancing at her watch, she swore and seemed to panic. She searched the hull for a second, lifted a gas can from the rubble, and smiled. "A little no-no I had hidden."

Olivia's fear turned to sheer terror.

This maniac was going to set fire to the boat!

While she was trapped inside.

"No," Olivia sputtered behind the tape. "No!" Angrily, she pulled her hands to her face, scratched at the duct tape until she'd lifted a corner. Then, willing her fingers to work, she yanked the tape off her mouth, peeling skin from her cheeks and lips. "No!" she cried again, but her captor ignored her pleas and hurried up the stairs, her footsteps ringing on the metal rungs.

Oh, God, oh, God, oh God!

"Don't do this!" she cried.

At the top of the stairs, the woman hesitated for a second. Had she heard Olivia's pleas? Was she considering giving in to them?

"Please!" Olivia screamed, desperate.

Then she heard the madwoman say, "Screw it!"

Oh, no! Sheer terror coursing through her veins, Olivia screamed and pulled on the gate, hoping to open it. But her hands slipped, her motor skills still affected by the shock. "No! Please."

With a click, the woman flipped a switch.

The lights went out.

Olivia's prison and the entire hull of the boat was suddenly black as pitch.

A door clanged shut.

Tears rolled down her face.

Olivia waited for the sound of liquid being splashed above, for the horrendous *whoosh* as a match was tossed and hungry flames ignited.

But there was only silence.

CHAPTER 32

Hayes figured he was in for a long night as he drove to Encino. While Bentz and Martinez stared at the passing landscape, he called Corrine and bagged out of their late-night plans. Corrine had known he'd be working late and had suggested that he come over and crash at her place. Normally a good idea, but now that he had no idea what time he'd be done, he let her off the hook.

"You're working overtime *again?*" He heard the irritation in her voice, hoped the others in the car couldn't hear her. "I guess I'll take a rain check. Again."

Corrine wasn't happy, but there was nothing he could do about it now, on his way to Encino with two other detectives in the car.

He didn't like making personal calls in front of other cops. Martinez and Bentz had tactfully looked the other way, but it was awkward. Especially since Corrine used to be hooked up with Bentz. Still, it was a choice of call while he was working the case, or not call at all.

That's what happens when you have no life, Hayes thought as he took the exit for Encino. "Let's hope Yolanda and Sebastian Salazar are home," he said. A few blocks off Ventura Boulevard, the houses were small and compact, single-story, post–World War II, with big yards where the grass was beginning to turn brown.

The Salazars lived on a corner lot, the stucco covering their house painted a light color that resembled ash in the bluish glow from the streetlights. A large chain-link fence circled the side yard, where a sign in bold letters read: BEWARE OF DOG.

"Great." Martinez shrank into the front seat. "I hate dogs."

Hayes scowled. "How can you hate dogs?"

"Got bitten as a kid. Had to have plastic surgery and a lot of physical therapy. Harriet, the neighbors' dachshund. Nasty little thing."

"You can't judge all dogs by Harriet."

"Wanna bet?" she said as Hayes cut the engine.

"You know that they smell your fear, Martinez," Bentz persisted. "As long as you're afraid of them, you won't be able to go near them."

"Fine with me," she said. "I'm happy to keep my distance."

Before they opened the Toyota's doors the dog in question began barking and snarling wildly from the other side of the fence. The furious creature was black and tan, with jaws as wide as Arkansas and teeth that flashed angrily. A Rottweiler mix from the looks of him, Hayes guessed.

"Oh, yeah, he's gonna be a real sweetheart, this one." Martinez's hand was frozen on the door handle. "Let's just call him Fluffy."

In his rearview mirror, Hayes saw Bentz starting to get out of the backseat.

"Don't even think about it," Hayes told him. He couldn't have Bentz go off half-cocked. As far as Hayes was concerned Bentz was advising on the case, nothing more. Although he didn't side with Andrew Bledsoe and Dawn Rankin, who had insinuated that Bentz was somehow involved in the murders, he couldn't allow Bentz to investigate for the LAPD. Bentz was no longer on the payroll here, and it would seriously compromise the case. He probably shouldn't even have brought him here, but Hayes had to give the guy some credit. So far, Bentz had been the only one to make some real headway in this case.

Hayes barely glanced at the side yard as the dog created a ruckus loud enough to wake the dead. From the back of the house a man yelled, "Rufus! You hush!"

Rufus ignored the command. If anything, the big dog seemed more agitated than ever, running in circles and drooling anxiously as he kept up his incessant barking. Judging by the lack of grass on Rufus's side of the fence, this wasn't a new routine.

"So much for the element of surprise," Hayes said under his breath.

Martinez glanced at the fence. "Let's just hope the gate holds."

As they reached the porch, a light over the door flipped on and the cement steps were bathed in a fake yellow glow. The door opened, leaving the grillwork of a screen door separating them from a slim woman with dark hair falling past her shoulders. She was wearing a white tank top, orange capris, and a bad-ass expression.

Hayes recognized Yolanda Salazar from the information Montoya had sent over. Her driver's license didn't do her justice; she was a helluva lot prettier in person, even in her bad mood.

"Can I help you?" she asked without a smile.

"I'm Detective Hayes, this is my partner, Detective Martinez, with the Los Angeles Police Department." They showed their badges. "Are you Yolanda Salazar?"

A slight hesitation, then she nodded, barely moving her head. "Why are you here?"

"We'd like to ask you a few questions."

"About what?" In that instant her anger fled, to be replaced by fear. "Fernando? Is it my brother? Oh, *Dios*, don't tell me he's hurt or in trouble." Without thinking she made a quick sign of the cross over her chest.

"No, nothing like that," Hayes assured her. "We need to ask you about a car that you own, a 1999 Silver Chevrolet Impala, registered to Ramona Salazar."

"Hey, is something wrong?" From within the house a man appeared. He was twice her size, all muscle and brawn, his tight T-shirt stretched over the broad span of his shoulders. His denim shorts hung low, almost falling off his slim hips. "What's going on?"

"It's the police," she said, casting her husband a fearful look.

"You're Sebastian Salazar?" Martinez asked.

"That's right." His accent was thick.

"We're here to ask your wife a few questions about a car that belongs to her."

Sebastian flinched. He turned to his wife and said something in rapid-fire Spanish that Hayes didn't catch, but he figured Martinez might understand.

"Can we come in?" Martinez asked.

Husband and wife looked at each other, then Sebastian muttered something in Spanish before opening the door. "Please," he said, white teeth flashing beneath a thick moustache. "Have a seat." He waved them into matching chairs.

Remaining at the door, Yolanda peered out curiously. "Is your friend coming in?"

Glancing over his shoulder, Hayes suppressed a groan. Bentz was out of the car, standing in the pool of light at the chain-link fence, murmuring something to Rufus, who had finally stopped barking. "He's fine out there," Hayes said, trying to distract Yolanda Salazar. "Sorry to bother you, but if you could just—"

"Wait a minute." Yolanda's eyes were cold, black pebbles as her face hardened into a scowl. "Sebastian!" She motioned him toward the door, a stream of Spanish erupting between them. *"Bastardo!"* she hissed.

Alarmed, Sebastian crossed to the door and gaped at the atrocity his wife indicated.

Hayes ground his teeth together, knowing what this was all about. Bentz.

Yolanda wheeled on Hayes and Martinez. "Get out of my house! You bring a baby killer into my home? The *hombre* who killed my brother? Shot him dead?" She pointed an accusing finger to the street. "He is the cop who shot Mario, a twelve-year-old boy! An innocent." Her upper lip curled into a snarl of distaste. "Leave now," she insisted. And then, to Hayes's horror, she flew out the door.

Pacing along the chain-link fence, Bentz was on the phone. ". . . I think her name was Judd. Yolanda Judd," he said to Montoya as Yolanda herself burst out of the house. Bare feet flying, she cut across the yard and lunged toward him. "Baby killer!" she accused. "What are you doing here?"

Hayes and Martinez were on her heels with a big guy, most likely her husband, following.

"I'll call you back," he said to Montoya and hung up.

"Can't you leave us in peace? Isn't it enough that you killed my baby brother and ruined my mother's life?" she said as Bentz swung around to face her.

She spat then, hitting him square in the face.

Bentz's hands clenched into fists. *Crazy bitch!* He could barely contain his fury.

"Back off!" Hayes shouted. He waved Bentz toward the car, motioning for him to return to the backseat in a feeble attempt to defuse the situation. "Mrs. Salazar, we just need to ask you some questions about your car," he insisted to Yolanda.

"Then why is *he* here?" She hooked a finger at Bentz as he wiped his face.

Certainly not to endure your abuse, Bentz wanted to say.

"Do you know where your car is now?" Hayes stepped between Yolanda and Bentz.

"With Fernando . . . oh, *Dios.* Fernando. Where is he?" Her anger appeared to morph into genuine fear.

"I don't know, Mrs. Salazar. But we have your vehicle."

"Where?" She seemed stunned.

"At the police lot. We're looking through it for evidence."

"Evidence of what?"

"It could be linked to three homicides."

"What?" She glanced at Bentz, but some of her hostility had evaporated. "Homicides?"

"That's right. Who usually drives the car?"

"I–I do."

Hayes looked at the driveway where a pickup with a canopy was parked beside a shiny Lexus. "Who drives those?"

"The Nissan truck is mine," the husband said and Yolanda sent him a withering look. "Yolanda drives the Lexus. We use the Chevy as an extra car, bought it from Carlos because it was a good deal. Lately Fernando has been borrowing it."

"He lives here?" Martinez asked.

Yolanda's lips pinched in disapproval, but Sebastian nodded and answered, "Most of the time."

"Does he have another vehicle?" Martinez had taken out a small notepad and was jotting down the information.

"His Blazer is in the shop; needs a new transmission. He hasn't decided if it's worth it yet."

"Where's Fernando now?" Martinez asked, risking a look at the dog, who was now standing on his hind legs and digging at the meshed steel of the fence.

"I don't know." Yolanda shot a nervous glance up the street, as if she expected her brother to appear at any second.

"Is he at work?" Martinez asked.

"School," Sebastian said, wrapping a big arm around Yolanda's shoulders. "He takes night classes at the junior college. Like my wife. He usually comes home after work at the restaurant, The Blue Burro, but today he didn't. Called and said he was going straight to school."

"You got a phone number for him?"

"No!" Yolanda said, obviously scared, but Sebastian placed a hand on the back of her neck and rubbed it as he gave Martinez the number.

"Damn it, Sebastian!" Yolanda said, pushing his hand away.

Her husband wasn't put off. "If he's in trouble, we need to know about it."

Hayes tried a different tack. "Does Fernando have a girlfriend? Anyone he would loan the car to?"

"No one serious," she said.

Sebastian scowled. "Fernando, he knows lots of girls. But I don't know about loaning the car to any of them. He should know better than that, you know? The car, it belongs to my wife."

Hayes asked, "Do you know a woman named Jennifer Bentz?" When Yolanda shrugged, he continued. "Come on back inside, I have some pictures I'd like you to see."

Yolanda shot Bentz one last hateful glance, then begrudgingly returned to the house.

Still seething, Bentz climbed into the back of the Toyota, leaving the door open so that a breeze slid into the car.

He wondered about Yolanda and the damned car.

She hadn't been driving it earlier today.

Nor had Fernando.

But Fernando Valdez was the next person on Bentz's list to interview.

Despite Hayes's warning, he put in a call to the phone number, but Fernando didn't pick up.

Bentz leaned against the seat, wondering if Yolanda was telling the truth. Something he doubted. He watched a bicyclist in reflective gear whiz past while a cat in a neighboring yard slunk through the shrubbery, hunting.

Meanwhile, Rufus had settled down to whining and pacing.

Bentz used his cell phone to reserve another rental car. He also called the So-Cal Inn, hoping against hope that Olivia might have slipped through the cracks and come looking for him there.

No such luck, of course.

He rented another room, one facing the interior pool this time, and gave Rebecca specific instructions to phone him if she heard from his wife. It was a long shot, of course, but he had to cover all his bases, even the most obscure.

Twenty minutes later, Hayes and Martinez were emerging from the house when Bentz's phone rang. He picked it up, hoping to see Olivia's number on the screen. Instead he saw Montoya's.

"Bentz."

"You were right," Montoya said. "I pulled up some records on Yolanda Valdez in Los Angeles County, dug a little deeper, and it seems that she was married to an Erik Judd for a short period of time. Erik was a roofer and he had an accident; fell four stories and died before the divorce was final."

"They were getting a divorce?"

"Had filed the papers."

"How do you know this?" Bentz said, looking outside to the night. No county offices would be open.

"You just have to know what you're doing, who to call, and how to work the Internet. Public records can be located."

"If you say so."

"I do, and the kicker is this: He had a five hundred thousand dollar insurance policy on him. Half a million. The beneficiary, none other than his soon to be ex-wife."

"Anything fishy about the accident?"

"The insurance company didn't balk. According to bank records, Yolanda owns her house in Encino outright and still has eighty thousand in the bank." Montoya sounded pleased with himself. "No student loans for this girl."

"Thanks," Bentz said. "Now, do me a favor. Find out what you can about the brother. Fernando Valdez. He's been using the car that *Jennifer* was driving. I think he lives with his sister and brother-in-law, but right now he's MIA."

"I'll see what I can find."

"Thanks."

"You owe me a beer. . . . No, wait, I think the debt is more than that. You're up to half a case already."

"I'm good for it," Bentz said. "You haven't heard from Olivia, have you?"

"No. Why? Didn't she show up?"

"Nope. She landed at LAX. We talked on the phone. She was meeting Officer Petrocelli and I haven't heard from her since."

"You're sure she was on the plane? If she was on her cell, she could have been anywhere."

"Yeah. I checked with the airline."

"So what happened?"

"I don't know," Bentz admitted, refusing to be defeated. "But I'll find her."

"Of course you will, man," Montoya said but there was an undercurrent of worry in his voice, one that was echoed in Bentz's own fears.

I have to work quickly, and I'm getting a little rattled. I feel it and I don't like it. It's not that I'm not fast on my feet; it's that I prefer to have everything worked out to the finest little detail. That's why it's taken twelve years to execute this plan. Twelve, long, torturous years.

I can't blow it now, I think, stripping off my clothes in a cabin on the boat and seeing my reflection in the slim mirror. I'm in good shape, better than anyone would guess or know, and I give myself credit. It's taken years to hone my muscles, to look just how I want.

Like so many things in my life, my strength and appearance took patience, timing, and determination. I didn't give up cigarettes for nothing.

Sometimes, unfortunately, it's necessary to take chances, to react to the moment. It's nerve-racking, I admit as I stuff my hair into a baseball cap. So after those risky moments, I just have to gain my equilibrium again, retain my focus, remember my ultimate goal.

I pull on my running pants and zip up my jacket, then sneak off the craft. No one's around at this hour, so I slip into the car unnoticed.

In the backseat, Sherry is all ready to go. Her clothes, badge, and purse sit beside her. "It's very quiet back there," I tell her.

Checking the rearview mirror, breathing slowly, I drive to a dead-end street about a mile from the restaurant where I met Sherry earlier. She and I go way back and it was a shame she had to be sacrificed, but the truth of the matter is that she always bothered me, a cop without any grit.

I park in a back alley and wipe off the areas where I might have left prints when I drove her away from the restaurant. I drop the latex gloves onto the backseat, douse it all generously with gasoline, and strike a match.

Hisssss!

The little flame glows bright for a second and I toss it through the open window onto the gloves. Combustion! The backseat ignites, burning quickly, setting the entire vehicle aflame.

Perfect, I think, starting to run when I see him. A guy on a motorcycle, cutting down the street behind me.

Oh, hell. My pulse skyrockets. Sweat beads on my forehead and hands. What if he saw me at the car? What if he can describe me? What if . . .

Calm down! He didn't see you. He might find the burning car, but that's what you want, remember? Just keep running.

Spurred by my own pep talk, I head out, cutting down back alleys, jogging at my regular pace, fast enough, considering everything I've been through.

I'm almost at the restaurant when I hear the sirens screaming. Fire trucks. Police cars. Probably a rescue vehicle. "Have at it," I say as I spy my own car parked in an alley several blocks from the restaurant, as it has been for hours, patiently waiting.

I drive home without a hitch. After stripping off my running clothes and tossing them into the washer, I take a long warm shower, giving myself a little time to think about Bentz and how he's suffering now. He's sick with worry about his precious little wife. He's all messed up about his dead one.

"Having fun yet, RJ?" I laugh while the steam rolls through the bathroom. As I shampoo my hair, then wash my body, my mind seizes on my next move, tomorrow's plan. Bentz is in for a few more heart attacks before I'm done. Olivia is going to die . . . oh, yes, I think, running the loofah over my back and down my arms, inhaling the scented soap. But before she bites it, I want Bentz to twist in the wind until he nearly breaks.

I scrub my feet, then let the warm water cascade over me, washing away all traces of dirt, grime, and sweat. Finally, I step out of the shower and towel off, thinking of Olivia rotting in the bowels of the boat, scared to death, probably screaming her lungs out to no avail.

Didn't I tell her not to waste her time? After grabbing my robe from the hook on the back of the bathroom door, I throw it on and cinch the waist.

Now, time for the news. I walk to the living area with a quick pause at the refrigerator where I find a chilled pitcher of martinis waiting for me. I drop two olives in my stemmed glass, pour the cool concoction over them, and settle in the living area where I click on the television. There should be a lead in with "breaking news" about a car fire at Marina del Rey. I cross my legs and wait and see a familiar face on the screen.

Donovan Caldwell, that whiner, is being interviewed about the most recent double homicide—the Springer twins. He and the reporter are seated in a studio, backdropped by a huge screen upon which pictures of the two sets of twins are displayed. Four girls, their eyes wide as puppies'.

An obvious tug at the viewers' heartstrings.

The reporter, a young woman with dark hair, huge eyes, and a concerned expression asks, "Do you think the killer who murdered your sisters is also responsible for the latest double homicide?"

"That's exactly my contention," he says fervently, an irate brother jabbing the air passionately. He's a small, fit man in an Izod golf shirt and khaki pants. A perfect little goatee covers his chin and a faux-hawk of dirty blond hair keeps him "hip." But he's not out to impress anyone with his looks. No, he's upset and flushed, all bristly anger. "I'm saying that if the LAPD had done its job right the first time and arrested the killer who murdered my sisters, two other lives wouldn't have been lost."

The camera zooms in on the victims, pretty girls with smiles so full of life.

"Oh, wah, wah, waah." I take another cool, calming sip and search for another channel with my remote. Of course I realize that the dead twins are news, but they're old news. Especially those Caldwell girls. They've been dead for over a decade . . . ancient history. And the little prick on the screen bugs the hell out of me. The nerve—grabbing *my* headlines. And that crack about the police department. He doesn't know what he's talking about.

I stare at the television and take a swallow.

Let's get to the good stuff.

Where in the hell is the reporter who should be covering the car fire on the streets of Marina del Rey?

That's the only story worth my time.

CHAPTER 33

"We need to find Fernando," Bentz said as Hayes drove back to the Center to drop off Martinez before taking Bentz to pick up his rental car. "I put in a call to him, but he didn't pick up."

"I thought I told you to back off." Hayes was irritated. "This is my case."

"And *my* wife." Bentz was equally upset, worried sick.

"I know." Hayes sighed, loosening the tie at his neck. "We'll put a tail on Yolanda as well as watch the house for Fernando."

"I'll check with his job and school," Martinez said. "We'll try to track what he did today," she was saying when Hayes's phone rang again and he took the call.

In the backseat, Bentz was quietly going out of his mind, trying to piece together the disjointed case. Though it had started out with him being lured to Los Angeles in search of his first wife, it now involved Olivia, he was certain of it. And now finding her was his number one priority. But with no leads to go on he figured the best way he could find her was through working this case, tracking down the person who obviously had a vendetta against him.

If he could pull his emotions out of it and study what was happening with a cool, cop's eye rather than his own passionate ardor, he could see that he was at the center of the case in the eye of a murderous hurricane. The person behind it all, the mastermind of the operation, was targeting Bentz.

From the ongoing investigations, the LAPD could find no reason for either Lorraine Newell or Shana McIntyre to be murdered individually; the link was Bentz. Though it was too early for the police to connect Fortuna Esperanzo, Bentz knew the deal. She wasn't left in the ocean in clothes identical to those that "Jennifer" had been wearing because she'd decided to go swimming. No, she'd been murdered, and the killer wanted to make certain that Bentz knew Fortuna had been a target, linked to this mess with Jennifer.

However if the woman who looked so much like his ex-wife were behind it all, then why hadn't it all come to a head earlier today, before she'd leapt into the ocean? Why risk her life? And how could she have been at the airport at the same time Fortuna had been dumped into the ocean?

Everything that had happened had taken calculation. Patience. Long-term planning.

Someone who held a very personal grudge was playing him, had spent years creating the perfect scenario. He discounted anyone he'd sent to prison. Most of those guys, if they had escaped or been released, would have run in the opposite direction as far and as fast as they could go. If they wanted to satisfy a grudge, they would have killed him and been done with it. Whoever was behind this string of horrifying events was getting off on his torture, watching him take the bait of Jennifer over and over again.

And that fact made his blood congeal. *Yolanda Salazar?*

Did she have the burning hatred to serve up her revenge ice cold? It didn't seem so. She seemed too much of a hothead, as witnessed by her act of spitting on him. She'd been scared and angry, but that wasn't the reaction Bentz expected from the killer.

So if not Yolanda, who?

What about someone close to the Caldwell twins?

Maybe this is the old "eye for an eye" thing.

Again, he was stopped by the killer's intimate knowledge of his ex-wife, of his relationship with her.

And now . . . Olivia was missing. Someone had the balls to call her and taunt her until she felt compelled to fly to L.A. That took confidence. Knowledge. And pure damned luck. How did the killer know Olivia would hop a plane?

Because whoever is behind this knows everything about you, about your life, about your wife. Damn it all, Bentz, this is your fault. Yours.

Absently he rubbed his leg as it had been aching since the chase down Devil's Caldron. He felt like a fool, following some woman down the ridge. Chasing an elusive truth while his wife had felt obligated to fly to California to reconnect with him, her ever-distant husband. Hadn't she mentioned they needed to talk? Hadn't he, too, felt the rift in their marriage?

Guilt tore a hole in his heart and all their arguments now seemed petty. Stupid! Even the one about kids. Hell, if she wanted kids, he'd give her a whole passel of them.

If he got the chance.

Hayes hung up. "We're not going back to the Center yet."

"What's up?" Martinez asked.

Hayes frowned, searching for the next exit. "Someone torched Sherry Petrocelli's car."

"Oh, Jesus." Martinez pressed her face in her hands.

"It gets worse. Looks like they found a body in the backseat."

"What? No!" Bentz shouted, coming up in his seat so fast, his seat belt clenched around him. Sick inside, rage and fear burning through him, he thought of Olivia. Beautiful, fun-loving, wickedly smart Olivia. *Oh, God, please, no!* He could hardly draw a breath. "Swear to God, Hayes, if something's happened to Olivia, if she's the person in that car—" He couldn't finish the sentence, couldn't think. Dread tore at his soul as the miles sped by and Hayes, breaking every speed limit, sped toward Marina del Rey, where the fire had been reported.

Bentz tried to calm himself. *It's not Olivia. It's not Olivia. She's alive and well. Somewhere. It's* not *Olivia!*

But he was frantic, fear eating him from the inside out.

The street was cordoned off, police barricades in place. Two fire trucks idled, their hoses snaking over the wet pavement, water running in sooty rivulets to the gutters. The blackened shell of a car still smoldered while the horrid stench of burnt rubber, melted plastic, and, worse, charred flesh filled the air.

Bentz flew out of Hayes's 4Runner the minute it stopped. Ignoring the barrier, he found a policeman in charge and demanded, "The body inside the vehicle. Who is it?" he demanded, frantic. Oh, dear God . . .

"Who the hell are you?"

Bentz pulled out his badge just as Hayes and Martinez showed up and identified themselves. Satisfied, the officer said, "We don't know. The body's already been taken to the morgue, but I gotta tell ya, it'll be hard to make an ID."

Bentz thought he might be sick. "A woman?" he asked.

"We think so. There was ID with her, most of it consumed in the fire, but she had a badge with her. It's pretty blackened, but I already checked the numbers. It belongs to the owner of the car, Officer Sherry Petrocelli. I'm thinking it's her body we found in the back-seat."

Bentz nearly sank to the ground in relief. He closed his eyes and clenched his fists, trying to get a grip on his own sanity. Desperately he clung to a thread of hope that Olivia hadn't met such a horrible, grisly end.

Yet, with that relief came an onslaught of guilt. Someone had died tonight. If not Sherry Petrocelli, then some other woman who had parents, possibly children, a husband, or friends who loved her. And he knew, deep down, that the victim was dead because of him. Because of his ego, his obsession with his first wife. His tunnel vision about Jennifer had brought death to several women and thrust his wife into harm's way. Someone had personally damned him to a living hell.

"I have to see," he said to Hayes, his voice rough, his teeth clenched.

"What?"

"I have to see the body."

"You're sure about this?" Hayes obviously disagreed. Shook his head.

"I need to know, Jonas. You understand."

"No I don't. For the love of God, Bentz, this ain't gonna be pretty." Hayes was still shaking his head, then seemed to realize he wasn't going to dissuade his mule-headed friend. "All right, I'll take you. But, for the record, I think this is a big mistake. Shit man. Oh, hell. We'll do it and afterward, *then* we'll pick up the rental and you can go back to the motel and get some sleep. You look like hell."

At the morgue, the Assistant Coroner tried to warn them. Her pre-liminary examination indicated that the Jane Doe's fingerprints had been burned beyond recognition. Eighty percent of the body had been charred, and there were no visible scars or tattoos. "We'll probably use dental records to confirm her ID," she said.

Still, Bentz had to see for himself.

The attendant, a different one from the person who'd pulled back the sheet on Fortuna Esperanzo hours before, waited for a sign from Hayes.

Bentz braced himself as a thunderous sound like a train in a tunnel roared through his brain. Powered by dread, it clamored down his spine and caused the back of his throat to turn to dust. What if he were wrong? What if the stiff, blackened body hidden by the thin sheet was actually Olivia? Oh God, no! He nearly backed down, but clenched his fists and set his jaw.

With a nod from Hayes, the attendant drew back the cover.

"Oh, shit," Martinez said and turned away.

Hayes winced.

Bentz's stomach roiled at the sight of burned flesh and white, staring eyes. Singed hair surrounded a nearly unrecognizable face. Teeth visible through blackened burned lips.

"Not Olivia," Bentz said, swallowing back the bile rising in his throat. He was certain. Felt relief tinged with guilt. Thank God she hadn't suffered the fear and pain this poor woman had endured.

"It's Petrocelli," Hayes said. "Officer Sherry Petrocelli. Oh, man, I wasn't expecting that." He was shaken, his lips flat against his teeth as he motioned for the attendant to cover the scorched remains again. "I know they found her ID, but somehow I didn't believe it." Hayes wiped the sweat from his brow with the back of one hand. "Her husband needs to know. I guess I'd better make the notification."

"I'll go with you," Martinez offered, casting a horrified glance at the draped gurney as it was rolled away. "What a friggin' nightmare. I hope to holy hell she was already dead when that car was ignited."

"Amen," Hayes agreed. He took one last look at the gurney then said, "Come on, let's get out of here. I'll take you to pick up that car if the rental place is still open. Then Martinez and I will go and give Jerry Petrocelli the bad news." He let out a long sigh. "God I hate this."

"You and me both," Martinez said.

*   *   *

The pink light of dawn was just streaking through the small port-hole in the hull of the ship, a tiny window Olivia hadn't noticed until daylight began to stream into the foul place. Vermin had taken over the boat during the night. The sounds of tiny feet on the floorboards and claws scratching at the wood had accompanied the creaks and moans of the boat moving slightly on the water. At one time during the pre-dawn hours Olivia had thought she heard someone come aboard. But if that had been the case, no one had hurried down the stairs to either rescue or attack her, despite her yells and screams.

She'd barely slept. Her nerves had been jangled all night, expect-ing the boat to be ignited into a hideous conflagration that would kill her with deadly smoke, squeezing the air from her lungs, or, worse yet, burning her alive.

She couldn't let that happen. And yet, when she closed her eyes it overcame her . . . the horror, the pain. She saw her skin crinkling and charring, felt her muscles and tissue consumed by hungry, excruciat-ing flames. Her eyelashes and hair would singe as she screamed deep in the belly of this empty boat.

And no one would ever hear her.

The vision was so horrifying, so vividly real that Olivia tried to keep her eyes open. Even the grim reality of this dank, smelly hold was preferable to the images her willing mind conjured.

However, facing reality meant dealing with the inevitable. Olivia knew she would have to fight. When the time came, she would have to attack the woman who had detained her here. She'd rather take her chances against a knife or gun rather than be caged like an ani-mal, forced to wait while the sick bitch decided her fate.

At least now, after enough hours, not only was her brain working again, but her limbs were doing what she asked of them and she felt no residual effects from the stun gun.

As the sun rose, she tried to plot her escape. She refused to be in-timidated by a weapon if her abductor brandished one. Let her try.

Who was this sick, deadly woman?

What did she want?

Why was she holding Olivia prisoner?

Worse yet, what did she have planned?

Nothing good, Olivia knew that much.

And that scared her to death.

Don't let it paralyze you. Think, Olivia. Figure out how to get out of here. You're a smart woman and there are tools available. You just have to figure out how to retrieve them, use them.

She eyed her surroundings, but they were sparse, only cluttered by bits or debris and rat droppings that confirmed the presence of tiny beasts living in the nooks and crevices of the boat. *Great.* She tried not to dwell on the vermin. She assumed that she was in a cargo hold of some kind, locked in a cage used for hauling animals. She was supposed to use the bucket to relieve herself, the jug for drinking water.

She hadn't used either.

So far.

But that would change soon.

A mop hung on one of the walls, a harpoon and life vests and oars on the other. There was a built-in cabinet, the doors shut tight. Otherwise the hold was empty, bisected by the narrow, steep stairs.

She checked the steel bars surrounding her. They were firmly attached, too strong to move, too close together to slip between. The gate, too, was solid. It wouldn't budge without a key. She lifted her bound hands and tried to prod the pins in the hinges, but they were set firmly. She couldn't knock them loose.

No. Right now, she was locked up tight.

And going out of her mind.

Cuffed as she was, Olivia was able to test the strength of the cage, but she couldn't get out. She'd tried to reach through the bars to grab the spear gun or oars from the wall, but of course, it was impossible. The valuable potential weapons stared at her, taunted her.

No, she had to find another way out. If her abductor returned, which Olivia assumed she would, then Olivia had to lure her into the cage, somehow steal the keys or physically restrain her.

It wouldn't be easy. The woman who'd abducted her was not only clever, she was tough. Athletic. Stronger than she looked, Olivia knew, by the way the woman had wrestled her into this prison of a boat.

You'll have to outwit her. It won't be easy, but you'll have to feign that your spirit is broken, gain her trust, then ambush her. Do not let it slip that you're pregnant. She'll use the baby against you, against Bentz, so not a single word.

Whoever her captor was and whatever she wanted, the bitch had planned her revenge on Bentz, step by step.

She wouldn't be easily duped.

But Olivia would find a way. She had no other choice.

I can't sleep. I am too keyed up, too excited.

Now, more than ever, I can't afford a slipup. One wrong move and everything will be for naught: all the planning, all the waiting, all the salivating at the thought of Bentz's unraveling. Caution is the word for the day. I must look normal, as if my routine hasn't been altered.

Just in case anyone is watching.

After staring at the clock all night long, I get up only half an hour early. I make a quick power shake for me and a sandwich for *her*. I would like to kill her and be done with it, but I can't, not yet. So I have to go through the motions of keeping her alive.

I even manage to drive to the club for a quick workout, including time on the weight machines and swimming a mile in the pool. The people I swim with recognize me, nod, and chat. It reminds me how important it is to stick to the schedule. Routine is everything.

So far, nothing I've done appears suspicious.

I wave and talk to the few type-A early risers I know, then get on the scale and make a loud disgusted sound as I read the results. Of course, my weight is perfect, my body fat lower than most female athletes.

Afterward, though I'm anxious and eager to see how Bentz's pathetic wife is doing, I shower and change as if I'm not in a hurry, not rushed. But I can barely restrain myself from running to the car. I drive five miles over the limit to the storage unit, where I grab a few essentials. Checking my watch, I return to the car and race as fast as traffic will allow to the dock where the boat is moored.

People are out and about, dockworkers and fishermen predominantly, but no one is really watching me or giving me the least bit of attention. Why would they? It's not as if I don't belong on the boat; I've boarded a thousand times before.

I am pushing it time-wise, but can't wait to see how little "Livvie" is doing. I have my taser with me, just in case she somehow gets violent. But really, she doesn't have a prayer.

Which is perfect.

I love having that power over Bentz's wife.

With my athletic bag slung over my shoulder, I head inside and check to make certain I'm alone. Then I climb down the staircase, my shoes ringing on the metal stairs.

She, of course, is waiting for me, sitting on the floor, and from the looks of her, I'd say had a worse night's sleep than I did. Dark smudges underline her eyes. Her hair is a matted mess. The area around her mouth where she's torn off the tape is still raw and red in one patch. Her clothes are wrinkled and dirty. In a nutshell: she looks like crap.

Which warms the cockles of my heart. If only her loyal husband could see her now.

Despite it all she isn't screaming. She's not begging or crying, which is more than a little disappointing. I'd like to break her spirit. Would love to see her grovel and plead. In fact, it's one of my most cherished fantasies. Obviously it isn't going to happen today.

But her time is running out. It won't be long before she'll be pleading for her life. Right now, it is still early. She doesn't really know what she's in for.

"Good morning," I say sweetly.

"Who are you?" Defiance in her tone. Even belligerence.

"I thought you might want breakfast."

"Why did you bring me here?"

"Let's see, I've got a sandwich. Peanut butter. Nontraditional for the morning meal, but it's all I could scrape together." As I reach in my bag I feel her rising in the cage.

"Let me out." She's on her feet, facing me through the bars, staring me straight in the eyes. She's calmer than I'd expected or hoped.

I lift my chin. "I don't think so." What kind of idiot does she take me for?

"I won't press charges."

She's serious. Desperate. Good. I like that attitude much better.

"Oh, yeah, right. I believe that," I mock. She's being stupid. "After all the hard work I went through to get you here, do you really think I'm just going to release you? Give me a break, you're smarter than that."

"Why are you doing this? Who are you? Not Sherry Petrocelli."

"Ding!" I say, pushing an imaginary button. "Score one for the blonde in the cage."

"What do you want from me?" she pressed. She was single-minded. Just like Bentz.

"Nothing," I say honestly. "From you."

"This is about my husband."

"Bingo. Now you're up to two right answers. Another one and you'll be in the bonus round."

"You think this is a joke? A game?" she asks, glaring at me as if I'm crazy, when she's the one locked up.

"A joke? No." I feel the boat sway a little, smell the scent of the beasts who were locked up before her. "A game? Possibly. Only I know the outcome and you, I'm afraid, don't."

"Fill me in."

God, she's ballsy! What the hell is she doing trying to get information from me? Asking questions when she should be submissive and fearful and begging for her life? I'm the one in charge. Doesn't she get it? "You don't need to know anything."

"Do you know my husband?"

"RJ? Oh, yeah."

"So you've been pretending to be Jennifer?"

I can't help but laugh. Then I make a low, flat sound. "Meeeep. Sorry, you just lost. No lightning round for you! And not even lovely parting gifts. You just get to stay here. Alone. That's your prize." She doesn't even break a smile, the humorless bitch. "Look I don't have a lot of time, so I thought I'd show you something, give you something to eat, and get going. Let's see." I make a big deal out of looking through my bag, then slide the wrapped sandwich and a can of Dr Pepper through the bars. I'm wearing gloves, just in case something goes wrong. You can't be too careful. I leave her miserable breakfast in the cage, but she ignores it.

Fine. If she wants to starve herself, it's no skin off my nose.

But I'm sure her tough facade is about to crack. She'll have more interest in the family album, I'm certain.

I open the scrapbook carefully and turn to one of my favorite pages, the Christmas section. There's a photograph with Jennifer sitting in an overstuffed chair, Rick at her side, his hand placed possessively on her shoulder. A lit Christmas tree fills one corner of the shot and Kristi, a toddler with a big smile and a cockeyed red bow in her hair is balanced on Jennifer's lap. "I know it's not the holiday season, but I thought I'd share this with you."

I lay the open album on the floor, just out of reach, on my side of the cage. She glances down disdainfully, but her hard shell cracks a little. Fear and outrage begin to show as she looks at the photos in the open album.

"What is this?" she asks in the barest of whispers. The album got to her. Finally. "Where did you get it?"

"Just something to think about," I say.

"Why?"

"So you can see for yourself that the man you married was obsessed with his first wife. I think everyone should have a little clarity; a little understanding before they die." I smile again. "It's only a matter of time, you know."

And then, while she's still stunned, I reach into my athletic bag again and retrieve my digital camera. Aiming and shooting quickly, I catch her horrified expression.

The picture is perfect.

"Your husband? He's going to love this shot," I assure her, as I look at the picture I've captured. "Just love it." Then, feeling victorious, I pack up my things and hurry up the stairs.

Let her think about her bleak future.

The woman was mad, Olivia thought. Cold, calculating, and mad as a hatter.

And obsessed with Bentz.

As Olivia stood imprisoned in the cage, gently rocking with the boat, fear slithered through her like a nest of tiny worms. She stared at the photo album left only a few feet from her cell. Opened to the page with the twenty-odd-year-old Christmas picture, the leather-bound volume was thick. Its plastic-coated pages had been filled with snapshots and clippings and cards, the work of an obsessed, sick mind.

Why?

Who was she?

Why was she so intent on Bentz?

Not that it mattered; the important thing was that Olivia had to escape. And soon. How, she didn't know, but she had to find a way because she was certain that she was scheduled to die.

She just didn't know when.

She noticed something else on the pages. Red smudges like . . . drops of blood? Crimson drips staining the photographs and smeared over the plastic. Oh, God. Whose blood? This maniac who held her? Or someone else's?

Jennifer's.

This woman is consumed with her.

No way! Jennifer was long dead.

Olivia was suddenly and violently nauseous. In an instant, she knew she was going to throw up. She scrambled across her cell and barely made it to the bucket before she retched though there was little in her stomach but acid and bile.

Again!

Her insides protested and she felt weak.

It couldn't be morning sickness. Not like this.

No, she was certain, this had nothing to do with her pregnancy. She was reacting to the horror that had become her life.

CHAPTER 34

Bentz felt as if he hadn't slept a wink. He'd spent most of the night trying to find a clue as to what had happened to Olivia. Where she was. If she were still alive.

He'd pulled up Olivia's cell phone records online and seen that the last call she'd taken was right after he'd spoken with her after she'd landed at the airport. No doubt the brief call was from Sherry Petrocelli's number. He'd dialed that number just in case he was wrong, but a taped recording threw him into Petrocelli's voice mail.

According to phone records, after the call from Petrocelli, Olivia hadn't spoken to anyone; there were only short, one-minute calls from a couple of numbers: his and Hayes's. "Shit," he'd said, frustrated as hell. He'd called Hayes, given him the info, then reminded the detective that there was a G.P.S. locator in his wife's phone.

Bentz had gotten nowhere with the cell phone company on that one; Hayes would have to use his police department influence to pry out any information he could from them.

After digging through the cell phone info, Bentz had been up most of the night on the computer, searching for anything he could find on Yolanda Salazar and Fernando Valdez. He studied the DMV photo of Fernando that Montoya had sent, wondering what the kid was up to. Most of the information Yolanda and Sebastian Salazar had given them the night before had checked out, including the name of the restaurant where her brother worked. Sebastian had told Hayes that Fernando worked the afternoon shift at the Blue Burro, and Bentz intended to pay the guy a visit later in the day. Bentz was tired of playing by the rules; he just wanted answers and he wanted them fast.

Before it was too late. *If it's not already,* his mind mocked now as it had all night. In the morning, he tried to wash away the grit from his eyes and wake up his tired muscles by showering and shaving. Then he walked outside to an overcast L.A. day. It was only seven-thirty in the morning and already a thick layer of smog accompanied an unlikely chill in the air, a surprising drop in temperature. He paused at the office door and looked down the length of the porch toward the doorway of the room he'd called home for the better part of a week. In the parking lot, the blue Pontiac was missing; Spike and his owner had probably moved out. A beat-up red pickup was parked in the Pontiac's spot.

Time marched on.

Things changed.

And Olivia was missing.

Anger mixed with fear, twisting his guts. She had to be safe; *had* to.

He ducked into the So-Cals' office for a cup of coffee, then, cup in hand, walked onto the porch to make some calls. Sipping coffee that settled badly in his stomach, he phoned Montoya, who, too, had worked most of the night and had dug up some more information on the Valdez family. Apparently Fernando was a theater major, interested in writing plays, while his sister Yolanda was studying accounting. Nothing out of the ordinary.

Except for the damned car. The one that Jennifer had been driving. He hung up, not knowing much more than he had last night.

Nothing made any sense. Nothing. In a haze of misery Bentz walked to his new rental car, a white Honda hatchback. He stopped at a mini-mart and bought two doughnuts that he ate on the way to the cemetery. He couldn't remember his last meal, but decided it had to be better than this breakfast.

The backhoe was already at work, men with shovels waiting for the big machine to do its job before they handled the final excavation by hand. Workers stood talking together in the rising fog, laughing, leaning on their shovels, telling jokes, and smoking, while Bentz felt his world collapsing around him.

As the huge machine scooped up dry earth, Bentz flashed back to the day of the funeral, when he had stood next to his grief-stricken daughter and watched as Jennifer's coffin had been lowered into the ground. The people who had come were a blur now, but he remembered Shana and Tally. Fortuna had attended, as had Jennifer's stepsister Lorraine, along with other family and friends. Bentz's brother had presided over the ceremony, looking stricken and ashen. As he'd mumbled prayers, a bank of thick clouds had rolled in, blocking the sun. James had loved Jennifer, he'd said, but, though only a few mourners had known the truth, he'd loved her in ways unbefitting a man of the cloth. His vows of celibacy had choked him far more than his clerical collar ever had. Bentz had clutched Kristi's hand and locked gazes with Alan Gray, the man Jennifer had nearly married before she'd fallen in love with Bentz and become the wife of a cop. At the burial Alan had stood back from the crowd, a millionaire who really didn't belong. His expression had been bland and void of emotion, as if he were playing poker in a high-stakes game in Vegas. Bentz had looked away and Gray had left before the final prayer had been intoned. Bentz had thought Gray's appearance had been odd at the time, but he had forgotten that detail.

Now, watching the back hoe extract soil from his wife's grave was surreal, the low-laying fog making it more so. Bentz believed with all his heart that the decaying body inside the coffin belonged to his wife.

Who else?

And yet he was jittery. Tense. Expecting the worst. He began to sweat despite the cool temperature. The men with shovels were just getting to work when Hayes arrived in a tan suit that looked as pressed and crisp as if it had just come from the dry cleaners. Dark shirt and matching tie finished the outfit and complemented the polish on his shoes. Always a dandy.

"No word from your wife?" Hayes asked.

"I was hoping you knew something."

"Working on it." Hayes touched the knot of his tie. "Tracked down the phone with the G.P.S.," he said.

"What?"

"No, don't get excited. Obviously the phone was dumped. We found it in the sand beneath the Santa Monica Pier."

"Shit!"

"We're checking with the webcam people again. So far nothing, but it's still early."

Santa Monica. Again. Bentz's guts twisted because he knew why the phone had been left there. Because of Jennifer. Because that pier and town were so much a part of her life, their life together. Whoever had kidnapped her was pointing that out, rubbing salt in the wounds, laughing at him.

"Son of a bitch." Bentz couldn't stop the black fury that overtook him. "Jennifer," he spat out. "She's playing with me."

"It's not Jennifer," Hayes said, hitching his chin toward the coffin.

"I know . . . you know what I mean. The woman I was with in the car. She looked a lot like Jennifer. A lot, but her voice was off and she was too young, and once I was that close, I knew she wasn't my ex-wife. But damn it, she knew so much about Jennifer . . . about us." His skin crawled at the memory of kissing her, of touching her. His stomach roiled at the thought of the taste of her and how he'd been duped. Furious with himself, he tried to focus, to move on, to think like a cop, not a husband. "Okay. So the phone's a bust, what else are you doing?"

"Backtracking mostly. Talking to people at the airport who might have seen Olivia connect with Petrocelli at baggage claim. We're checking security cameras at the airport and piecing together Sherry's schedule yesterday."

It's not enough, Bentz thought. "Have you called the FBI?"

"The captain's taking it up with—"

"It's a kidnapping case, Hayes."

"It hasn't been twenty-four hours. Not that our Missing Persons Department plays by that rule."

"I hope not. Jesus H. Christ! A police officer is dead. Along with a lot of other people. So, not only do we have kidnapping, we've got a serial killer on the loose. A cop-killer. I think the Feds should be involved."

"They're already checking into the Springer twins' murder. We're just not sure that all these incidents are connected," Hayes admitted. "Bledsoe's working that angle."

"Great." Bentz couldn't stand to think that Olivia's safety might hinge on Andrew Bledsoe's investigative work. "What about Fernando Valdez? Have you talked to him?"

"Still trying to find him. He didn't go back to the Salazars' house last night. We watched." He glanced at Bentz. "I talked to Jerry Petrocelli. He was devastated."

"I bet," he said, hoping to high heaven that he wouldn't be the next husband to learn that his wife had been murdered by this whack job. Not if he could help it.

Bentz watched as the casket was carried to the van by six strong guys . . . so reminiscent of the burial when Jennifer was originally laid to rest. The dusty box was slid into the back of the vehicle. "At least now we'll know if it's Jennifer inside," he said as the back doors of the van were slammed shut.

"It won't take long," Hayes said. "We've already received the records from her dentist. Got an expert who's going to compare them to what we find in the skull."

And then what? Bentz wondered. No other body had washed onto the beach, so they still didn't know what had happened to the woman who'd teased him, lured him to the cliffs, and jumped into the sea. God, why would anyone do that? Who was this woman who looked so much like Jennifer? Why was she tormenting him? And what the hell had she done with Olivia?

As if reading his mind, Hayes said, "We'll find her." His cell phone chimed. "Later, Bentz." He fished the phone out of his pocket and took the call as he walked back to his 4Runner and the vehicle carrying the casket took off. Bentz was left staring into the dry, empty hole where he'd thought he'd buried his first wife forever. Even in the hazy morning light, he felt a chill snake down his spine, as if someone were watching him, unseen eyes observing his every move. He looked up and turned, searching through the fog. A human form seemed to materialize, then fade, leaves and limbs of trees shivering. Was someone watching him from the shrubbery on the other side of the fence?

He told himself that he was imagining things, that the exhumation had weirded him out, but he walked toward the area where he'd thought he'd seen the branches move. As he approached he was certain he caught a glimpse of eyes peering at him! Green eyes, so like Jennifer's, studying him through the thick mist.

His pulse skyrocketed.

"No way," he said between clenched teeth. But despite his denial, he had to check it out. Picking up speed, he broke into a jog, his gaze fastened on the area where he'd first caught sight of the voyeur. As he spurred himself forward, his knee and thigh protested, but he gutted it out. Upon reaching the fence, he vaulted over, landing with most of his weight on his good leg.

No one was in the scrub brush of the vacant lot. No green eyes were staring at him. But he'd been certain someone had been here, watching . . . waiting, anticipating that he'd be at the exhumation; someone who knew where Olivia was.

Hell.

He pressed forward to a small copse of trees that stood still and quiet in the swirling fog. But he had seen her here, before she slipped through the sycamores and scrub brush.

A ghost in the mist.

"Where are you, you bitch?" Methodically, he searched the area, a strip of trees, grass, and brush between the cemetery and the sub-division abutting it.

He strained to listen. No twig snapped, no footstep over the sound of his own heartbeat and breathing. He heard only the sounds of muted traffic and voices from the men working on the exhuma-tion.

Frustrated, he peered over the fence that edged the tree line and again saw nothing. No one.

No one was here, he told himself. *Just you and your paranoia. A mirage you conjured in your tired and willing brain.*

He took one last sweeping look, but found nothing.

"Hell." He climbed over the fence again, paid no attention to the pain in his leg, and decided he was going to take the law into his own hands. He knew that Hayes and the LAPD were doing their best to lo-cate Olivia, but they were playing by the rules, doing everything by the book, and he didn't give a damn about what protocol should be used, or whether he was compromising the damned case.

Olivia was missing.

Maybe already dead.

Bentz wasn't going to mess around any longer.

He'd do whatever it took to find his wife.

*   *   *

"Screw this." Montoya hung up the phone. He wasn't one to sit on the sidelines when the action was elsewhere. Bentz was in trouble, seeing ghosts, for God's sake. Now Olivia was missing. Bentz was going even further around the bend, and there wasn't a whole helluva lot he could do from here in New Orleans.

So California, here I come.

He had the next two days off anyway, and there was some leave he could use if he needed it. He didn't even wait for the end of his shift, just told Jaskiel that he wanted to take a few hours comp time, and walked out the door.

On the way home he called Abby at work and gave her the same word. Fortunately she was cool with it.

"Do what ya have to do," she told him. "But be careful, would you? Come back in one piece. I'm not great at playing Nancy Nurse."

"You got it." He hung up smiling. At the house he packed a quick bag, then jumped into his Mustang again and headed to the airport.

Hayes returned to the office to find Bledsoe on a rampage, trying to build a case to nail Bentz for any and all crimes committed in L.A. and the surrounding area for the last week.

"I'm tellin' ya," Bledsoe reiterated when Hayes ran into him in the men's room. "If Bentz hadn't shown up, five people that we know of would be alive today." He zipped up, then made a pass at the sink. "Ask the family members of McIntyre, Newell, Esperanzo, and the Springer twins what they think."

"They're not cops."

"Oh, and add Donovan Caldwell, Alan Gray, and even Bonita Unsel to the mix. I've talked to them all; they think Bentz is our doer."

Hayes shook his head. "Again, not cops."

"Unsel was."

"With a major grudge. She and Bentz had a thing."

"Big deal. Bentz was quite a swordsman in his day. Cut a pretty wide swath through the department." Then with a smarmy grin Bledsoe added, "Even your girlfriend hooked up with him a few times."

Hayes had expected the zinger; it was just Bledsoe's style. "You talked to Alan Gray?" Hayes asked.

Bledsoe nodded. "He's back in town. Well, back in Marina del Rey, where he's got his yacht moored. Hates Bentz."

"Then maybe he's setting him up," Hayes suggested.

"Gray has too much money and power to be bothered with a pissant nobody like Bentz."

"Didn't he steal Jennifer from Gray?"

"You think he cares?" Bledsoe scowled. "Alan Gray has enough girls to make Hugh Hefner jealous."

"Don't tell Hef," Hayes said. "And Gray's a competitive guy. My guess is he doesn't like to lose. Nobody does."

"But to wait so long? What is it . . . like twelve or thirteen years?"

"Longer," Hayes said. "Jennifer was with Gray before she and Bentz were married. More like twenty-five or thirty."

"Alan Gray has better things to do than harbor a thirty-year-old grudge. Christ, Hayes, get real."

Hayes couldn't help the irritation that crawled into his voice. "You and I both know that Bentz is innocent. You're just pissed at him." Hayes took a position in front of another urinal. "Let it go, Bledsoe. You're a better cop than that."

"And you're not looking at this clearly. You've got blinders on, man. We're searching the wrong direction; we should be looking at Bentz with a freakin' electron microscope." Bledsoe pushed open the door and stepped into the hallway as a toilet flushed.

Trinidad, newspaper tucked under his arm, emerged from the stall and glanced at the doorway. "Bledsoe's a prick," he said, moving to the sink to wash his hands.

"Old news, Russ."

"But he's a good cop. His instincts are usually right on."

"He's tryin' to make a case against Bentz."

"No, he's not." Trinidad reached for a towel. "He's sayin' look at the man more closely." He wiped his fingers and wadded the towel, tossing it into the wastebasket with the skill of a high-school jock. "Wouldn't hurt." He paused. "Bentz thought he was saving my life and killed a kid. An honest mistake, but it doesn't make me think Bentz is a saint. He's made his share of mistakes just like the rest of us. Personally, I think some sick son of a bitch is setting him up. That's who we should be trying to find."

Hayes finished peeing and shook off as Trinidad left the room. Maybe Bledsoe and Trinidad were right. There was a chance that, in his efforts to defend Bentz, Hayes hadn't really looked at him, seen his flaws, put together a *complete* history of the man. He believed that someone was setting him up, he believed that it had to do with his ex-wife, and therefore it was personal.

Someone had a razor-sharp ax to grind.

It was just a matter of finding out who.

Bentz squeezed the steering wheel, trying to reaffirm the line between reality and delusion.

Had he seen Jennifer?

Was that crazy woman who dived into the ocean really still alive and taunting him, or had her vision been a figment of his tired but overactive imagination? He didn't have an answer as he drove directly to Encino. All he knew for certain was that his last hope, that of locating Olivia through her cell phone's G.P.S., had been destroyed.

Crushed.

He'd staked so much on the possibility of being able to locate her through her cell phone.

But he'd been wrong.

Again.

So here he was back in Encino, chasing another ancillary lead. He was tired to his bones, lack of sleep and worry eating at his guts, but he couldn't stop. Not until he found Olivia.

The junior college that Yolanda Salazar and her brother Fernando Valdez attended was only five miles from their house in Encino. And the Blue Burro where Fernando worked stood smack-dab in the middle between home and school. It wasn't too much of a leap to think that Fernando could walk, bike, or run to the JC, work, and home. He could also take the bus that stopped four blocks from the Salazar home, passed directly by the restaurant, and stopped at the main entrance to the college. Or, if everyone at the Salazar house was lying or hiding information, he could have easily borrowed one of the other vehicles or caught a ride with Sebastian or Yolanda.

The question was, as it had been from the moment Bentz had awakened from the coma at the hospital: who was the woman he'd seen driving Fernando's car? Today, come hell or high water, he meant to find out. He figured he didn't have a whole lot to lose. He was already persona non grata at the LAPD, and back in New Orleans, his job was still in question.

Besides, he didn't give a flying fig about either; all that mattered was his wife's safety.

He parked in the visitor lot, found the registrar's office, and by flashing his badge and wearing his dead-serious cop face, convinced a frightened-looking girl of about twenty to give up Fernando and Yolanda's class schedules.

With the help of the free campus maps on the counter, he was able to determine where and when both of Mario Valdez's siblings were scheduled to be during the day. As luck would have it, he had missed the early class in Fernando's schedule but the kid was supposed to be in Sydney Hall for an evening lecture.

Good.

Bentz planned to return before that class started.

He couldn't wait to have a chat with the kid.

I don't have a lot of time. It's broad daylight, the damned fog is lifting, but I have to take the risk.

So I leave work and drive straight home, download my picture of Olivia, and print it out. I'm wearing thin gloves . . . no reason to get sloppy now. The result is superb. I captured the horrified expression on Olivia's face perfectly and cropped out anything that would give a hint of where she is being held captive. All you can see are the bars of a cage and a pathetic, broken, frightened woman looking desperately at the camera.

"Phase one," I say, pleased with myself. Then, before too much time slips by, I erase the image from my hard drive and slip the photo into a manila envelope. Rather than using up a day by mailing the picture to him, I decide it's time to ramp things up. Push him hard. Let him know what it's like to feel the hollowness, the despair, of losing someone he loves.

Oh, yes. Rick Bentz will soon learn what it's like to be truly and horridly alone.

I put on my sweat pants and jacket, tuck my hair into a baseball cap, then find my running shoes and a pair of oversized sunglasses. Not the best disguise, but it will have to do. Even though the sweats will look out of place on this warm day, they help alter my shape, along with a sports bra that's two sizes too tight. Satisfied, I scribble Rick Bentz's name across the envelope, then drive quickly to that horrible dive of a motel where he stays in Culver City.

One sweep past the So-Cal Inn assures me he's not in; his new rental car is not in the lot.

I park several blocks away, then, with the envelope tucked into my jacket, take off at an easy lope. Hiding my face from any traffic camera, I time the lights just right so that I barely have to slow to cross a street. When I reach the corner near the motel, I cut across the parking lot and drop the envelope at the door of the office. From the corner of my eye I see a kid at the desk, but he's not paying any attention to what goes on beyond the television screen mounted in the corner.

I feel a rush of anticipation as I jog back to the car. From there, I find a place to fill up with gas. I duck into their restroom to change into work clothes. Looking in the cracked, dull mirror, I fluff my hair and pat on some powder to hide the fact that my cheeks are flushed.

Then I pay for the gas with cash, climb into my car, and head back to work. For the first time in years, I long for a cigarette, just to calm my nerves, but I ignore the craving.

How I would love to make a swing by the motel to make certain that stupid kid sees the package. But I restrain myself. No reason to take any unnecessary chances.

I only wish I could be a fly on the wall when Bentz opens the envelope. Oh, dear God, his expression will be priceless!

CHAPTER 35

Bentz was on the road when he got the call. Caller ID flashed the number and name of the So-Cal Inn. "Bentz."

"Hi, this is Rebecca, the manager of the So-Cal. You asked me to call you if anything odd happened?"

Bentz's free hand gripped the wheel. "Yeah."

"We found a package with your name on it at the front door."

"A package?" he repeated.

"Well, an envelope. You know one of those manila things. Around eight by eleven. I thought you might have dropped it when you left."

"No." He thought about the last manila envelope he'd received with pictures of Jennifer and a marred death certificate. He didn't doubt for a second that whatever was in this one, too, had come from the same source. "Hold on to it. Don't open it and I'll be right there. Ten minutes, fifteen tops." He searched for an exit, switched lanes, and sped to the next off-ramp, barely slowing as he left the freeway until he hit the red light at the cross street.

Another set of pictures? More documents? Oh, Jesus . . . please let this be about Jennifer, *not* Olivia.

His guts were grinding, his fingers tapping nervously on the steering wheel.

What now? Just what the hell now?

As soon as it turned green, he made a quick left turn under the freeway, swinging around to the southbound entrance of the 405. The light was with him and he gunned it.

He knew he hadn't dropped an envelope or anything else at the motel.

So someone had left him a surprise, this time without mailing it. "Son of a bitch."

Whoever was behind all this madness was getting bolder.

He couldn't shake the feeling that this time the packet had something to do with Olivia. A ransom request? Or worse? His heart nose-dived and he wasn't able to drive fast enough to eat up the miles to the Culver City exit. Time seemed to stand still and dread burned a hole in his stomach but ten minutes after taking the call, he pulled into the familiar, pockmarked parking lot, cut the engine, and strode into the office.

Rebecca was waiting.

The envelope in question sat on the registration desk. Across the yellowish face was his name written in the same block letters that had addressed the envelope containing Jennifer's death certificate and pictures.

"I found it when I walked in. I was out checking a room where the key wasn't working and Tony was at the desk. He didn't see who left it."

Warily Bentz handled the thin package. She offered him a letter opener and he sliced the seal carefully. Rebecca watched as he tipped out the single sheet of paper within.

"Oh, God," she whispered, her hand flying to her mouth as a picture of Olivia slid onto the desk's Formica surface.

Bentz's knees nearly gave way. His stomach turned over. He stared at the shot of Olivia, his beautiful Olivia, who eyed the camera dead-on with an expression of stark, cold fear. Pale as death, she was looking through bars, as if she were in some old western jail. Her hair was mussed; her eyes round and bloodshot, a red patch evident over her mouth where it seemed a gag had been taped. All of the life, the fire of her personality, had disappeared. Instead her expression was of pure terror.

"Goddamn it!" he said, his jaw tight, every muscle in his body clenched. If he ever found the psycho who did this, Bentz would personally tear him limb from limb.

But she's alive, he reminded himself. *That's something!*

Insides twisted, he checked the envelope further, expecting a letter or note, but there was nothing more. Just the devastating photograph.

You did this, Bentz. She's been captured, maybe tortured, and held in this jail because of you and your insatiable need, your damned obsession to chase down your ex-wife.

Guilt and fear ripped through him.

"What . . . what is this?" Rebecca asked.

"This," he said, his voice nearly cracking, "is my wife."

"Oh, God . . . I'm so sorry." She licked her lips nervously as she continued to stare in horror at the picture. "Where is she? What is happening to her? This could be a joke, right? A sick one, but a joke?" When she met his gaze, she knew the truth. "Oh, mother of God." She blinked against a spate of tears.

"Is Tony around?" Bentz asked.

"Oh . . . yeah . . . Sorry." She turned her head and yelled over her shoulder for her son. "Tony!"

"Do you know if Tony got a look at the person who left this?" he asked, motioning to the envelope.

"I don't think so." She cleared her throat and took a step closer to the door separating the lobby from the business office and staff quarters. "Tony!" she called again, more sharply. "He's got a cold, that's why he's not in school."

Yeah, right.

A few seconds later, Tony appeared plugged into an MP3 player, grooving out to music loud enough that Bentz heard the sharp cadence of a rap tune. Hands in his pockets, the kid shuffled into the office from the back as Bentz slid the picture into its heavy envelope. To the boy's credit he did sniffle and snort a bit as if his nose was threatening to drip. A cold? Or maybe the results from snorting some drug? Coke? Meth? At the moment Bentz didn't care.

Rebecca pulled one of the earbuds from her son's ear. "Mr. Bentz wants to know if you saw anyone leave this?"

"Uh-uh." Tony was looking down at his feet.

"You sure?" Bentz asked.

The kid shrugged. "Nah, I don't think so."

"But you're not sure," Bentz said, urging him to think of something, *any*thing that would help him save his wife.

"I, uh, I heard something," Tony said, clearing his throat. "You know, like a slap. Maybe when she dropped it?" He didn't sound certain.

"She?" Bentz asked.

"Or him." Tony frowned, concentrated, then acted as if he were afraid to give the wrong answer. "I dunno."

"But you saw someone?"

"Not really, but there was a runner going by. You know, jogging."

"And you thought it was a woman?" Bentz's heart was beating double-time. He wanted to shake the words from the kid's body. A jogger had been caught on the webcam at Santa Monica Pier the night Bentz had jumped into the water after Jennifer, and he thought he'd seen a runner on the street near Lorraine Newell's house on the night she was killed. And now?

"Look she, he, was wearing sweats and a cap. I really couldn't tell. Can I go now?"

"No," Bentz said. Sweats and a cap on a warm morning . . . had to be a disguise. *Had* to. Bentz knew he was grasping at straws but he'd take anything, the tiniest shred of a clue that might lead to his wife. It was all he could do to appear calm, keep his voice even when he was screaming inside. "Look, Tony, I think I might want you to go to the police station and talk with a police artist."

"Hey, no." Tony shook his head as if a police station was the very bowels of hell. "The cops? Nuh-uh."

"He'll be there if you need him," Rebecca said firmly.

"No, Mom. I didn't see nothing, not really. I'm not even sure about the runner. She was crossing the street . . . I mean, I don't think she came to the door."

"But you don't know."

He shook his head, bit his lower lip.

"Tony has a tendency to watch TV or play video games when he's supposed to be working." Then as if realizing he was underage, she amended, "I give him his allowance if he watches the desk for me."

Tony's employment or lack thereof wasn't any of Bentz's concern. Not now. Though he was still reeling from the photo of Olivia, he now felt a grain of hope. A drop of adrenaline coursed through his blood. Here, finally, was something solid to go on. "Do you have a security tape?" Bentz asked and Rebecca nodded. "Of the parking lot and front door?"

"Sure, and of the lobby, too. Our security equipment is pretty cheap, but you're welcome to a copy of the videotape."

"Right now, can you play it back? So we can watch it?" he asked, suddenly on fire.

"Yeah, sure." Rebecca was on board.

"I'll need a copy for the police."

"No problem." She gave Tony instructions to watch the front desk and led Bentz to a small area with a TV monitor and tape machine. As Rebecca said, the security system was hardly state of the art, but Bentz didn't care. He just wanted something, anything, that would help him find Olivia.

Rebecca sat at the tiny desk, pushed a few buttons, and rewound the black-and-white tape. Images reversed quickly on the monitor, people walking and running jerkily backward, cars in reverse. "There," she said as a jogger appeared. She rewound the tape until the runner was caught in the camera's eye.

Just as Tony had suspected, the jogger cut across the parking lot, slid the envelope from inside a jacket, and dropped it by the door.

But watching her on tape, Bentz didn't think it was the woman who pretended to be Jennifer. He wasn't even certain it was a woman, but it seemed that way. Her clothes were bulky, hiding her shape, but there was something about the chin and neck, no Adam's apple visible, not a hint of peach fuzz or beard shadow, although it was hard to be sure considering the indistinct quality of the moving image.

Nonetheless, it was something.

"Ever seen this person before?" he asked Rebecca.

"I don't think so, but it's hard to tell with the baseball cap and dark glasses."

"Tony!" Bentz called and the boy, looking bored as hell, returned. "You were right. This is the person you saw, right?"

"Yeah." He lifted his shoulder again, as if it were his signature move. "I guess."

"Did you notice anything else about the runner? Color of clothes or hair or car nearby?"

"Nah, but that's the person. See there? She's dropping the package."

"*She?*"

"Yeah, I think. Hey, I don't know, man."

"Tony," Rebecca said sharply. "This isn't just Mr. Bentz. He's a detective with the New Orleans Police Department and his wife is missing.

Kidnapped. There's a good chance this jogger," she pointed to the monster, "is involved, so please think. Think real hard."

"I am!" he said, throwing up his hands. "Holy crap, Mom, don't you *ever* listen to me? Didn't I tell you that was everything I knew? And there . . . there she is on the tape. I didn't see any more than that." He eyed Bentz suspiciously, as if he expected to be busted at any second.

"What about the color of her clothes?"

"Nah . . ." He snapped his fingers. "But I think I thought she was a woman because of her shoes. They . . . they don't look like a guy's."

Bentz glanced back at the screen and saw a glimpse of a running shoe, not one he would necessarily describe as being made for a woman, but definitely small. A woman's foot. Or that of a very small man. "Thanks, Tony."

"Hey, no prob." The kid shrugged and retreated through the doorway, trying to put as much distance between himself and the cop as possible.

Bentz turned to Rebecca. "You said you can make me a tape?"

"Yeah. *No prob,*" she said, mocking her son.

Rebecca copied the tape quickly and handed it to him. "Good luck," she said. "I hope you find her. Soon."

"You and me both." Bentz hurried back to his car and didn't add what they both were thinking: *Find her before it's too late.*

"I checked the roster of recent parolees with a history of violent crimes. Looking for suspects who might fit the profile of the Twenty-one killer," Bledsoe said as he approached Hayes's desk.

Hayes leaned back in his chair. Martinez perched on the edge of his desk. They were waiting for a call from Doug O'Leary, the forensic dentist who'd been called in to compare Jennifer Bentz's dental records with the body that had been buried in her coffin.

Bledsoe continued, "These are the guys that have been locked up since the Caldwell twins were killed and before the Springer twins became homicide victims. There are only three who even remotely meet the profile.

"There's Freddy Baxter. He got out last January, had pled down to Man-One for running over his girlfriend with his car. But he has an alibi, solid. Was with his brother in Vegas when the Springer girls were abducted." Bledsoe was holding up three fingers on his right hand, his thumb holding his pinkie down. With the dismissal of Baxter as a suspect, the ring finger went down.

"Then we've got Mickey Eldridge, cut up his old lady during a fight and was released in December, just in time for Christmas. But that wife, who almost died because of his butcher job on her, swears he's changed, found religion or some such lame excuse, and she was at his side on the night in question." Bledsoe's index finger curled into his fist, leaving his middle one poking straight to the heavens.

"Our last nut job with enough balls and rage to do the job is George St. Arnaux. He's my personal favorite. Remember him? The whacko who systematically cut off his victims fingers and toes. How the hell did he get out, I ask ya? Because some legal eagle swears she found an eyewitness who claims the killer was a white guy, not a black, so our friend George was released, though the taxpayers are going to be paying for a new trial, I'll bet. But George, he was with the lawyer, or so she claims. I think there's something going on there, ya know what I mean?"

"Not everyone's mind is in the gutter like yours," Martinez said. "You already said she's his lawyer."

"And she's boinking him, let me tell you." His voice lowered, "Some women get off on all that crazy, dangerous stuff, know what I mean?"

"*Boinking?* Grow up, would ya? We're not in the seventh grade." Martinez was not one to hide her feelings. "And your point was . . . ?"

"Yeah, right." Bledsoe put his hand down and sent her a scowl meant to cut her to the quick, but she held her ground. No matter how hard he tried, he couldn't intimidate her. "Anyway, I've got no parolee in the state of California I can hang this on. Shit."

Hayes felt the weight of the investigation. It had been too many days since the coeds had been found dead. The trail was getting cold, not that it had been hot or even warm to begin with. The Springer twins' murders had moved from page one to further back in the paper, but the killer was still out there. Justice was a long way from being served.

Bledsoe wasn't finished. "I talked to everyone who knew the Springer twins, retraced their steps. We had officers questioning all the neighbors, friends, relatives. We tried to establish some kind of connection between them and the Caldwell twins, but came up with nada." He rubbed his face with one hand. "Which brings me back to our 'friend.'" He made air quotes with his fingers. "And I use the term loosely when I call him a detective. This can't be random."

"Even if it's not random, it doesn't mean he's the perp," Martinez said. "If you want to pin it on him, you've got to come up with some proof, Bledsoe. Do your job."

Just then Hayes spotted Rick Bentz, who strode into the squad room and made a beeline for his desk. "Looks like you'll get a chance to ask him about it yourself." Hayes smiled for the first time that day. "Knock yourself out."

"I will." Bledsoe stepped away from Hayes's desk, making way for the detective from New Orleans. "Bentz," he said by way of greeting.

Bentz was having none of it. He sent Bledsoe a scathing glance as he brandished a large manila envelope. "I received this at the motel this morning," he said and dumped the contents of the envelope onto Hayes's blotter. A photograph of a terrified woman staring through bars settled near his calendar.

Every muscle in Hayes's body constricted.

Bentz looked over his shoulder to Bledsoe and said, "My wife."

Martinez didn't say a word, just stared at the frightened, captive woman.

"And this is a tape from the So-Cal Inn, where the package was left. The security camera caught a runner who dropped the envelope at the door and took off. I'm hoping you can check the local traffic cameras, find out if they photographed her image anywhere. Maybe caught her getting into a car."

"Her?" Bledsoe said, his eyebrows becoming one line.

"I think so. The tape is inconclusive, but I thought you might be able to enhance it, get a close-up of the face, though it's mainly turned away from the camera."

"Another jogger," Hayes said.

"That's right. You can compare the image to the photo taken by the webcam at Santa Monica." He shook his head. "As for the runner I saw on the street at Lorraine Newell's house the night she was killed, I don't know. It was too dark. But I'm willing to bet my badge that she's involved."

"Is this the woman who you drove up above Devil's Caldron?"

"No." Bentz appeared sure of that fact. "But, trust me, they know each other."

"Holy shit," Bledsoe said.

"Come on, Jonas." Bentz stared straight at Hayes. "Let's nail this jogger. Let's go find my wife."

Hayes's phone rang. He held a finger up to indicate for Bentz to wait a second, then answered. "Detective Hayes."

"Hey, yeah, this is Dr. O'Leary," the forensic dentist on the other end of the connection said. "I've got your results, detective. No big surprise here. We've got a match. The woman you exhumed this morning is definitely Jennifer Bentz."

CHAPTER 36

Bentz was stunned. And yet it was what he'd expected. Of course the body in the grave was Jennifer. So everything he'd believed for twelve years had been the truth. Jennifer was dead and the imposter had only been a part of a wide scheme to get him to return to Los Angeles.

Why?

To torment him?

To kidnap and torture Olivia? To start a killing spree?

"So this whole thing has been a wild goose chase?" Bledsoe shook his head.

"A smoke screen," Bentz corrected.

"And you dragged your wife into it? For the love of Christ, it's dangerous being married to you, Bentz. Not only for your spouse but for the people who knew her."

If Bledsoe wanted to twist the knife, he was doing a damned good job, Bentz thought. The glint in Bledsoe's eyes told Bentz the L.A. detective was enjoying his discomfiture. "So let's go after the person who's been staging this debacle," Bentz said.

"Meaning of course that you're not a suspect." Bledsoe took a swallow of his coffee to hide his smile.

"I didn't kidnap my own wife." Bentz warned himself to play it cool; Bledsoe was just looking for a reason to make him the scapegoat. Again.

To make matters worse, he saw Dawn Rankin walking through the squad room. She caught his gaze and her lips tightened a bit before she forced a smile and approached. "Back again?" she asked. "You just can't seem to stay away, can you?"

"It's business," Hayes cut in, saving him. Dawn, as always, ran hot and cold. One minute Bentz thought she was long over him, had buried the hatchet; the next she was hissing with a forked tongue. He felt lucky that their relationship had been short.

"Let me know if I can help," Dawn said with just a touch of sarcasm before she left.

"Piece of work," Bledsoe said. "Maybe you were lucky to have hooked up with Jennifer Nichols after all."

Bentz didn't buy the other detective's stab at camaraderie. Bledsoe, he knew, would just as soon kick him to the curb as help him. Fortunately Bledsoe's cell phone rang and he drifted off, cradling a cup of coffee.

"So this is what we know," Hayes said once he, Martinez, and Bentz had a little privacy. "The body in the grave was Jennifer's. The prints on the Chevy are many and varied, but other than yours, Bentz, they don't match anyone in the system. We're still trying. There was no other evidence in the car and our search-and-rescue team did not recover the body of the fake Jennifer in the Pacific Ocean."

"That's because she's alive. I saw her again."

"What?"

"This morning," Bentz said. "At the cemetery."

"And you didn't think it was important enough to tell anyone?" Martinez said.

"I wasn't sure, okay?"

Hayes waved the dissension away. "So now we've got this photo and the envelope it came in. Since our perp has been careful so far, I'd be willing to wager these materials will be clean, but we'll check for prints or DNA. And then there's this." He held up the security tape. "Let's have a look, compare it to the pictures we got from the webcam at the Santa Monica Pier. And you," he said to Bentz, "file a report with Missing Persons. Make it official. I'm sure the FBI is going to want to talk to you, too."

Hayes as ever was dotting all his Is and crossing his Ts. Running the case by the book. All of which wasted time. As he had from the beginning of this madness, Bentz felt the grains of sand running in a river through the hourglass. The more time that went by, the more likely he would never find Olivia and that thought brought him to his knees. "What about Yolanda Salazar and her brother?"

"Still trying to locate him. He didn't show up for work today, skipped his early class."

"On the run."

"Looks like."

Damn! He'd thought Fernando was the key. The kid was the one person who would know the identity of the Jennifer imposter. He was probably working with her, an accomplice. They had to flush him out.

"He has to surface some time," Bentz said. "Let's go."

Martinez hopped off the desk.

Hayes rolled his chair back and said, "Maybe we'll get lucky."

Martinez was already walking down the hallway, but she paused to throw a glance over her shoulder at Hayes. "Oh sure. And maybe my boyfriend, Armando, will get down on one knee with a three-carat diamond ring and propose tonight." She snorted a laugh. "Forgive me if I don't hold my breath."

The boat had never been set on fire. Not before or after her captor's visit.

Olivia did not know why she had been spared a fiery death, but now that the day had worn on and she was still alive she felt calmer. Slightly. She knew the maniac who had duped and abducted her would eventually kill her, but not before she got what she wanted.

Which was . . . what?

Olivia had no idea, but she would be damned if she'd give the woman the satisfaction of killing her.

Reluctantly, Olivia had eaten the sandwich, which she'd half expected to be tainted. But no, she'd survived. And she'd drunk the can of soda as well as used the bucket to relieve herself. It was gross, but worked.

And all the while, she considered her fate.

One way or another, she had to escape. She couldn't hope for Bentz or the police or someone else to come and rescue her. Nope, she thought, staring at the oar on the wall; she had to do it herself.

She looked around the hold, searching for anything that could help set her free, but there was nothing. Her eyes were drawn back to the oar. If she could somehow get hold of the long-handled blade, she could smack her jailer and knock her down and grab her damned keys. If the woman ever got close enough.

Oh, Olivia would like nothing better than to turn the tables on the bitch and lock her inside this stinky cage, then walk around with a damned stun gun and a gas can.

Again she studied the oar. Wooden, with narrow red, white, and blue bands painted near the blade, it looked heavy enough to knock a five-foot-six woman to kingdom come. And that was exactly what Olivia planned.

If she could just figure a way to reach it.

She felt the rock of the boat on its moorings and knew they were in some marina. She'd been told no one could hear her if she made a ruckus, but that was a lie. She heard seagulls crying and people shouting, engines catching and rumbling, but all the sounds were muted and it was probably because she was alone, aware of every little scrape of a rodent's claws, or anticipating the sound of footsteps on the ladder.

She had cried out earlier, after the psychopath woman had left and she was certain she was going to be burned to death. She had removed her shoes and banged on the bars of her prison, creating a dull clang. But no one had heard her. No one had boarded the boat, the *Merry-Anne* if the faded name scrawled on the life jackets could be believed.

Now, her throat raw from screaming, she sat in a corner of the cell, watching the sunlight fade and the hold become dark again. It was unnerving. Creepy. And she refused to let her imagination run away with her.

Instead, she tried to figure a way out of her dire situation. There had to be a logical solution to the problem of how to save herself as well as her unborn child.

As a psychologist, she had studied the human mind. She had learned various therapeutic approaches for people who were losing a grip on reality. That was what she needed: a plan.

Right. She would have laughed aloud if she had the energy. Psychologists did not treat unwilling patients; at least, not with any degree of success.

She pulled her knees up and hugged them to her chest. How do you deal rationally with someone who has lost touch with reality? Someone lacking in sound moral judgment? Someone inherently evil?

"God help me," she whispered as night fell and, once again, she was alone in the thick, stygian darkness.

"I'm sorry about your wife," Corrine O'Donnell said as she finished with the Missing Persons report. Bentz had already spent several hours with the FBI and had ended up here, in Missing Persons. The paperwork was necessary, but he was crawling out of his skin, watching the minutes tick by.

"Yeah." "Sorry" didn't begin to describe the fear that slithered through him, the cold, stark terror of knowing that Olivia was in the hands of a madwoman.

"Try not to worry. We'll find her." She offered a smile and he remembered fleetingly that he'd cared for her, more as a friend than a lover, but they'd shared a lot in their on-again, off-again affair.

"You happy with Hayes?" he asked.

"Well . . . I'd like to say *ecstatic,* but, you know, at this age, we're both carrying a lot of baggage, both careful because we've been hurt. Maybe too careful." Then, as if she realized she'd fallen too easily into the trap of shared confidences, she said, "Just sign, here." She pointed to a spot on the form, where Bentz scribbled his signature.

"I'll see that this gets out there," she said with a smile, and Bentz nodded.

"Thanks."

"Good luck." She was already turning away from him, ready to do her part to find his wife.

God, he hoped he didn't have to rely on luck.

But he'd take whatever help he could get. If it was good luck. Or divine intervention. Or even a deal with the devil himself. No matter what it was, just so that Livvie could be safe.

Montoya landed at LAX, picked up his bag, and went straight to the rental-car desk. As he was taking steps to collect the Mustang, a much newer model than the one he had in New Orleans, he put in a call to Bentz. "I'm in Los Angeles," he said when his partner answered.

"What? Here?"

"Couldn't stand being your goddamned gopher another minute. Figured I could help out here. Be more hands-on."

Bentz barked out a hollow laugh.

"Fill me in," Montoya said. He listened to the latest in the chain of events that revolved around Jennifer Bentz's ghostly appearances and Olivia's abduction, ending with the picture Bentz had received and his fears for his wife.

"So now the FBI is on the case," Bentz finished.

Montoya snorted through his nose, signed the required paperwork, and grabbed the Mustang's keys. Bentz got along fine with the Feds, but Montoya would rather work without them. Yeah, the bureau had smart agents, state-of-the-art equipment, and a wide net, but still, Montoya preferred to run his own cases. His way.

"Where are you now?" he asked, heading to the lot.

"At Whitaker Junior College. Fernando Valdez didn't show up for work or any of his day classes, but I'm hoping he appears tonight."

"He works at the Blue Burro, right?"

"Yeah."

"Been there?"

"Not yet. But the LAPD paid them a visit."

"I might just check it out anyway. Then I'll try to get a room at the dive you've been calling home the last week," Montoya said. "Once you collar Fernando, call me."

"If I find him."

"He's got to be somewhere. You just have to dig a little, think like the prick to find him. Be a cop, man." He hung up and tossed his bag in the tiny space for the backseat. He had a map and a G.P.S. system that would lead him to Encino. Once in the Encino City limits, he'd check out the Mexican restaurant where Fernando worked.

Thanks to his heritage Montoya spoke Spanish as fluently as he did English. With a little luck and some patience, he might just learn something.

At Whitaker Junior College, Bentz parked near the gym, then found his way to the student union. After waiting in line behind two giggling female students, he grabbed an order of twin dogs and fries, bought a bottled Pepsi, and took a booth in the corner, behind a fake potted palm. As he ate he kept his gaze fastened on the door. Clusters of students came and went. Some looked young enough to be in high school, others much older, picking up the missed college credits of their youth or returning to college to make a stab at a new career. Goths, punks, beach babes, computer geeks—you name it—a small mixed bag of a student army attended the JC. He checked each face, but he didn't see Fernando Valdez in the groups of students who were studying, eating, or listening to music as they filtered in and out of the student lounge.

He wasn't surprised. Fernando was obviously trying to avoid the cops.

Though he hadn't eaten all day, he barely tasted the wilted fries or the Polish dogs that had probably been spinning under a heat lamp for hours. His mind was elsewhere, on Olivia, hoping beyond hope that she was alive. Safe. Unbroken.

She's tough. Remember that. She's dealt with a homicidal maniac before.

It seemed like a waste of time to sit here on the off chance that Fernando Valdez would show up for his night class, but Bentz didn't have many leads. Fernando was his best.

But Valdez wasn't visiting the student union tonight.

Getting up from the table, Bentz felt a twinge in his leg. He ignored it as he tossed the remains of his dinner into a garbage can. Following the instructions posted near the waste cans, he placed his empty plastic basket in a bin marked for baskets and utensils, then carried his bottled Pepsi through the glass doors and into the coming night.

It wasn't quite twilight, but the fog was rolling in again, settling over the walkways that bisected lush gardens and lawns.

As he thought about his wife, he kicked himself to hell and back again for being such a fool, for wearing blinders about Jennifer, for not realizing what he had in his marriage to the one woman he truly loved and trusted.

"Idiot," he muttered as he made his way to Sydney Hall, a two-story concrete building that had all the style and grace of a county jail. Exterior stairs led to the second floor and the doors on the ground level opened outward to wide porches. In a quick check of the building, Bentz noticed that there were no interior hallways. Fernando, registered for "Writing the Play," an English class located on the first level, would have to pass this way if he wanted to get to class.

Finishing the remains of his soda, noticing bugs already gathering near the globe lights at the doors, Bentz waited near the stairs while the students trickled into room 134. There was a chance Fernando wouldn't show. No doubt Yolanda had warned him about Bentz. And the fact that he was MIA from his job and earlier class indicated he was wary.

Hell, he could be in Tijuana or deeper into Mexico by now. The border wasn't that far south.

Still, Fernando was a U.S. citizen, born and raised in L.A. Bentz was betting that sooner or later, the kid would surface.

And when he did, Bentz intended to nail him.

Maybe tonight.

Maybe later.

But Bentz wasn't about to back down.

He only hoped that he'd get lucky. No way could he spend another night in his motel room waiting for the damned phone to ring, staring at that bone-chilling picture of Olivia. And the thought of Olivia spending another night as someone's captive . . . he just couldn't let his thoughts go there.

Bentz leaned on the wall near the stairs and watched as the door to the classroom opened and closed, slamming behind each group of would-be playwrights as they hurried inside.

The purple haze of dusk deepened into night.

No Fernando.

Come on, you bastard. Show the hell up.

But the noise of footsteps and conversation faded as the stream of students dribbled to nothing. Bentz checked his watch. Ten after seven. No one had entered the room for over five minutes.

It appeared that Fernando was a no-show. Again.

"Damn it." Bentz drained the dregs from his bottle, watched a moth beat itself against the globe light and was about to toss his empty sixteen-ouncer into the trash when he spotted someone running through the mist. A man, he thought. The guy hurried past the gym and cut across a wide expanse of grass.

Bentz froze. Squinted into the night.

As the runner drew closer, Bentz recognized Fernando Valdez. The little prick was actually showing up.

Gotcha, Bentz thought, his pulse elevating. *Finally. A break!* Every muscle tense, his gaze glued on the kid, Bentz slid silently to a place beneath the stairs. Peering through the steps he fought to hold himself in check. He had to wait until the kid was close enough to nail. He couldn't risk scaring the little creep off.

Fernando was breathing hard, running as if the devil himself were chasing him, sweating as if he'd been running for a while.

He was close now.

Just a little bit further.

Fingering his badge, Bentz waited for just the right moment.

Fernando reached the staircase.

Now!

Bentz sprang from under the steps. Holding up his badge, he blocking the kid's path. "Fernando Valdez? Freeze. Police!"

"Shit!" Fernando started to turn, but Bentz was ready and grabbed him by the forearm. Hard enough to make Fernando cry out. "Ouch! Hey! Let go of me!"

"I wouldn't resist, if I were you," Bentz warned him, his leg acting up. *Not now! His knee couldn't give out now.* "You've got no priors, a clean record. You might even have a future if you cooperate now and give up your girlfriend."

"What? You're crazy! Let go of me!" Fernando yanked hard on his arm, but Bentz held on tight.

"Look, you're going to tell me who, what, when, and where, everything you know about this freaky scam involving the Impala and the woman who is pretending to be my ex-wife. Who's behind it. Where the hell the girl who's pretending to be Jennifer is and most importantly where my wife is."

"I don't know what you're talking about, man."

"Give it up, Valdez, it's over."

Recognition finally registered in the kid's eyes.

"I mean it."

"You?" he said, his lips curling in revulsion as he finally put two and two together, putting Bentz's face to his name. "I should trust *you?* The pig who killed my brother?"

"You'd better, or I'll haul your ass into jail so fast your head'll spin."

"I have nothing to say to you."

"Fine. We'll do this at the station." Bentz started marching him to the parking lot, figuring he could get some assistance from the guard in the booth there.

As they moved away from Sydney Hall the kid tried to worm away, pulling with such force that Bentz had to will his leg not to buckle as he yanked back.

"Look, don't think you're going to get out of this," Bentz growled. "I'm not messing around."

"Leave me alone, you prick!"

"Can't do it."

"What the hell do you want from me?" The boy's face was set. Hard. Dusk shadowed the sharp angles of his jaw.

"I already told you, just the truth."

"I don't know what you're talking about."

"Yeah, right." With his free hand, Bentz pulled out his cell phone and pressed the speed dial button for Hayes. It rang. Once. Twice. "Come on, come on!" Three times. "Hell."

For once the detective picked up. "Hayes."

"It's Bentz. I've got Fernando Valdez." They were still marching toward the gym. A few passing students eyed them curiously, but no one stopped to ask what was up.

"What?" Hayes asked. "You found him?"

"At Whitaker College." He glanced at Fernando. "Seems he didn't want to miss his seven o'clock."

Fernando gave a tug and Bentz reciprocated, his fingers digging deep into muscles and tendons.

"Shit, man!" the kid whispered, but he quit trying to break free.

"I'm already on my way," Hayes said. "I'll be there in ten minutes. Fifteen, tops."

"Just get here," Bentz said. "I'm armed, but I don't want to have to hurt him."

Bentz felt the younger man tense, heard him swear under his breath in Spanish. The kid was finally scared, too.

"Meet us at the west parking lot," Bentz said. "Near the guard booth."

"Got it."

Bentz ended the call. As he tucked his phone back onto his belt, the kid tried once more to break away, and Bentz felt the strain on his sore leg. He growled, wincing. Strain caused beads of sweat to form on his brow.

"I didn't break any laws," Valdez insisted. The curl of his lip suggested he was glad to cause Bentz some pain.

"I can't help you until you help me," Bentz said. "If you've got a brain in your head, you'll start talking about the girl you loaned your car to. The one you set up to pretend to be my wife."

"You're crazy. Loco. I have no fucking idea what you're talking about!" Fernando insisted, but there was a hint of fear in his dark eyes, a second of hesitation, as if he, too, felt the night and justice closing in.

"It'll go a whole lot easier if you give it up before you're arrested."

"Arrested? Are you out of your mind?"

"You tell me." They reached the edge of the parking lot. From here he couldn't see the campus security guard who had been patrolling the area on foot earlier. *Where are they when you need them?* Bentz wondered, scanning the parking lot as he warned Fernando, "You've got about three minutes to talk before Detective Hayes shows up," Bentz said, wishing he could squeeze the words out of this kid. The truth . . . the answers . . . the location where he'd find Olivia. "If I were you, I'd want to go on record as being cooperative. Right now the LAPD wants you behind bars."

"Let them arrest me," Fernando said. "I got nothin' to hide." He glowered at Bentz with a dark gaze of pure hatred. "But you . . . look at you, sweating like the pig that you are. I hope whatever you're going through, it stings like a bitch."

Bentz didn't release his hold on Valdez to wipe the sweat from his forehead. The Jennifer imposter had escaped him, but he was not going to let this one go. "Cut the theatrics, kid. You don't have a chance of seeing sunlight from outside a prison wall if you don't start talking. Tell me where your girlfriend is, and where are you holding my wife. You've been working with her from the start, right? Are you the runner? Do you take care of the dirty work?"

"Again, you're talking crazy!"

"If I'm crazy, why are you the one going down for kidnapping?" Bentz said, thinking of Olivia trapped somewhere in a prison. His grip on the boy tightened. "Kidnapping . . . and just maybe a few counts of murder."

CHAPTER 37

The Blue Burro was hopping, the dinner crowd spilling into the bar where colorful piñatas and fake parrots hung from open beams painted in bold primary colors. Dressed in dark slacks and white shirts with bandannas at their necks, the waitstaff bustled through the connecting rooms, skirting around each other and patrons. They carried trays laden with food or opened up portable serving tables to prepare homemade guacamole. Every so often they stopped serving to assemble, plunk a huge Mexican hat on a customer's head, and sing a special Mexican birthday song.

The place was festive and fun and brimming with customers.

Montoya suspected the police had been here searching for Fernando, so he decided to tread carefully, try to blend in. He pocketed his wedding band and took a seat at the bar, grabbing one of the few open stools next to the doors swinging into the kitchen. He ordered a scotch from a bartender who looked as if she could barely be twenty-one herself.

Lively Mexican music could barely be heard over the hum of conversation and clink of glasses, but Montoya listened intently, trying to hear something that might help him learn more about Fernando Valdez, his sister, the silver Impala, or the woman who had last driven it. Slowly, he sipped his drink, his gaze wandering to the mirror mounted over the bar so that he could unobtrusively watch the action behind him.

For a while inane chatter floated past him. But as he was close to finishing his drink, he heard Fernando's name come up in bits of conversation floating through the swinging doors from the kitchen.

Something about him not calling in and a waitress complaining about being forced to stay through the crush of dinner to cover his shift. Though she liked the money, she was really inconvenienced and pissed as hell that *he,* of all people, would make her work a double, which was a real pain in the ass with the baby and all. She'd had to call her mother to bail her out and babysit the kid. Or something close. It was hard to tell, and Montoya only heard parts of the conversation: her side because her voice was so shrill.

Trying not to appear interested, Montoya watched from the corner of his eye. The door to the kitchen swung open again, and Montoya caught a glimpse of the girl with a round face and tight lips. Her near-black hair was streaked with contrasting stripes of platinum and pulled tightly away from her face to a tight knot at her crown. She was seething, and Fernando seemed to be the cause of her exasperation.

"Ouch," he said to the bartender when the door swung closed again and the girl's voice still shrilled from the kitchen. "Someone's not happy."

"Never. Acacia's never happy." She gave him a smile as she filled glasses with ice.

"Not with Fernando," he said.

She quit scooping and studied him. "You know him?"

He shook his head. "Not that well. I took a couple of classes at the J.C., business classes at night, for my job. Insurance adjustor. Fernando was in one. He mentioned he worked here."

"He won't much longer if he doesn't show up," she said, shaking her head as she pushed the scoop through the ice and drizzled cubes into glasses set on the counter below the bar. "He's a player. A ladies' man. Acacia doesn't like it. Wants him to settle down."

"With her?"

The barkeep threw him a look that told him his question was asinine. "Of course with her. He's the father of her child."

"Is he? Didn't tell me about a kid."

"Figures. Acacia, she claims they were together a couple of years back. They hooked up at a company party and she got knocked up." She glanced at Montoya. "The kid looks just like him. Fernando isn't arguing about it, he's just not stepping up."

A new wrinkle, Montoya thought, as a slightly flustered waitress hurried to the bar and rattled off her order. "Can you hurry that? I forgot to turn it in and the women at table six are getting pissed."

"Got it." The bartender nodded and started mixing drinks, first for the waitress, then for a party of four at the far end of the bar.

Montoya decided he'd probably gotten all the information he could from her and he didn't want to tip her off by talking too much about a guy he "barely knew."

The door to the kitchen was pushed open by the same harried waitress and Montoya caught sight of Acacia stepping out a rear door.

Quickly, he paid for his drink, left a generous tip, then wandered outside to the cool night, a breeze blowing across the parking lot. Montoya waited for a rush of traffic to clear, then crossed the street to a convenience store. He bought a pack of Camels and returned to the restaurant.

Hoping to catch Acacia on her break, he headed toward the back of the building, where he caught sight of the small crowd of cooks and waiters clustered under an awning near the delivery door of the Blue Burro. Montoya unwrapped his pack and placed an unlit filter tip in his mouth. He patted his pockets, pretending to be looking for a light as he approached the group of half a dozen workers who were smoking and laughing, telling jokes, and ribbing each other.

Acacia stood among the group, just finishing her cigarette. Under the security light she looked more angry than ever, frowning as she took a final drag.

The laughter and jokes dissipated as he moved closer.

"Can I bum a light?" Montoya asked in Spanish.

One of the cooks, a big guy with a thin moustache and dirty apron, nodded. "Why not?" Shrugging, he flipped a lighter through the air and Montoya caught it on the fly.

"Thanks, man."

Acacia stubbed out her cigarette and seemed about to walk inside.

Montoya lit up and said, "Anyone seen Fernando?"

Everyone went stone silent.

"No?" Montoya frowned. "I heard he worked here and he owes me money. Thought I might collect."

At first no one said a word; they'd all apparently heard the cops were searching for him. The big cook in the dirty apron looked as if he wanted to dart inside. He dumped his butt in the overflowing ash can.

"Something wrong?"

No one said anything until Acacia, unable to contain her irritation with the guy, shook her head. "He owes you money? Get in line."

Montoya flipped the Bic back to the cook. "So he owes you, too?" he asked Acacia as the big guy slipped through the screen door to the kitchen, a shorter waiter on his heels.

"You wouldn't believe."

"Try me." He offered her a cigarette from his pack.

She shrugged, then took one and lit up as a scruffy cat stole through the shadows, slinking under the Dumpster in the back alley.

"He owes me a life, okay? Oh, and his son. He owes his son a life, too." She drew hard on the cigarette, then shot a stream of smoke out the side of her mouth.

"You have a boy together?"

"Mmm. Roberto . . . well, I call him Bobby, but Fernando, do you think he cares? Does he come and see his son? Pay me child support?" She sighed. "Not when he's running around with that woman."

Montoya didn't say anything, just took a long drag on his cigarette and listened.

"She's poisoned him, you know. Driving his car, meeting him at school. *College.* He was going there to better himself, become an accountant like his sister and then . . . then he met this . . . this *actress* and all of a sudden he wants to write plays!" Her eyes narrowed suspiciously, her nostrils flared. "And what does he do for me? Dumps on me, that's what. Doesn't even take his own damned shift because he has to be with Jada." Her lip curled in disgust and she flicked the rest of her cigarette onto the gravel. "You know, if it weren't for Roberto, I swear, I'd kill that son of a bitch!"

Olivia heard the steady thump, thump from above.

Over the creaking and settling of everything inside her floating prison came the sound of footsteps.

Someone was on the boat.

She didn't doubt for a second that it was her tormentor, so she didn't cry out, didn't want to risk the chance that the psycho would gag her again.

God, if she only had some kind of weapon.

The best she could do would be to fling her jug of water on the woman and soak her through the bars. But other than startle her or infuriate her, it would accomplish nothing.

Suddenly the lights snapped on and Olivia blinked hard, her eyes adjusting to the sudden brightness.

Her captor slowly descended the stairs, lugging a case with her. "So how're we doing?" she asked with feigned cheer.

Olivia wanted to respond with "just peachy," but thought better of it. Olivia reasoned that the best way to deal with the woman was to stand her ground. Not so easy when she was the one confined to this disgusting cage, but if Olivia could keep the woman talking, she could work toward extracting information while letting her abductor vent her frustrations.

If she could keep her cool. Reign in the terror that ate at her.

"So you ate, I see. Good, good. Necessary to keep your strength up."

Olivia froze. Where was this going? The woman didn't know about the baby, did she?

Of course not. No one knows. Not even your husband, and the way things are going, he may never know.

She closed her mind to that train of thought. She would find a way out of this damned boat. She had to. For the baby.

"So, hungry?" the woman asked as she pulled a plastic bag from her case. She tossed another wrapped sandwich and plastic bottle of soda into the cage.

Once again Olivia, wanted to slap her.

But she couldn't.

Keep your cool. Keep her talking.

"Who are you?" she asked again.

"Wouldn't you like to know?" She smiled to herself, as if amused at playing the part of a smarmy seven-year-old.

"Yeah, as a matter of fact, I would. And that coy thing you're doing? It's not working."

The woman's lips twisted in a rare moment of fury. "Oh, I think it is. I'm the one *outside* the cage."

"Who are you?"

"A friend . . . well, make that a close friend of your husband's," she said with a trace of bitterness.

"But you knew Jennifer."

The woman's eyes darkened.

Olivia had hit a nerve. Why? What was she to Jennifer?

"I really wasn't too into that bitch," her captor said as she smiled at a sudden thought, "but I've become, over the years, close with some of her friends. You know, the kind that just love to share secrets."

Olivia's stomach dropped. "You pumped them for information and then you killed them?" Of course she'd suspected this evil maniac was behind Shana and Lorraine's deaths but saying it aloud in the gently swaying hold of a boat, confirming what she'd surmised, observing this woman's smug self-satisfaction made it all the more real. More terrifying.

"They never saw it coming."

Olivia wanted to throw up.

Stay cool. Use your wits.

"And they just got in the way." She was assembling a camera and tripod, adjusting the legs, securing them with clamps she screwed into the floor and clipping all the pieces into place. Her nose wrinkled and she looked around. "God, it still smells down here. My father, he used to haul his dogs from port to port. Great Danes."

"So you called me? You're the one behind the phone calls, right?" Olivia asked, forcing the woman on topic, trying to learn more.

"My, God, you are just so sharp," her captor mocked. "Your IQ must be in the stratosphere. Except you can't be all that clever, can you, considering the circumstances? Here—" She bent down, flipped the photo album to a new page, one of Rick and Jennifer's wedding, the bride in a white lacy dress and long train, the groom, so much younger than he was now, proud and handsome in a black tux. Again, there were blood drops on the plastic, drops that had been drizzled and smudged over their faces. "Here's a good one." She nudged the book forward with her toe and turned back to her camera.

Olivia's skin crawled. "What are you doing?" she demanded.

"Setting up things so that you can pay."

"Pay?"

"For your husband's sins."

"I don't understand."

The woman glanced over her shoulder and smiled smugly. "Of course you don't."

"Listen. Why don't you just let me go?"

"Oh, right, after twelve years of planning, of waiting, of searching for just the right person to play the part of Jennifer, I should give it up. Because you think it would be a good idea?" She stared straight at Olivia, her eyes narrowed and cold as a demon's touch. "You don't get it, do you? I want Bentz to pay. To feel the pain that I felt. To know what it's like to lose someone dear, to go forward each and every day of his life realizing that he not only let you die, but he destroyed his own life as well. To be alone, totally and infinitely alone." She was working herself up, talking more loudly, more vehemently, more passionately, her face reddening, her fists clenching.

She had to visibly force her rage down, straighten her fingers. When she did, she spoke in a harsh whisper. "That man put me through hell, 'Livvie,' and now it's his turn. Time for him to feel a little pain. To know what it's like. He never knew that I killed Jennifer, didn't so much as suspect. Some great detective he is! All his awards for acts of heroism? Ridiculous!" As if reading the shock registering on Olivia's face, she let out a disgusted laugh. "That's right. You didn't know, did you? Jennifer is still rotting in her grave, at least she was until she was exhumed.

"It's her all right, in the coffin. That sick, twisted bitch who had Bentz wrapped around her little finger. He *loved* her, you know. Was obsessed with that two-timing slut! It was sickening. Despite the fact that she cheated on him over and over again . . . fucking betrayed him, he loved her." Still assembling the camera, she was shaking in rage. "Even after her affair with his half brother, a goddamned priest, the real father of his kid! Jesus H. Christ, he still came back for more. Talk about a masochist!"

This woman was really off her nut. Filled with hate and a craving for revenge.

"It's all ancient history," Olivia pointed out.

"Don't you even want to know how I did it? How I took care of her?"

"Jennifer."

"Of course, Jennifer! We're not talking about the friggin' queen, are we? It was so easy," she bragged. "I doctored her pills, and her vodka. Waited. Then followed her as she drove and made certain she had an accident." She paused, savoring the memory. "It was an impersonal attack, I know. The coward's way out with the car, chasing her down, freaking her out. But it worked."

"You really killed her." Olivia wanted to hear the complete confession.

"Uh-uh-uh. She killed herself. Remember? And as for the suicide note, I didn't even know about it. It was something she'd written a while before. Not very stable, our Jennifer. But Bentz . . . he just couldn't get enough of her. Divorce wasn't enough for him. He had to start up with her again. Some men just never learn." She chuckled coldly. "But he will. Tonight."

Sick inside, fear congealing her blood, Olivia could barely speak, but she forced the question over her lips. "What the hell did he do to you?"

"You really don't know?" She paused, thought for a second. "He left me. Not once, but twice, for the same bitch that kept breaking his heart." She looked toward the wall, but seemed to focus on the middle distance, to a place only she could see. "I loved him, I took him back, I trusted him, believed in him . . ." Her voice faced and tears welled in her eyes. "And he left me. Alone. And after Jennifer died, the son of a bitch poured himself into a bottle. Would he let me help him? Hell, no!" She sniffed loudly, straightened her shoulders. "That coward left L.A., went to New Orleans, and found you." She was shaking her head. "He never looked back. And you, the wife who should know all his secrets, you don't even know who I am, do you?"

That was the truth. Olivia couldn't place her.

The spurned lover said ruefully, "Maybe it's best this way. You don't need to know," she said. "But Bentz. He will. He'll get it and he'll live with it for the rest of his life."

Olivia stared at the camera and felt a wave of nausea. Oh, God, she was going to be sick. From the pregnancy? From fear? "What are you planning to do?" she asked in a voice that she didn't recognize as her own.

"What does it look like? I'm going to film. Well, it's not really film, all digital, but I'm going to make a movie of you."

Olivia flashed to all the prisoners of wars she'd seen with the enemy, forced to say things they didn't mean, beliefs they'd never held, at the point of a gun or risk of being beheaded. She started to shake inside and had to talk herself down. Think rationally. Nothing had happened yet.

"It's for posterity." Satisfied that the camera and tripod were secure, the woman checked the viewfinder, and squinting, angled the lens to her satisfaction. "There we go, now we can begin." She flipped a switch and turned the camera on, then she stood in front of the cage, just out of Olivia's reach, but in front of the camera's eye.

"Hi, RJ," she said, without any of the breathy tone she'd used in her phone calls. "I hope you find this, along with the boat and your wife."

What? Oh God, no!

"You should," she continued. "The camera's not only waterproof, it's meant to film underwater. As you can see, I captured Olivia . . . She's been my guest here on the *Merry Anne* for over a day now and I was hoping she and I could hang out a little longer, but . . . gee, I think I'd better not waste any more time and the truth of the matter is, she bores me." She looked at Olivia. "Say 'hi' to Ricky, Livvie. Wave. Show him that you're fine. So far."

Olivia didn't move. Not only was she scared to death but she wouldn't give this lunatic the satisfaction.

"Oops, seems like *Livvie* is in a bad mood. Maybe she'll talk when I leave. You'll have quite a bit of time alone while I sail out into open water.

"I could kill her as easily as I did the others. My good friends Shana and Lorraine and Fortuna. I did miss Tally, but you know, sometimes you just can't win 'em all, and I do have Livvie, now, don't I? They helped me, those friends of Jennifer's. They helped me learn so much about you, RJ, about Jennifer and your life together. Poor Jennifer. She just couldn't keep her mouth shut. Told her friends every detail, from what you did together over the weekend to where you first made love. And her friends, they remembered."

Olivia was dying inside, feeling the betrayal, knowing this psycho set them up to be used, then murdered.

"So you killed them?" Olivia said as the boat rocked slowly, creaking a bit with the motion of the water.

"Of course!" She shot Olivia an irritated glance that suggested Olivia was a moron. Or worse. "For a shrink, you sure have trouble connecting the dots. I had no choice but to kill those women. They might have put two and two together and ruined everything. And this way, the police department had to look at your husband again as the doer."

"So you murdered five people, three of Jennifer's friends and those twin girls."

"Please!" She turned then, her face florid. "I did *not* have anything to do with that. That idiotic Twenty-one killer, he killed those twins. A repeat of the killings all those years ago, the Caldwell girls. That sick son of a bitch picked one helluva time to resurface," she said, visibly shaking. "I can't believe you would even suggest I would be a part of that! He's a serial killer; gets his rocks off by killing innocents."

"Not like you," Olivia said, trying to keep her voice cool and calm.

"This is all part of a plan. It's all about Bentz understanding."

"But you killed innocents as well."

"Shana McIntyre? Innocent? Never. Jennifer's friends, they had to die. It's different."

"Dead is dead."

"This is revenge. The Twenty-one, he's just a sicko. *He* deserves to die."

"You're as sick as he is."

For that she caught a malicious glare. "You stupid, stupid bitch. You don't know what you're talking about. You just don't get it, do you?" She took in a big calming breath, her hands clenching and unclenching into fists as if she might fly into a rage at any second.

Which would be fine. Olivia would rather take her chances in a one-on-one fight than be trapped in this god-awful, foul-smelling cage.

"This *isn't* about the Twenty-one, you idiot! Not tonight. This is about you," she said, then looked into the camera. "And you, RJ. This—" She swept her arm in a gesture that indicated the hold with its cage.

"This is the final act. It ends tonight. All the charades, all the pretending, all the years of waiting. All the time of being alone." Her voice quivered a bit: "It's finally going to be over. And do you know how?" She gloated into the camera. "Well, let me tell you." Her smile widened. "I'm going to sink this boat. Tonight."

"What?" Olivia gasped. A new terror crushed the breath in her lungs. Oh, dear God, she couldn't be serious. But she knew in her heart that this woman, this killer with her vendetta against Bentz, was just demented enough to pull it off. "No," she whispered, her insides turning to water. "Please, please, no."

"Oh, yeah, I think so. The *Merry Anne* is sailing for the last time. With you on it." Turning to face the tripod again, she added to Bentz, "I'm going to make sure this boat sinks slowly, and the camera will be trained on your wife, so that you can watch as the hold slowly but surely fills, water inching upward. Olivia, she'll be cold at first, shivering and knowing that there is no escape, but she'll try to find a way out, be desperate to save herself. You'll see her panic and scream and cry, see each detail of her torturous, pathetic struggle as she gasps and chokes for air, treads water, forcing her lips and nose above the rising water, as she takes her last, dying breath and accepts her fate. You'll witness the terror in her eyes, Bentz, and know that her fate was in your hands."

"No! Oh, please." Olivia was frantic. She had to stop this woman. "You can't do this," she said without thinking. "I'm . . . I'm pregnant." Surely this sicko wouldn't knowingly take the life of an unborn child.

"Impossible." But she was shaken. "Bentz is sterile."

"I'm not kidding! I'm going to have a baby! Another innocent life. You don't want to be responsible for something like that." It took all of Olivia's strength to steel herself and not reveal that she was crumbling inside. "You don't want to be a serial killer, right? A lunatic like the Twenty-one killer. You said that yourself. You're different!" She was trying to find any way to reason with the killer.

"A baby?" she said, almost to herself, disbelieving. "Bentz's? No . . . but . . ."

"It's true!" Maybe she was making headway, appealing to this woman's warped sense of values. "Please, really, you don't want to hurt an unborn child."

Still blindsided, the woman narrowed her eyes on Olivia. "What a sick, pathetic lie. You are not pregnant!"

Olivia moved closer. "I am. I'm going to have a baby!"

Her captor waved wildly in the air to dismiss the thought, but her equilibrium was shaken, her voice tinged with a new anger. "It doesn't matter anyway. Even if by some miracle you are with child, well, all the better. Bentz can watch you and the baby die, all in living color. Hear that, 'RJ'? Her death, and this fictitious baby's, will be on tape and you can relieve her agony and fear and desperation over and over again. This is just so perfect. Worth every minute of the damned wait."

"No! Listen, I don't know who you are or why you're doing this, but please, don't," Olivia said, screaming inside, but trying to keep her voice level. She saw that pleading for her life only fed into this maniac's ego; she had to try a different tack, a diversion. "Tell me what your problem is with Bentz. Maybe I can talk to him—"

"Talk to him? Haven't you been listening to me?" The woman clapped her hands over her ears, as if she needed to hold on so her head would not burst. "Don't you get it?"

Olivia sensed that her captor was at a meltdown point, but she refused to cower. She kept her gaze trained on her would-be killer. "Don't do this," she said evenly. "Please. Don't—"

"Enough!" Her round eyes blazed with renewed fury. "You can blabber and beg all you want, but I'm not falling for it. Got that? It's over. You're going to die, 'Livvie,' and you're going to die tonight."

Jaw set, seething, but in control again, she double-checked the camera, then hurried up the stairs.

This time, she left the lights on.

Now the camera caught Olivia's every move.

Staying perfectly still she heard noises above and then the sound of a big engine roaring to life. The floor below her shifted as the boat began to move.

"Oh God," she whispered, spurred into motion. She paced the perimeter of the cage, checking and rechecking each bar, knowing they were sturdy. Immoveable.

No way out.

Her blood congealed as she considered her fate: Doomed to die at the hands of this twisted, deranged maniac, her baby never having a chance at life.

Olivia's throat grew thick with regret.

She would drown on camera.

Her death recorded for posterity.

To be used to torture Rick Bentz for the rest of his life.

She knew it.

The maniac knew it.

And soon, unless some miracle occurred, it would be over.

Then Bentz would know it, too.

CHAPTER 38

Bentz drove back to the So-Cal wired on caffeine, adrenaline, and just plain lack of sleep. And overriding all that sick energy was fear for Olivia. He was scared to death. The minutes were ticking by and he knew nothing more than he had earlier tonight.

Fernando Valdez had stonewalled them.

Bentz had stood on the other side of the glass ready to tear his hair out as the kid was interrogated for three hours. Hayes and Martinez went after him with questions peppered with some indication of the trouble he might be in, but Fernando responded by slouching in the chair, folding his arms, closing up.

"Who was this woman you loaned your sister's car to? The silver Impala?" Martinez asked.

"Just . . . someone I know. A girl at school."

"You got a name?"

"Jada. I don't know her last name."

That sent Bentz flying into the squad room, asking Bledsoe—who, unfortunately, was the only detective available—to run a search on a female, first name Jada, with a criminal record. Back in the interrogation room, Martinez was playing the good cop.

"Nice of you to help her out when she's low on cash and everything," she said. "Sounds like you're a good friend. But did you know that Jada has been linked to several murders?"

Unbroken, sullenly Fernando shook his head.

"Did you help her kill some of those people?" Martinez asked. Her dark eyes softened. "Maybe you didn't realize it. Maybe you just gave

her a ride somewhere, not knowing what she was doing." She
shrugged. "As far as you know, you're just helping out a friend."

"I didn't do anything wrong. I didn't kill anyone."

Finally a response.

"Come on, Fernando," Hayes nudged. "We've got your fingerprints now." The kid had tightened up earlier when Hayes printed
him. "I'm sure they'll match up with prints found in the Impala.
Maybe even with prints found at some of the crime scenes."

"No! I swear." Fernando turned his body away from them, refold-
ing his arms across his chest. "I didn't do anything wrong."

"No one is saying you did, Fernando," Martinez said in a soothing
voice. "Your sister, your professors . . . everyone says you're a good
kid. That's why I was thinking you might help us. We need help finding someone. A woman named Olivia Bentz. Blond hair, dark eyes.
Did you ever meet her, Fernando?"

Bentz had watched through the one-way mirror and felt his life
unraveling while the kid shook his head no.

"Olivia Bentz is missing," Hayes said, "and we have reason to believe your friend Jada is involved in her kidnapping. What can you tell
us about that?"

"Nothing!" Valdez insisted.

Frustrated, Bentz had wanted to smash his fist through the glass
and curl his fingers around the kid's throat to shake the truth from
him. Since Fernando hadn't lawyered up, the detectives continued
questioning him, and Bentz stayed for every second of the tedious
process.

Bledsoe checked on the name Jada, but hadn't found any females
with that name who had been booked in the past eighteen months.
Another dead end. Bledsoe would get Jada's photo ID and records
from the college in the morning, but he couldn't work on that until
the college's administrative offices opened.

Finally Bentz left the surly youth to Hayes and the FBI, who would
probably release him, then have someone follow him. There was
nothing more he could do at the Center.

As he drove he thought about the photos the LAPD lab had been
working on. The pictures of the runner from the Santa Monica webcam looked enough like the same jogger who had been caught on

the security cameras of the motel. Something about the runner seemed familiar to Bentz, as if he should be able to visualize her face.

A woman? Yeah, they were all pretty sure about that. The police were checking traffic cameras and parking tickets issued in the area around the motel at the time of the letter's delivery, along with the pier where Jennifer had jumped into Santa Monica Bay and the security cameras near the place where Sherry Petrocelli's car had been torched, but Bentz didn't hold out much hope. This person who had killed so easily seemed to know how to avoid detection.

A master criminal?

A cop?

He drove by instinct, his hands on the wheel, beams of headlights washing over him as his mind spun.

It's someone with a personal grudge.

Someone who's enjoying this.

Jada, the girl who looks so much like Jennifer, she has the answers. And Fernando won't give her up.

And right now Olivia was locked behind bars, a prisoner, because no one could find a shred of a clue that led to her captor. Bentz felt his life unraveling, everything that he believed in falling away, the woman who had turned his life around, made him a better man, now suffering because of his actions.

He saw his exit and rolled off the freeway, picking his way through traffic. He wondered if he'd find another disturbing, dark photo of his wife waiting for him back at his dive of a motel.

"Just keep her alive," he said to the car's interior. The dash lights glowed on his face as he glanced in the rearview mirror and caught his reflection. The man staring back at him looked older than he remembered. Haunted. By the ghost of a dead woman.

He pulled into his parking spot, yanked the keys from the engine, and looked in the mirror again.

This time, he saw past his own face to a person behind his car, standing on the far side of the parking lot.

Jennifer!

No way. She wouldn't appear now. He swung around to look.

She was gone.

Shaking inside, he slid out of the car and stood next to it, hearing the ticking of the rental's engine as it cooled and the night closed in.

Where had she been?

Under the streetlamp?

Near the ficus tree?

He started walking faster and faster across the dusty, uneven lot, beneath the flickering, humming neon lights of the So-Cal's advertising board offering free wi-fi and cable TV.

Was that a movement on the other side of the planter?

Someone running?

It might not be her.

But he was jogging now, his eyes trained on the image ahead, a fleeing woman with dark hair.

Déjà vu.

The eerie sensation tugged at his mind. He remembered following her down the steep trail over the sea, how she'd turned and blown him a kiss before leaping from the cliff to the ocean below. He recalled chasing her shadow through the decrepit mission in San Juan Capistrano. Following her earlier today in the woods beyond the cemetery.

What do you want, you bitch? I know you're not Jennifer. You're a fraud.

He broke into a sprint, barely aware of the traffic lights glowing red and green, or the cars whipping by. Keeping her in his sights, he crossed traffic against the light, heard a horn honk in protest, and someone shout. But he ignored the driver and picked up his pace. He felt the pain in his leg. Gutted it out. He was gaining on her now, but she was still a block ahead, running full out.

What the hell?

An old memory surfaced and a feeling of *déjà vu* settled over him. Another time. Another place.

He remembered chasing Jennifer, through the sun-dappled park at Point Fermin. How he'd caught her, breathless at a pergola, where he'd kissed her madly, both of them sweating, her breasts, beneath a thin blouse, pressed up against him. He'd hoisted her hands over her head, pushed her back against the rough trunk of a tree, and proceeded to strip her and make love to her in the shadows.

Oh . . .

Hell . . .

Another memory surfaced. Of running after her along the beach at Santa Monica just after sunset, the western sky ablaze, the tide lapping at their ankles, as the Ferris wheel spun on the pier jutting over the ocean . . .

Fool. Stop it! Forget her. Nail this woman and put Jennifer out of your mind forever. It's Olivia you love, Olivia who is your life.

He saw Jennifer turn, cutting into a parking structure.

Gritting his teeth, breathing hard, his leg throbbing, he ran, faster and faster.

Within seconds he reached the entrance to the parking garage, its florescent bulbs sputtering weak light. No one on this level. He stopped, listened.

Over the sound of his own pumping heart, he heard the sound of feet madly slapping concrete, running up stairs. Spying the staircase, he followed, his knee screaming, as he pounded upward, looking into the spiraling stairs above and catching sight of her dark hair. As if she felt his stare, she glanced down at him, managed a wicked smile over the rail, then turned toward the interior lot.

Damn!

Was she on the third floor?

The fourth?

Grabbing the rail, hauling himself upward, he pressed on, his heart thudding, his lungs tight, his skin damp with sweat. *Don't give up. Don't let her get away. This is your chance!*

On the third floor, he turned into the shadowy lot, but saw no one, only a few abandoned cars, their paint jobs shimmering beneath the watery lights.

Back to the staircase, running upward, straining to hear anything over the pounding of his pulse. On the fourth floor he thought he saw a glimpse of her, on the far side of the structure, and definitely heard her racing footsteps. He flew toward the sound, rounded a pillar and saw her, still fifty feet away, clicking a keyless remote.

The lights on a dark blue SUV flashed.

No!

He couldn't let her get away.

She pulled the door of the car opened, then turned back to Bentz and grinning provocatively, blew him a kiss.

"Jennifer!" he yelled.

In that second a man stepped out of the shadows, a gun leveled at her head.

Bentz nearly stumbled.

"Police. Freeze!" Reuben Montoya ordered, his face a grim mask, his hand steady as he held his pistol. "Jada Hollister, you're under arrest."

As long as the boat was moving, there was still time.

Olivia could find a way to escape . . . somehow.

Of course she'd been around this cage, searching for a means of escape over and over again with no luck. Now the camera was just out of reach and the only thing close enough for her to touch outside her cage was the damned photo album with its faded pictures and bloody smears. Apparently this psychotic woman got off on dripping her blood, or *someone's* blood onto Bentz's life.

At least the leather-bound album was near. Extending one arm through the bars, she managed to flip the pages. Her horror magnified as she viewed the history of Bentz's life in photographs: Rick as a child with James, his half brother. Photos from high school showing Rick in boxing shorts and gloves, posing by a punching bag. His college graduation photo and one from the police academy. Then a shot of a younger version of the woman who held her hostage, a faded snapshot of her with Rick at a bar, drinks and cigarettes in hand, all smiles and very much together.

Just as she'd said.

This psycho and Rick had been lovers.

She was a woman scorned—twofold, as Rick apparently had dumped her twice:

For Jennifer.

She'd said as much, of course, but these pictures were confirmation. Biting her lip, Olivia sifted through pages of his life with Jennifer, and pictures of him with other women, presumably after he'd split from his wife. Again, this woman surfaced. And this time her smiles weren't as wide; not as trusting.

How could someone be so obsessed?

Olivia felt sick to her stomach.

She flipped a few more pictures, seeing the family together again and then . . . and then there were snapshots of her. The wedding. Photos of Bentz and her at charity events.

Tears filled her eyes as she saw the love that they'd shared, caught in these pictures. The twinkle in her eye, the sexy grin on Rick's jaw.

Oh, God, what had happened to them?

Her heart twisted when she thought of all she'd lost. And now it was too late. This sick killer's rage hadn't stopped with Jennifer's death. If anything it had intensified, her obsession with Rick Bentz more focused, and Olivia had become her target. Now, just like Jennifer before her, she was going to die in some carefully plotted and executed horrific "accident."

Olivia closed her eyes and felt a pang deep in her abdomen.

So sharp she sucked her breath in through her teeth. Oh, dear God. She collapsed forward against the cage and held tight onto the bars, her fists clenching, knuckles showing white as the pain ripped through her.

She felt the boat pick up speed, knifing through the water to its deadly destination, water rushing against the hull.

The pain began to subside. She lifted her head and took a long breath. She was going to be fine. She and the baby. Somehow she'd find a way to save them. She just had to work on it—*Oh, sweet Jesus!*

Another razor-sharp pain ripped through her.

Like a knife twisting deep inside.

She gasped.

The baby?

A miscarriage?

No! No! No!

She pulled in a shaking breath, tried to think, to get hold of herself. She was overreacting.

She pulled in a shaking breath, tried to think. She was overreacting.

Nothing was wrong with the baby or her pregnancy. *The baby's fine.*

But the pain didn't let up. She cast a glance at the open photo album and fought another hard, wrenching abdominal cramp.

The baby's FINE!

She began to pant, to let out her breath in short little huffs as the cramping continued and she could barely think.

The baby's fine, the baby's fine, the baby's fine!

She gritted her teeth against the pain and the horrid, deplorable thought that she could be losing the tiny life within her.

And then she felt the blood.

Warm and oozing, just a trickle.

She was bleeding. Damn it all, she was bleeding.

"What the hell are you doing?" Bentz demanded as he crossed the stained concrete slab of the parking structure.

"Covering your sorry ass." Montoya had his service weapon trained on the suspect.

Walking up to her, Bentz still couldn't believe how much she looked like Jennifer. "Jada . . ." Beyond her resemblance to his ex-wife, he was sure he didn't know her. "Who are you?"

When she didn't respond, Montoya filled him in. "Her name is Jada Hollister and she's a theater major at Whitaker Junior College. A wannabe actress. Friend of Fernando Valdez."

"I bet." Seething, Bentz stared at the imposter. He had to restrain himself from tearing her limb from limb. "Where's Olivia?"

"What? Who?"

"My wife. My *real* wife. Where the hell is she?" he demanded.

Her cool demeanor, the act she'd perfected, remained in place. "I have no idea."

Bentz's temper exploded. "I'm through fuckin' around, you got it? Now where the hell is my wife?"

"I'd tell him, if I were you," Montoya said.

She put her hands on her hips. "But I don't know."

"Think real hard," Bentz advised.

"Oh, shut up," she snapped at him. "What is that, like a line from a really bad B Western?"

A car drove down from an upper level and the driver, an African-American woman with a flamboyant scarf wrapped around her head, saw the gun in Montoya's hand and hit the gas of her Mercedes wagon. As she wound her way down, Bentz saw that she was on her cell. She'd be calling 9-1-1.

"The LAPD is going to be here shortly," Bentz said, his voice deathly quiet. "And I guarantee they'll go so much easier on you if you tell us where we can find my wife. Now."

"But I don't know," Jada insisted, her brow furrowing. She followed the path of the disappearing Mercedes.

"Your name is Jada Hollister?"

"Yeah, yeah."

"And you're friends with Fernando Valdez."

"If you can call it that."

"He paid you to pretend to be Jennifer?" Bentz asked.

She hesitated and he said, "I'm not kidding about the police. You're involved up to your neck in several homicides and my wife's disappearance. If you don't start telling the truth, I'll see that you're arrested, locked up, and kept in prison for the rest of your life."

"Bullshit! I haven't done anything!"

"Really? Because the way I see it, you and Fernando, you're in this together and you're both going down."

Jada looked from Bentz to Montoya before focusing on the gun still trained on her. "Oh, crap," she said, biting her lip and obviously struggling with her decision.

"It'll go much easier on you if you tell us about your boyfriend," Montoya urged.

"Boyfriend? Fernando?"

"He's the mastermind."

She laughed. "He couldn't mastermind his way out of a open bag. He's not behind it," she said with a sneer.

"Then who?"

Her eyes narrowed a bit. Calculating. Then she tossed more guilt Fernando's way and let out a long-suffering sigh. "It was someone he knew, okay? A woman."

"What woman?" Bentz asked.

Jada sent Montoya a go-screw-yourself glare. "You can put that down now."

He holstered his weapon, then stripped the keys to the SUV that Jada still had clutched in her fingers.

"Someone paid you to mess with my mind."

"I guess." She lifted a shoulder, showed some more of her attitude.

"You *know!*" God, he wanted to shake the truth from her. "Listen, you're in big trouble." How could she not get it? "People are dead." He yanked out the picture of Olivia being held captive, looking scared out of her mind, and stuck it under Jada's nose. "Meet my wife. The one who's missing. Your friend, the person who hired you, abducted her." There was a tremor of rage in his voice and his hands, holding the picture, shook.

"She's *not* my friend." Jada's face paled as she stared at the copy of the picture. She cringed as he noticed the terror in Olivia's eyes, the raw skin around Olivia's mouth.

"We have other pictures," Bentz said, his voice low and threatening. "Of the corpses. Maybe you'd like to see Shana McIntyre in her pool, or Lorraine Newell with her brains blown out, or Fortuna Esperanzo—"

"Enough!" she said, tears welling in her eyes. "For the love of God, I don't know anything about any murders, okay? I mean . . . I did get involved with this freak of a woman who wanted me to play someone. An acting role, that's all. She claimed that if I dyed my hair darker, curled it, wore some green-colored contacts, and put in some cheek prostheses, I would be a dead ringer for this Jennifer woman." To prove her point, she took out her contacts, her eye turning a pale blue, then she extracted false teeth and cheek prostheses, changing her appearance. "She had a vial of perfume she wanted me to wear and so . . . so I did. You have to trust me. No one was supposed to get hurt."

"Like hell."

"Really. She said it was just an elaborate prank. She wanted to scare an old boyfriend. And she was going to pay me big money."

"How big?"

"Twenty-five grand. Thirty if I'd do the jump into Devil's Caldron. She thought of that after she heard I used to high dive."

"Thirty thousand dollars," Bentz spat out, disgusted. "What is that, about eight thousand a life?"

"I told you I didn't know anything about anyone getting killed!" she said emphatically. Suddenly she was serious as she started to finally see how dire her situation was. "I tried to get out of it, but she wouldn't let me. I really thought it was a joke, one of those elaborate pranks you see on TV. I figured I might get some exposure out of it, jump-start my career. She gave me a script and coached me over the phone, and I got a couple of free trips to New Orleans out of it. Her one rule was that I *not* get caught. I guess I blew that." She parted, looking ruefully at the oil-stained concrete floor. Bentz decided she was sorrier for the loss of her fee, as opposed to the loss of life. What a piece of work!

"Who is she?" Bentz demanded. "Who hired you?"

"I don't know. I never saw her. We just talked on the phone."

"How did you get paid?"

"Cash . . . " Jada reluctantly gave it up. "She said she'd been saving it for years. She left it for me in a locker at my gym in Santa Monica, not far from the Third Street Promenade."

"You got the money already?"

"Part of it. Only five thousand, to help me pay my rent . . ." Her voice faded as she finally understood the gravity of her situation, and it was finally hitting hard.

"I'll want the address of the gym where she left the money. You're a member?"

"Yeah. It was . . . a perk. I had to look good, be in shape, be able to swim, you know."

Bentz wanted to throttle the selfish bitch, but he controlled the urge by reminding himself of Olivia. He had to save his wife.

"And we'll need the script," Montoya added.

"Yeah, yeah."

Montoya asked, "How does Fernando Valdez fit into this?"

"He doesn't," she said with a shrug. "I was supposed to use him, get to know him, pay him some attention, get him to do things for me."

"Like loan you the car."

She rolled her eyes and sighed.

"A smoke screen," Bentz said, "so I wouldn't be looking in the right direction."

Jada said, "I guess. She didn't want me to have anything to do with the police department, either. And I was told to avoid some-body named Hayes. He was totally off limits."

"Hayes?" Bentz said barely able to draw a breath.

"Yeah. I thought maybe he was in on it with her."

Jonas Hayes? A bad cop? No way.

"You think?" Montoya said, as if reading Bentz's mind.

Bentz shook his head. "No. Couldn't be him."

"I'm just sayin'." Jada shrugged as if she didn't have a care in the world, her bad attitude returning. "She said something once, like, I don't know, when I asked about what was going on, she told me not to worry, that she had it handled that Jonas would take care of things, or tell her about it."

"Pillow talk?" Bentz said with mind-numbing certainty.

"I don't know." Jada rolled her now-blue eyes. "Maybe."

Not just maybe. It made sense. Bentz had suspected a cop. And if it was a cop with access to police intelligence, someone with a position at Parker Center, someone who could learn through Hayes how the investigation was going, he or she could be one step ahead.

Someone like Corrine O'Donnell.

A woman he'd dumped twice. For Jennifer. Bentz cringed inside, not willing to believe . . . then he remembered Corrine's overly concerned smile and words of encouragement when he'd filed the Missing Person's report on Olivia. How could he have missed it? Corrine, involved with Jonas, Bentz's link to the LAPD.

It explained how Jada had anticipated Bentz's every move. Bentz's throat went dry as his mind sped through the past week, the images of dead women, car chases, "Jennifer" sightings.

Was it really possible?

Was Corrine the one behind all this?

And Hayes, holy Mother of God, how did he fit in?

Jonas Hayes had known everything Bentz was doing, had insisted they play it by the book. The wail of sirens split the night air, reverberating through the parking garage, snapping Bentz back to the moment. The LAPD was on its way. "You'd better not be bullshitting me," he warned Jada.

"I just want to get paid." She eyed him expectantly.

Montoya sent her a look of pure disgust. "Yeah, well, I wouldn't bet on it. I want to be Brad Pitt, you know, but sometimes things don't work out the way we plan."

Her lip curled. "Yeah, well, too bad about the Brad Pitt thing," she said and Bentz could almost see the wheels turning in her mind. "And by the way, I want my lawyer. I'm not saying another word until we have some kind of deal."

* * *

Martinez stopped by Hayes's desk and handed him blowups of the picture of Olivia. "This is the hard copy of what they came up with in the lab."

Technicians in the lab had analyzed the shot, which they'd enlarged and enhanced in an attempt to bring out every detail of the picture, even images that were hidden.

"They sent it to you via e-mail, too."

"Got it," Hayes said, bone tired. He compared the images, on the screen, on paper.

"It's a boat, obviously," Martinez said. Sliding her finger a bit, she touched the corner of the picture over Olivia's head. "These puffy things stuffed in here? Life jackets. And take a look at those curved lines on the walls. Seems to be painted with stripes." She pointed to a detail in another blowup. "They make that out to be the handle of an oar."

"A boat. So she's being held on the water somewhere?" Jonas touched the knot of his tie, thinking about that. "So in a marina probably? Or private boat slip? Or . . . even dry-docked?" He eyed each shot, looking for more details.

"Or out to sea."

"Damn." Something about the blowup nagged at him, tugged at his mind.

"We might have to coordinate a search effort with the Coast Guard." Martinez brought him back to reality as she tapped another shot. "There's an image that isn't visible to the naked eye in this one. The lab thinks it's a script, probably the name of the vessel on a life preserver. It ends in *n, n, e.*"

Hayes closed his eyes for a second, then looked again. She was right. The image resembled a life preserver. With the letters *n, n, e* stenciled on faintly.

The end of a boat's name?

He blinked again, feeling a sense of dread crashing over him as he studied the original photo. It couldn't be.

No way.

No fuckin' way.

But the boat looked so damned familiar.

He'd seen those preservers, those oars. His insides turned to ice . . .

no, it couldn't be . . . but the proof was right in front of his eyes. Those letters on the life preserver, they were the last letters of the *Merry Anne*, the boat he and Corrine had used a couple of times . . .

Panic swept through him as his mind turned back to all the cancelled dates, the cell phone calls from God-only-knew where, the hot sex that never really became warm affection, the understanding of his job and the questions about his cases, and her keen interest in his work.

"It is a boat," he said finally and the realization cut to his very soul. How could he have been so stupid? So blind? "It's the *Merry Anne*. It was named after Corrine O'Donnell's mother, Merry, by her father."

"Corrine?" Martinez repeated, looking at him as if he'd gone around the bend. "But, she—"

"Is my girlfriend. I know." Bile crawled up his throat, bitter with betrayal.

"I was going to say she's a cop."

"Which makes it worse, because she's our killer, Martinez, and she's got Olivia Bentz held captive in the hold of the goddamned *Merry Anne*." His eyes held hers for a second before he picked up the phone. "I'll call the marina, make sure the boat is still in her slip."

"And if it isn't?"

He didn't want to think about that, how far Corrine, an excellent sailor, could be out to sea. "Then we'll call the Coast Guard."

CHAPTER 39

"The way I figure it, you've got two choices," Montoya said as he followed the flashing lights of the police cruiser hauling Jada Hollister to Parker Center. "One, you can tell Hayes straight out that his girlfriend is a freakin' killer. Or two, you do an end run around him and tell someone else in the squad about it, just in case Hayes is involved."

Bentz tapped his finger on the window ledge of Montoya's rented Mustang. "My gut tells me Hayes isn't in on it. How could he be? With all the hours he put in with me trying to crack this case? A guy can't be two places at once."

"So go with your gut." Montoya nodded as he took a corner a little too fast and the tires chirped. He slowed for a second, then punched it again as he hit the freeway. "It's worked for you so far. But we've got to cut through the crap fast and get to this Corrine. If she's the one who's got Olivia, we need to find her now."

Bentz nodded, unable to clear the image of his wife, peering through the bars of her prison, from his mind. All because of him.

Hang on, he willed her. *Just keep it together. We'll be there soon.*

"What really gets my goat is thinking that another cop is behind all this," Montoya said, staring ahead to the dark road. "Someone from the inside. That'll be a black eye on the department."

Another cop. That burned Bentz the most. A woman he'd once cared about, made love to. Corrine. She was behind all the death and destruction. She'd kidnapped Olivia and was planning no doubt to kill her, if she hadn't already.

To hell with playing by the book.

They planned to follow the squad car to Parker Center, blow the whistle on this cop gone bad, and enlist every hand they could to help them find Corrine O'Donnell.

"We'll get her," Montoya said, his face grim in the lights of the dash. "We'll find Olivia and we'll nail O'Donnell's hide to the wall."

No backing off.

No excuses.

No leniency if she pulled the "I'm a cop" card, or looked at him piteously.

And if Hayes was involved, then he'd go down, too.

A muscle worked in Bentz's jaw. He just kept tapping his finger, his gaze straight ahead as they flew down the freeway.

His cell phone rang, and he glanced at the caller ID—Jonas Hayes. "Hayes," he said to Montoya, bracing himself for a bevy of lies. If that son of a bitch was involved in the least . . .

Beside him Montoya glowered, his hands holding the wheel in a death grip.

He cleared his throat. "Bentz."

"Look, man, I know where Olivia is," Hayes said, his voice quiet and restrained, as if he were seething with a slow, black fury that was eating him from the inside out.

"Where?" Bentz was wary, slid a glance at Montoya.

"Olivia's being held on a boat. We got that much from the lab and . . . oh, hell, there's more to it than that," he said tightly. "I recognize the boat from some of the equipment hanging on the walls."

"You do."

"It's the *Merry Anne* . . . That's merry as in Merry Christmas, A-N-N-E. Corrine's old man owned it. She inherited the boat."

"O'Donnell?" Bentz asked carefully, though he knew the truth. He had to hear Hayes's theory word for word so there would be no mistake. "Corrine O'Donnell's holding Olivia captive on a boat somewhere?"

"Shit, Bentz, I can't believe it myself but . . . goddamn it, she's played me for a fool. Anyway, I'm on my way to the marina now, but it sounds like she's a step ahead of us. According to the security at the Marina del Rey docks and the harbor patrol, the *Merry Anne* isn't in her berth."

"Where? Where is this marina?" he asked and Hayes gave him the info, which Bentz repeated to Montoya then entered into the G.P.S. "You're sure it's Corrine?"

"Fucking Corrine was behind it all. I think . . . oh, hell I think I fed her information. You know how that is, cop to cop. I never thought she'd . . ." Hayes's cool facade cracked. "She's killed people, people she considered her friends."

Bentz felt his jaw harden. "Sounds that way."

"Shit." In the silence, Hayes seemed to be working to pull himself together. "I've called the Coast Guard. They're on the lookout for her, but she knows how to run that boat. She could be on her way to Mexico by now."

"And Olivia might be dead."

Hayes waited a beat and said, "Yeah." His voice was filled with regret. "Christ, I'm sorry, Bentz."

"We'll meet you at the marina," Bentz said stiffly.

"I'm on my way. Already called backup. Got a boat waiting at the marina."

As Bentz hung up, his partner was already hitting the gas, following the navigator's voice on the G.P.S. to head west, toward the Pacific, though Bentz knew the route.

Toward Olivia.

Olivia felt a shift.

The boat's engine changed speed.

Her heart leapt to her throat. This was it!

The engines died, and the big vessel slowed to a stop. For a few seconds within the hold, it was deadly quiet, the gentle movement slow and eerie. Then she heard the creaking sound of the boat rolling softly with the vast, silent ocean.

How far out to sea were they?

How far from anyone?

She bit her lip and listened. No one knew where she was. No one would ever find her. In the cavernous vessel, Olivia felt more alone than she ever had in her life.

Her cramps had eased, though the twisting ache still hit her every few minutes. Pushing herself up from the floor of the cage, she knew she had to fight.

Somehow . . .

Don't give up. Do not!

Fighting her fears, Olivia tried to pull herself together. She tried not to think about the fact that she was still bleeding, slowly yes, but bleeding nonetheless. No doubt miscarrying the baby she wanted so desperately.

She forced herself upright as she heard the heart-stopping noise of a running chain, metal being spun out. *Oh Lord!* The killer was dropping anchor.

For a second, Olivia couldn't move.

This, wherever it was off the shore of California, was where the killer had planned for her to die. A slow and torturous death.

Think, Olivia, think! You're not dead yet!

She reasoned that the boat couldn't be too far out to sea if the killer expected the boat to be found, her body located, the camera intact.

Her captor was, if nothing else, precise, her plans comprised of minute details, her timeline plotted to the last second. A control freak to the nth degree, she'd chosen this particular spot carefully, had anticipated and savored this moment for years, fantasized exactly how Olivia's death was to be executed.

"Like hell," Olivia said. She wasn't going down without one helluva fight. What was it Grannie Gin had always said when Olivia was growing up?

Where there's life, there's hope.

And Olivia wasn't dead.

Yet.

There had to be a way to outsmart this twisted maniac . . . maybe fake that her spirit had been crushed, pretend that the killer had "won," breaking her psychologically, so that her captor would become overconfident, perhaps slip up.

Really? You think for a second a diabolical woman who has been planning this moment for twelve years will make that kind of error?

No way, you have to make sure it happens. You, Olivia. You can't count on anyone but yourself.

Olivia had to beat the maniac psychologically.

And quickly. Dear God, time was running out. All too soon the boat would start sinking. Wasn't that her plan? Mother Mary, Olivia couldn't think of a worse death than trying to save herself, feeling the cold water rush in, push her off her feet, force her to tread water in the cage knowing there was no way out while she was gasping for an ever-dwindling supply of air.

Her heart was pumping crazily and her skin was sheathed in a cold, clammy sweat as she frantically searched the hold for any means of escape.

Stop it! Calm down. Do not panic! That's what she wants you to do, what she's counting on. Take a deep breath, count to ten, and think rationally.

Above, the woman was moving around, setting her plan into motion. Olivia had to work fast!

Drawing in a shaky breath, forcing back the terror eating at her, Olivia tried to get hold of herself. She knew the killer wanted her to appear miserable into the camera, for Bentz to be able to watch his wife's desperate, horrifying confrontation with death over and over again. This woman's goal seemed to be to haunt Bentz for the rest of his life: first by raising Jennifer from the dead, then by slowly and excruciatingly killing Olivia.

That was her whole game.

Control.

Terror.

To thwart the killer, Olivia would somehow have to deny her the ultimate fantasy, her coup de grâce over Bentz.

The answer was simple: She had to stop the filming.

But how?

If she could reach the oars to knock down the camera and attack her jailer . . . but that was impossible. Olivia had already tried to stretch through the bars and grab them, only to fail miserably. The same was true of her attempt to reach the fishing poles. Or the tripod.

Out of the question.

She could only use the tools she had handy. A bucket, a water jug, and a photo album.

She tried with the water jug, hurling the contents at the camera through the bars.

Water splashed wildly, drenching her hands and wrists.

The camera with its incessant red light didn't so much as shudder.

"Great." Hurriedly, she tried pushing the plastic jug through the cage, but even pressing the sides together to make it thin enough to get through the bars proved impossible.

She tried to swing it from her hand, stretching her arm through the iron rails so that she could beat the tar out of the camera.

No luck.

"Damn it."

Determined, she eyed her surroundings one last time and her gaze landed on the album. Faux leather-bound and stuffed with pictures and articles bound in plastic, it was too thick to pull into her cage.

But that didn't mean it couldn't be torn apart, the individual pages used somehow. Heart pounding wildly, her mind spinning with her desperate, newly hatched plan, Olivia reached for the album. Her fingers brushed against the pages and she pressed her shoulder into the bars, straining, barely touching. Gritting her teeth, she stretched as far as possible and the pad of one finger touched the album. She pressed down, dragged it forward but her finger, sweaty from her exertion slipped. Another pain ripped through her and she winced.

"Damn." Determined, she kept at her task, forcing one hand as far outside the cage as possible, touching the faux leather, inching it closer only to lose it. As she strained, perspiring, she heard the sound of footsteps ringing overhead as her tormentor walked on the deck above. Moving things. Getting ready. To ensure that she and the baby drowned.

No! Olivia wouldn't allow herself to concentrate on anything but her escape. Nor could she give into the cramps that were wracking her body, reminding her of the fragile life within.

"Be tough," she said and didn't know if she were talking to herself or her unborn child. Finally the album was close to the cage. Using both hands, she worked to tear the pages out of their bindings, unfastening the hooks that held the album together.

Her hastily conceived plan had to work!

It *had* to.

For her.

For Bentz.

For the baby.

*   *   *

Montoya stood on the brakes and the Mustang screeched to a stop at the marina, the frame shuddering. Before the car completely stopped Bentz was out, hitting the ground running, his leg aching, reminding him that he'd already abused it.

He didn't care. Across the pavement, down the boardwalk, and aboard the sleek Coast Guard cutter, Montoya right behind him. Within seconds, the skipper set sail, easing out of the marina, heading toward open water, moving much too slowly.

Hurry, damn it! Hurry.

He was worried, his eyes trained on the vast, dark Pacific. God, how could they possibly find her? He swallowed back his fear, told himself that there was time, but he was sweating, his heart beating with dread.

As soon as they were away from shore, the captain hit the gas, and the boat roared to life.

Behind them, the lights along the shore were brilliant and festive, reflecting in the water and thankfully receding as they headed out to sea. The cutter knifed through the water, salt spray and wind pushing against Bentz's face as he searched the darkness, silently praying that his wife was alive. Safe. That there was still time.

Montoya and Hayes were talking over the thrum of the engines and the swish of water.

Strategizing.

But Bentz could only think of Olivia and what she was going through. He felt impotent and weak. All his training, all his years working as a cop, and he couldn't save her.

His hands curled over the railing. *Hang in there,* he thought. *Oh, Livvie, hang in there.*

With each sound from above, a footstep, a chair being scraped against the decking, a rattle of chains, Olivia jumped. "Focus, Olivia," she told herself. "Focus."

But things had changed, something with the engines . . . a different noise . . . Then she saw it. Water seeping across the floor, soaking the pages of the album . . . still just a little but . . . "Please, please . . . no." Spit rose in her mouth as she thought of drowning.

Where was it coming from? Could she stop it? Plug the leak? Oh, God, where was the source? In a frenzy, she spun around, staring at every inch of the flooring, but saw no gaping hole in the hull, no split in the seams of the vessel. There was nothing she could do to stop the inevitable. Whatever the psycho had planned was already happening. Olivia had no choice but to hope beyond hope her plan would thwart the killer's deadly intentions. She just had to stay the course.

Setting her jaw, she yanked the last pages from the album and dragged each, along with the leather bindings, into the cage with her, where she pulled the plastic from each thick cardboard page. Then, with bloody pictures of Bentz and his family falling onto the wet floor, she rolled one piece of cardboard into a small bat, leaned far through the iron bars again and started whacking at the camera. It took several swipes in midair before she actually connected.

Bam!

The camera didn't budge.

"Damn it!"

Again!

Nothing.

The camera remained unscathed. Standing. The red light a small malicious and mocking eye staring at her, recording her futile movements. "You son of a bitch," she said and took another swipe.

Another hit.

Still the camera stood.

"Bastard!"

Now, there was more water. Sloshing over the floor, wet and cold under her feet. She swallowed hard. How long for a boat of this size to sink?

An hour?

Two?

Or less?

She took in a long, calming breath.

Concentrated.

Gave the camera another shot.

Whack! A solid blow, but the camera barely shimmied. Maybe she was going at this all wrong . . . she eyed the tripod and took stock.

Come on Olivia, you can do better than this. Hurry up! You're running out of time.

The legs of the tripod were bolted into the floor, yes, but they telescoped and, she thought, might be weak at the joints.

Only one way to tell.

Rolling up and using page after page of the album, she beat at the tripod's closest leg, shaking the contraption, making it wobble as the water and her panic rose. "Die, you bastard," she muttered, then grabbed the plastic-bound cover. It was stronger, the frame beneath the smooth simulated oxblood leather either plastic or metal or wood.

It didn't matter which.

She only stopped to listen once, trying to discern where her jailer was, but she couldn't get a bead on the woman, heard only the groan of the boat as it began to list slightly and the horrifying slosh of water as it rose, splashing her calves.

The boat was going down.

Fight, Olivia! You can do this!

Terrified, she started swinging like crazy, smashing the cover into the tripod's legs, swinging with all her strength, her fingers clenched over her makeshift weapon.

Whack! Whack! Whack!

All sounds above stopped.

No footsteps. No scrapes of metal on metal. Nothing but the spookiness of the empty, rapidly-filling hull. Olivia's teeth were already chattering, her fingers numb, her fear at the quietude complete.

Give me strength, she silently prayed. *Please.*

Then the sound of footsteps. Fast and furious.

Olivia froze, the album cover raised for a final assault, cold water sloshing around her knees. Her pulse was pounding in her brain, her senses heightened as she strained to listen. More footsteps. Her gaze turned to the stairs as the door above opened.

"What the hell?" the woman yelled. "What's that banging? What's going on down there?"

Damn!

Suddenly the footsteps were ringing down the steps.

No!

Olivia wasn't ready.

She threw another blow at the tripod, hitting hard as her attacker descended. Wearing a wet suit, she dropped to the floor of the hold, splashing water.

The camera teetered.

Olivia gave the tripod a final whack!

The legs gave way and the camera flopped off its base and fell into the water.

"Noooo! What the hell is this?" her attacker demanded, an expression of sheer horror on her face. "You miserable bitch, stop it!" She was sloshing through the salt water, trying to reach the camera as it sank.

Olivia fell to her knees, her hands scrabbling outside the cage, trying to reach the camera, water splashing around her face. She held her breath. Scrabbled frantically. Her finger grazed the side of the camera. It floated off. She tried again, sweeping it with a paddling motion toward the bars.

"Hey!" the woman screeched. "No! Stop! What do you think you're doing?" She lunged through the water to the cage.

Olivia's fingers curved over the handle and she pulled. The camera hit the bars and she nearly dropped it.

Her attacker sprang forward.

Gulping salt water, Olivia adjusted the camera so that it slipped through the bars to the inside of the cage.

Freezing, she was coughing and choking on the briny seawater, but she didn't care as she turned the lens on the woman who'd abducted her, the woman glaring at her and standing knee-deep in water.

"Give it back."

Olivia, seeing the red light was still glowing, kept filming.

"I said, give it back to me right now, you little bitch!"

"Come and get it." Even if she pulled out a gun, or the Taser again, Olivia wouldn't give up her prize.

The woman was freaking. "I said . . ." Her gaze swept the interior of the cage where her pictures were floating in the water. "What? You tore up my album!" Her eyes rounded in pure horror. "No! You couldn't." As pages reached the edge of the cage, she reached through, plucking them up. "No . . . no, this isn't right! This isn't how it's supposed to go." She picked up each page and held it high overhead, shaking them off. "Oh God, what's wrong with you? You can't . . ." She spied more of the pages inside the cage, far from her, the pictures scattered, the bloody plastic sheaths cast aside.

"No!" She was fumbling with her keys, desperate to retrieve the album. "No, this is all wrong."

Olivia just kept on filming.

"Look what you've done!" She was frantic, desperate to retrieve what was left of the soggy, disintegrating album. "You screwed everything up! You're ruining everything!" Her frustration and paranoia mounted and for the first time, it seemed, she realized her actions were being caught on camera.

"Give that back to me now!"

Olivia wasn't in the mood. Shivering, keeping her tormentor in her viewfinder, she said, "You want it, bitch? Then come and get it."

"There she is!" the skipper yelled over the cutter's engines and the rush of wind. They were jetting through the dark water, leaving a white wake behind.

"Oh, shit, she's listing."

Bentz squinted into the night, saw the *Merry Anne* in the powerful beam of the search light.

His heart fell to the floor as he saw the skipper was right; the vessel was leaning hard to one side, sinking fast.

"No," he whispered, disbelieving. "Oh, God, no!" Against everyone's protests, he'd donned a wet suit with the intent of boarding, but now the captain was pulling up short. "Get closer!"

"No. We'd better leave this to the Guard," he said. Already rescuers were trying to board the smaller craft. "Just wait."

Not a chance.

"Pull up closer," Bentz insisted.

He thought Montoya would argue. Instead, he turned to Hayes and ordered: "Do it."

The cutter drew alongside the listing boat. "Really Bentz, you should leave this to the professionals," Hayes warned. They were less than twenty feet from the sinking *Merry Anne*. "You'll only get in the way."

"I am a professional," Bentz reminded him as he climbed onto the railing. "And it's my damned wife."

From the corner of his eye, he saw Hayes lunge, ready to restrain him, but Montoya caught the L.A. detective's arm. "Let him go."

Bentz focused on the boat, looming larger as they closed in. Twelve feet away . . . eight feet . . . five . . . At that second, Bentz jumped.

The killer's plan was falling apart.

As her precious photos swirled on the surface of the rising water, she gathered them, one by one. "No, no, no!" she whined, temporarily forgetting her prisoner. "All my work . . . years . . . oh, God, this can't be happening . . . my photographs!" She seemed near the brink of tears as water sloshed around her waist and Olivia, fighting cramps and freezing, caught her paranoia on film. Plastic pages floated past, photos curled as they became saturated with water. Olivia's back was pressed against the bars, the boat tilting at a frightening angle. In a few minutes it would be over. She had to get the damned keys!

Plastic pages floated past.

Olivia thought she heard a noise, a thud. Oh, Jesus, was the boat breaking apart?

The woman heard it as well and she seemed to snap back to reality, noticed again that she was being caught on film.

"Give me back the camera!"

"I said come and get it." Olivia stood firm, propped by the steel bars, the camera trained on the bitch's face. Water was splashing above her waist now, weighing her down.

"Damn it!" the woman held the wet photos against her with one hand and struggled with her keys in the other.

"Who are you?" Olivia said. "You might want to tell the viewers your name so you get all the credit that's due you. Let's see, is your name . . . Dawn?" Olivia guessed, remembering that Bentz had once been involved with a cop by that name.

"Stop it."

"Or are you Bonita . . . was that it?"

"That bitch? No way!" She snorted in disgust. "Bentz must have mentioned me."

"I don't think so."

Another thud . . . oh, God, the boat was going down!

"Sure he did. Corrine. Right?"

Olivia shook her head. This woman was Corrine O'Donnell? Of

course she'd heard the name before, but she wasn't going to give this twisted killer the satisfaction. The boat groaned menacingly.

"Corrine. I worked with him. Dated him. Jesus, we slept together and . . . he loved me. We . . . we dated twice, almost lived together but then he left me. Both times for Jennifer . . ." Her voice trailed off. "They all leave, you know. Every one of them but Bentz . . . I was fool enough to have trusted him twice and he left me alone . . . all alone . . ." She shuddered, then, as if realizing she was letting on too much, focused on Olivia again. "I should have used the stun gun on you again!" Another picture passed by, this one of her with Bentz.

She let out a little squeak of denial, then snatched it up. She nearly lost the keys, trying to unlock the gate, "But I wanted you to fight. I wanted 'RJ' to see you straining to breathe your last pathetic breath, and now . . ." She gasped as the keys fell from her fingers, drifting through the bars to the inside of the cage.

Panicked, she tried to stretch her hand into the cage to take hold of them.

Olivia, seeing her chance, shoved the woman back. If she could snatch the keys and unlock the gate, maybe make it to the stairs . . .

The boat let out a long, low moan and the lights flickered. Olivia's heart sank. It was now or never!

Taking in a gulp of air, Olivia spotted the fallen keys, then dove down. Her hair and clothes floated around her. On the floor of the cage, the keys glistened enticingly as she reached for them.

To her horror she saw the killer's hand snake through the bars even further, her index finger catching the ring!

No! Olivia thought, her lungs protesting, her abdomen still cramping. No!

She surfaced at the same moment the killer did and thrust her arms through the rails, her fingers tangling in the woman's hair and pulling her under.

Her assailant struggled, wrenching back, whipping her head around.

Olivia hung on. If she was going to drown, by God, this woman was going to drown, too! Struggling, fighting, splashing, they fought. Twisting, turning. Olivia's lungs felt as if they would burst. *Oh Lord, help me . . .*

Again she thought she heard something.

But not the boat keening. No . . . it was different. *Shouts?*

Footsteps?

Could someone be on the boat? *Oh, God, please!*

The lights flickered again.

She took in another huge gulp of air mixed with salt water.

Coughing, sputtering, hanging on for dear life, she dragged the killer's head closer to the bars and swung hard with the camera, connecting with the woman's skull. *Thud!* A sickening crunch.

Blood stained the water.

More shouts from above!

"Help," she screamed. "Help! Down here!"

Corrine grabbed her by the neck and dragged her down. Olivia, gasping, took in air and water as together they sank below the surface.

No! No! No!

Olivia thrashed wildly.

Corrine's grip tightened. Their eyes met. Corrine was smiling beneath the water, her dark hair and a spreading plume of blood fanning around her, her eyes bright and psychotic. *I've got you,* she said without words. *You and your baby are going to die right now!*

Olivia's lungs were on fire.

The world was swirling, swimming. She tried to pry Corrine's death grip from her throat.

She couldn't hold on. She needed air!

Feebly, Olivia struck again with the camera, connecting with Corrine's forehead.

Then the lights went out.

Were those footsteps? Frantic voices? The sound of angels calling?

In the darkness she felt the camera slip from her fingers . . . felt Corrine's hands on her throat . . . felt herself drifting away in the cold and the blackness . . .

Her abdomen ached and she thought of the baby and of Rick Bentz. *I love you,* she thought and saw the light, the round white light as if it were in a tunnel.

We're dying, she thought, floating upward. *My baby and I . . . we're dying.*

The lights went out just as Bentz and two rescuers from the Coast Guard entered the hold. He caught a glimpse of the two women struggling, separated by the horrible cage, Olivia trapped inside, Corrine on the outside. Blood diffusing in the salty water.

"No!" His voice ricocheted through the dark, cavernous hold as he raced down the stairs, his feet splashing in water covering the lower rungs.

"Hey, wait up, man," one of the divers said, flipping on a flashlight that gave the interior of the listing bolt a weird, macabre look.

Bentz sprang, diving into the water, thrusting himself toward the cage, guided by the eerie light. He was vaguely aware of the others behind him, rescue workers with flashlights and crow bars and floatation devices.

A horrid gash cut across Corrine's forehead, still oozing blood as she looked up at him. "Bentz," she said with a ghastly smile. "You son of a bitch. This is all your fault . . . she's going to die, her and her baby, because of you."

"No way," he growled and pulled her away, flinging her toward one of the divers. "Arrest her!"

"No! You can't!" Corrine was sputtering, blood coming up with her spittle.

Bentz ignored her, reaching for Olivia, who was drifting away from him, so blue and cold . . . He pulled Corrine away, then reached for Olivia through the bars. "Livvie!" he cried, holding her face above water. "Olivia!"

The boat let out a long groan, like a whale in death throes. "Let's move it!" One of the rescue workers switched on a high-intensity underwater light, illuminating the hold, showing Olivia floating inside her cage, her hair a golden mane on the waters' surface.

"We've got her, sir!" one of the divers said as he found the keys and unlocked the cage. The other diver had dealt with Corrine, dragging her up the stairs, bracing himself against the wall as the boat sank deeper, shuddering. "Let her go . . . we'll take care of it."

"No!"

"Sir, please!" the order was sharp but Bentz ignored it. Olivia was his wife. She was barely breathing, but alive. He carried her up the stairs and she coughed.

"Olivia?"

She coughed again, a deep, racking cough, and he held her tight while she spewed salt water all over him as the boat shuddered, a horrid cracking sound ripping through it.

"Let's get out of here now!" The divers pushed them forward, across the steep deck.

"Hold on," he said, feeling the seams of the vessel, giving way.

"NOW!" With the help of the rescuers, Bentz helped Olivia into the cutter, just as the *Merry Anne,* with a final horrifying groan, cracked apart, timbers and glass sliding into the sea.

A medic attended to her while another worker wrapped Corrine in blankets in the next berth. She was barely breathing, her eyes fixed. "She's still got a pulse," the medic said, though Bentz didn't care.

He was only concerned about Olivia and the baby . . . isn't that what Corrine had said, that she intended to kill both his wife and un-born child?

"Rick?" Olivia whispered as they stripped off her wet clothes and wrapped her in blankets. She was blinking against the bright lights, her hand searching for his, lying on a bunk only six feet from where Corrine lay, handcuffs surrounding her wrists.

"Right here, honey," he said, his throat thick, his eyes hot from the threat of tears.

"I . . . I lost the baby." She looked up at him and swallowed hard. "I was pregnant. I should have told you."

"It doesn't matter." He clung to her hand. "You're all right. That's what counts."

"But the baby . . ."

"There will be others, Olivia," he said, bending down to kiss her lips. "I promise."

EPILOGUE

Olivia opened her eyes slowly, against soft lights that seemed impossibly bright. She was in a hospital room of sorts and there was someone in the room with her, a glow near the window.

You're going to be all right, the emanation said to her without making a sound. *You and the baby, you're going to be fine.*

"Excuse me? Who are you?"

But the figure only smiled.

"Olivia?"

She blinked. Bentz's voice jarred her back to reality.

"Did you see that?" she asked, turning to the window that was now just a view of pink sky streaked with orange and lavender as the dawn rose.

"See what?" he asked, glancing at the window.

"There was someone . . . something . . ." But when she caught the look on his face to see if she was pulling his leg, she shook her head. "I think I was dreaming."

"How're you feeling?"

"Like I *need* to get out of here." She'd been in the hospital for two days now, under observation for the ordeal she'd been through, but the baby was still viable, and she had suffered nothing more than trauma.

"I'll see if I can spring you."

"Please use *all* of your powers of persuasion."

"You got it." He leaned over and kissed her on the lips, a sweet lingering kiss that promised more to come, once they were home in New Orleans again.

She couldn't wait to get back, to plan for the baby, to put the trauma of Los Angeles behind her. "City of Angels," she muttered sarcastically, then looked at the window again, wondering about the spirit that she could swear had been there.

According to Bentz, Corrine's attack was recorded on the camera that was found on the *Merry Anne* just before it had sunk. No doubt she would be in prison for the rest of her life.

In the two days since then, details about the deranged woman had emerged in the newspapers. Olivia glanced over at the *L.A. Times* on her night stand, which had published an updated piece today.

Apparently Corrine had faked an injury to get a desk job at Parker Center—a way to gather information about new cases and about former LAPD Detective Rick Bentz. There was now evidence linking O'Donnell to the murders of Shana McIntyre, Lorraine Newell, Fortuna Esperanzo, and Sherry Petrocelli.

"O'Donnell wrought a trail of death and anguish," the article stated, "which included the kidnapping of a New Orleans woman who is married to O'Donnell's former lover, New Orleans Police Detective Rick Bentz."

Poor Hayes, Olivia thought. He'd been duped. He'd repeatedly told Bentz that he'd been a fool not to have seen the signs and that he was swearing off women for the rest of his life.

"Won't last long," Bentz had predicted.

Montoya had already returned to New Orleans to be with his wife and the Los Angeles Police Department was returning to a routine without the agitation of Rick Bentz. Though Fernando Valdez and Yolanda Salazar seemed to have been duped, rather than participants in Corrine's grand plan, the LAPD was taking another look at them as well as Jada Hollister.

As for the Twenty-one killer, Bledsoe, with the help of two female detectives as decoys and a lot of searching Internet chat rooms, had run a sting operation and caught someone who fit the profile—Donovan Caldwell, older brother of someone the LAPD had thought might have killed his sisters. It looked like he was their guy. The speculation was that the return of Bentz to L.A. had set him off and that he loved all the attention he was getting.

Corrine had been adamant that she hadn't been a part of his

vicious attacks against twins, so the LAPD was treating the case as if it had nothing to do with the string of murders perpetrated by Corrine O'Donnell, one of their own.

Still, Corrine's killing spree was more than another black eye on the department.

She was alive, in a hospital, under police custody, and the most anyone could speculate was that she was paying back Bentz for dumping her twice, and for the fact that after the second time, her mother, Merry Anne, had been killed on the way to consoling her daughter. Hayes said that Corrine, who had been an orphan and suffered through a string of foster homes before being adopted by the O'Donnells, hated being alone, feared growing old by herself, though she'd put on a pretty good act of independence. She'd admitted to him once that after her adoptive mother died and her father, who'd been having an affair for years, married his second wife, she'd felt alone and abandoned.

Her love affair gone sour with Bentz, twice no less, only confirmed that fact.

Apparently she'd targeted not only Jennifer Bentz, whom she'd murdered, but then Olivia as well, the woman Rick had married.

Although Bentz's leg had not completely recovered, he needed his cane less and less, and he'd been able to hold his own during his Los Angeles investigation. Melinda Jaskiel had called and offered him his job again, as long as he kept up with his physical therapy and a doctor approved his work schedule. "Since you're bound and determined to get yourself into trouble, then do it here, where I can keep my eye on you," she'd said.

"Good news," Bentz said as he strode back into Olivia's hospital room, barely limping. "As soon as the doc takes another look at you, we're outta here. Personally, I just think he wants to take another peek at that gorgeous body of yours."

"Yeah, Ace, that's it," she said, but laughed.

"I called Kristi. Brought her up to date," he said. "Guess who's excited about being a big sister?" He laughed at the thought. "So Kristi will be married before we know it. And next she'll have a kid. And our baby will be playing in the sandbox with her own niece or nephew." He touched his chin. "What's wrong with this picture?"

"I get it, I get it." Olivia suppressed a smile. "You're too old to be a father again. But that's just too damned bad, because like it or not, Hotshot, a baby's on its way. Get ready!"

"I am," he assured her with a wink as he leaned down to kiss her. "You're the one who doesn't know what she's in for."

"Then bring it on!" She wrapped her arms around his neck and grinned. "I've been waiting for this all my life!"